BURN FACTOR

BOOKS BY KYLE MILLS

Rising Phoenix

Storming Heaven

Free Fall

BURN FACTOR

KYLE MILLS

HarperLargePrint
An Imprint of HarperCollins*Publishers*

FIRST HARPER LARGE PRINT EDITION

Printed on acid-free paper

Library of Congress Cataloging-in-Publication Data
Mills, Kyle.
Burn factor / Kyle Mills
p.   cm.
1. Women computer programmers—Fiction   2. Government
investigators—Fiction.   3. DNA fingerprinting—Fiction.
4. Serial murders—Fiction.   I. Title

PS3563.I42322   B87   2001
813'.54—dc21   00-059734
ISBN 0-06-019334-4 (Hardcover)
ISBN 0-06-018558-9 (Large Print)

01 02 03 04 05 10 9 8 7 6 5 4 3 2 1

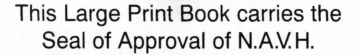

This Large Print Book carries the
Seal of Approval of N.A.V.H.

ACKNOWLEDGMENTS

In no particular order I'd like to thank my wife, Kim; Darrell and Elaine Mills; Robert Gottlieb; Matt Bialer; Caitlin Blasdell; Pete Groseclose; and Chris Bruno for their contributions and support. Special thanks to Bruce Budowle, the FBI's DNA guru, for speaking slowly when explaining the science behind CODIS to me and for his (anticipated) tolerance of my occasional flights of fancy.

BURN FACTOR

PROLOGUE

The combination of the tall wooden fence surrounding them and the trees spreading out above filtered enough street light to turn everything to shadow. The cold wasn't deep enough to penetrate Brad Lowell's jacket as he stood patiently at the base of the steps, waiting. Until the quiet click of the door opening and the gentle rush of warm air that followed, the most overwhelming impression was the scent of accumulating dew.

Lowell looked around him one more time as his people moved cautiously into the house and fanned out in a practiced pattern. The small backyard was completely still. It was just after four A.M. and a good two hours before this generic suburban neighborhood would begin to stir. He wished he had more time, but there was little he could do about that now.

The only light on inside—coming from the living room, he assumed—went dark as he stepped through the door and closed it behind him. He dug a penlight from his pocket and switched it on, briefly illuminating a man running up the stairs on rubber-soled shoes.

"We're clear. Blinds are down," came a voice through the tiny microphone nestled in Lowell's right ear. He shaded his eyes as he started for the second floor, dulling the glare of the lights being turned on throughout the house.

One of his men was already busy in the bedroom, sifting through the contents of drawers and shelves with gloved hands and practiced efficiency. There was nothing unusual or suspicious about the room, as Lowell had known there wouldn't be. The bed in the center was covered with a floral quilt that matched the dust ruffle perfectly. Stuffed animals seemed to have migrated off it as the room's occupant had aged, but hadn't made it far— they were lined up neatly on a shelf built into the wall.

The man searching the room started in on the closet, carefully pulling shoe boxes from a stack on the floor and removing the top from each. When he paused and glanced back over his shoulder, Lowell let his expression go blank, effectively hiding the rage, frustration, and fear building inside him. As long as he was in command, he had to remain passive—to project at least the illusion of control.

"I don't think we're going to find anything here, sir."

"But we're going to look, aren't we?" Lowell responded.

"Yes, sir."

Lowell descended the stairs, listening to the quiet rustling of the rest of his team as they moved efficiently around the living room. There was a barely perceptible break in their rhythm when he entered, acknowledging his presence. By the time he'd taken a position along the back wall, though, he seemed to have already been forgotten.

The woman's body was spread-eagled on a large plastic dropcloth in the middle of the floor next to a bloody industrial apron and two used condoms. Her wrists had been wired to the sofa with coat hangers and her feet were similarly bound to either side of a heavy-looking bookcase.

She had once been pretty—Lowell could still see it in her unmarked face. The full lips parted just enough to expose dry white teeth, the long auburn hair spread out beneath her head, the blue eyes fixed on the ceiling above her. He moved a little closer and crouched. If he hadn't already known the woman would be in her mid- to late twenties, her age would have been almost impossible to estimate. Her naked body had the graceful curves and undefined muscle tone of youth, but the sleek lines of her were distorted by countless razor-thin cuts crisscrossing her skin. A few were still wet—shocking red streaks in the uniform dull brown of dried blood that covered her and much of the black plastic she was lying on. The flesh seemed to hang a little too loosely on her dead face, hinting at the hours of agony she had endured before finally giving up and slipping away.

When Lowell finally stood, he saw that the young man in front of him was frozen. He was holding a powerful vacuum used for collecting evidence, but his knuckles had turned white around the handle and his stare was fixed on the body.

"Is there a problem, Mr. Geller?" Lowell kept his voice steady, matter-of-fact. The kid was new and sure as hell had never seen anything like this before. While the reaction was understandable, it couldn't be tolerated.

"No, sir," Geller replied, still staring dumbly at what was left of the young woman at his feet.

"Then get to work, son."

Lowell felt a hand on his shoulder as the muted whine of the vacuum started and the young man began carefully running it over the carpet around the body. He turned and started toward the hallway, followed by another one of his men.

"Who was she, John?" Lowell said when they reached the kitchen.

"Her name was Mary Dunnigan, sir." He laid a leather purse and day planner down on the dining table. "She was twenty-six years old and some kind of economic analyst working for a private company in D.C. There's nothing showing on her calendar for tomorrow or the weekend. I found a number of pictures of her with the same young man, though they cover a lot of years and I'm guessing that he's a relative—probably her brother. No messages on her machine . . ." He let his voice trail off, obviously finished.

"That's it?"

"For the moment, yes, sir. We—"

An angry wave of Lowell's hand silenced the man. "This is what happens when things get fucked up, John. Right?"

"Yes, sir."

Another wave of his hand and the man gratefully scurried off toward the living room to help his colleagues.

Lowell touched his forehead and his fingers came back soaked with perspiration. This whole situation was fucked. Dawn was two hours away and he was standing in a nice, neat, middle-class house, in a nice, neat, middle-class neighborhood, with the shredded body of a well-educated, well-employed young woman. It was getting harder and harder to imagine how things could get any worse.

Lowell used his sleeve to wipe away the sweat bleeding from his hairline and went back into the living room, where two of his men were using pliers to detach the corpse from the furniture.

"Are we ready?" A woman's voice.

Lowell turned to face Susan Prescott as she entered the room. She was wearing a wig of long dark hair and had changed into a pair of slacks and a casual blouse from the victim's closet. The fit wasn't perfect, but it wasn't bad either. Lowell had chosen Prescott for this detail on the basis of her height and build as much as for her ruthless efficiency.

"I've got pretty much everything from the bathroom and enough of her clothes and shoes to make it obvious," she continued, adjusting the suitcase in her right hand. "She had three months' worth of birth control pills in the medicine cabinet. I took them all."

Lowell looked down at the two men kneeling on the floor. They had freed the victim's hands and feet and were struggling to overcome the onset of rigor mortis and push the woman's legs together. "Did you find any other meds, John?"

He shook his head as he secured a strap around the woman's ankles and yanked it tight. "I went through the other two bathrooms, her nightstand, and the kitchen. Nothing prescription. I think we're okay."

Lowell focused on the younger man again as he helped wrap the woman in the plastic she was lying on, taking care not to let any still-wet blood flow onto the carpet. His face had taken on a noticeable pallor and his jaw was quivering dangerously.

"Geller," Lowell said.

He didn't seem to hear.

"Geller!" Lowell didn't actually raise his voice

from the muted volume made necessary by their situation, but the intensity of his tone got the young man's attention.

"Are you going to be sick?"

"No, sir!" He straightened and met Lowell's gaze with a forceful stare of his own. He looked like he was going to make it, but there was no way to be sure.

"We don't have time for a problem, Mr. Geller. If you have to leave the room, do it. Nothing will be said. Do you understand?"

"I'm fine, sir."

Lowell turned his attention back to the woman standing next to him, looking her over one more time. "Okay, Susan. Go."

She gave him a short nod and started toward the garage.

Lowell stayed planted in the middle of the living room, trying to concentrate. Had anything been missed? He scanned the carpet as his men secured the plastic around the body with a roll of duct tape.

It looked clean. There would be no prints, he knew, and their cleanup had removed any physical evidence that would be detected under normal scrutiny. Witnesses? There was no way to know at this point. Unforeseeable problems? Always. They would just have to be dealt with as they arose.

"Easy," he cautioned, dropping to his knees and examining the underside of the plastic as the two men lifted the body. "Okay, you're clean. Go."

He followed them into the garage, where Susan Prescott was already behind the wheel of the victim's Ford Taurus. He saw her lean forward and a moment later the trunk popped open.

"How's the car look, Susan?"

"Less than twenty thousand miles, sir," she said through the open window. "Plenty of gas. No mechanicals that I can find. All the lights and blinkers are functioning."

"Uh, sir?"

Lowell turned toward the back of the garage, where the two men were struggling to get the stiffening body into the car's small trunk. It was obvious that there was no way it was going to fit in its current configuration.

"You're going to have to break the legs, Mr. Geller. Susan, get out and help him. John, you're with me." Lowell started for the door leading back into the house, but not before noting the speed with which the young man's face had once again blanched. He didn't have the luxury of sympathy or the time to hand hold Geller while he came up to speed. He'd either handle it or he wouldn't. Best to find out now.

Lowell pointed down at the carpet as he entered the living room. "We're going to have to go over this one more time before we can get out of here. And I want a preliminary report on this situation by midmorning. By tonight I want to know everything about her. Do you understand me?"

"Yes, sir."

"And I'm to be told the minute the police get involved. After that I want daily reports on their investigation."

"I'll take care of it, sir," John said, cocking his head slightly at the sound of the garage door going up. "With a little luck, she won't be reported missing until Monday."

"I'm not interested in luck," Lowell growled, letting a tiny fraction of the rage that was eating a hole in his stomach leak into his voice. "There will be no more fuckups, John. Do you understand me? **No more.**"

1

Quinn Barry glanced at her watch and grimaced. Only eleven-thirty in the morning and she was already on her fourth cup of heavily caffeinated tea and her fifteenth rice cake.

"So you're going to have it running today, then?"

Quinn jumped, knocking the last of the strawberry-flavored cakes from her carefully organized desk. It seemed to fall in slow motion, turning end over end before fatally impacting the floor.

"Quinn?"

"I didn't say that, Louis," she said, turning in her chair. She could hear a hint of a southern accent creeping into her speech. No matter how much she practiced, it always seemed to come out when she was stressed. Or drunk.

Louis Crater leaned forward a little, causing the

lights in the ceiling to fluoresce on his bald head, but didn't look at her. Instead he stared at her computer screen with the stern expression that seemed to be his reaction to everything.

"Tomorrow?" he said, continuing to focus on the screen, though she knew the code filling it was complete Greek to him.

"Like I told you, I'm running a full-scale test on the Forensic Index today and I don't anticipate any problems . . ."

In her previous life as a corporate programming consultant, Quinn had dealt with people like this every day. And that, combined with the endless hours of solitude, dark cubicles, bottomless pots of coffee, and truckloads of junk food, was why she'd bagged programming a year and a half out of college. She'd taken a support position at the FBI a few weeks later, hoping to learn the ins and outs of the organization and improve her chances of becoming an agent as soon as she was eligible.

"So you're saying tomorrow, then. Right, Quinn?"

About the same time Crater, the man in charge of the FBI's Combined DNA Index System and the man now hovering over her like a vulture in an updraft, had canned the private contractor maintaining the system in the face of budget cuts. Then, undoubtedly only moments later, he'd uttered those fateful words spoken by department heads to their bosses all over the world: "If we keep it in-house we can do a better job for less money."

"Right, Louis. No problem." Quinn sighed.

So now she was pretty much right back where she'd started—reprogramming an enormous and convoluted computer database, but with a government paycheck that came in at about half her private-industry income.

"Well, I'm glad to hear that you're on track," Crater said, rising again to his full six feet three inches while Quinn gnawed on what was left of her pencil's eraser. "Tell you what. Why don't we go grab a drink after work and you can fill me in on what you've done."

Now, that sounded unpleasant. And if the code gnomes weren't asleep at the switch, it almost guaranteed a system-wide crash during her test.

"I'd like to, Louis, but I can't. I've got plans."

"Lunch?"

"You know, I promised a friend of mine that I'd grab a bite with her," Quinn said truthfully. "You're welcome to come along. It ought to be fun . . ."

He shook his head—a little angrily, she thought—and started walking back toward his office without another word.

Bad. Very bad. Every time he left her desk, he seemed a little more teed off. As near as she could tell, everyone she'd ever worked for had two things in common: first, they heard only what they wanted to, and second, they always made impossible promises to their own bosses. Louis Crater's chances at career advancement hinged at least partially on this project getting done right and fast, while her own prospects hinged almost solely on his happiness. And what a rusty little hinge it was.

She centered herself in front of her keyboard again and took a deep breath. Fifteen minutes till lunch. If she hurried she could get the test routine running before she left.

"Guess who?"

It was fifteen minutes almost to the second when a pair of ring-laden hands covered her eyes, briefly blocking out the lines of code scrolling across the screen.

"Hi, Katie."

Quinn regained her vision again as her friend flopped into an empty chair.

"What about lunch, babe? We still on?" Katie said, taking a brass paperweight from the desk and examining it with feigned interest.

"Yeah, we're still on. I've just got to finish this one thing."

Katie leaned forward and tried to get a look at the computer screen. "Pac-Man?"

Quinn frowned deeply and began tapping commands into the computer again as her friend spun around in her chair like a hyperactive child. "I like the no-window look," Katie said, motioning around her. "I've never been this far under the

J. Edgar Hoover Building before. I always thought this was where they tortured suspects."

Quinn shook her head but kept her attention focused on what she was doing. "Nah. That's down the hall. This is where they torture the employees."

"If you think it's any better on the fourth floor, you're crazy." Katie leaned in a little closer. "Done yet? I'm starving over here."

"I've just got to get a search running so it'll be finished when I get back."

"What are you searching for?"

"A good man."

"Stop. You're killing me. Seriously."

"Phantoms."

"What—you can't tell me? Like, it's top secret or something?"

Quinn slapped the enter key and rolled her chair back a foot or so, letting the computer digest the search parameters. "No, really. I'm serious. Do you know what the Forensic Index is?"

"Part of the DNA database, right?"

"I'm impressed. Actually, it's the section of the system that stores information on unsolved cases. Like if a guy commits a crime in Michigan and leaves some blood or saliva or whatever there, his DNA signature would be entered into Michigan's police database, which would at some point then be uploaded to our central computer. Let's say someone left the same DNA at a crime in—oh, I don't know . . . California.

The Forensic Index would find the match and notify the two states that the cases are related."

"So whose ghost are you looking for?"

"My own. We had to upgrade some of the hardware in the system and I've been modifying the code to accept it. Anyway, I planted a fictional DNA signature in the databases of all fifty states. Now I'm going to run the search routine I wrote and see if it finds them. With a little luck I'll get to keep my job."

"You call that luck?" Katie said, looking around her again. "So I take it, then, that **this** is the problem?"

"What do you mean? What problem?"

"Why you've spent the last week looking like someone just ran over your cat with a lawn mower."

Quinn turned her attention back to the screen and pretended to tap commands on her keyboard, trying to ignore the fact that her friend was staring intently at the side of her face.

"No, it's not, is it?" Katie said finally, drawing out each word dramatically. "It's David. It is, isn't it?"

"I don't know what you're talking about."

Katie feinted left then made a grab for the calendar sitting next to the computer monitor. Quinn was just a little too slow to stop her.

"Come on, Katie, give that back!"

"Oh, you want this, do you?" she said, rolling herself out of range and starting to flip through the calendar's pages.

"Katie, I'm serious . . ."

"'June sixteenth,'" her friend read. "'Dump David.'" She turned a few more pages. "'August tenth. Cut David loose.'" A few more pages. "'September second. Drop David like a hot potato.'"

Quinn pushed herself out of her chair and snatched the calendar from her friend's hand. "Okay, okay. So I'm a wimp. No need to rub it in."

"My God, girl, what's this hold he's got over you? I mean, I can see how the gorgeous, sophisticated, perfect-butted CIA type would have looked pretty flashy to a bumpkin like yourself—"

"Hey, I'm not a bumpkin. I'm a redneck."

"Oh, right. Sorry. The bottom line here is that the guy's turned into kind of a jerk. I mean, what is it this time?"

Quinn sighed and fell back into her chair. "Oh, it's just another one of his work parties. You know how they are, a bunch of guys with well-defined hairdos, whose job is to bring coffee to people in Langley, acting like they run the world. And whenever David's around them he gets that show-off, know-it-all voice and talks to me like I'm an idiot."

"So what else is new?"

Quinn stared over her friend's shoulder at the men and women milling around the large, crowded room that housed most of the FBI's computer equipment. "We were supposed to go skydiving this weekend."

"Skydiving? You mean actually jump out of a plane?"

Quinn nodded. "I found this really cool place—you go to ground school for a day and then they let you jump. Two guys jump with you and one of them films you. I've been trying for months to get David to go, and he promised we'd do it this weekend. Now he says we have to be at this party and then he's going to be too busy."

"If God had meant for us to jump out of planes, He would have made us impact resistant."

Quinn shrugged. "I just thought it would be something new, you know? Exciting."

"So your problem is that you have to go to a party, get drunk, and eat free food instead of plunging to your death."

"That's not all of it."

"Give."

"He wants me to wear **The Dress**."

Katie's hands flew to her face in horror. "Oh, my God! Not **The Dress**!" Her squeal was loud enough for everyone in the office to stop and turn in their direction.

They both leaned forward, partially obscuring themselves behind Quinn's desk and fighting to stifle a giggling fit. Finally, when she had regained some control, Katie gave Quinn's hand a sympathetic squeeze. "Not **The Dress**!" she repeated—in a whisper this time. "Dear God, anything but that."

2

Brad Lowell could feel the secretary's eyes on him, but that wasn't enough to get him to open the door and walk through. He took a deep breath and looked around at the spacious outer office, careful to avoid her curious gaze. The furniture was expensive but sparse and overly efficient looking. Walls were a little too white and completely devoid of artwork, making the room look like a work-in-progress. He knew that it wasn't, though. The office suite hadn't changed in years. And neither had the man it was built for.

"You can go right in," the secretary prompted.

Lowell glanced at her and she gave him a sympathetic smile. While she would have no way of knowing what he was there for, it was obvious that he was not the only person who had ever hovered reluctantly outside her boss's office.

Lowell straightened his shoulders and buttoned his jacket, then pushed through the door, immediately closing it behind him. The air inside seemed different—denser somehow. He knew it was his imagination, but he still couldn't shake the sudden oppressiveness of it.

Richard Price acknowledged his entrance with a formal nod—no more or less than common courtesy demanded—and then went back to writing something on a legal pad centered on his desk.

The half glasses he peered through were a recent addition, appearing with more and more frequency as Price climbed into his late sixties. Beyond that and the hair graying at his temples, though, he was the same man Lowell had met fifteen years before. His broad shoulders were still evident through a meticulously pressed dress shirt, as was the dramatic narrowing of his torso as it disappeared into a rock-solid waist. The combination of his build and the wide, flat nose supporting his glasses left him looking like an impossible mix of retired boxer and intellectual—which, in fact, wasn't far from the mark.

"What happened, Brad?" Price said, still not looking up. Lowell watched the gold pen in his weathered hand as it looped gracefully across the pad.

"We ran into a problem, sir."

"I gathered that. I was led to believe that we'd set up an airtight operation."

"We didn't have cooperation from the subject, sir."

Lowell resisted tugging at the tie that suddenly seemed to be a little too tight. Price's unique ability to intimidate him was undiminished by the years.

"Are we going to spar here, Brad, or are you going to tell me what happened?"

"Sir. He didn't show up. He chose an alternate victim and location."

"What 'alternate victim'?"

Lowell pulled a small notebook from the pocket of his jacket and read directly from it, despite the fact that its contents were already branded into his memory. He knew better than to risk making a mistake. Price had an uncanny ability to zero in on the slightest misstep. And he never forgot.

"Mary Dunnigan. She was a twenty-six-year-old economist working for a think tank in Washington. She'd been there for a little over a year—she took the job right after receiving her Ph.D. from Georgetown."

Lowell glanced up for a moment when Price removed his glasses and placed them on the desk. His expression was completely opaque. "She has a boyfriend of three months—a young lawyer with no criminal record. It doesn't appear to be a particularly serious relationship, but there is no evidence that she was seeing anyone else. He's left two messages on her machine so far, but doesn't seem particularly worried yet—"

"What about her office?" Price broke in.

"They left a single message on her machine when she didn't show up for work this morning, but it was more a question they wanted her to get back to them on than concern about her absence. It seems that she sometimes worked from home and kept a fairly irregular schedule."

"The police?"

"Not involved yet. I believe it's likely that we have until Monday, maybe even Tuesday, before she's reported missing. When the police finally do get involved, it will look like she just took off. Eventually, they'll have to begin an investigation, but I think we can be confident that they'll focus on her current boyfriend and a few prior ones. They won't be able to nail down a very narrow time frame for her disappearance, so alibis will be hard to come by. In any event, we'll be monitoring the official investigation closely."

"So we're clean?"

"I believe so, sir."

"Then we got lucky."

"Yes, sir. In fact, there's more. Her medical records indicate that she was treated for clinical depression during her undergraduate years. Overwork was one of the causes, as was a bad relationship.

That will make a rigorous police investigation even more unlikely. They will simply assume—"

Price pointed to a chair in front of his desk. "You know how I feel about luck, Brad."

"Yes, sir," Lowell said, taking a seat. For some reason, it made him even less comfortable. "And I agree. But in this instance we—"

"Family?"

"Both parents are still alive and married, and she has a younger brother. All are living in Texas, none with any discernible connection to politics or law enforcement. No extraordinary financial resources."

Price's face tightened. He pressed his fist to his lips and seemed to concentrate on the thick carpet beneath his feet. Lowell was familiar with this particular mannerism and knew to keep quiet while Price considered the problem. He used the time to silently rehearse the rest of what he had to say. It was almost a minute before Price spoke again.

"How did this happen, Brad? How did we lose him?"

Lowell had been expecting the question and knew that he had to answer carefully. Price tolerated explanations but not excuses. It was a fine line that was sometimes difficult to tread safely.

"I'm working with only three people, sir. One is new. I don't have manpower to spread around, and that means I have to rely almost solely on electronic surveillance . . ."

"And this is a problem?"

"Sir, he discovers our bugs and tracking systems as fast as we can plant them. The truth is, I think he always has."

Price rolled his chair back and concentrated on the floor again, but this time Lowell decided to chance interrupting his train of thought. "Sir, I think we're losing control."

Only Price's eyes moved, flicking up for a brief moment and then returning to the floor. "This is a bad situation, Brad, but it's not a new situation. We need to guard against overreacting."

"That was different, sir." Lowell surprised himself with the volume and force of his own voice. He adjusted his tone to something more respectful, but wouldn't be silent. Not this time.

"Before, sir, there was a vector. We saw it coming. This was different. Random. I don't know exactly how to explain it . . . It was like a game. Sir, I don't know where this is leading. I think it may be time to reevaluate our position . . ." Lowell let his voice trail off into the long silence that ensued. He had more to say—ten years' worth of pent-up frustration. But now wasn't the time.

"We're just stealing time now, Brad. We both know it," Price said finally. "This has to be held together until the last possible moment."

"Yes, sir. I understand." Lowell had known that his words wouldn't change anything. But he'd felt compelled to speak up, to go on record.

"If we double the size of your team? Will that do it?"

Lowell shifted uncomfortably in his chair. He knew what Price wanted to hear, but he wasn't willing to hide the uncertainty he felt. "I don't know, sir. I just don't know. There's a risk to bringing in more people. And I can't guarantee that the benefit will be worth that risk."

"Well, I don't see that we have any alternatives at this point." Price jotted something on his calendar. "Draw up a short list, Brad. We'll meet at four to make the final decisions."

3

Quinn Barry was still smiling when she walked back into the FBI's computer center. Even the drab gray of the cavernous room and the solemn air of the people who worked there couldn't wipe it from her face. After almost a full hour of Katie's manic energy, half-baked theories, and shameless flirting with their undeniably gorgeous waiter, it would take more than the ever-present ghost of J. Edgar Hoover to bring her down. And if her test on the Forensic Index had worked, well, she might just be able to get through David's work party tonight with fewer than her customary dozen watered-down vodka tonics.

She didn't look at the screen as she slipped into her chair, instead reaching for her mug and casting a furtive glance around her. When she was reason-

ably certain that she was enjoying a brief moment
of anonymity, she turned the cup exactly one full
revolution and then tapped it twice on the desk. It
was an obsessive-compulsive ritual she'd picked up
in her computer consulting days. Silly, sure, but
still a lot less elaborate than some of the ones her
fellow programmers had developed.

She picked up a pencil and used it to give her
mouse a gentle nudge. A moment later the screen
came to life and she watched the dim images on it
sharpen into words.

SEARCH 1 COMPLETE
SEARCH 2 COMPLETE

Letting out a deep sigh of relief, she punched a
few commands into the system and confirmed that
the two separate search engines had indeed completed their tasks. And, more importantly, that the
second—hers—hadn't crashed, exploded, shut
down, or looped. Quinn started a print job and
went over a few final details as the search results
began to spew from the communal printer against
the wall. Her smile widened as she read the program stats. Her engine had run a full seventy-five
percent faster and had used significantly less
bandwidth.

"Oh, baby. You are **so** good," she said quietly as
she kicked the floor and set herself to spinning

lazily in her chair. When it stopped, she jumped to her feet and jogged over to the printer. The results of the first run—the search engine that had originally been programmed into CODIS—were already lying in the tray. As expected, it had performed in its customarily efficient but unremarkable fashion, connecting each of the fifty imaginary DNA signatures she'd planted in the states' databases and outputting the location of the crime lab and case numbers. When the results of her search engine were spit from the printer, she snatched them up and quickly scanned through the output.

The two reports looked identical.

"Yes!" she shouted, thumping the printer triumphantly and then looking around at the upturned and slightly annoyed faces of her coworkers. "Sorry." She struggled to look sincere and not laugh as she walked back to her desk.

Once settled back into her chair, she ran a finger down the data columns on her printout. It was all there—her phantom DNA signature and case number, as well as the lab locations, starting with Alabama—number one—and ending with Wyoming, number . . . Another joyful exclamation died in her throat when she saw the number next to the Wyoming entry. Fifty-five.

Her brow wrinkled involuntarily and she pushed her glasses up her nose, bringing the printout into better focus. Fifty-**five**?

She ran her finger up the sheet, finding the first culprit almost immediately. The Pennsylvania lab was showing two hits. One with her now-familiar phantom DNA signature and another with one she didn't recognize. She pulled out a pen and circled the mysterious data, then began searching for the others.

Two minutes later she had them all highlighted. The same unidentified DNA signature had shown up in Pennsylvania, Oregon, Oklahoma, Maryland, and New York. It just didn't make sense—it should have worked. She stared silently down at the print-out, mouth slightly open, trying to figure out where she'd gone wrong.

Her search engine had done exactly what it was designed to do—correctly connect the imaginary DNA signatures she had planted in each state's computer and spit them out as a fictional interstate crime spree perpetrated by a single, nonexistent in-dividual. So what the hell had caused the other hits? The DNA signature was definitely the same in all five cases—but hadn't ever been identified as a match by CODIS before. She put her head in her hands and closed her eyes, blocking out the data in front of her. Where had she screwed up? She'd pretty much used the same search algorithm as be-fore—the main modifications related to hardware compatibility.

After five minutes of uninterrupted concentra-tion, it still didn't make any sense. She wouldn't have been surprised if the whole system had crashed. Or if her program hadn't found any connections at all. Or even if it had found an infinite number of connections. But five? What was that all about?

The sudden pressure of a hand squeezing her shoulder startled her enough to make her throw her pen at her computer screen. She jerked her head around to find her boss's normally stern expression replaced by one of amusement.

"Louis. You **have** to stop doing that."

"Feeling a little tense, Quinn? Maybe you should cut down on all that tea you drink."

"I figure anything with so much hippie sentiment printed on the box can't possibly be bad for me," she said, trying to keep her tone light.

"Uh-huh. I could hear you yelling all the way from my office. It sounded like you had something to tell me. Good news?"

She froze for a moment, but made a quick save by forcing a smile. "Good news. Of course. Definitely."

"You've got the system working, then?"

"The search engine test on the Forensic Index worked great," she lied. "Way more economical than the old system."

He slammed a hand onto the back of her chair, jerking it and her back a few inches. "Great! That's great, Quinn. Can I pass that up the chain?"

"Uh, yeah, Louis. Sure. But you understand it's

not completely done, right? Like we talked about, there are still some details that need to be ironed out and bugs always come crawling out of the cracks during beta testing—"

"Sure, of course," he said, obviously not listening to a word she was saying. "Great job, Quinn. Great job."

She watched him scurry off and felt her will to live slowly drain from her. In retrospect, that hadn't been the smartest thing she'd ever done. Undoubtedly he was already mentally dialing his boss to tell him the new system was "fully operational." Computer neophytes just loved that phrase—"fully operational." Tomorrow she'd be up to her eyeballs in old guys in suits wanting a demonstration.

And what did she have to show them? A system that split out nonsensical data caused by a glitch that she wasn't sure how to even start to look for. No doubt they'd just be falling all over themselves to send her to Quantico for agent training. Right after hell froze over.

Quinn glanced at her watch. She had five hours before David would be at her house to pick her up. She considered calling him and backing out, but this would be the fourth time in a row and she just didn't have the energy for a fight.

She dropped another tea bag in her no-longer-lucky mug and went straight for the coffee machine to get some hot water. She'd have to make the afternoon count.

4

Get out."

Geller did as he was told, throwing open the side door of the van and jumping into the ankle-deep mud.

According to the radio, Hurricane Bart had been downgraded to a tropical storm, but the difference seemed academic as he ran through the fifty-mile-an-hour winds. Sheets of rain instantly soaked through his clothes and amplified the chill he didn't seem to be able to shake anymore, even in his own bed.

He tried to stay in the path of illumination cut by the headlights but found that it just reflected off the rain and blinded him. He turned back toward the van and ran a finger across his throat. A moment later the lights died and he was left with nothing but the darkness and the static of the storm.

Geller moved forward cautiously, finally spotting the chain-link fence when he was only a few feet from it. It took a few moments of searching and a few more of fumbling with a ring of keys, but he managed to get the heavy padlock open and pull off the chain that held the gate closed.

"Go!" he yelled as he fought the wind and dragged the gate open. The van started moving again, a dense shadow splashing slowly past him.

"Did you lock it?"

Geller ran a hand through his short hair, wringing what water he could from it as he slid into the passenger seat. "No, sir. I looped the chain through the gate and hung the lock on it open. Just like you told me."

Brad Lowell didn't acknowledge the reply, other than to step on the gas and propel the van forward. The darkness, rain, and fogging windows didn't seem to affect him as he weaved through the partially flooded streets at an ever-increasing speed. Geller started to wonder how many times he must have driven through this abandoned army base to be able to maneuver so precisely under these conditions. After some consideration, though, he decided he didn't really want to know.

"How much further, sir?" Geller said, more to

break the silence in the vehicle than anything. Lowell apparently didn't feel the same need.

Geller finally just leaned his head against the window and stared out into the darkness. For the most part, all he could see was the chaotic motion of the rain. But every few seconds there would be a slight ebb or change in direction that would allow him a glimpse of his surroundings. The ghostly outline of square, tightly packed buildings would appear and then just as quickly fade back into the storm. Everything looked dead. Just like their cargo.

He put his hand out to brace himself as Lowell skidded the van to the right and then slammed it in reverse for a few seconds before coming to an abrupt halt. "Okay, let's move," Lowell said, throwing his door open and jumping out. Geller was still frozen with his hand on the dash when he heard the back doors of the van being pulled open.

"Geller! Get your ass in gear. Now!"

He took a deep breath and slid between the front seats, moving into the back of the van. The interior lights had been disabled, leaving him to maneuver by the reflection of headlights through the windshield.

"You got ahold of it?"

Geller reached down and grabbed his end of the plastic-wrapped parcel, lifting its considerable weight and waddling forward as Lowell worked the other end out of the back of the van.

Geller managed to maintain his grip as he jumped the two feet to the ground but the plastic became increasingly slick with rain as they moved toward a set of double doors in a dilapidated concrete warehouse. Still ten feet from the building, his hands burning from the strain, he dropped his end into the deep water flowing around his ankles.

"Jesus Christ, boy!"

"I'm sorry," Geller said weakly, feeling the heat building beneath the cool rain running down his face. "I—"

"Pick it up!"

Geller crouched and fumbled uselessly with the wet plastic, unable to get enough of a grip to lift the weight. Lowell spoke slowly this time, enunciating each word. His normally controlled, almost mechanical countenance had completely disappeared and Geller could clearly hear the anger in his voice. "So help me if you don't fucking pick that—"

Geller closed his eyes and forced himself to wrap his arms all the way around the plastic, locking his hands underneath. He could feel everything now. Every edge, every curve. The rigor was completely set now and their package felt like a statue. A statue of a dead woman a few years younger than he was.

A sense of weakness suddenly washed over him but he forced it back, refusing to relinquish control of his body to his struggling mind. At least he hadn't gotten the other side, he told himself as they pushed through the doors and teetered down the hallway. That would have been worse. He didn't know if he could have handled the feel of her broken, folded legs.

"Up here."

Geller helped swing the woman's body onto a steel conveyor belt in the otherwise empty room and stepped back. "Sir, I'd like to apologize—"

"You did fine." Lowell had regained his composure and seemed completely detached as he pushed one of the buttons set into the concrete wall. The sound of the storm penetrating the desolate building was suddenly drowned out by creaking metal wheels and hissing gas.

Geller stared at the package—the woman—as she was carried toward a small opening in the wall surrounded by two heavy metal doors. The black plastic and duct tape dully reflected the jets of flame that sprang from the pipes lining the hole at the end of the conveyor.

"How long does it take, sir?" Geller heard himself say.

Lowell slammed the doors behind the body and locked them shut.

"Not long. An hour. Maybe a little more."

Geller nodded dumbly, unable to take his eyes off the small doors as the gas continued to hiss audibly through them. He could feel the heat on his exposed skin and moved back, trying to escape it.

5

What?" Quinn yelled, leaning forward and bringing her nose to within a few inches of the bottom of the bathroom sink. The contact lens she had dropped seemed to be purposely hiding.

"I'm telling you, Quinn, the old man was pissed!" David was in the living room, unwilling to move from in front of the TV, but still trying to carry on a conversation. "I don't know what Bob was thinking, but he really screwed up."

Quinn finally spotted the lens and managed to get it to stick to her finger. After rinsing it off, she held her reddening eye open and tried to insert it for the third time. People just weren't meant to have to poke themselves in the eye to see better. It wasn't natural.

"At this point I don't think he's going to get that slot. And you know what that means, Quinn."

The lens got caught on her eyelash and a blink sent it back into the sink. That, combined with the glee in her boyfriend's voice and the fact that she still couldn't come up with even a stupid idea about where she'd screwed up the CODIS search program, was enough to finally push her over the edge. "Jesus, David. Bob's a friend of yours!"

"Hey, I'm not wishing him ill here," David called back. She heard the channels changing on the TV set. "But if **he** isn't going to get the job, it might as well be me."

She grabbed the faucet and turned it on in one, angry jerk. A satisfied smile crept across her face as the offending lens disappeared down the drain.

"I guess," she said, putting on her black, slightly horn-rim glasses and walking into the bedroom. She didn't have a full-length mirror, so she had to step up on the bed to center her image in the one over her dresser.

She stared at herself for a few seconds and then took a deep breath in preparation for a sigh. When she did, the ultrashort dress David had bought her scooted up slightly, revealing a glimpse of white underwear. She grimaced and gave the dress a violent downward tug as she took a step back on the soft mattress to get the full-body view.

"Hey, Quinn? Do you smell something burning?"

She didn't answer. It was the blow dryer that she'd turned on tonight for the first time in a year. She wore her dirty-blond hair at a pretty much uniform length of one and a half inches, normally making it blissfully low maintenance. But the slightly spiky, disheveled look didn't work with fire-engine-red microdresses any better than the glasses did. She looked like she should be turning letters on a game show or something. And that was without the matching fuck-me pumps David had so thoughtfully provided to increase her already overly tall five feet eleven inches to well over six feet. Outstanding.

David froze for a moment when she walked into the living room, almost dropping the remote in his hand. She adjusted her glasses self-consciously and looked down at herself. A chiffon skirt flowed from her waist almost to her ankles, but stopped short enough to reveal a pair of leather clogs. She tried her best to smooth out the formless sweater she now wore as David extricated himself from her sofa and slowly approached.

"What's this?"

"What's what?"

"Where's the dress I bought you?"

"Yeah. The dress. Well, David, about that . . . It's sort of . . . You know, I think . . . It doesn't quite—"

"You told me you were going to wear it."

"I'm sorry, David. I just don't feel comfortable in it, okay? I figured we'd meet halfway." She jabbed her hair with her index finger. "Look at this. Wouldn't move if you hit it with a sledgehammer. And I'm wearing makeup—lots of it, in fact."

He silently circled her, obviously unimpressed by what she thought was a terrific compromise. "I just don't get it, Quinn. I really don't."

"What don't you get?"

"Why you want to go through life looking like a fat, hippie librarian."

Quinn wasn't sure how to respond to that, or if it indeed demanded a response. She just stood there and blinked a few times. When David stopped directly in front of her and slid his hands into the pockets of his unimaginative but vaguely stylish slacks, she finally managed to shake off her stupor. "Look, David, I realize that you're not exactly on speaking terms with your feminine side, but do you think maybe that wasn't exactly the right thing to say?"

Though he was not the most perceptive man she'd ever met, the coldness in her voice wasn't lost on him. He actually stepped back to a safer distance. "Quinn . . . I . . . It's just that you would have looked so beautiful . . ."

"Beautiful," she said. "David, I would have looked like a mid-priced hooker drowning in a sea of Laura Ashley."

She saw the surprise on his face melt back into

anger. David Bergin was accustomed to having the upper hand—particularly where women were concerned.

"What are you trying to prove with this, Quinn? That you're so smart you don't need your looks to succeed? A little reality check here. You aren't living on a farm in Dog Patch, West Virginia, anymore. This is D.C. What you look like and how you act is just as important as what you can do. I'm sorry, let me take that back. It's more important. If you really want to be an FBI agent, you better learn to play the game."

Quinn crossed her arms in front of her chest. "'Dog Patch, West Virginia'? We're just full of compliments tonight, aren't we?"

He started to look a little worried again, obviously realizing that he'd gone too far. She held up her hand, silencing him before he could start backpedaling.

"You know, David. I don't think tonight's such a good idea."

"What are you talking about?"

She let out a loud, frustrated breath and brushed by him as she headed for the door.

"Where are you going? QUINN! Where are you going?"

She stopped with her hand on the knob and turned back to him for a moment. "I'm going for a drive. I need to do some thinking. Okay?"

"No way," he said in that cautioning, authoritarian tone she hated so much. "We are going to this party. You've blown too many of these things off, Quinn. People are starting to wonder about you. How is it going to make me look if you don't show up?"

"I guess it's going to make you look single," she said. "Lock the door when you leave."

6

Quinn scooted her stool forward a bit and rested her elbows on the torn felt of the pool table. The small pub was nearly empty, inhabited only by her, a man who looked remarkably like Abraham Lincoln, and the tall-haired woman serving him. Quinn had discovered the place by accident when she was attending the University of Maryland. Stumbling through a cobblestone alley with some friends at one-thirty in the morning, she'd decided that they needed another beer before leaving Baltimore and returning to the dorms. They'd pushed through the door of the first place they'd come to and spent the next two hours laughing hysterically and trying to play pool without falling on their faces.

The next weekend they'd found themselves back

at the little bar, locating it only by combining their spotty memories and patching together a crude map. After that, probably no more than a week passed that they didn't at least come by and drink a quick beer.

When Quinn and her roommates graduated, they'd spread out across the country and more or less fallen out of touch. But for some reason, Quinn couldn't leave this place behind. There was something about the claustrophobic feel of the stained ceiling tiles hovering just over her head, the smell of old wood and mold, the Elvis memorabilia spilling from every shelf. It took her back to a time in her life when everything was new and exciting. Before reality had so ruthlessly attacked.

Quinn straightened up for a moment and stretched her back before she started in again on the papers strewn across the pool table. She shuffled back to the beginning of the Forensic Index search subroutine she'd written and squinted through tired eyes at the endless lines of code. It was hard to read in the dim light, but the eyestrain headache threatening to take hold of her had been beaten back by the three and a half pints of beer she'd been through. There was nothing like the combination of unfathomable programming glitches and booze to take a person's mind off a disastrous personal life.

Across the room, Elvis's hips rocked hypnotically and the clock set into his stomach read one A.M.

She'd been there for four hours going over the same thing again and again. The search system algorithm was a complete no-brainer—a problem you'd give a high school senior. All the computer had to do was open a database and compare the numbers representing strands of DNA. If there were any common strings, it spit them out. Dead simple. So where were these other five hits coming from and why hadn't the original search engine picked them up? The two systems worked in essentially the same way.

She dug through the loose papers on the table until she found the data her new program had output. "Maryland, New York, Oklahoma, Oregon, and Pennsylvania," she said quietly to herself. What was the connection? She'd already gone through the literature on each state's individual database, finding no meaningful incompatibilities between their hardware and programming. And with that, she was rapidly running out of places to look.

"Okay, closing time. Everybody out."

Quinn glanced up and saw the old man turn unsteadily on his stool to stare glassy-eyed in her direction. The bartender grabbed his chin and pulled his face toward her. "Not her, Barney. I meant you."

He was a little too out of it to mount any kind of meaningful protest, so, with a little help, he staggered through the door and out into the dark alley.

The bartender slammed the door behind him and sagged against the wall. "Why do I do it, hon? Shouldn't I be living the good life?"

Quinn smiled. Bertie was the other reason she couldn't stay away from this little dive bar. Half mother to everyone who came in and half working-class philosopher, Quinn went nowhere else when she had a problem. She raised her glass in a mock toast. "I thought this was the good life. Isn't that what you told me?"

"Never believe anything I say, hon." Bertie leaned over the bar and poured herself a pint. "You'll live a longer and happier life that way."

Quinn started gathering her papers into a single, disorderly pile as Bertie dragged a stool over to the pool table and sat down across from her.

"Working on a case?"

Quinn shot the woman a stern glance. "Bert, I've told you a hundred times that I'm not an agent. I'm just a clerk. A doormat. An insignificant speck of dust blowing around the basement of the J. Edgar Hoover Building."

"Just a matter of time. Don't you worry. You'll get there."

"Sometimes I wonder," Quinn said as she stuffed her papers into a worn knapsack and tossed it under the table.

"So what are you doing here, hon?"

"Can't I just come by to say hello?"

Bertie looked a little skeptical as she lit a cigarette. "There are more comfortable places to work. Am I right?"

"I guess," Quinn said, sounding a little dejected even to herself.

"So? Problems with David?"

Quinn nodded without lifting her eyes from the floor. "We got into a fight."

"About what?"

"A dress he bought me."

"A dress he bought you? Now, how'd you kids manage to turn that into a fight?"

"I couldn't legally sit in it in most states."

Bertie took a thoughtful drag on her cigarette, followed by a rattling cough.

"You should quit those things, you know," Quinn said.

She ignored the advice. "What are you going to do about it?"

"Maybe get you some of those nicotine patches."

Bertie frowned. "About the dress."

"Burn it. Strangle him with it. I don't know . . ." Quinn fell silent as Bertie continued to work on the cigarette, knowing that the woman was gathering her thoughts and would have them assembled into some kind of sage advice before the ashes reached her fingers.

"You know, Quinn, I think you're getting too worked up over this. Men like to show off their women. They don't mean nothin' by it. If I were as beautiful as you, I don't think I'd spend so much time trying to hide it. Hell, I'd have married a movie star by now. Or maybe one of those good-looking baseball players . . ."

"It's not just the dress," Quinn said before Bertie could sink into one of the Cal Ripkin fantasies she liked to indulge in. "It's a lot of things. I'm starting to think he's just not right for me. I don't know, I guess I've changed. Grown up a little. Did you know that when I started at Maryland I'd never even eaten Chinese food? The tallest building I'd ever seen in person was a grain silo."

Bertie nodded but didn't interrupt.

"I guess what I'm trying to say is that some of the newness has worn off. When I first met David, all I could think of was his great clothes, his good looks, his Ivy League education, his job at the CIA. I'd never met anyone like him before. He seemed so perfect, so exciting. I couldn't believe a guy like him would even give me the time of day."

"You were starstruck."

"Yeah. Starstruck. Exactly. And I thought I wanted the same things he did. But now I'm not so sure." Quinn sighed quietly and rubbed her eyes beneath her glasses. "I don't know. Maybe I'm just a malcontent, huh? That's what my mom used to tell me before she left my dad—that I was never satisfied with anything. That I thought I was too good for her."

"Well, that's just nonsense, Quinn. The world wouldn't be a very interesting place if everyone was

just satisfied with what life had handed them, now
would it?"

"Maybe not, I don't know."

Bertie jabbed her cigarette out on the edge of the
pool table, leaving yet another burn mark in it.
"Well, I **do** know. I got this bar when my dad
died—that was in '62. I was about your age; told
myself that it was just a short-term thing—that I'd
sell it and move on. Do something with my life.
But there was always a reason not to, you know?
Always a reason to wait just one more year. And
now here I am. And here I'll stay."

"Come on, Bert, you—"

The woman stood and snatched her beer from the
table. "Lock up when you leave, hon."

"Wait! Where are you going?"

"To bed. It's late."

"But this is where you tell me what to do. Remember how it works?"

"Oh, you don't need me, Quinn. This is a decision you can make all by yourself."

7

Quinn leaned back in her chair, rubbing the bridge of her nose and scanning the gray walls around her. It was exactly twelve-thirty on a dreary Monday afternoon and the spacious office around her had nearly emptied out for lunch. She followed one of the last stragglers with her eyes as he walked back from the coffee machine to his cubical.

It wasn't going to get any deader, she knew, but she still couldn't seem to unglue herself from her chair. She'd spent most of her weekend planted in it, trying to figure out where her code was screwed up and avoiding David Bergin. And while she'd been joyfully successful with the David thing, she had reached an utter dead end where the program was concerned.

There was just nothing there. She was almost

starting to wish it was some kind of ultracomplex, cutting-edge piece of code. Then she could call some old friends, fill them with beer and chili con queso, and stay up all night figuring it out. But there was nothing **to** figure out—there just weren't many algorithms simpler and more time-tested than the one she'd used.

Quinn tilted a little further back in her chair so she could see around the watercooler. The top of Louis Crater's bald head was just visible through the door to his office. As always, he was trying to steal a little time for paperwork while his people were at lunch. This was it—everyone was going to start filing back in before long and she didn't want any more witnesses than necessary. Humiliation in and of itself sucked bad enough without adding the public part.

Quinn grabbed the stack of papers containing her code, more as a security blanket than an exhibit, and started for Crater's office. She stopped in the doorway but didn't immediately say anything, instead opting to prop herself against the jamb and chew her lower lip. It took an excruciating twenty seconds or so for Crater to finally look up from what he was doing.

"Quinn? What can I do for you?"

When she didn't answer, he raised his eyebrows and tilted his head a little to the right. The body language wasn't hard to translate. He had better things to do than watch her stand around.

"I was wondering if I could have a few minutes, Louis. To talk about CODIS."

"Of course. Grab a chair."

"Thanks," she said, but didn't move from her position at the door. "Remember I ran that test on the forensic search engine Friday?"

"Sure. I told the guys upstairs about it. They were impressed."

She was forced to fake a sneeze to keep him from seeing the wince that suddenly spread across her face. "Well, like I told you, it found all the test data. Fast. It worked really well."

His smile and nod clearly said "get to the point."

"You see, there's this little problem . . ."

He straightened in his chair, suddenly giving her his full attention. "You just said it worked perfectly."

"No, I said it worked **really well**. It's just that it also connected five other DNA signatures from five different states. The old search engine doesn't, uh, seem to recognize them as matches."

He was silent for what seemed like a really long time. When he finally spoke again, his palms were flat on the desk. Quinn wasn't sure if it was her imagination or not, but he seemed to be pressing down hard enough to make his arms quiver.

"What the hell are you talking about?"

Quinn resisted the urge to look behind her to see who was eavesdropping. "I was in here all weekend, Louis, and I haven't been able to figure—"

"Shut the door."

She reached behind her and pulled it closed, leaning against it to keep the maximum distance between her and her boss.

"Are you telling me that this goddamn thing doesn't work? Is that what you're telling me?"

"No, it works, it's just that—"

"It works, but it doesn't work right? That's what you're saying?"

She looked down at her clogs. "I guess. Yeah."

"Jesus Christ!" Crater said, jumping up from his chair. His hands had balled into fists now but remained firmly planted on the desktop. "Quinn, you told me you had this thing done!"

That, of course, wasn't what she'd told him; it was what he'd **heard**. But this probably wasn't the time to point that out.

". . . and that's exactly what I passed on to my boss. What the hell were you doing messing with the goddamn search engine anyway? This was nothing more than a hardware compatibility issue."

"Louis, I had to—"

He held up a hand and silenced her. "All I want to know is how long?"

Her voice was starting to quaver a little, but she managed to even it out by sheer force of will. "I don't know. I can't find the problem. I'm not sure there is a problem. I'm thinking now that it could be an error in the state systems, or some kind of weird echo. Maybe there's a glitch in the original search eng—"

"Oh, right. Of course. That must be it," Crater said sarcastically. "The system we've been using successfully for ten years must be the problem. I mean, a woman with your experience couldn't have made a mistake, right? Hell, you've been out of college for what? Almost two years?"

"Louis, I thought it was going to work. There's no reason for this to be happening." She took a step toward him and held out the highlighted copy of her program. "Let me show you—"

"Shut up."

She stopped short after covering half the distance to his desk. "What?"

"Do you have any idea what kind of a position you've put me in, Quinn?"

"Louis, I—"

"**Don't talk.**" He looked around him at nothing in particular. "I don't believe this. I've supported you throughout this whole thing. Other people were skeptical, but I told them you could handle it. How do you think this is going to make me look?"

Quinn felt her nervousness fade a little and her irritation start to grow. How dare he make this sound like he had been doing her some kind of favor? She hadn't asked for this job. She'd told him that doing a modification on someone else's system by herself would be a difficult and time-consuming process. But as usual, he hadn't listened. All he'd thought about was how many brownie points he could collect for getting the work done for free. If she had miraculously brought it in on his ridiculous timetable, he would undoubtedly have taken all the credit. And now that things weren't going quite right, it looked like she was going to take all the blame.

"Look, Louis, I can still—"

"Out."

"Excuse me?"

"We're already past our deadline and you're telling me we've got nothing. Right? Because that's what I'm hearing."

Quinn felt her irritation grow into anger at the melodrama of it all. "It's not nothing, Louis. I've done a lot of work here. It's just a bug. They happen, you know?"

"Look . . . just get out of my office. I've got to think about what I can do to salvage this situation."

Quinn stood her ground for a moment, wanting to grab him by his tie and force him to have a productive conversation about this. But she could see that it wasn't going to happen. For now, it looked like it would be better just to run away and let him cool off.

8

There was nothing about this project that Senator James Wilkenson felt even remotely comfortable with. That hadn't always been the case, but the jittery feeling at the bottom of his stomach got worse every year. Was it the project itself—the technology growing with the speed and inevitability of a virus, and the impossible levels of secrecy and security that were made necessary by that growth? Or was it just him—older, wiser, and more aware of the possible consequences of his involvement?

He bent over a drinking fountain and tried to wash away the vaguely metallic taste that filled the sterile halls and labs around him. It didn't work.

"If you could just step this way, Senator, we'll continue your briefing in the main project center."

Wilkenson nodded regally at Richard Price, the chairman and Svengali of Advanced Thermal Dynamics, Inc., and followed him through a security checkpoint into yet another lengthy corridor. The senator's head moved slowly from side to side as they walked, surveying the busy men and women working on the other side of the heavy glass that passed for walls.

It was yet another thing he hated about this project—the physical layout. Scientists and techs scurrying freely through gardens of unfathomable machines and devices, working unsupervised, discussing technical problems, failures, and successes. He had chaired the Senate Intelligence Committee for longer than he cared to remember but had never come to terms with scientists—their eccentric behavior, their arrogant dismissal of political and military realities, their penchant for sharing their discoveries with colleagues.

Price seemed to read his mind as he inserted the card hanging around his neck into a slot in the wall.

"We've done what we can to keep the separate areas of research completely independent of one another, Senator. "Different physical locations, limited access, and the like. Only a handful of people have a grasp of the project as a whole, but as we've discussed in the past, good science is about the exchange of ideas . . ."

"I guess it all depends on who you're exchanging

with," Wilkenson replied coldly. He had never liked Price. He was as arrogant as the eggheads who worked for him. It seemed that his tone was always skirting the edge of condescension.

"I believe that our security record over the last ten years is perfect, sir."

Wilkenson nodded, more to acknowledge the fact that he had heard than in recognition of Price's accomplishments.

"You haven't been here since we completed this section, have you, Senator?"

Wilkenson stepped through the door and surveyed the room. It was probably the size of two football fields placed side by side, with stark, unblemished walls, floors, and ceilings. Stainless-steel rails hung fifty feet above them, efficiently moving and storing a multitude of enormous devices constructed of titanium, carbon fiber, and space-age ceramics. The hundred or so people flowing back and forth across the lab seemed to have no other purpose than to humbly serve their creations. They stood on tall scaffolds, polishing and adjusting; they pounded furiously on computer keyboards feeding the mysterious objects knowledge and direction. They worshiped.

"As you know," Price said, putting a hand on the senator's back and prompting him forward, "the pace of development here has continued to accelerate, and that made the addition to the main facility necessary. We've outgrown straight computer simulation and now we're going to combine some real-world systems with our imaging capabilities. It's a very exciting time."

Senator Wilkenson rubbed his eyes, partially to try to ease the pressure building behind them and partially because of the ungodly hour. He'd had to rise at four A.M. to make the drive to this back-country nowhere in the southern Virginia mountains. Never again would he let Price talk him into a seven A.M. meeting.

"And how much are these real-world systems going to cost me, Richard?"

Price smiled a little uncomfortably—more for show than for anything else. Despite the pretense, they both knew that these meetings were always about the same thing. Money.

"Ninety million."

Wilkenson let out a long breath, not bothering to keep his surprise and irritation hidden. "In addition to what we just paid for the modifications to the facility?"

Price nodded.

"Richard, I don't think you're fully aware of what you're asking. Where do you think this money comes from? Do you think I just walk in and ask Congress for funding for this project? No, it has to be bled off other contracts and funneled here without their knowledge. Do you have any idea how difficult it is to make ninety million dollars just disappear into thin—"

"I think you have me to blame for that, Senator."

Wilkenson turned toward the voice and examined the man striding across the concrete floor toward them. He didn't seem to fit in with the other people working in the facility. For one thing, he wasn't wearing the obligatory lab coat, having forgone it for an expensive-looking maroon sweater and beige linen slacks. His silver hair was longer than the senator was comfortable with, but it was neatly combed and perfectly suited to his sharp features and tanned skin. Mostly, though, it was his relaxed confidence that set him apart from the acne-scarred introverts infesting this project.

"Senator," Price started, "I'm sure you remember Edward Marin, our project coordinator."

"Of course. It's good to see you again, Doctor."

Marin's smile showed a mouthful of straight white teeth that intensified the dignified aura that surrounded him, making him seem a few years older than the forty-four Wilkenson knew him to be. They'd met twice before, and each time Marin had made him feel vaguely uncomfortable. He was a little too smooth, a little too charming. Wilkenson was used to gauging the insincerity of his political brethren, but he had no criteria by which to judge Edward Marin.

"So you say this is your fault, Doctor? Can I assume we've had an unavoidable setback?" Wilkenson wondered how many times he'd heard that little phrase in his lengthy career overseeing countless government contracts.

Marin motioned a little too graciously toward the center of the lab, and the three men began moving again. "On the contrary, Senator. We've had a major breakthrough that I didn't see coming and didn't budget for."

Wilkenson stopped and turned to Marin, waiting for a team of lab techs to move out of earshot. "Now, I thought I'd heard it all. But that's a new one on me."

"Like I told you, Senator, there have been some exciting things happening," Price cut in.

"Would you care to be more specific, Doctor?"

"Of course. We have a very talented young man doing some theoretical work for us, and I have to admit that he surprised even me. We had a problem with the HF Overtone System that I think you're aware of, and I assumed that we were a couple of years from solving it. To make a long story short, he pulled a rabbit out of his hat a few months ago and that problem no longer exists."

Wilkenson nodded thoughtfully when Marin fell silent and graced him with another flash of those brilliant white teeth, though he wouldn't have known an HF Overtone from a hole in the ground. He had a tendency to lose interest when things went the way of details. That's what aides were for.

"And what does this mean to us, Dr. Marin?"

"Other than the ninety million dollars?"

Wilkenson frowned. "Yes. Other than that."

"Frankly, it means that this project is starting to

wind down. Obviously, we still have some problems to work out, and we'll know more—"

"What are we talking about in time, Doctor?"

Price looked nervous but had the good sense not to speak as his project coordinator ran an index finger back and forth over his smooth-shaven chin. CEOs didn't like their technical personnel making these kinds of statements. They were generally a little too honest.

"With funding and a little luck, I'd say we could have a working system ready for installation inside of three years."

Wilkenson immediately started walking again, setting a pace that forced the other two men into a half jog to keep up. They continued in silence for about a minute before Price, looking uncomfortable, started a running explanation of the systems surrounding them. Wilkenson tuned him out and concentrated on the problem at hand.

As far as most of the government knew, none of this existed. Even the president was unaware of the scope of their research. Wilkenson had considered it politically expedient for him to continue support of the project, as it would make him look conscientious and forward-thinking should the delicate balance the world was currently enjoying suddenly fail. But he'd never really considered the possibility of ATD actually producing anything workable during his career. He'd always treated this as another black hole that it made sense to occasionally throw money into.

Forgetting for a moment a potentially dangerous response from the Chinese and Russians, what would the reactions closer to home be? How carefully would people want to scrutinize the less-than-aboveboard financing of Advanced Thermal Dynamics? What about the unwavering, and perhaps illegal secrecy? And finally, when all the dust had settled, would anybody want what had been built? At that point it would be too late to turn away and pretend it didn't exist.

A hand on his shoulder pulled Wilkenson back into the present. When he refocused his eyes, he saw a bright red strip running along the floor in front of him.

"I'm sorry, Senator, but for your own safety, we won't be going into this section. There's a buffet set up in the boardroom. Why don't we finish our discussion there?"

9

"Quinn? You all right?" The young man had stopped in the middle of the hallway, blocking her path to the FBI's computer lab and evaluating the dark circles under her eyes.

"Late night, you know?" she answered, taking a tentative sip from the Styrofoam cup in her hand. Her miracle tea wasn't working anymore. Always a bad sign.

"Doing something fun, I hope."

She grimaced and tried desperately to remember his name. They'd been introduced a few months back and now knew each other well enough to say hi, though it was obvious he was interested in deepening that relationship a bit.

"No such luck, Charlie," she said when the caffeine finally started to reanimate her dead and dying brain cells. "Work, work, work, you know?"

"Tell me about it."

She made a show of glancing up at the clock on the wall and started forward again.

"Try to get some sleep tonight," he said, moving out of her way.

"Not much chance of that."

Quinn continued down the hall and reluctantly stepped through the door of the computer center. She kept her head down as she walked toward her desk, embarrassed to acknowledge the eyes that she could feel following her. She'd started getting the slightly uncomfortable looks and nods yesterday afternoon, and by now pretty much everyone would know she had been read the riot act by Louis Crater.

She dared a glance to her right and, sure enough, got a queasy smile from one of the clerks seated against the wall, though he seemed to be looking past her. She followed his gaze to her desk and stopped in the middle of the floor.

The two men huddled around her terminal seemed to have already made themselves at home. One was sitting in her chair with his feet on her file boxes and the other had moved her personal effects to the floor and planted his butt on the edge of her now-empty desk.

"Excuse me," Quinn said as she approached. "Can I help you?"

The one sitting in her chair turned his head

lazily, giving her a brief, disinterested smirk before going back to the screen of her terminal. "You're Quinn?"

"Uh, yeah. And that's my chair."

"You're supposed to go in and talk to Louis," the one leaning against her desk said.

"Who are—"

"Quinn!"

She turned and saw Louis Crater poking his head out of his office. "Can I have a moment?"

She knew it was stupid, but she couldn't help feeling a little violated. She didn't want to leave these rude jerks spread out across her space . . .

"Quinn! Now!" Crater said when she didn't move. Aware of the silence that had descended on the computer center, she started obediently across it.

"Take a seat," Crater said, shutting the door behind her.

"Who are those guys, Louis?" she asked, though she was pretty sure she already knew the answer.

"They're from Advanced Thermal Dynamics, the system's original designer."

Quinn felt the muscles in her jaw tighten and didn't bother to mask her indignation. "You called ATD?"

"I said have a seat."

She stood her ground for a moment but then decided that belligerence probably wasn't going to improve her situation any. "Louis—"

He held up his hand. "Don't bother. This is the way it's going to be. This project has to get done, and as of yesterday it was dead in the water."

"I can finish it, Louis. By the time those guys figure out where I'm at, I could have the thing up and running."

"Come on, Quinn. Last time we talked you didn't even know where the hell to begin."

"I'd start with the ATD code and the individual lab systems. I still don't think my stuff is the problem—"

Crater let out a short laugh and shook his head. "I admire confidence, Quinn. I even like a certain amount of stubbornness. But let me give you a little piece of advice: there's such a thing as too much. Nobody respects a person who refuses to admit she's wrong. And it's not a quality we can afford in our agents. We're team players here, Quinn."

Quinn's eyes narrowed but she didn't say anything.

"I know you've done your best on this thing, and I appreciate all your hard work. But it's obvious now that you're in over your head. And that's probably as much my fault as anybody's . . ."

There was no point in arguing; as stupid as it was, he'd obviously made up his mind. And the implied threat in his comment about agents and the team was fairly obvious.

"Where are you going?" he said when she started to stand.

"To get those guys up to speed. There's a lot of background we're going to need to go over before they can get to work."

Crater shook his head. "They assure me they have it under control."

"Excuse me?"

"Look, Quinn, these guys are professionals, they don't need your help."

"Louis," she said, careful to keep her voice even, "**I'm** a professional and I'm telling you right now that—"

"I'm reassigning you to a programming job in Quantico. Nathan Shale in the Investigative Support Unit needs a modification to his system."

Quinn just stared at him as he walked around his desk and plopped down in his chair. "Louis, you can't be serious. Whatever this bug is, it isn't obvious. Without my help, these guys are going to be completely lost."

He didn't seem to hear. "Why don't you gather up your stuff and take the rest of the day off? I told Nate you'd be there first thing in the morning, ready to work."

10

The feeling of decay that had been plaguing him was almost gone now—the heaviness in his limbs that made it seem as if his blood had become too thick to flow, the alarming deterioration in his ability to concentrate, the brief moments when his emotions fought their way to the edge of his control.

He rolled down the car window and leaned his arm on the door, letting the wind rush in. It would have been uncomfortable to most people but he enjoyed the sensation as his body reacted—the nearly imperceptible tightening of his skin, the follicles of his arm hair stiffening to hold in body heat.

The late-morning air seemed to be perfectly clear, though he couldn't be sure if the cause was atmospheric or just the result of his enhanced senses. He could discern the subtle changes in odor as he sped along the gravel road from one grouping of trees to the next—as if he could smell their color as the leaves were slowly killed by the fall.

He glanced in the rearview mirror for no real reason—just to see the emptiness of the road as it twisted through the bright reds and golds of the landscape. He already knew that there was no one behind him. The people whose job it was to follow him, to try to control him, were a hundred miles away.

It had taken years of slow, often painfully frustrating work, but he had finally turned everything against them. Their endless procession of electronic devices and carefully planned surveillance programs were now completely subverted. It was ironic, really. The more sophisticated their techniques had become, the easier it had been for him to take control of them. And now that control was absolute. They saw and heard only what he allowed them to see and hear, while he was virtually omniscient— privy to their phone conversations, e-mail, family histories, medical records. There was nothing they could hide from him.

He pulled back on the steering wheel, a smile spreading across his face when it flexed dangerously in his hands. His strength was coming back to him. He'd almost forgotten what it felt like.

The car seemed to slow by itself as the first house came into view. Sometimes he wondered if this wasn't the best part. The years of anticipation, building to an unbearable crescendo as he watched and planned. And then those final moments just before the act itself, when time seemed to stop and all that existed was the pounding of his heart and the strange contradiction of dry throat and overactive saliva glands.

The road steepened and he finally crested on a pronounced ridge that he knew to be the highest point for miles. Below him, the floor of the small valley looked like a quilt, cut into neat geometric shapes by the farmers who still lived and worked in this part of the country. He followed the straight lines of the crop divisions with his eyes, pausing briefly whenever they converged at one of the antique homes sparsely dotting the rolling land.

He was pushing them too far now, he knew. Jolting them too suddenly from the complacency he'd lulled them into. There was a point when the stupid became unpredictable, like a mortally wounded animal that didn't yet realize its life was over. But that was just part of the game. Part of the excitement. Part of finally coming back to life.

The car rolled to a stop alongside the road, again with seemingly no prompting from him. There was no breeze and the sun burned into his back as he stepped out and started up the road. The driveway wasn't far, maybe five hundred meters. He turned up onto it, running his hand along the sun-heated metal of the mailbox at its edge.

As he continued toward the little house, the rest of the world seemed to dim. A normal person wouldn't have noticed, but he did. The color bled from the landscape, making the tiny, gabled home and the carefully tended flower gardens around it seem to glow with a subtle intensity.

The effect became more pronounced as he drew closer. He paused before knocking on the door, looking out over the faded world around him. The nearest house, probably a quarter of a mile away, had almost disappeared into the corn that surrounded it.

He wasn't completely aware that he had knocked until the woman opened the door. Her T-shirt and jeans were splotched with dirt and she wore a pair of tattered gloves on tiny hands. Her long brown hair was tied back, but a few errant hairs had escaped and were hanging in her face, accentuating her smooth skin and youthful features.

She worked as a marine biologist, he knew, studying the environmental impact of industry on the Chesapeake Bay. By all reports, a very bright and very talented young woman.

"Can I help you?" she said, pulling off her gloves and stuffing them partway into the front pocket of her jeans. The muscular flesh on her thigh compressed seductively under the brief pressure and then instantly rebounded.

Her smile was confident, relaxed. She felt completely safe, as all the ones before her had. They only saw what he allowed them to see. Later he would show her more, but right now he projected only kindness, tinted with just a shade of distress and uncertainty. It seemed to be the mask that worked best.

11

Quinn Barry threw her gym bag at the stairs leading to her apartment, landing it with an unsatisfying thud about halfway up. A solid kick sent it the rest of the way to the open walk that ran along the front of the building. She'd stopped at the gym on the way home to blow off some steam and to try to forget the heinously crappy day she'd had, but even with a twenty-minute attack on the heavy bag, she was still pissed off.

Emptying her desk had been one of the most humiliating experiences of her life. She'd approached the two guys from ATD again after Louis had basically canned her, and made what she'd thought was a magnanimous offer of a little background on what she'd done and where she kept things. Their only reaction had been a condescending stare and a shake of the head. Then they'd just turned their backs on her and gone back to what they were doing. She'd actually had to push one of them out of the way so she could get into her drawer.

Arrogant bastards. They'd treated her like she was some kind of idiot—a government hack who didn't know her keyboard from her elbow. Well, she'd pit her programming skills against theirs any day of the week. Hell, if she'd started with ATD out of college, **they'd** probably be working for **her**.

The wind was starting to blow as she scooped up her bag and moved along the walkway toward her second-floor apartment. When she passed by the window of the office she kept in the tiny guestroom of her place, she registered movement out of the corner of her eye. She stopped and stepped closer to the window, cupping her hands on the glass and trying to peer through the half-closed venetian blinds. It took a moment for her eyes to adjust to the weaker interior light, but when they did her breath caught in her chest.

There was a man standing with his back to her going through the papers next to her computer. She watched, frozen, as he shuffled through a teetering stack of bills at the edge of her desk and then sat down in her chair. She adjusted her hands to more efficiently block out the glare of the sun when he spun a half turn to the left and revealed his profile.

David.

Quinn took a step back from the window and let out a long breath. This was not what she needed today. She glanced over the railing into the parking lot, focusing on her vehicle for a moment. It was looking a lot like a getaway car.

"Oh, grow up," she said quietly to herself, and then marched the rest of the way to her front door. She entered as quietly as possible, laying her gym bag on the carpet and leaving her tennis shoes by the sofa. Her stockinged feet didn't make a sound as she moved across the apartment and stopped in the doorway to her office.

David was still in her chair but now he was doubled over, going through a stack of papers on the floor.

"Looking for something?"

As was her plan, David jumped out of the chair and spun around, narrowly avoiding falling back into her computer.

"Quinn, Jesus! What are you doing here?"

"I live here. What are you looking for?"

"Something to write on. I was going to leave you a note," he said. There was a nervous uncertainty in his voice that she'd never heard before, but she couldn't be sure of the cause. Was he concerned about the future of their relationship or was he still trying to shake off the effects of her sneaking up behind him?

He seemed to want to back away as Quinn

walked up to him and dug a legal pad out from under the mess on her desk. She slapped it into his chest. "What was it going to say?"

"It was going to say I'm sorry."

Her suspicion notched a little higher. As long as she had known him, those words had never passed his lips. He was a lawyer by schooling and his apologies were usually long, complicated, and full of disclaimers.

"I see," Quinn said. Then they just stared at each other. He didn't seem to know what to do, and for different reasons, she didn't either. What she **didn't** want was to give the impression that she was in an apology-accepting mood. Cupid's evil twin was clearly offering her a way out of this relationship and she was pretty much inclined to take it.

"Quinn, look . . . What I said. I was wrong."

Another first. This day was just full of surprises.

"Look, David," she said, purposefully dulling the edge in her voice. "I'm not trying to be a bitch here. But we've got to talk . . ."

"I know. I know we do. That's why I made reservations at Tony's. I thought we could have a quiet dinner—just us."

She sighed quietly, knowing what she should say. She should say no. She should tell him that they didn't want or expect the same things out of life and that it was time to run away from each other before it was too late. But she was having a hard time getting the words out. They'd been together for almost a year and the bottom line was that he was a pretty good guy—smart, ambitious, and in his own way, a loyal friend. Just not the right one for her. "Sure, David," she heard herself say. "Sounds good."

"Great. Great. Hey, what are you doing home in the middle of the day?" he said, obviously anxious to change the subject.

"I got transferred to Quantico," she said, walking out of the room and taking a seat at the kitchen table.

"Really? That's great. It'll give you a chance to press some flesh." He seemed distracted, like he was thinking of something completely different. In any event, it was unlikely that he was going to ask her how she felt about her sudden career change.

"What about you, David?"

"Huh? Oh, I just took a late lunch. Like I told you, I wanted to leave you a note, since you, uh, haven't been returning my calls. See if we could get together for dinner tonight."

Neither one of them seemed to have anything else to say but David didn't move from his position at the edge of the kitchen. He looked like he was deep in thought but trying to hide it with a rather vacant smile. Quinn wondered if he was actually starting to feel committed to this relationship. Great timing.

He finally went for the door, but stopped with his hand on the knob and stared down at her gym bag. "Quinn . . ."

"Yeah?"

"No. Never mind."

"Come on, David. What?"

"I was going to ask you a favor. But now probably isn't the . . ."

"Spit it out, David."

"My car does this shaking thing when I stop . . ."

Quinn rolled her eyes. She'd grown up on a farm and spent a good portion of her childhood with her head under the hoods of trucks and other farm equipment. From a free-advice standpoint, being a mechanic was surpassed only by being a doctor.

"Your rotors probably need to be turned. If you'd get rid of that monster truck, you wouldn't have this problem."

"It's not a monster truck. It's an SUV."

"Whatever. I'll tell you, David, I don't really have the tools to—"

"No, no. I was just wondering if you could check it out and tell me exactly what's wrong and how much it should cost to fix. You know how those guys at the garage are if they think you don't know what you're talking about."

Quinn briefly wondered if he was more concerned with smooth braking than the fact that their relationship was coming unglued, and then silently admonished herself for her cynicism. While she'd pretty much come to the conclusion that they weren't even close to being right for one another, that was no reason to turn into a shrew. "Sure, David. No problem." She tossed him her keys and he dropped his on her gym bag.

"Thanks, babe. I'll meet you at the restaurant at seven."

It took a few minutes, but Quinn finally mustered the energy to peel herself from the chair and grab a carton of ice cream from the freezer. She ate directly from the container, trying to put David out of her mind and sort through everything that had happened to her over the last few hours.

In light of the big black blot that Louis was undoubtedly painting on her performance review, did she still have a realistic chance of becoming an agent? Hell, had she ever? The fact was, David hadn't been completely wrong during his tirade on Friday. Her look didn't exactly scream "federal government" and neither did her attitude. She had already started to bristle at the powers-that-be constantly sticking their noses into her business—and she'd been working with nearly complete autonomy compared with what a street agent had to deal with. What would happen when she had some old guy telling her he didn't like the shade of her suit? That her shoes weren't shiny enough? That she had to call him sir?

Maybe she'd been a little overzealous in her desperate effort to escape from small-town West Virginia. She'd promised herself in the second grade that she would get out at the first opportunity—that she'd see the whole world and try everything it had to offer. But maybe this **was** what it had to offer. Maybe the best she could hope for was a decent private-sector job for decent money. A decent house. A decent husband. A couple of decent kids. Maybe a decent dog—nothing too unusual—a Lab or a Golden.

Maybe she could get her old job back. She'd been doing really well before she'd quit to work for the FBI. The compensation had been a hell of a lot better, the work environment was totally casual, and the job was actually pretty interesting. Well, kind of interesting. She grimaced and shoveled a snowball-sized scoop of ice cream into her mouth. Who was she kidding? The most exciting thing that happened in private industry was when someone sprang for the doughnuts with the little sprinkles on top.

Quinn dropped the scoop and rubbed her forehead, trying to dissipate the ice-cream headache that had snuck up on her. This was all a bunch of crap. The more she thought about the modifications she'd made to CODIS, the more convinced she became that it wasn't her fault. After getting the cold shoulder from those two asses ATD had sent to "fix" her mistake, she was starting to think that maybe the problem was with them. Maybe their system wasn't all that it was cracked up to be and they were just there to cover their butts.

Quinn walked into her office, opened her fire hazard of a closet, and started digging through the papers stored there. It took about half an hour but she finally found it—a copy of ATD's code. She'd gone through the relevant sections before she started her modifications but hadn't really given it a whole lot of thought. Now, though, maybe it was time for a second look. She wasn't going to give up her dream of gunfights and glory for a computer terminal and a minivan. Not without a fight, anyway.

12

It was eleven P.M. by the time Quinn eased off I-95 and headed into the lights of Baltimore. She continued to accelerate through the off-ramp, waiting until the last second to slam on the brakes. Her seat belt tightened painfully over her full stomach as the antilock system kicked in and David's truck glided smoothly to a stop. It was her third attempt at reproducing the complaint he had, and for the third time she'd found nothing. She decided to give it up and pronounce the car healthy before a cop noticed her erratic driving and shoved a Breathalyzer into her mouth.

Their dinner had been unusual, with David on better behavior than she thought possible. He had apologized again, offering no qualifications at the end of it, and had looked appropriately uncomfort-

able and penitent the entire evening. She, in retrospect, had probably come off like a perfect bitch,
but she just hadn't known how to react. Was he
being possessed by a charming demon with a thing
for tall blondes who dressed like fat-hippie librari-
ans? Was he cheating on her and feeling guilty?
Had he actually seen the error of his ways?

Whatever it was, it was enough of an improvement to confuse her and strip her of her will. She'd
remained uncharacteristically silent for most of the
dinner, letting him talk and trying to build her
courage. In the end, though, everything had been
left unresolved.

When they'd finished dinner, he'd invited her
back to his apartment but she'd begged off, using
her first day at her new job tomorrow as an excuse.
He seemed genuinely disappointed and had gotten
even more upset when she told him she was driving
straight to her dad's farm after work Friday. He
hinted at wanting to go, but she pretended not to
notice. Then he told her that he had hoped they
could spend some quality time together that weekend. He'd actually used those words: **quality time**.
Possessed. That had to be it. The man was clearly in
need of a good exorcist.

Quinn surveyed the broken buildings around her
as she weaved through the familiar streets of Baltimore's industrial area. What was it about this city
that always drew her back? She'd never been entirely comfortable with the atmosphere of D.C.; it

had always struck her as a self-important and superficial place. Baltimore, though, felt real.

Quinn squeezed the truck down a narrow cobblestone alley and jumped the passenger-side wheels up on the sidewalk, knowing that David would cringe at the maneuver. Grabbing her knapsack from the backseat, she jogged over to the battered door of Bertie's bar. It was locked, but she could hear the muffled strains of Patsy Cline inside. A full minute of pounding finally brought Bertie to the door.

"Quinn? Girl, what are you doing here on a school night?"

"I was in the neighborhood."

"Uh-huh." Bertie looked both ways down the street and then let Quinn slip by her.

"I thought I'd grab a drink, but if you're closing early . . ."

"It's been dead all night, no real reason to stay open. Go ahead. Make me one, too."

Quinn walked around the bar, threw her knapsack on a stool, and opted for a glass of water. "Had dinner with David tonight," she said, starting to mix Bertie a gin and tonic.

The older woman stopped sweeping the floor for a moment. "Did you, now? How did that go?"

"It was amazing. He was like a different person. He seemed so . . ."

Bert leaned against her broom, looking amused enough to make Quinn lose her train of thought.

"What?" Quinn asked.

"It's just that sometimes I forget how young you are, Quinn."

"What's that supposed to mean?"

"Men don't change, honey. You either like them the way they are or you don't."

Quinn took her glasses off and rubbed her eyes, accomplishing nothing but a further blurring of her vision. In the hour she'd spent helping Bertie clean up, the only real conclusion they'd come to was that she was a chicken. The David Issue, as it had come to be known, clearly wasn't going to solve itself.

Bertie had gone upstairs to bed but Quinn stayed, brewing some tea and strewing her copy of ATD's CODIS program all over the tiny bar. That had been three hours ago.

She put her glasses back on and flipped the sheet of code she had just read to the floor. She'd already been through the search algorithm twice and found exactly what she should have—a simple, efficient search engine. Now she was in the middle of the input subroutine and finding pretty much the same thing. The deeper she got into it, the more she wondered if Louis was right. The ATD system had been in place for years. What were the chances she was right and it was wrong?

It was another hour before she found it. As tired as she was, she would have read right over the in-

nocuous line of code if it hadn't had a single, recognizable term in it: 30,33.2. She dug through her
knapsack and found her printout with the five mysterious hits on it and ran her finger down the page,
finding the unidentified DNA signature.

15,16/30,33.2/16,20/20,25/11,17/14,16/
8,13/11,11/9,11/10,10/8,11/7,9.3/9,13

The single line of code she had found was fairly
straightforward—if the DNA string had the term
30,33.2 in it, which this one did, the system would
skip it forward to another place in the program.
Quinn started to paw through the documents
stacked on the table, suddenly realizing that she
was smiling for the first time in three days.

She finally found what she was looking for in a
pile of papers lying on the floor next to the broken
pinball machine. At the designated address, there
was another line of code almost identical to the first
one. This time, though, it queried for the term
8,13. And if the string included that term, the program skipped to a line of code that looked like it
was embedded in one of the printer drivers.

"We have a winner," she said aloud as she slid her
finger over the mysterious string and found the
term 8,13.

Four hours later she was sitting in the middle of
the floor surrounded by fourteen loose pages representing what seemed to be random sections of

ATD's program. Thirteen of the fourteen included one of the terms in the DNA string her modified search engine had turned up. If the string held any one of those terms, it kicked the program to the next line of code, which queried another single term. If all thirteen terms matched, it kicked the program to a last line of code, which decided if the terms were in the right order. And then the most interesting part. If they were in the right order, the computer was instructed to just ignore them.

Quinn looked down at the pages and the lines of code she'd highlighted on them, trying to figure out what it was exactly that she was seeing. There was no doubt about one thing; the original CODIS system had been programmed specifically to exclude a single DNA signature. If the FBI searched for or tried to match up the DNA string 15,16/30,33.2/16,20/20,25/11,17/14,16/ 8,13/11,11/9,11/10,10/8,11/7,9.3/9,13, CODIS would simply not recognize it, causing the query to turn up negative. And there was one more thing she was certain of—whoever had created this little bypass had intentionally hidden it, spreading pieces of it out all over the system.

The question was why?

Quinn stood and walked over to the bar to get another cup of tea. She was about to take a sip when she noticed the dim glow struggling through the shutters closed over the front window.

"Oh, shit!"

She slammed the cup down and looked at the Elvis clock over the bar. It was almost seven in the morning! She ran back into the center of the room and started desperately collecting the papers covering the floor.

It looked like she was going to make a hell of an impression on her first day. Late, no shower, no change of clothes, and no sleep.

13

He could see the cracks.

They'd be invisible to anyone else, but they were there, marring his perfection. He tried again to reconfigure his face into the impenetrable mask of gentleness and distress that had so effectively gained him access to the little house, but he could still see himself at the edges of his eyes. The eyes had always been the hardest. There was something in the faded white surrounding his green irises and the way it combined with the tiny wrinkles in his skin, the position of his eyebrows. It had a surprising capacity to convey . . .

What?

He remembered as a child thinking it was something that lived inside him. Something small and weak. Something he could suppress. It had taken him a long time to realize the truth. Or had it? Maybe he'd always known. **He** was that thing inside him. Everything else was just a disguise.

He moved a vase full of flowers and leaned in closer to the mirror set into the back of the sideboard. It would get worse—he remembered that from before. People he knew would start to avoid him, wondering what it was about him that had changed. Even people he met in passing—at the store, on the street—would become vaguely uncomfortable when he was near and would find a reason to turn away, to try to escape the vague sense of dread that preceded him. It felt like nothing else—like being a species distinct from the rest of humanity. Like his entire physical being was just a costume, a flesh-and-blood host for what he really was. But he knew that it couldn't last. It was an end, not a beginning. An end that he should have let come a long time ago.

He ran his hand through his hair, still mesmerized by his own reflection, and let the incomplete mask fall away. It was as though he was the master of shadows, conjuring and directing them to play across his face, to wipe away the facade he wore for the rest of the world and leave only the bare skull underneath.

He finally turned away and looked down at the floor. The sun was just beginning to stream through the bay window, illuminating the small eat-in kitchen and glinting dully off the black plastic beneath his feet. She seemed to be staring up at him, though he knew she saw nothing. He watched as the angle of the light continued to change subtly, revealing the cloudy dryness of her eyes. Her hands were wired to the heavy oak table in the middle of the room and her feet to the sideboard behind him, one to each side.

He stepped carefully between her spread legs and ran his bare foot up her thigh. Her skin's dramatic fade from the pleasant brown of her legs to the creamy white of her pelvis was barely visible anymore. Narrow cuts covered her in straight, deep red lines that fanned out randomly, partially hiding her nakedness with the dull brown of dried blood. He closed his eyes as he moved his foot through her thick pubic hair and across her abdomen. In places, the blood was just the right consistency for his sole to stick slightly, tugging at her young skin for the briefest moment. How he loved that sensation.

But it wasn't enough anymore. And that was something he remembered from before, too—the feeling that he was dancing at the edges of the experience. The desperate need to crawl inside them, to be a part of their fear and pain, to feel the ebb and flow of it. To know what they saw in those last few moments. To follow them into death.

He lay down next to her, curling into a fetal position and resting his head on her left breast. The morning sun was beginning to heat the room and he could feel the warmth moving along his bare skin.

He'd let himself be caged. He'd let himself be fed, trained, cared for. He'd let them bleed the danger and unpredictability from his experiences. But that was over. It had taken years, but now he was in control.

He wouldn't act right away. He'd let the anticipation slowly build, as he always did. And when it became unbearable, when his hands shook with the adrenaline constantly leaking into his bloodstream and his mind begged for release, that would be his moment.

14

Quinn held up a temporary pass and the guard waved her through the gate without making her roll down her window. That was a minor stroke of good luck, since she'd dropped the Life Savers meant as a substitute for a toothbrush between the seats and had yet to find them.

Traffic had been light, thank God, and as long as she didn't get lost trying to find her building, she was actually going to make it with a minute or two to spare. Quinn held the car to the maximum speed allowed, barely noticing the widely spaced buildings and colorful trees that made up the FBI's Quantico facility as she examined herself in the rearview mirror.

Her hair looked fine—at an inch and a half long, it couldn't go too far astray. Lack of sleep had left a slight pallor to her skin, but the real offender, the dark circles beneath her less than clear eyes, were mostly hidden by the thick plastic frames of her glasses.

She had almost convinced herself that she looked fine when a group of FBI agent trainees jogged by on the other side of the road. They looked tan, fit, and bright-eyed. It was almost like they were doing it on purpose. Jerks.

Fortunately, the directions she'd been given were relatively simple and she found herself easing her car into an empty parking space three minutes before zero hour. She grabbed the fuller of two cups of tea in the drink holder, found the missing Life Savers, and jumped from the car in a less-than-graceful motion. She was about to slam the door when she spotted the knapsack containing ATD's CODIS program in the passenger seat. It didn't have the dignity of a leather briefcase, but it seemed marginally better than walking into a new assignment with nothing but a Styrofoam cup and minty-fresh breath.

She snatched it from the seat, slung it over her shoulder, and jogged toward the utilitarian building she'd parked in front of. By her watch, she still had thirty seconds before she was officially late for her first day.

"Can I help you?" the woman at the front desk asked. Like those joggers, she looked just a little too perky.

"I'm trying to find Donna Feldman."

"You've succeeded. I'm Donna. You must be Quinn." She stood and offered her hand. "Nate's morning meeting just started, I'm afraid, so I'm going to have to run you down to your desk myself. He should be done by eleven."

Quinn smiled her understanding and Donna motioned for her to follow. The stairs they descended seemed too long for the little building; it was obviously much deeper than it was tall.

"Sorry about the office space," Donna said. "You've got to fight for your windows around here."

"No problem," Quinn mumbled. "The only thing that kills a computer programmer faster than sunlight is a stake through the heart."

Donna laughed as she walked through an open door and negotiated the maze of gray cubicles on the other side. "This is you," she said, pointing to a small cube containing a metal desk and a single blue chair.

Quinn tossed her knapsack on the desk but didn't sit or relinquish the grip she had on her tea.

"Nate said he wanted to give you the tour and then buy you lunch if you don't already have plans. I'll try to get ahold of some office supplies for you. Other than that, let me know if you need anything."

"Thanks, Donna."

"No problem. I'll see you later."

Quinn watched her hustle off and then sagged

into the chair and stared at the ceiling. The buzz of voices coming from the cubicles surrounding her was a little quieter and less defined than it had been in D.C., but the atmosphere seemed pretty much the same.

What now?

She didn't have a thing to do for the next couple of hours and boredom wasn't an option—she'd be dead asleep in her chair in five minutes. After a few moments of consideration, she emptied her knapsack onto the desk and spread the pages it contained out in front of her.

She'd thought about it the whole way there and was more convinced than ever that the strange subroutine she'd found in ATD's code had been intentionally concealed; there was just no other reason someone would spread it out all over the system like that. And as near as she could figure, that left only one explanation: ATD had used the same testing method she had—they'd planted a phantom DNA signature in the separate state computers and then searched for them as they debugged their program. Then, when they were finished, for some reason it had been more trouble than it was worth to remove the phantom from five of the state systems. And instead of doing the right thing and putting forth a little effort, they'd just programmed around it.

Quinn smiled and picked up a thick stack of papers, bringing them close to her face as she examined the tightly packed lines of code. Sloppy sloppy.

"Quinn? Nate Shale."

She slammed the papers down a little too hard—caffeine—and jumped to her feet. "Mr. Shale," she said, sticking out her hand. "It's nice to meet you."

His skin was cool and dry, and his grip pleasantly firm but not overpowering. "Call me Nate. I'm really glad to see you. Surprised, but glad."

"Surprised?"

"I just put in the request a couple of weeks ago. It's not exactly what I'd really call important, just an idea I had to make one of our applications run a little more smoothly."

Quinn's eyes narrowed and she felt her lip curl up a bit before she could stop it.

"Are you all right?" Shale said.

"Fine. Why do you ask?"

"For a second there it looked like you wanted to cut my heart out with a spoon."

Nice. Clearly, she was well on her way to impressing the heck out of her new boss.

"Actually, I'm just getting over the flu and didn't sleep very well last night."

"Sorry to hear that," he said in a tone that suggested he believed her and actually cared. "Like I said, this isn't all that pressing. Maybe you should just go home and get some rest."

"Thanks, Nate, but I'm fine, really."

He glanced down at his watch. "I'm just on a

quick break here and wanted to say hello. Why
don't we plan on getting together for lunch at noon
and I can tell you what I'm thinking on this thing."

Quinn smiled and bobbed her head as he ducked
back over her cube. Her mood darkened significantly as she watched him hurry back to his meeting. If Louis thought he was going to put her out
to pasture for something that wasn't her mistake,
he was sadly mistaken.

She threw herself back into her chair and jabbed
at the buttons on the phone.

"Hello, Louis Crater."

"Louis, it's Quinn."

"Quinn," he said, sounding less than happy to
hear from her. "What can I do for you?"

"I'm calling about that glitch—"

"Not your job anymore. I met with the guys from
ATD this morning and they have your system
pretty much up and running."

"I'll bet they do."

Her tone seemed to throw him for a moment, but
he recovered. "Uh, yeah. Anyway, they said you
did a pretty good job. They seemed genuinely impressed. Apparently the problem you couldn't find
turned out to be no big deal."

Quinn frowned deeply. **They seemed genuinely
impressed** . . . It made sense. The last thing ATD
wanted was her making an issue out of this. They
had to pacify her, get her to drop the whole thing.
And they figured that if they put in a good word for

her with the old boss, that would do it. Unfortunately for them, she was dead tired, hungry, sitting in an empty cubical in Quantico, Virginia. And she was pissed off about it.

"That's not entirely true, Louis. I put some work into this last night and it turns out it wasn't my fault—"

"What did I just say?"

"What I mean is—"

"Just stop right there," he said, cutting her off again. "This is getting ridiculous."

"Louis, I—"

"Look, Quinn, there was a bug in your system and you couldn't fix it, okay? **You couldn't fix it.** And I had to bring these guys in to bail you out. Now, they said that you did an okay job and I'm going to take them at their word on that. Just let it go, for God's sake."

"But—"

"Quinn! Let it go. Remember what I said about not being able to admit when you're wrong being a quality we don't much like in our agents? You've got a new assignment. Concentrate on doing a good job with that."

Dial tone. He'd hung up.

The plastic handset made a distinct cracking sound when she jammed it back in place.

"'You couldn't fix it,'" she mocked, and then kicked the side of the cubical. That's what he'd be passing up the chain of command and what her performance review was going to say. "She did her best, but in the end we had to call in the pros to get things done."

Quinn folded her arms across her chest and glared at the papers covering her desk. That was it. She was screwed and there was nothing she could do about it. Louis obviously had no interest in listening to her. He'd already made up his mind.

She sat that way for a long time, staring at the gray fabric walls surrounding her. It was probably five minutes before a sly smile started to spread across her face.

The case files. That was it. That was the answer. All she had to do was use the credibility of her new Quantico address to order up copies of the five case files her system had spit out. And when it turned out that none of them existed, her theory would be proven. Then she could shoot off a concerned-sounding memo to ATD suggesting that their leftover test data could cause problems with the system she'd set up. Copy Louis and his boss and voilà— she would not only be vindicated but look downright conscientious. And that **was** a quality the FBI looked for in their agents.

15

Richard Price stood in front of a large window that looked out over the uninhabited Virginia mountains surrounding the Advanced Thermal Dynamics research facility, but he didn't really see them. "The second woman in a week, Brad. What the hell happened?"

Brad Lowell's reflection in the glass shifted uncomfortably. His dark suit and red tie were impeccable, as they always were, but there was something different about him. His stare, while respectfully trained on an empty wall, was a little too intense, his chin was thrust a little too far forward. And then there was his silence.

Price turned away from the window and looked Lowell directly in the eye. "Don't make me ask twice."

He couldn't tell if the action weakened the man's resolve to remain silent, or strengthened his resolve to speak. It didn't really matter.

"I told you this was different, sir."

"I don't think that's what I asked you, is it? What I asked was how this happened. I just doubled the size of your goddamn team—"

"Yes, sir!"

Price settled into the leather chair behind his desk, keeping a watchful eye on the man standing statuelike on the carpet. "I don't want to play this game with you, Brad. If you've got something to say, say it."

"Sir. Three of my people are brand-new and one has only been on the job for a few weeks. They're good men, all of them, but they're not pre-pared . . . not for this. And even when I've had time to fully train them, I still have nowhere near enough people to effectively cover the subject—particularly with your edict that we not be seen."

"Come on, Brad. You know damn—"

"Sir!" Lowell's voice, nearly a shout, stunned Price into silence. "Sir, he seems impervious to elec-tronic surveillance—we've discussed this before. We found a computer chip hardwired into the tracking device on his car this morning. It sends out false data—he had us tracking nothing. So far my people can't even figure out how it works . . ." Lowell started to look a little uncertain and his voice lost some of its forcefulness.

"Are you through?" Price said.

"No, sir. Based on the constraints I'm working under, I believe it's impossible to maintain control of this situation."

"The situation is what it is. I'm not interested in excuses."

"And I won't stand here and provide them, sir. If you don't feel my work has been adequate, I can have my resignation on your desk by this afternoon."

Price let out a long breath and motioned to one of the chairs in front of his desk. Lowell sat, but a bit stiffly.

"I don't want your goddamn resignation, Brad. You know that."

"Yes, sir."

Price let his forehead sink into his hand. "The end of this operation is coming, Brad. You and I both know it. Every day now is precious; we just have to hold on."

"I understand, sir. I'm just not sure it's possible."

Price stood and walked around his desk, taking a seat in the chair next to Lowell. The time for relying on hierarchy and the power of intimidation as a motivator was over. He needed Lowell focused. He needed him to be a believer for just a little longer.

"What's our situation, Brad?"

"The house is clean and the body is being taken care of . . ."

"But?"

"Any more and someone is going to notice the pattern. Young, well-educated, attractive women disappearing over a short period of time in a relatively small geographic area. There's nothing we can do to counteract that."

Price rubbed his lower lip with his thumb but didn't speak.

"Do you think there's anything you can do, sir?" Lowell asked.

"I don't know, Brad. I honestly don't know."

"Then perhaps if we alter some of the guidelines I work under, I could—"

Price shook his head. "No. We're not there yet. We may be soon, but not yet. What about the woman from the FBI?"

"Quinn Barry. We're watching her as a matter of routine, but I'm not anticipating any more trouble. She's been transferred to Quantico and we've corrected the problems with CODIS."

Price stood and Lowell rose a moment later, correctly interpreting that he was being dismissed. When he turned to leave, though, Price reached out and gripped his shoulder. "Brad. You have my confidence. You always have."

The surprise on Lowell's face wasn't completely unexpected. Price had always been sparing with his praise, finding that infrequency significantly increased the impact when it was given.

"This is obviously an extremely difficult situation," Price continued. "But you know what's at stake here. We're just stealing time. Every second counts now. You understand that, don't you, Brad?"

Lowell gave a short, jerky nod and walked out of the office, leaving Price standing motionless in the middle of the floor.

An extremely difficult situation.

He wondered if it had ever been that. Or if it had been impossible from the start.

Price nodded a silent greeting to the five men sitting at the conference table and took his customary place at the head of it.

"I'm glad you're here, sir. We're just about ready to start." The lab tech closed a glass door on the six-foot-high stack of audiovisual equipment and backed away, intent on the remote in his hand. The enormous screen covering the far wall flickered from black to gray to green, and a moment later a hazy image appeared.

"Okay, we've captured the satellite feed," the young man said, laying the remote on the table. "If you have any problems, I'll be outside." He shut the lights off as he left, bringing better defintion to the large image.

There was no scale, only the faded greenish white of rolling sand dunes moving slowly by, captured by the night-vision video camera in the bottom of an F-18 Hornet. Occasionally, a calm voice would mingle with the static hissing from the speakers built into the walls. To most of the men in the room, it would have been indecipherable, but to Price it was perfectly clear. Twenty years in the military had made aircraft radio chatter his second language.

The lifeless terrain began slowly to change. Dim, widely spaced bursts of light started to appear—perhaps the campfires of shepherds or nomads—then the geometric shapes of small man-made structures, and finally the lights and easily discernible pattern of a city.

The hiss of static diminished as the pilot eased back on his throttle, making the increased chatter even easier to decipher. Price glanced around him for a moment, watching the degree of concentration on the other men's faces increase in the eerie light.

The F-18 released its payload over a large cube of a building near what looked like the center of the city. Price watched the small object fall, guided with deadly certainty by a laser painting the structure. An approving murmur erupted around him when the bomb impacted, blowing the building apart in a silent, light-suppressed flash.

The world seemed to tilt as the F-18 began a lazy turn back the way it had come. The camera beneath it was able to compensate partially, and remained trained on the impact site as long as possible, recording the hazy white of fires as they were spread by the desert wind.

"What a waste."

Everyone turned toward the back of the room and the source of the voice.

"Excuse me?" Price said as a previously motionless figure leaned forward and allowed itself to be illuminated by the glow still emanating from the screen.

"I said, what a waste."

"Would you care to expand on that, Dr. Marin?" one of the other men in the room said, obviously angered by the scientist's disgusted tone.

"The Afghans are years from developing anything even mildly threatening," Marin said.

"And how can you be so damn sure of that?"

"Oh, please. Everyone in this room—including you—knows that the Afghans aren't a threat. If any one country is, it's North Korea. But they're too well connected to the Chinese to make them a practical target, aren't they? They aren't completely helpless."

Price chose not to involve himself in the heated argument that ensued. The fact was, Marin's assessment was essentially correct. Paranoia in the U.S. was continuing to build as the media gleefully played up the threat of rogue nations developing delivery systems that could put one of their crude nuclear weapons inside American borders. It could be argued that this threat was the gravest the country had ever faced, eclipsing even the Cold War, when the complete irrationality of the enemy was taken into account. Over the next ten years, countries run by madmen and religious zealots would become nuclear powers. The president had to look like he was doing something, and this was the best his advisers could come up with.

What no one else in the room knew was that the building the navy had just destroyed probably wasn't even involved in weapons development—the CIA had been completely unsuccessful in locating Afghanistan's missile research facility. But that wasn't really important. As Marin had so eloquently pointed out, the Afghans weren't much of a threat anyway. What **was** important was that something blew up and the media got the footage.

Dr. Edward Marin suddenly stood and pointed at the men grouped around the table, a vaguely threatening gesture that once again imposed silence on the room. "This is my fault. My fault and the fault of men like me. We've sterilized war, made it easy. Stripped it of the smell of infection and the silence of death. We've bled off the terror and the sorrow. And because of us, the power to wage war now rests in the hands of cowards and hypocrites."

The shouts started almost immediately, but again, Price did not participate. His own anger and his personal feelings about Dr. Edward Marin were no longer relevant. Emotional displays were not a luxury he could afford.

What was done was done.

16

As far as programming problems went, this one was pretty simple. She'd only been in Quantico for a day and a half and she was about ready to compile her changes. Quinn glanced at the edge of the desk out of habit but then remembered that her lucky mug was still at home, shoved in a box with the rest of her stuff from headquarters. There seemed to be no point to bringing it out here. If things went her way, she had maybe another day of debugging and then two or three more of training. Then . . .

What? She still had nearly a year before she was eligible to test for agent training—assuming that was still going to be an option given her now somewhat checkered FBI employment record. Hopefully, she'd get a chance to vindicate herself and restore her reputation. But, in the meantime, she'd probably end up in Iowa programming the special agent in charge's VCR.

It was a shame, really. She'd taken to Quantico almost immediately. Her new boss seemed to be a great guy and very supportive of her aspirations. The area was beautiful—brightly colored trees and widely spaced buildings instead of concrete and urban clutter. And best of all, her hour-long commute was against traffic.

The easy driving gave her some time to think and the distance had given her an excuse to avoid David. Immature? Yes. But helpful. She was nearly clear of the uncertainty and emotional conflict that had been bogging her down for the last week. And after a do-nothing weekend relaxing on her father's farm, she fully expected to have mustered the courage to finally end it with David.

While she wasn't looking forward to actually sitting down with him and doing it, she couldn't imagine he'd be all that upset. After all, he was gorgeous, intelligent, successful, and didn't watch sports on TV. It wasn't like he went unnoticed by women much more ambitious, conformist, and professionally dressed than she was. In the end, he'd thank her.

Quinn reached out and spun the Styrofoam cup sitting next to her keyboard and tapped it once. It wasn't her lucky mug but it would have to suffice. She smacked the enter button on the keyboard and headed for the stairs and a quick lunch.

The compilation wouldn't take long. She wanted to wrap this job up as quickly as possible. As much as she'd have liked to stick around Quantico for a few weeks, at this point it was more important to make herself look as efficient as possible.

When she arrived back at her cubicle, she spun her chair around to sit but found it stacked with Federal Express packages. Assuming it was a mistake and that they were for the cube's prior occupant, she scooped them up and turned to take them to the front desk. When she did, though, she noticed her name scrawled across the thick envelope on top. She must have forgotten something at her workstation in D.C.

Quinn tossed the packages on her desk and dug her veggie sub out of an otherwise empty drawer, carefully unwrapping it from the foil it was cocooned in. She gnawed off the end of the sandwich and struggled to open the first package with greasy fingers. It contained a single file that she'd have sworn she'd never seen before. Maybe it had something to do with her next assignment?

She flipped the file open and then jerked back, breathing in a green pepper and almost choking on it. When she got control of her coughing, she looked around to see if anyone was watching. There was no one. The inhabitants of the surrounding cubes had, for the most part, bailed out of there at noon. Satisfied that she was alone, Quinn reached tentatively for the open folder and slid it onto her lap.

The photograph was small, stapled to one of the many other documents neatly arranged inside, but it was well lit and sharply in focus. The woman it depicted was spread-eagled on the floor. Her naked body was brutally slashed and she was lying in a pool of her own blood.

Quinn slammed the file shut and snatched the envelope it had come in from the garbage can. The return address was a little difficult to read and she held the light carbon copy directly under her desk lamp. New York. The police crime lab.

"Oh shit," she said under her breath as she shoved the file and the other unopened envelopes under her desk. She looked around again to make sure no one had seen her and then put her feet on the stack to further obscure it from prying eyes.

Her mouth suddenly felt a little dry and she took a sip of her lukewarm tea, trying to think. Someone had obviously made a serious mistake. That had to be it. A mistake.

She pulled her CODIS search engine output from a drawer and then leaned under the desk and compared it with the case number on the file folder she'd received.

They matched.

"Shit," she whispered again. No, it could still be a mistake, she told herself. A transposed number or something. It happened all the time. She tore into the next envelope. And then the next.

Less than a minute later she had shoved her printout back in the drawer and had her feet propped up on five very real case files. Case files she'd had absolutely no authority to request and that could get her fired, or worse. Case files that were supposed to be a figment of CODIS's electronic imagination.

Quinn sat there for a long time, forcing herself to make a show of eating her sandwich as her coworkers began to wander back in from lunch. What was she going to do? Send them back? That was certainly an option—maybe nobody would ever notice. While the FBI undoubtedly received some kind of report or record of case file requests, surely no one really paid attention to it. Every month or so it would just get shoved into an archive somewhere, never to be seen again. Right?

As she chewed her thumbnail, attempting to figure a way out of the predicament her stubbornness had gotten her into, another thought intruded on her mind. What did these files mean? What if there really was someone out there committing horrible crimes, and because of some lazy programming by ATD, no one knew about it?

She continued to work on her thumbnail, thinking about the photograph she'd seen, the case numbers, the strange subroutine she'd uncovered. The damage was done; she'd not only ordered the files, but opened them. There would be no harm in taking a quick look, confirming that it was just a computer error—a bug relating unrelated cases. It made sense to be sure.

Quinn pulled the top folder from under her desk and turned her back to the door of her cubical, using her body to conceal what was in her hands.

Years of dreaming about being an agent and another actually working for the FBI, and she realized she'd never even seen a case file, except on TV. She flipped through the separate sections quickly, figuring out how it was organized and gleaning some general information. The dead woman lying on the floor was Shannon Dorsey, a twenty-five-year-old biologist working for Dow Chemical. Quinn paused at another photograph of her, this one looking like it had been cut from a college yearbook. She was pretty, with a thin face framed by long dark hair and highlighted by equally dark eyes. Her smile was a little self-conscious, but still exuded warmth. Quinn took a breath and flipped again to the front of the file, forcing herself to look down at a very different picture of Shannon.

The photos were color, not black-and-white like in the movies. The young woman's body was covered in the uniform brown of dried blood and crisscrossed with thin lines that looked almost black. Beneath her, the beige carpet was stained crimson and must have still been slightly wet; it reflected back some of the light from the camera's flash.

The woman was completely naked and her hands

had been secured to the sofa above her head with something that didn't look like rope. Her feet were tied to either side of an entertainment center and a dishrag had been taped into her mouth, leaving her helpless and silent for the last moments of her life.

It took another minute or so, but Quinn found a crime-scene report and ran her finger down the various details it contained. Coat hangers. She'd been tied with coat hangers. For some reason, that fact, even more than the dead woman's photograph, made the hairs on the back of her neck stand up.

Cause of death was blood loss—the coroner hypothesized that a razor had been used and that the woman had been alive while the killer had repeatedly cut and raped her.

Quinn felt a tear welling up in her eye as she unwillingly imagined what this woman had gone through. Had she been happy to die? Had she still been afraid at the end, or just grateful?

Quinn shook her head violently, clearing it and trying to refocus on the less sensational aspects of the case. The woman had died in her own home around ten A.M. on November 11, 1991. The middle-class neighborhood had been almost deserted at the time, with children at school and parents at work. The police had questioned all known sex offenders within a two-hundred-mile radius but had never come up with a good suspect.

Quinn felt another little surge of adrenaline when she came across a report on skin cells found beneath the victim's fingernails. CODIS, only two years old at the time, had found no matches to the DNA of convicted felons or other unsolved crimes. She chewed at her lower lip as she read that section over again. It had to be a mistake. This couldn't be real . . .

The next file seemed to support that theory. It was much thinner, from a police department near Allentown, Pennsylvania. It told the story of Catherine Tanner, a twenty-seven-year-old computer hardware designer. Another pretty young woman with long dark hair but whose death was completely different. She'd been killed in 1989 when she failed to negotiate a curve on a winding Pennsylvania road and plunged into a shallow canyon.

Quinn flipped past the pictures of the burned car, stopping at the coroner's report. On the basis of the condition of her lungs, she had died in the crash and not the ensuing fire. Quinn started to feel a sense of relief wash over her as she skimmed down the report. The two deaths seemed to have little in common, supporting her theory that the connection between them was nothing more than some kind of bizarre glitch in the database.

It was near the end that she came upon it. A single sentence across the bottom of the report:

A number of narrow cuts were observed on the front (but not the back) of the body;

these lacerations may or may not have been caused by the crash and/or ensuing heat.

Quinn swallowed hard and pawed through the file until she found the report on the DNA sample sent to the FBI. The police had found pieces of the woman's passenger-side window in a place on the road that seemed inconsistent with the crash. A small amount of blood not belonging to the victim had been lifted from one of the shards and sent in for a CODIS evaluation. The database search had, of course, come back negative.

Quinn hovered over the third file, not sure she wanted to know what was inside. Finally, she opened it and almost immediately felt the perspiration begin to form on her forehead.

Lisa Egan, a grad student at Johns Hopkins University, had been found dead on the floor in her living room. Her throat had been cut by a single stroke from an extremely sharp instrument in January 1992. There had been no other injuries and no evidence of sexual assault.

The thing that really stood out, though, was the fact that the investigating officer, a Detective Roy Renquist, was more or less convinced that he had found the killer—a seventeen-year-old physics genius on staff at the university. Despite his certainty, though, Renquist had been unable to produce enough hard evidence to bring his suspect before a grand jury.

Quinn tossed the file back under her desk and pulled out the last two. They were more recent—1995 and 1999—and seemed very different. Both were disappearances and no body had ever been found in either case. The women, while both young and attractive, were poor and relatively uneducated. Also, both were living with men who had a history of abusing them. In the 1995 Oklahoma death, the DNA sample in question had been procured from a bloodstain on the carpet. One of a number of samples taken; the police hadn't given it much thought, particularly in light of CODIS's failure to recognize it. The obvious suspect in the case had been the boyfriend, but it turned out that he'd been in a serious accident at work the day before the woman died and had spent two weeks in the hospital with a piece of rebar through his leg. An airtight alibi.

The 1999 disappearance, in Oregon, was a similar scenario. The unidentified DNA sample had been from a single hair found on the sofa and the main suspect had been the boyfriend. Based on his lack of an alibi, history as an abuser, and lengthy police record, he had been taken to court. The fact that there wasn't a witness or a body, though, had been too much for the prosecutor to overcome. He was found not guilty.

Quinn scanned the man's police record, noting a number of violent crimes and several incarcerations. She paused at a description of a bar fight that had landed him in jail for the last half of 1991 and most of 1992, reading through it twice. It would have been impossible for him to have been involved in the death of Lisa Egan . . .

"How you coming along?"

Quinn whipped her head around and must have looked terrified, because Nathan Shale started to chuckle. "Sorry 'bout that. Didn't mean to scare you, there."

"That's okay. People do it to me all the time," Quinn said, hoping that also explained the slight shake in her voice. She swiveled her chair toward Shale, careful to keep the file hidden behind her on the desk. "I'm pretty much done, Nate. The program's compiling and tomorrow I should be ready to go over it with you—make sure it's what you wanted."

"Wow, already? That's great."

"There wasn't that much to do," she said, having a little trouble concentrating on the conversation. "Of course you may want some tweaking done and I'll need to train everybody that's going to be using it . . ."

"Fantastic."

For a moment he looked like he was going to come into the cubicle and Quinn instinctively scooted back to cover the file better. Instead, he turned away and started for the stairs. "Let me know when you've got it running, Quinn. I'm anxious to see what you've done."

17

Quinn reached over to the stack of books lying next to her on the bed and selected one bristling with sticky notes. She scanned the chapter defining the different types of sexually motivated killers, focusing again on the one describing the sexual sadist. It was a near-perfect fit.

She tossed the book on the floor and looked around her at the reference material covering her bedspread. Crime-scene photographs of dead bodies, pictures of infamous serial killers, transcripts of prison interviews with Ted Bundy, Charles Manson, and David Berkowitz; speculation on the psyches of murderers still at large. The investigative support offices at Quantico were overflowing with this stuff and Nate Shale had been more than happy to encourage her interest in his unit by lending her some of it.

Quinn pulled her sweatpants up a little higher around her waist and wrapped her arms protectively around her torso. She'd started this little research project four hours ago in her customary bedtime clothes—a pair of panties and an old University of Maryland T-shirt. As she'd pored over the gory details of America's most brutal killings, though, the sweatpants, sweatshirt, and socks had appeared. She peered out her open bedroom door for the hundredth time, searching the visible areas of the kitchen and living room for movement and resisting the urge to check the doors and windows again. Too much imagination and too little sleep were a bad combination.

Quinn moved a few of the books to the floor and centered one of the case files she'd smuggled out of Quantico in front of her. Of the five, this was the only one with a reasonable suspect—a seventeen-year-old physics whiz working for Johns Hopkins University. She flipped it open and extracted a slightly yellowed article from the Hopkins school paper, reading it carefully for the third time that night.

In 1986, at the age of twelve, Eric Twain had been accepted to NYU, where he had pursued an art degree. Despite his success there, and for reasons that were somewhat murky, he had dropped out a year later. A brief quote in the article she was reading suggested only that he had become "disillusioned with the art world."

Quinn tried to remember what she was doing in art class when she was that age. It would have been seventh grade. Probably drawing horses in colored pencil and coercing her dad to stick them to the fridge.

After leaving NYU, Twain moved back in with his working-class parents, despite a poor relationship with them, and continued to work on his art. When he wasn't painting and sculpting, he apparently liked to do a little light reading in the areas of quantum mechanics, unified field theory, and gravitation. It was this hobby that had prompted him to write down some ideas he had about nuclear fusion, building on the work of a professor at Hopkins.

He'd sent the paper in to a physics journal he subscribed to, hoping to get some feedback from the editors. Instead, they published his article in its entirety. Based on that work, Eric Twain, at the ripe old age of thirteen, received his Ph.D. in physics—all without the benefit of ever taking a class. A year later he was on staff at Hopkins teaching and doing research.

Lisa Egan, the woman with the slashed throat, had been Twain's assistant. At the time of her death, she had been twenty-three. Her boss had not yet reached his eighteenth birthday.

The first police interview with Twain had been routine, mostly questions about whether he knew if Lisa had any enemies or disgruntled former lovers. Across the bottom of the report, though, the investigating officer, a man named Renquist, had jotted down some personal thoughts. Eric had been extremely nervous, distracted. He'd had difficulty expressing himself in a straightforward manner. Overall, he'd seemed maladjusted and uncomfortable.

Quinn reached for the cup of tea on her nightstand, remembering a PBS special she'd once seen on child geniuses and trying to remember if Eric Twain had been one of the subjects. The whole thing had struck her as just plain creepy—little kids, clothed in well-pressed suits and dresses talking with prodigious vocabularies and lifeless, mechanical precision. Ventriloquist's dummies. They'd reminded her of ventriloquist's dummies.

That first interview had been enough to prompt Renquist to look a little more closely at the young physicist. His alibi for the night of the murder seemed shaky; he'd been in his apartment working with a grad student. According to police, though, this particular student worshiped his young professor and would likely lie for him.

Quinn adjusted herself into a slightly more comfortable position and flipped forward in the investigative reports. The most damning evidence against Twain had come when it was discovered he had lied about his relationship with the victim. During an interrogation by the police, he had finally admitted that he and the twenty-three-year-old Egan had a friendship that went beyond the purely professional. A week later he'd admitted that they had been sleeping together.

After that revelation, the investigation had centered almost completely on him. He had refused to provide the police with a DNA sample, stipulating to the fact that his DNA would undoubtedly be one of the many found in her apartment, and might even be found on her body. Later he had refused to take a lie detector test on the advice of his attorney.

Despite an exhaustive investigation, the police had never been able to obtain enough hard evidence to bring Twain before a grand jury. In the end, Detective Renquist had more or less abandoned the matter. He was convinced that Twain was the killer but he was equally convinced that he would never be able to get a conviction.

The most recent entry in the case file was years old and related the fact that Twain had moved from Maryland to D.C.

Quinn took a sip of her lukewarm tea, reading his last known address again. It was less than twenty miles away.

She leaned back against the headboard, letting the file slide off her knees and staring again at the old newspaper article. The picture of Eric Twain was grainy but still good enough to read his T-shirt. It depicted the Milky Way galaxy with an arrow and the slogan **You Are Here**. His hair was uncombed, hanging a little haphazardly over his ears and collar as he leaned self-consciously against a bench covered with countless vials and beakers.

Quinn gazed at the photo for a long time, trying to get into his head like the profilers did, trying to see if what set him apart from other people was reflected in his eyes. Genius, cruelty, hate—anything. The longer she stared, though, the less she saw. He just looked like a kid. Braces, acne, and all.

She flipped the newspaper article off her lap and began adding to the already voluminous notes she'd taken, crossing out some conclusions she'd made about Twain that now seemed a little sloppy and writing down some speculation about his childhood.

It all seemed to fit: his geographic location, his personality and background, the evidence uncovered in the police investigation . . .

Or not.

Quinn slid down the headboard and lay motionless among the reference materials covering the bed. What the hell did she know? She'd spent a total of four hours reading—or, more accurately, skimming—a few books and files on serial killers. Compare that with the years of schooling and on-the-job training of a typical FBI profiler. And they were still the first to admit that they sometimes got it completely wrong.

So what now? Drop the whole thing? That was the smart move. Fed Ex the five case files back where they came from and keep her fingers crossed that no one ever noticed she'd had them.

It was all just a figment of the computer's imagination. Right? The system had connected a group of unrelated deaths that happened to have a few similar elements. Maybe something goofy had happened at the state level during their countless hardware and software updates. Or maybe ATD had planted their test DNA string signatures into actual files for some reason. There were countless explanations she could come up with.

But what if it wasn't a bug? What if there was someone out there brutally killing young women? As unlikely as this was, it was possible. Could she just forget about it? Quinn stared at the blank white of her ceiling for a long time, mulling over that question.

It didn't take long. She knew herself well enough to know that she couldn't just let this go. Not after reading about those women, seeing the pictures of them smiling and alive, and then imagining what they had gone through before they'd finally died.

She reached for her tea again and took a sip, though the taste and temperature didn't really register with her. She had less than seven hours before she had to start getting ready for work. She pushed the rest of the books and papers off the bed and began reaching for the light, but thought better of it. After everything she'd seen and read that night, she'd rather keep it on.

18

The shadows weren't getting any shorter.

Despite that rather obvious observation, Quinn Barry didn't move. She just sat there peering through the windshield, letting her fear and the wind's gentle rocking of the car make her increasingly nauseated.

It wasn't actually a neighborhood she found herself in. That is to say, it didn't look like anyone lived there, or for that matter, ever had. She was parked behind a partially collapsed stone wall that effectively hid her car but still allowed her a reasonable view of the surrounding area.

Based on the artistic embellishments on the brick buildings crumbling around her, she guessed the place had been built at least seventy-five years ago—before utilitarianism had completely won out

over aesthetics. And based on their state of disre-
pair, she guessed that they had been abandoned for
at least half that time.

Quinn leaned forward, peering out at the collapsed roofs, rusted doors, and shattered glass of the
old industrial park. Her eyes slowly tracked right,
searching for evidence of any human presence, but
not finding any until they fell on the building directly across from her.

At first glance, it hadn't seemed much different
from the others. Upon further inspection, though,
it became obvious that the structure was still intact, as were the tall, narrow windows set into its
faded brick walls. It was surrounded by a stone
fence with rusted but still formidable-looking iron
pikes growing from it. At one time they had undoubtedly provided effective security, though now
all that was left of the gate were some twisted
hinges.

What really made the building stand out,
though, was its metal door. Instead of the uniform
color of rust one would expect, it was electric blue
with a strange yellow geometric symbol three feet
wide painted on it.

Quinn took a deep breath and let it out. Time to
make a decision. What already seemed really dumb
would move quickly into the insane category when
the sun hit the horizon and darkness started to
spread.

She'd spent most of the day at work just going

through the motions of her job. Her mind had been too preoccupied by CODIS and the case files to really do anything. After hours of contemplation, she had finally been forced to accept that she had only three options and that none of them were good.

The most obvious was to quietly return the files and forget the whole thing. Then she could spend the next year working her butt off and hope Louis didn't completely trash her on her review. Her chances of being accepted for agent training would still be at least fair. But could she just forget about this? While it was unlikely that the cases were really related, stranger things had happened. How would she feel if she found out years from now that this was real—that more women had died horribly because she was worried about her career prospects?

Another option was to take the files to her new boss and tell him the whole story. It hadn't taken long to find the holes in that plan. If it turned out to be nothing, which it probably would, all management would remember was that she had illegally ordered the files. She'd be lucky to stay out of jail and could pretty much forget about ever being an agent.

The bottom line was that she needed to be sure. If she could obtain evidence that Eric Twain was guilty of these crimes, then she could take the files to Nate and be fairly confident in her position. What could the FBI do? Fire her for tracking down a serial killer that they didn't even know existed?

No way. They'd be forced to pin a medal on her and forget about her bending of the rules where the files were concerned.

Quinn opened the car door and picked her way quickly through the shattered asphalt of the road, slowing only when she came to the empty archway in the building's protective wall. She managed to keep moving through it but stopped in the middle of the large courtyard to stare up at the tall, intricate sculptures surrounding her.

They seemed to have been welded from the discarded materials that littered the area—gray and brown sheets of metal, the jagged edges of old machines, rusted chains rattling quietly in the wind. Some rose as much as fifteen feet over her head, cutting dark silhouettes against the reddening sky. After a few moments she started forward again, trying to shake the feeling that they were twisted grave markers and that she was walking through a cemetery.

Beyond the bright paint, there was nothing on or near the door that would suggest the building was occupied. Quinn stopped in front of it and stood there for almost a minute, summoning her courage. It would be all right, she told herself. The story she'd concocted would protect her. Wouldn't it?

She finally shot a hand out and slammed it into the door, rattling it on its rails. For some reason, the sound calmed her, so she continued to pound for a few seconds, making sure that anyone inside could hear.

A minute went by, then two, with no response. She had pretty much decided that no one was inside when the door started to rattle and move on its own. She took a step back as it began sliding straight up, the sound of metal grinding on metal slowly being overpowered by music pouring from the opening.

The man standing in the doorway wasn't the one she'd been prepared for. His nearly black hair was long, tied back in a loose ponytail that she guessed went a good ways down his back. He was wearing a pair of denim overalls and no shirt, exposing thin muscular arms and broad shoulders—one of which was adorned with a black tattoo of a geometric symbol similar to the one on the door. A closer inspection, though, proved it to be a complex intertwining of different animal and bird images that looked vaguely American Indian. But then, so did he. His delicate features were sculpted from dark skin that looked more genetic than sun-enhanced. Or maybe it was just the effect of the thin layer of dust that covered him.

"Wow. A secret agent."

"Excuse me?" She tried not to sound startled.

The edges of his eyes crinkled slightly as he examined her. He started with her face, pausing at the horn-rim glasses perched on her nose, then moved down her formless sweater and skirt, and finally reached the tennis shoes she'd chosen for this particular outing. "I don't get many visitors out here.

Particularly beautiful women in disguise." His expression and voice were totally neutral. His words
clearly weren't meant as a come-on, or even a compliment. Just an observation.

Quinn reached into the bag hanging from her
shoulder, finding her ID badge and holding it up.
"I'm with the FBI, sir. I'm looking for Eric Twain."

"Eric Twain," he repeated quietly. "What could
you possibly want with him?"

"It's a private matter, I'm afraid. Is he home?"

He hesitated, and in that brief moment of uncertainty, Quinn saw the uncomfortable little boy in
the newspaper article.

"You," she said, taking another half step back before realizing that she'd already put too much distance between them to seem natural. "You're Eric
Twain."

"What's left of him."

"I'd like to—"

"Do you have a warrant?"

"No, I—"

"Good-bye, then." He reached up and started to
slide the door shut. Before Quinn knew what she
was doing, she'd jumped forward and blocked it
with her hand. And that impulsive little maneuver
brought her to within six inches of a man who had
almost certainly slit his girlfriend's throat and may
have tortured, raped, and murdered any number of
other young women.

He wasn't much taller than she was, Quinn noticed, trying to return his intense stare. The truth was, she was frozen with fear, but he seemed to mistake it for resolve. His eyes turned toward the floor for a moment and then he started walking away from her. She still hadn't moved when he disappeared around a corner in the hallway. She considered taking off, running back to her car, and getting the hell out of there. But she knew she couldn't. If she was going to risk throwing away her future over this, she needed something a little more solid than a screwy computer printout and a few police files.

She finally forced a compromise between her mind and her rattled nerves. She'd go in but she'd leave the door open. Just in case.

The music grew louder as she moved down the wide corridor, a disorienting wall of sound with elements of the country music she'd grown up on, twisted almost beyond recognition. By the time the hall opened up, she couldn't hear anything else.

The room she found herself in was probably a hundred feet across and forty feet high, mostly brick and glass, but with original pipes and machines still integrated into the ceiling and walls. They had been painted in bright primary colors, though, and now created a stark contrast to the large paintings hanging around them.

"Can I look?" She had to shout to be heard over the music.

"I thought you didn't have a warrant," he yelled

back, taking a seat in front of a large table covered with tools.

"I mean at the pictures." She was trying to seem calm, to hide her nervousness. A routine visit, backed by the full force of the Federal Bureau of Investigation. That's what she had to portray.

It seemed to be working. He waved a hand dismissively and turned away from her.

She moved along the walls, making sure that she always kept him at least partially in sight, and looked around for anything suspicious. What exactly that would be, she wasn't sure. According to the books she'd read, this type of killer often kept souvenirs. Underwear, jewelry, body parts. She couldn't help wondering what was lying just beyond her view.

The paintings were actually kind of spectacular and she felt herself concentrating more and more on them as she continued her search. They were a bizarre mix of influences blended together into an unlikely whole. The subject was always simple: a woman, a child, a landscape. But the style was much more complex. The one she was standing in front of started at the left side of the canvas looking like a Picasso, then faded seamlessly into a Matisse, then ended as a Rembrandt.

"Are these yours?" she yelled.

He turned away from what he was doing and squinted at her for a moment, then jabbed at some-

thing on the table. The music faded into the background.

"What?"

"Are these yours?"

He nodded.

"They're amazing," she said, starting back across
the room toward him. She paused for a moment in
front of a state-of-the-art computer terminal
framed by two blackboards. The boards looked like
they had never been used but the walls behind
them were covered with complex mathematical
graffiti.

"Do you have a name?" he said, turning back to
the table he was sitting at and starting to work
again. It looked like he was drawing on it.

"Name? I'm sorry, sir. It's Quinn Barry."

When he spun on his stool to face her, she
stopped short with ten feet still between them. It
wasn't a pen he was holding; it was some kind of
woodcarving tool that looked a lot like a scalpel.

"Are you all right?"

He was beautiful—there was no other word for
it. Smooth unblemished skin, full lips, and white
teeth framed by long, dark hair that shone in the
fading sunlight coming through the windows. Had
he learned to use his physical appearance to draw in
his victims?

"Ms. Barry? Can I get you a drink of water or
something?" he said.

She smiled reassuringly. "I'm sorry. Thank you, but I'm fine. So are you an artist or a physicist?"

"There's no real difference." When he laid the knife down on the table next to him, Quinn took a step forward. The carving on the top wasn't complete enough to be identifiable yet, just a series of graceful lines.

"I don't mean to be rude, Ms. Barry, but why are you here?"

"Just to confirm that this is still your primary address and to open a line of communication."

"A line of communication," he repeated. There was no curiosity in his voice, just an increasing melancholy.

"Yes, sir. Based on some new evidence, we're going to be actively looking into the death of your assistant Lisa Egan again." She examined his reaction carefully. Someone smart enough to get a Ph.D. at thirteen would be smart enough to know that this kind of direct involvement by the FBI might mean that Egan's death had been connected to the deaths of other young women.

"You want the killer brought to justice, don't you?" she said when he didn't respond.

He wouldn't look at her, instead staring over her shoulder at the back of the room. "The killer. That'd be me, wouldn't it? The maladjusted little freak who turned on the woman he was sleeping with. Cut her throat from ear to ear for no reason.

Listened too carefully to the voices in his head, right?"

"We're . . . we're interested in the truth."

His mouth curled up a little, but she wasn't sure she'd actually describe it as a smile. "You'll excuse me if my ten years dealing with people like you makes me doubt that."

"You lied about your relationship with her," Quinn said.

He suddenly looked even more distant, like he was slowly falling into himself. "I did do that. I lied."

Quinn found it impossible to tear herself away. She was captivated—by him, by the danger he represented. It was like looking at a predator in a zoo, but without the bars. "May I ask why?"

"Why I lied?"

"Yes."

She could almost see pain in his eyes. An amazing illusion.

"Lisa was a friend to me when I needed one more than anything. But she wasn't comfortable with our relationship being public—I was still pretty young then. In fact, she used to joke that it wasn't even legal in Maryland. Anyway, she was dead. I decided to respect her wish that our relationship remain between us. And because of that, the cops arbitrarily decided that the person I was with when she died was lying and marked me a killer . . ." His voice trailed off for a moment. "I'm not sure why I told you that."

"Is that why you live out here?"

"I tried other places—back when I thought I could still have a life." He eyed her accusingly. "But no matter where I went, somehow people found out about my past."

"You live alone, then?"

He nodded. "Renquist and your colleagues have made sure of that."

Quinn recognized the name of the Baltimore cop who had headed the investigation into Lisa Egan's death. As near as she could tell, the FBI's involvement had actually been minimal—nothing more than a little consulting.

"Where do you work now, Mr. Twain?"

He folded his arms on his chest and leaned against the wall behind him, obviously trying to decide whether or not he wanted to continue to participate in her little interrogation. Quinn was starting to think she'd pushed it too far when he finally answered.

"I still work for Hopkins. I don't teach anymore, of course. We have an understanding: as long as I continue to provide them with interesting math and I don't get within a mile of their campus, they continue to pay me. We mostly communicate through e-mail."

"I see." She reached under her sweater and pulled out a small pad, making a show of jotting down a few notes. "Well, thank you for your cooperation, Mr. Twain."

"That's it?"

"I think so . . . Well, one more thing."

"Yes?"

"Do you mind if I use your bathroom before I leave? I've got kind of a long drive."

He shrugged and pointed to the far corner of the room.

"Thanks," she said, trying to look natural as she backed away far enough to feel comfortable turning away from him.

When she got into the bathroom, she locked the door and sagged against it, suddenly drained of energy. She took a few deep breaths and told herself over and over how well she was doing—the performance of a lifetime. When she'd calmed down a little, she moved to the sink and, thanks to the length of Eric Twain's hair, easily found a few samples with good follicles still attached.

She stuffed them into a small plastic bag and tucked it into the waistband of her skirt before flushing the toilet. Her hand wasn't even on the doorknob when the incredibly vivid image of Eric Twain standing just outside with a couple of coat hangers and his carving knife filled her mind. She froze for the second time that afternoon, feeling her heart pounding in her chest.

Pull it together.

She went back to the sink and splashed some

water on her face. Her eyes looked a little bloodshot in the mirror as she dabbed her face dry.

A quick search of the bathroom yielded nothing she could use to defend herself that was more deadly than a hairbrush. Finally, she just walked up to the door and jerked it open.

He hadn't moved.

Quinn let out the breath she was holding and plastered a serene smile across her face as she moved confidently across the ancient wood floor.

"So you're not an FBI agent," Twain said as she approached. He didn't look up from the tabletop he was working on. "What is it you do, exactly?"

"Excuse me?"

"Wrong ID," he said. "And they all dress like morticians."

She'd hoped to make it out of there without being asked that particular question. "Technically, I'm a researcher. Like I told you, I'm just here to verify your address and get a little background."

"And how'd you happen into a job like that?"

"It seemed like it would be exciting."

He finally repositioned himself so that he could look up at her and began spinning his carving knife along the backs of his fingers with dexterity that would make a professional magician envious. "Is it?"

"You have no idea."

He nodded thoughtfully as she started for the hallway that led to the hopefully still-open front door. "Expect the investigating agents to be giving you a call in the coming weeks."

He didn't answer.

Quinn didn't stop until she had put a good ten miles between her and Eric Twain. She finally pulled over at an office complex with a FedEx drop box on the sidewalk, turned off her engine, and bounced her forehead gently against the steering wheel. She'd made it. And except for the slight panic attack in the bathroom, she'd more or less kept it together. Not bad. She'd like to see the guys at Quantico hit her with something worse than that.

Quinn slid the plastic bag containing Eric Twain's hair into an envelope she'd addressed earlier and leaned out the window to stuff it into the drop box.

That was it. In a few days she'd have her answer.

So this is all still a go?"

Richard Price looked around him at the cavernous lab and the titanium, steel, and carbon-fiber constructs that filled it. For the most part, their specific functions were a mystery to him. Ten years ago, his masters in physics had been sufficient to understand the project and even provide input as to its direction. Now, though, he had come to terms with the knowledge that he was presiding over something that was well beyond his intellectual grasp.

"The testing?" Dr. Edward Marin said, walking over to a computer terminal and tapping in a few commands. "Of course."

"When?"

"Three weeks at the most."

"And what do you expect to find?"

Marin turned to face him again. His smile was barely perceptible but Price could still see the shadow of condescension in it. "I expect to find problems, Richard. The advances of computers over the last few years have brought more realism to our simulations, but there are too many unknown terms to make them completely accurate. This mock-up should give us the last word on where we stand."

Price didn't let his impatience show. "And where is that, Dr. Marin?"

"If I knew—"

"Come on, Doctor. You're making me work too hard. All I'm asking for is a guess."

Marin leaned against a counter jutting from the wall, looking completely at home amid the unfathomable technology around him. "This isn't an accounting problem or a personnel issue, Richard. Do you have any idea how many moving parts I'm trying to make work together? A breakdown anywhere in the system could cause an hour's delay or a year's delay. I don't know."

Price affected a more subservient tone. Cowering in front of this bastard caused him almost physical pain, but in the end, it was expedient. "I'm not going to hold you to it, Doctor, but I need something. I have to keep the heat on, keep the money flowing . . ."

Marin held up his hands. "Of course you do,

Richard. My apologies. I think we're going to find that we're where we need to be with the on-board computers. There are going to be a few power-generation problems that we'll have the ability to resolve fairly quickly. If we run into anything difficult, I think it's going to turn out to be laughably mundane. Probably fine-tuning the mechanical systems to counteract jittering."

"But that can be done, right?"

"Absolutely. It's not architecture, it's carpentry. But painstaking work nonetheless."

"Money?"

Marin shook his head. "We've got what we need to complete this series. If things go well, we won't need Senator Wilkenson's ninety million until we're ready to start building a working unit."

"Time?"

"I'd say this phase of testing will be complete in two months. Then another year to clean up any problems we find. Then . . . well, then it will be up to you and the senator to decide how we proceed."

Out of the corner of his eye, Price saw Brad Lowell appear at the entrance to the lab. Even with the distance between them, Price could see that his business was urgent. "I thank you, Doctor. You'll let me know if anything changes?"

"Of course I will, Richard."

"Then, if you'll excuse me . . ."

Marin nodded politely and lit off across the lab, obviously anxious to forget the pedestrian issues of project administration and get back to his machines and theories.

"A moment of your time, sir," Lowell said, motioning Price to a quiet corner of the lab. "Sir, we have a situation that you need to be aware of."

Price nodded, prompting the man to continue.

"We got a call from our friend at the FBI."

"And?"

"The girl . . . she's digging."

"Quinn Barry? You told me we were rid of her."

"She was moved off the CODIS project to an unrelated programming job in Quantico."

"So what's she doing that I need to worry about?"

Lowell straightened, squaring his shoulders, a mannerism that always seemed to precede bad news. "She pulled the case files from the individual states."

"Shit!" Price said a little too loudly, and then looked around him to confirm that none of the techs inhabiting the lab had heard. "How many?"

"Five, sir. All the ones that had DNA evidence uploaded to CODIS."

"And she has them?"

"As far as we know, yes, sir."

"Goddammit! Is she doing this on her own? Does she have support from anyone at the Bureau?"

"She's all alone on this, sir. Our friend has deleted all references to her requests for the files—"

"You're sure. You're sure she's alone on this?"

"Yes, sir."

Price ran a hand through his close-cropped hair and let a breath hiss out between his teeth. This is how fatal screwups always started—as something stupid, insignificant. New hardware for the FBI's mainframe and a twenty-four-year-old programmer. It was a pebble dropped in a lake. And now the ripples were starting . . .

He tried to clear his mind. There was only one reasonable course of action. One more abhorrent, necessary act in what was quickly becoming a sea of them.

"Sir?" Lowell said. "Can I assume that this is a problem we need to correct?"

Price kept his eyes trained on a blank wall as he spoke. "Our friend at the FBI is aware of the threat this woman poses?"

"Yes, sir."

"And he understands what action we might be forced to take?"

"Yes, sir."

A slight nod was all Lowell needed.

20

The overcast skies had combined with the moonless night to turn everything around Quinn Barry's car completely black. The headlights seemed barely able to cut through the darkness and illuminate the quiet rural highway, but it didn't matter—she'd driven it hundreds of times before. She could do it with her eyes closed.

A week ago she'd really been looking forward to a quiet weekend on her father's farm; now she was almost desperate for it. After six years in the city, the pace of life back home seemed pleasantly slow. She'd convince him to let her sleep till noon. Then she'd make them some pancakes, maybe milk a few cows. And think.

Her problems with David—the main reason she'd planned this trip—seemed far away now, as did the calm that she normally felt as her car floated through the Virginia countryside. She had Eric Twain to blame for that, of course. She'd escaped from the warehouse he called home just over twenty-four hours ago, but she still had the jitters. If anything, they had grown in intensity as the reality of what she'd gotten herself into continued to sink in.

And what, exactly, **had** she gotten herself into? She wished she knew. The more she thought about the inexplicably compromised CODIS system, the more confused she became. She'd come up with countless explanations for the bizarre subroutine she found, but none held up very well to even half-hearted consideration.

The chance that five separate glitches in five separate state computer systems would relate five crimes with obvious similarities was about a billion to one. And the chance of ATD accidentally using an existing DNA signature as a test string—assuming they were stupid enough to make that mistake—was so low it was hard to calculate.

Quinn reached out and turned up the country station playing on the radio. The sound of Hank Williams Jr. filled the car but couldn't penetrate her mind and drive out the conclusion that she was trying desperately to suppress—that the crimes were real and the modification to CODIS was an intentional effort to cover up the connection between them.

Despite the evidence, it seemed impossible. What would the FBI have to gain by keeping secret the fact that a twenty-six-year-old reclusive Hopkins professor/artist was running around the country killing women? And if someone high enough up in the FBI to subvert CODIS was involved, where did that leave her? Nowhere good. Her strangely sudden transfer to Quantico was starting to look less like a random act and more like an effort to get rid of her. And if that was true, it made sense that she'd be sent someplace where she could be watched. Did someone at the FBI know she had the files?

"No," she said aloud, her voice swallowed up by the music filling the car.

She was just being paranoid. It was just a computer glitch that the FBI was completely unaware of. But they wouldn't be for long. The private DNA typing company she'd sent Twain's hair sample to would have her results by tomorrow—Monday at the latest. Then she'd have everything she needed to save her job and make sure that Eric Twain spent the rest of his miserable life painting murals on the walls of his prison cell.

Quinn rolled down the window and let the cold air wash over her as she thought back to her visit to Twain's home—the smell of wood and old brick, the bright colors and music, his physical beauty and disarming demeanor. She hated to admit it, but it had been incredibly exciting to be that close to someone so brilliant and so evil. To play cat and mouse with him and to have escaped.

The car lurched suddenly, bouncing Quinn against her seat belt and knocking her out of a daydream that had her showing up the other FBI trainees on the shooting range. She pumped the accelerator and the engine smoothed out, but it didn't last long. Less than a minute later she was coasting to a stop in the short grass growing alongside the road.

"Great," she muttered, grabbing a flashlight from the glove box and stepping out into the thick darkness. It sounded like it wasn't getting gas. She opened the hood and stuck her head beneath it, checking the fuel line and what she could see of the fuel injection system. Nothing. She slid back into the driver's seat and tried again to get the engine to fire, but with no success. She'd swear it had felt like she'd run out of gas. But that wasn't possible— she'd filled up on the way to work and the gauge was reading more than a quarter of a tank. She stepped out of the car again and looked down at her skirt and blouse, trying to remember what she'd paid for them as she sat down on the grass and slid under the back of the car. A couple of taps on the tank with a stick confirmed her suspicions. Empty.

"What's going on here?" she said aloud as she stood and brushed herself off. It seemed pretty un-likely that anyone with an inclination to siphon gas from parked cars would do it in the FBI Academy lot.

She poked her head back inside the open door of the car and, ducking under the dash, shined her flashlight directly on the gauge mechanism.

It looked new.

She slid in a little farther, getting a better angle. It looked like it had just been installed—and kind of a shoddy job at that. "What on earth . . ."

The sound of an engine became audible just before the headlights washed over her. Crawling out from under the dash, she saw an old pickup ease to a stop in the empty road alongside her. The man inside leaned over and rolled down the passenger-side window.

"Got problems, there, miss?"

Quinn shrugged, only half listening. No mechanic had ever touched her car; she did all the work herself and she was certain she'd never replaced any of the gauges.

"Yeah. I guess I do."

He grinned and jumped out of his truck. "Can I borrow that?"

Quinn handed him her flashlight and watched him examine the engine, still trying to make sense of what had happened.

"Yup," the man said, turning around and wiping his hands on already greasy jeans.

The sound of his voice knocked her back into the here and now. "What?"

"It's your carburetor."

"Excuse me?"

He motioned her over and she watched him point kind of randomly at her engine. "I know a fair amount about cars," he said in a relaxed drawl. "Your carburetor's clogged. It's not serious, but you ain't driving out of here." He took a few steps back toward his truck, leaving her looking at an engine that didn't **have** a carburetor, let alone a clogged one.

When she turned back toward him, she spotted a car approaching from the other direction. The man glanced up at it but didn't seem to notice when it came to a stop about a hundred yards up the road. "Tell you what—there's a town about twenty miles from here. I'll run you up there."

Quinn felt the palm of her hand sweating as she subtly began to unscrew the wing nut holding the jack to the side of the engine compartment. She could hear the nervousness in her voice when she answered. "Thanks anyway, but I called Triple A from my cell phone. They'll be here any minute."

The man smiled and she saw his eyes twitch right to confirm that the car across the road was still there. "Well, hell, I can't just leave you here. Why don't we leave a note for them?"

The nut came free and Quinn wrapped her hand around the cool metal of the jack. "Really, I'll be fine."

"I'm afraid I have to insist," he said, suddenly losing the drawl that had been so evident a moment before. When he reached out to grab hold of her arm, Quinn swung the jack. It caught him in the shoulder with enough force to throw him off balance and knock him back onto the road. She saw the surprise on his face as it was briefly illuminated by the truck's headlights and heard the squealing tires as the car across the street spun around and started speeding toward them.

Quinn stood over the man, gripping the jack but not knowing what to do. He took advantage of her indecision, reaching into his jean jacket and pulling out a gun.

This time the jack hit him in the chest, a full, desperate swing with Quinn's entire weight behind it. She could barely hear the air escape him and the clatter of the gun spinning across the asphalt over the roar of the approaching engine.

There was no time. She ducked into the open door of her car and pulled a heavy knapsack from it, then ran around the violently coughing man lying in the road to the driver's-side door of his truck. It was still running and she floored it just as the car behind came skidding to a stop. For a few moments it receded in the rearview mirror, but then it started to close fast.

She felt the impact as the car's front bumper slammed into the light back end of the pickup. Her hands were slippery with sweat, making it even more difficult than it should have been to bring the vehicle out of the dangerous fishtail that resulted. She watched in the rearview mirror as the car behind her slowed and then started to accelerate again. This time it was going to hit her hard—she'd crash for sure.

At the last possible moment she yanked back a lever on the floorboard and turned the wheel, sending the truck skidding off the road. The four-wheel-drive system engaged as she smashed through a wood fence and started bouncing wildly through a field of cut hay. The car tried to stay with her but went wide and was slowed considerably by the loose dirt.

Quinn continued to push the old truck, dodging obstacles as best she could at the speed she was going. When she looked back again, the car chasing her had stopped and she could see the brief dimming of its headlights as someone moved through their beam. She ducked her head and continued forward, finally jumping up on a dirt road and jamming the accelerator to the floor.

Quinn pushed the empty Dumpster forward a few more feet and then squeezed between it and an enormous propane tank. The truck was completely hidden from view now behind a closed gas station some fifty miles from where she'd broken down. She started to get into the cab but it felt too claustrophobic. Instead, she grabbed her knapsack and climbed into the open bed, hugging the pack to her for warmth as she pressed her back against the tailgate.

It had been planned. There was no doubt about that. Somehow they had known where she was going. They'd siphoned her tank so she would break down on the loneliest section of road between Quantico and her father's farm, and they'd replaced her gas gauge so she wouldn't know it.

Quinn suddenly realized she was shaking all over. Who were they? And what did they want? It had to be CODIS—what else could it be? Other than that, her life was completely ordinary. Whoever these men were, they didn't want that subroutine to become public. What was their connection to Eric Twain? Were they protecting him for some reason? Why? What possible reason could they have?

When she'd managed to calm herself down a little, she climbed out of the truck and walked quietly to the pay phone on the back wall of the gas station. Taking a deep breath, she dialed and willed David to answer.

"Hello?" His voice was groggy.

"David!"

"Quinn? Where've you been? I've been trying to call you all goddamn week."

"David, listen—"

"Hey, what the hell time is it?"

"David! For once, just shut up and listen."

"Jesus. What?"

"I think I'm in trouble and I need your help."

"What are you talking about?"

"Do you remember that place we used to jog sometimes when we first met?"

"You mean—"

"Don't say it!"

"Quinn, what the hell's wrong with you?"

"I think someone could be listening."

"You think someone could be listening? What—"

"Can you meet me there? In two hours?"

She heard him rustling around, probably turning a light on. "Yeah, I guess."

"Don't let anyone follow you."

"Follow me? Quinn—"

She hung up and ran back to the truck. She'd already been there too long. They'd be looking for her.

21

Quinn had started purposefully enough, but now she felt herself faltering. With each step, the sound of the crushed gravel beneath her feet was a little quieter, a little more hesitant. Finally, she came to a stop where the jogging path she was on intersected another. Her breath was coming in rapid, hazy puffs, illuminated by the faint light of D.C. working its way through the dense trees.

She still couldn't understand what was happening to her. And the harder she thought about it, the more paranoid she became. She tried over and over to tell herself that she was being irrational, that she was letting fear substitute itself for logic. But she just couldn't make it sink in.

She had to bring her watch up close to her face to read the hands: 3:15 A.M. David would already be waiting for her. David, the only person she'd told about going to visit her father. David, whom she'd found going through her papers the day she'd been dismissed from her job at headquarters. David, whose sudden interest in spending more time with her had coincided almost exactly with her discovery of the error in the CODIS system.

Stop it!

She willed herself to move, but her feet stayed firmly planted. The memory of David switching cars with her so that she could check out a nonexistent problem with his brakes suddenly came back to her. Had he wanted to search her car? Bug it?

She shook her head. Now she was really getting into straitjacket territory. Despite that admonishment, though, she edged off the path, letting the wet grass silence her footsteps as she climbed a short hill that she knew overlooked the rest of the park.

He was there, as she knew he would be, standing in a ring of light provided by a tall street lamp. Quinn edged through the semidarkness to a bank of pay phones, hiding behind them as she carefully scanned the area.

There wasn't anything to see. Just trees and the empty paths that crisscrossed the area. David was the only thing moving in the park, shifting impatiently from foot to foot as he waited for her to appear.

This was stupid—she was letting her recent anger with him get blown out of proportion. While he wasn't exactly a sterling "significant other," he also wasn't the kind of person who would turn on a friend. He could help. He worked for powerful men; he had powerful friends. He could get the files into the hands of people who could do something with them and who would be safe from reprisals.

"Come on, Quinn," she whispered to herself.

It was hopeless; she couldn't convince herself. She looked down at David one more time and then at the phone she was hiding behind. She'd call him. That was the answer. That would make her feel better.

Quinn dug around in her knapsack for some change and dialed David's cell-phone number from memory. She watched him as he suddenly jerked upright and began patting his tan raincoat.

"Hello?"

"David—"

"Quinn! Where the hell are you? I've been standing here in the rain for half an hour."

Quinn watched him as he lowered his head and began walking around the edges of the circle of light he had been standing in. "I'm sorry, David. I got delayed. I . . . I don't think I'm going to make it."

She could see the speed of his circling increase, but his expression and the other body language she'd become so familiar with was impossible to discern because of the distance between them.

"Are you kidding, Quinn? You got me up in the middle of the night to drive out here for nothing?"

His tone was taking on that authoritative tone that he slipped into when he was showing off for the people he worked with. She squinted and leaned forward a little, trying unsuccessfully to see his shadowed face.

"I said I was sorry, David."

His next words came quickly, as though he was trying to keep her from hanging up. The authoritative tone melted into one of concern. "I did what you asked—I made sure I wasn't followed. You said you were in trouble. Tell me what's going on, Quinn. I want to help. You know that or you wouldn't have called me."

Something about this just didn't seem right. She was willing to accept that her normally acute perceptions had been muddled a little by fear and confusion, but this was still obvious. He was almost begging. Begging to help her. It was just a little too out of character.

"Sorry about waking you up, David. I've got some thinking to do. I'll call you later."

He'd stopped moving now and was covering his free ear to hear better. "Quinn, wait—"

She hung up the phone and turned away, telling herself that she'd made the right decision. Better safe than sorry. That's what her dad always said. Of course her dad had probably assumed that there would be other options . . .

"Fuck!"

It was David's voice. His shout was loud enough to resound throughout the park. She stopped and looked back at him as he jerked his cell phone back and forth in what looked like a child's tantrum. Finally, he calmed down and started dialing, obviously unconcerned that it was three-thirty in the morning. A moment later he was circling the light again, speaking urgently, but inaudibly, into his phone.

The conversation lasted less than a minute and at the end of it he started sprinting across the park toward the street.

"Need a refill?"

Quinn turned away from the computer screen and faced the young waiter.

"Pulling an all-nighter, huh?" he said, topping off her teacup.

The Internet café was only a few blocks from Georgetown University and was frequented almost exclusively by students. She was still young enough to blend in with them, which was the reason she'd picked the place.

"Sorry?" Quinn said.

He nodded toward the computer screen. "Forget to study for a test?"

She gave him a smile she'd perfected her senior year. Polite but not inviting. "Yeah. My eight o'clock. You know how it is."

He got the hint and started toward one of the few other customers unfortunate enough to be there that early. "Good luck."

"Thanks."

Quinn looked around to make sure no one was paying her any particular attention and typed www.DNAssessment into the browser on the screen. The connection was a little slow and she had time to take a nervous bite of the bagel lying next to the keyboard before the page was fully loaded.

She felt her heart rate rise a little as she clicked on the results button—not because she had any doubts about what she was going to find, but because she wasn't sure what she was going to do with the information once she obtained it. Who could she go to? Not the FBI. Certainly not David. The press? The local police? Quinn tapped the password she'd selected into a white box at the center of the screen and hit the enter key. There had to be someone. She'd just have to figure it out.

She glanced down at the bagel again while the computer accessed her data, but couldn't bring herself to pick it up. Lack of sleep, adrenaline, and caffeine were starting to take their toll on her normally bulletproof stomach.

When the screen came up, she scrolled down through the mumbo jumbo, finally stopping when she came to the DNA signature taken from Eric Twain's hairs. She stared at it for a long time, not even bothering to look down at the killer's signature that she'd scrawled on a Post-It note.

They weren't even close.

22

The wind had continued to build throughout the day and was now giving the misting rain force, driving it through her sweater and the light skirt wrapped tightly around her legs. Quinn pressed her back a little harder against the crumbling brick wall behind her and heard the jutting piece of metal roof make a dull clanging sound. She looked up and decided it would hold—as long as the wind didn't pick up any more.

She'd been there for hours already and had no idea how much longer she'd have to wait. Minutes? Days? The scene around her was completely desolate. The only sound and motion was the work of the wind. She looked out of the little alcove that she was huddled in, once again trying to find something of visual interest in the dilapidated buildings and blowing garbage. She needed something to keep her alert; she'd already caught herself nodding off twice . . .

She wasn't sure what it was at first, but something snapped her awake. She jerked forward, swiveling her head back and forth in a quick motion, trying to see anything that hadn't been there before.

At first there was nothing. After a few moments, though, the hum of an engine became distinguishable from the drone of the wind. She jumped to her feet and picked her way through the rubble, keeping close to an old wall that ran almost the full thirty yards to the road. The stiffness in her legs slowed her down a little, but she made it to the end of the wall with time to spare. In front of her, a set of abandoned railroad tracks bisected the road. Over the years the asphalt had buckled around them, leaving a series of deep ruts.

The little gray Honda slowed as it came into view, approaching the tracks with necessary caution. She waited until it had passed by before she darted out and ran up behind it. She yanked the door open and threw her knapsack over the seats before diving in.

"Jesus!"

She slid partway onto the floor in front of the passenger seat as the car skidded to a stop, slamming her shoulder painfully into the dash.

"What the hell are you doing?"

She looked up into the startled face of Eric Twain. "Keep driving!"

He didn't move. "You people are a bunch of psychos, do you know that? Read my lips, Quinn Barry. **I didn't kill Lisa.**"

"Please, Eric—"

"Wait," he said. His face suddenly darkened and he ducked down in the seat a little, moving his head slowly back and forth. "Why are you on the floor?" He leaned forward, trying to see better through the slightly fogged windows. "They're out there, aren't they?"

"Eric, for God's sake—"

"You've got a bunch of SWAT guys with guns aimed at my head. You're going to kill me."

Quinn reached out and grabbed his arm. "Eric, no one's going to kill you! You have my word, okay? Now DRIVE!"

He hesitated for a moment but finally released the emergency brake and eased the rest of the way across the railroad tracks. "What do you want from me? Why won't you people just leave me the hell alone?"

She didn't answer, instead rising up enough to see out the back window. Nothing. Did that mean she was safe or did it mean that they just weren't stupid enough to be seen?

"Look, Eric. Listen to me carefully now, okay? I have conclusive DNA evidence that whoever killed your assistant also killed at least four other women across the country—probably more."

"What? What are you talking about?"

"What I'm talking about is that I know you didn't do it."

She watched him run a hand through his long hair, pushing it back and exposing the side of his face. He looked kind of confused.

"Eric? Are you all right?"

He seemed to lose the strength to keep the accelerator depressed and the car started to drift a little.

"No, no. Don't stop," Quinn said, putting a hand on his knee and pushing on it.

"I, uh . . ." He covered his mouth with his hand for a moment. "I'm sorry. I don't expect you to understand but I've . . . I've been saddled with this for so long. I'm having a little trouble . . . It's over? It's really over?"

Quinn peeked out the back window one more time and, satisfied that they weren't being followed, straightened up in the seat. When she did, he looked over at her. She wasn't sure if his eyes had softened or if it was just her perception of him.

"Thank you," he stammered. "Thank you."

"Don't thank me."

"Why not? I mean you can't imagine what it's like. To have everyone think you're—"

"I'm not exactly an FBI agent, remember?"

"So?"

"I discovered this myself."

The suspicion she'd seen the first time they'd met started to creep back into his face.

"Eric, I don't know exactly what's going on, but there's reason to believe that the FBI doesn't want this made public. That they're covering up—"

He slammed on the brakes again, pitching her forward. This time she managed to get a hand out before she hit the dash.

"I can't believe I let you do that to me," he said angrily. "Get out."

"What are you doing? Keep driving. I—"

He leaned over her and threw the passenger door open. "Out!"

"Eric, I've got proof—"

"Oh, hey, that's different. You've got proof?" He leaned his back against his door and fully faced her. "Do you have **any** idea how many of you conspiracy freaks I've had to deal with over the years?"

"Excuse me? I am **not** a conspiracy freak."

"You probably think JFK was killed by space aliens, don't you?"

"Of course not."

"The CIA created AIDS to kill gay people?"

"No! Look, I have—"

"A psychic."

"What?"

"That's it, isn't it? You're a psychic. You figure Lisa isn't really dead. She's being held underground by the Mole People or something."

She reached out and grabbed both his hands. He didn't resist, but his eyes narrowed perceptibly.

"Listen to me," Quinn started. She didn't look directly at him, instead surveying the empty landscape around them, looking for movement. "You saw my ID. I do work for the FBI. And in your backseat are police files that'll prove what I'm telling you. All I ask is that you give me a half an hour of your time."

"Why should I?"

"Because you want to know who killed Lisa. And because you don't have anything better to do."

23

Getting out of the car turned out to be more complicated than Brad Lowell had expected. With his right arm in a sling and still sending shooting pains down his side, even the simplest tasks had become a struggle. He grabbed the seat belt with his good hand and gritted his teeth as he propelled himself out onto Richard Price's driveway.

He moved more slowly than normal, not because of his injuries, but to give himself time to run through the responses he'd make to the questions Price would undoubtedly ask. Their phone conversation that morning had been uncharacteristically abrupt and had ended in a rather emphatic "request" that they meet. Lowell had been to his boss's new home only once, and certainly not under circumstances such as these. He had no idea what to expect. But what was worse, he wasn't sure he cared anymore.

Lowell knocked hesitantly and stepped back, straightening his jacket as best he could. A moment later a young girl pulled the door open.

"Colonel Lowell! Oh, my God. What happened to you?"

He smiled disarmingly and looked into the pretty, unlined face of Price's fifteen-year-old daughter. "I was showing one of my kids how to ride a bike, Rachel. I guess I'm a little rusty."

She motioned him inside. "Man, I guess so. Are you all right?"

"They tell me I'll live to ride again."

"Well, I'm sure your kids will be glad to hear that. Dad's out back."

Lowell moved purposefully through the hallway and entered a large kitchen to find a slightly plump woman of about forty rolling dough out on the counter.

"Brad?"

"He fell off his bike, Mom," Rachel said, gracefully hopping onto one of the stools lined up against the wall.

Lowell shrugged as best he could. "'Morning, Connie."

The woman shook her head and went back to what she was doing. "Getting a little old for that kind of thing, aren't we?"

"I know I feel old today," Lowell said, stepping

through the sliding glass door into the backyard. Price was reading in a lawn chair next to a half-installed pool. He looked up as Lowell approached but didn't comment on his obvious injuries.

"We'll talk in my study," he said.

"I think I've been pretty understanding, Brad."

Lowell closed the door behind him as Price took a seat at his desk.

"Yes, sir."

"Don't 'yes sir' me. Do you or do you not think that I have been sympathetic to your situation?"

Despite his preparation, Lowell wasn't sure how to respond. "You've been very supportive. And I appreciate it . . ."

He couldn't tell if this had been the right thing to say; Price's glare didn't waiver.

"Am I being unfair here, Brad? Is it unreasonable for me to be a little bewildered that you and two of your men couldn't capture a single twenty-four-year-old girl?" He motioned in the general direction of Lowell's arm. "That you would let her do this to you?"

Lowell stood his ground, shaky as it was, and remained silent.

"I'm waiting."

Once again, Lowell found himself in an impossible situation, walking a fine line between explanation and excuse.

"Sir. I believe she knew the car had been sabotaged."

"And how is that possible?"

"I don't know, sir. Because of the time constraints involved, we were unable to do any meaningful background on her. For all we know, she was an auto mechanic before she joined the FBI."

As Lowell could have predicted, a flush spread across Price's face. It was he who had created that urgency, he who had approved the plan, and he who had insisted on the use of limited manpower.

"So this is my fault, is it, Brad?"

Price's tone suggested that Lowell had overplayed his hand. "I'm not suggesting that, sir, I was—"

"Enough!"

Lowell looked behind him at the door. Price's shout was loud enough to have been heard by his family.

"What the fuck are we doing here, Brad? There's too much at stake for this kind of shit."

"I understand, sir."

"What about the boyfriend? You said she made contact?"

"David Bergin. Yes, sir. She set up a meeting with him."

"And?"

"She didn't show. She called him and told him she wasn't coming."

"Why?"

"We believe she suspects him of some kind of involvement, sir."

A loud rush of air escaped Price and he slumped back in his chair. "And what does **he** believe?"

"He's still okay—a good soldier and ambitious as hell. We told him that we're investigating her for espionage—"

"And he bought it?"

"That she's involved in any wrongdoing? No. But that works even better for us. He'll be anxious to help us get her so she can clear her name. And he'll keep it quiet; if it were to become public that a woman he's involved with is under suspicion . . . Let's just say he's aware of the effect that could have on his career."

"Okay. What are we doing about all this?" Price said.

"Sir, we're physically covering her father and what we consider to be her other three top potential contacts. We're covering all other potentials electronically. Obviously, we're working up some background on her now and will be expanding our coverage based on what we learn."

"And the press?"

"We're doing what we can to monitor them, but as you know, that's more difficult."

Lowell examined his boss as they both fell silent. The aura of calm control that always surrounded him had dissipated a little, letting Lowell see past it. For the first time since he'd known the man, he could see a glimmer of the same emotions and weaknesses that plagued normal human beings. And that worried him.

"What about the files?" Price said finally.

"We believe she still has those."

Price pursed his lips and nodded. "So what you're telling me is that you have no fucking idea where she is or what she's doing."

Lowell straightened a little but didn't respond.

"Brad, this is top priority now. I am holding you personally responsible for finding this girl and . . . and dealing with the threat she poses to us and the project. If you need any extraordinary resources to get the job done, contact me immediately. There is nothing—nothing—more important than this right now. I'll accept no more excuses. Do you understand?"

"Yes, sir."

Lowell knew he'd been dismissed, but didn't move.

"What?" Price said.

"Sir, I'll have to reassign nearly all the manpower available to me. That leaves no resources to—"

"I'll take care of it," Price said, cutting him off.

"Yes, sir. Thank you, sir."

24

Your clock just started," Eric Twain said, aiming his car at an uninhabited corner of the rest stop.

"Oh? Got a date?" Quinn countered, but instantly regretted it. "I'm sorry, Eric. That was just mean. I haven't slept in a while . . ."

He wagged a finger in her general direction as the car rolled to a stop in front of a group of empty picnic tables. "You only have nine minutes and thirty seconds left. And if Jimmy Hoffa or Area Fifty-one comes up, you're going to be hitch-hiking home."

Quinn knew she deserved that. She hadn't handled this very well. But that was going to change. She reached into her pocket and handed him her FBI identification.

"The ID's real," she said. "I work as a computer

programmer at the J. Edgar Hoover Building. Or at least I did until last week."

He turned the small piece of plastic over in his hand and seemed to be comparing the photo on it with her face. "You could have gotten this any-where. But I'm still listening."

"I was working on reprogramming parts of CODIS—the Combined DNA Index System. Are you familiar with it?"

He shook his head.

"Individual state law enforcement agencies have data banks of DNA signatures relating to crimes and criminals. The FBI's system is sort of a clearinghouse or central storage facility for all that—so separate states can have access to national data."

"I guess I do know something about it," he said, handing her back the ID. "They take blood from convicts and suspects so that they can use their DNA like fingerprints. They wanted me to give a blood sample when they were investigating Lisa's murder."

Quinn remembered that from reading the case file. "But you refused."

He shrugged. "Not to be vulgar, but I **was** sleep-ing with her. I think it was a foregone conclusion that they'd find my DNA lying around. Eight min-utes. I'd think about getting to the point if I was you."

"Look, you're going to have to give me a break

and bear with me for a few minutes, okay? Now follow me, here. Using DNA to sift through suspects and keep track of convicted felons is only part of it. I was working on something else, a subsystem called the Forensic Index."

"And what exactly does that do?"

"It categorizes DNA samples from crime scenes that don't have a suspect. That way, crimes can be tied together."

He seemed to understand, so she continued. "The FBI asked me to modify CODIS to work with some new hardware—they were too cheap to go back to the original contractor. When I did, my new search engine found five hits that had never been recognized."

"By 'hits,' you mean it connected five unsolved crimes that were considered unrelated before?"

"Exactly. Someone left the same DNA at the scenes of killings or disappearances involving five different young women. Lisa Egan was one of them . . ." Quinn fell silent, trying to find something in his opaque expression that would tell her if he believed anything she was saying or if she was just wasting her time.

"So what you're telling me," Eric started slowly, "is that Lisa was the victim of some guy on a multi-state killing spree and that the FBI didn't notice because of some kind of glitch in their system?" He pressed his knuckles against his mouth and talked around them. "If you're trying to convince me that the government in general and law enforcement specifically are completely incompetent, you aren't going to have to work very hard. But if what you're telling me is right, it sounds like you should be downtown talking to your boss, not sitting in a rest stop with me."

Quinn started to open her mouth to speak, but hesitated. Everything she knew about Eric Twain had come from an inaccurate police file and a few ten-year-old newspaper articles. Could she trust him? There was no way to know for sure. What she did know, though, was that if anyone was motivated to help her, it was him. Whoever killed Lisa Egan had not only taken away a woman he had been close to but had done a fair job at taking away his life.

"It's not a glitch," she said, reaching into the backseat and digging a handful of papers from her knapsack. She handed them to him and he immediately started flipping through the pages.

"The DNA sequences the FBI uses are numeric, thirteen two-term expressions . . ." She wasn't sure he was listening. The speed with which he was flipping through the code continued to increase, to a point at which it would be impossible to read and comprehend the sections she had highlighted.

"The lines I marked were inserted all over the

program—they were intentionally hidden. It's kind of complicated, but—"

"It's a sort," he said when he came to the last page.

"Excuse me?"

"If-then statements." He jabbed a finger at the top page. "Right here. If a DNA string includes the expression eight comma eleven then it jumps to the next embedded section." He flipped a few pages. "Then here, if the string includes the expression seven comma nine point three, it skips forward again. The last section queries the order. If it matches, then the computer just ignores it."

Quinn stared at him, suddenly even more uncertain. It seemed impossible that he could have figured all that out so quickly without prior knowledge. She must not have been very successful at hiding her apprehension, because when he looked up at her again he cocked his head a little to the right and said, "I'm pretty good at math, remember?"

She chewed her lower lip for a few seconds but then decided to give him the benefit of the doubt—for two reasons. First, she had no idea what a person who'd mastered calculus in the first grade could or could not comprehend. And second . . . she had no Plan B.

"You're exactly right."

"So what you're saying to me is that these lines of

code caused the system to pass over this particular DNA signature. But when you reprogrammed the system, your search engine didn't include those lines." He tossed the stack of paper back at her and landed it in her lap. "And what do you conclude from all this?"

"I'm not sure," Quinn said honestly. "All I know is that when I brought this up at work, I was pretty much instantly transferred and they called in the original programmers to finish the job. It took them about a day to 'fix' the system so it wasn't coming up with the additional hits."

Eric rubbed his chin and watched a young family walk toward the tables in front of their car. "I figured we'd get around to the conspiracy thing eventually."

"So you don't believe me?" she said, a little too defensively.

"I'm sorry, Quinn, but I met more than my share of FBI agents while I was being investigated for Lisa's murder. I'm no big fan, but if anything, they're overzealous. You're telling me that they're purposely protecting some nutcase who's going around killing people, and, well, I don't see it." He pointed to the pages of code in her lap. "I mean, that could be nothing more than the remnants of some test they were running."

"That's exactly what I thought," she said. "For security reasons, CODIS outputs really limited in-formation in response to queries—not much more than a case number and crime lab location. So I ordered the files."

"You figured they wouldn't really exist. That they'd be fictional."

Quinn nodded.

"And?"

She reached back for her knapsack and dumped it out on the console between them. "How do you think I found you? Five police files and five missing or dead women. Real cases, real people. And there's more connecting them than just a DNA signature."

Eric reached out and touched one of the files but didn't open it. His eyes clouded and he seemed to be somewhere else for a few moments.

"You thought it was me," he said finally.

Quinn felt a flush rising to her face. "Everyone else had alibis," she mumbled.

Eric's demeanor shifted a bit. For some reason, she seemed suddenly to have gained a little credibility.

"So, with no FBI support—all alone—you waltz into the house of a guy you think kills women for fun and start questioning him."

"I'm sorry, Eric. I—"

He held up his hands. "Don't apologize. I don't know, Quinn, I still think you may be a nut, but I have to give you credit for guts. I mean—" He suddenly went silent, a knowing smile slowly spreading across his face. "But you didn't really question me, did you? You just wandered around and . . . the bathroom. You were hunting for DNA."

Quinn stared down at the floorboard.

"I take it you found what you were looking for."

She nodded, but didn't look up. "I sent a couple of your hairs to a private DNA testing facility. They weren't a match."

"Uh-huh. Well, as much as I want it to, it still doesn't prove anything. I mean, the cases CODIS is connecting could still be nothing more than a hardware or software bug. That subroutine you found could just be some kind of half-assed patch. It wouldn't be the first time."

Quinn lifted her head and studied him. He seemed nothing like the person she'd met a few days ago. His eyes were as intense as before, but they were probing now, not threatening. The delicate features and athletic build that seemed so predatory before had lost their strange malevolence and regained their beauty. She knew that the change was just in her mind, but that didn't really make any difference now. She didn't have the ability or the time to look inside Eric Twain. She'd just have to take a chance.

"Someone tried to kill me last night."

"What?"

To his credit, he caught the amused little smile almost before it started.

"I know you probably don't believe me, but it's true.

Someone rigged my car to die on a road out in southern Virginia. A guy stopped and pulled a gun on me."

"So how'd you get away?"

"I hit him with a tire iron and took his truck."

That seemed to worry him. "Quinn . . . Think now. Are you sure he pulled a gun on you? Are you sure you weren't just freaked out by all this stuff and maybe thought he did? I mean, how do you know your car was rigged? Maybe it just broke down."

Quinn's mouth tightened and her eyes narrowed. The expression wasn't lost on Eric, who took the hint and shut up.

"I grew up on a farm," she said coldly. "I could take my car apart and put it back together again blindfolded. Take my word for it."

She had originally planned to tell him about David, too, but now she saw that it would be a mistake. He already looked like he was leaning toward the conclusion that she was a complete crackpot. Besides, she herself couldn't decide whether her suspicion of David was reasonable or not. She'd been so sure at the time, but now she was starting to wonder if it hadn't just been a product of everything that had happened to her that night.

"I'm sorry, Quinn. I just don't know what to tell you."

She started stuffing the files back into her knapsack. "I understand. All I'm asking for is a couple of hours. After you look at the files and the other stuff I have, if you still think I'm a nut—"

"Hey, come on. I don't think—"

"Yes, you do. And in two hours, if you haven't changed your mind, then you can just walk away. What have you got to lose?"

25

There was no sound in the windowless room except for the occasional rustling of paper as Eric continued his examination of the case files. Quinn hadn't said a word in over an hour—in fact she'd hardly moved except to make eye contact with Eric when he occasionally flicked his gaze in her direction.

He was nearly finished tearing apart the fourth file, and the table they were sitting at was strewn with its contents. Newspaper articles, DNA tests, gruesome photographs, investigative reports. The cynicism and suspicion that had been so visible in him when they arrived seemed to fade a little more with every page.

Quinn noticed his progress slow as he neared the end of the file and she felt a pang of sympathy. Only one was left unopened—the one relating the investigation into Lisa Egan's death. And into his life.

He didn't seem quite ready to look at it and Quinn briefly considered breaking the silence that had grown between them—to let him use it as an excuse to put off opening the file. In the end, though, she decided to keep her mouth shut. He needed to finish and to make a decision. Was he going to help her or not?

Eric stopped reading and let his head drop against the back of the chair he was sitting in. His breathing slowed and his body went slack, creating the illusion that he was sleeping with his eyes open.

He came out of this self-imposed trance about a minute later and sat up straight again, pulling out a few pages of yellow legal paper that had been hidden behind the file's back cover.

"Eric, wait!" Quinn said, jumping from her chair and sliding partway across the table toward him.

The sudden motion and sound startled him but didn't slow his reflexes. He scooted his chair back and yanked the pages away just as she grabbed for them.

"Is something wrong?" he said, moving back a little more and continuing to unfold the pages. "Something I shouldn't see?"

"It's nothing! Really." Quinn pushed herself off the table and moved quickly around it.

"'Eric Twain,'" he read, protecting the pages

with his body as she leaned over his back and tried to pry his hands from them.

"Eric, please. I forgot those were in there. I was just—"

His response was to jump out of the chair and jog to a safer distance as he scanned the pages. "Your handwriting, I assume. My psyche according to Quinn Barry?"

"Come on, Eric. It was just a bunch of speculation. It doesn't mean anything anymore—"

"Don't you want to know how you did?"

Quinn fell dejectedly into a chair. This was really no way to make friends.

"Now where was I?" he said. "Oh yeah. Me."

Quinn let her head sink into her hands.

" 'Eric Twain,' " he read. " 'IQ too high to accurately measure. Enters college at age twelve. Would have felt alienated in grade/high school. Would have expected it to be better in college. It's worse. People around him form relationships/bonds—he can't. He's an outsider—going into adolescence with no women around him anywhere near his age.' "

"Come on, Eric. Give me a break."

"No, no. You're doing great so far . . ." he said, and then started reading again. " 'Early 1989. Fifteen years old. Hires Lisa Egan as his assistant. They begin a relationship.' " Quinn winced when he turned the paper to the side so he could read what was scrawled in the margin. " 'Young for a sadistic rapist. He's been living in an adult world for years, though.' "

He glanced up at her. "I've always been an overachiever, you know? Let's see . . . 'Egan is older; dominates him, causing resentment—perhaps withholding sex. This resentment grows. He kills Catherine Tanner, June '89—probably his first murder. Tanner resembles Egan—is similarly highly educated. Twain covers this murder up. While killing her, he feels the control Egan has taken from him and is able to act out his repressed sexual fantasies. The next victim is another facsimile of Lisa, but the murder is not covered up—he has become more comfortable and angry. Finally, he gains the courage to kill Lisa, but it is not premeditated or planned like the others. He is somehow frightened away and almost prosecuted.' "

Eric smirked as he turned the page and continued reading. " 'Or maybe not. Doesn't seem exactly right for a sadistic rapist. Perhaps this anger was building independent of Egan? The general un-availability of the women around him? Despite catharsis of killing the woman who held power over him and unlike Ed Kemper . . .' " He looked up from the page. "Ed Kemper?"

"He, uh, dissected college girls, 'cause he hated his mom," Quinn mumbled. "Finally cut her throat out and shoved it down the garbage disposal. After that, he gave himself up."

"Nice . . . 'He is still shunned by the women around him—young physicists aren't exactly ladies' men . . .'" That got her another well-deserved smirk. "'He misses the absolute control he had over them during the killings. In 1995—perhaps before—he begins again. More calculated now. No longer near his home—victims no longer facsimiles of Lisa. Victims chosen now to minimize possibility of discovery/arrest . . .'"

Quinn heard him carefully refold the pages, but by now her face was almost resting on her knees.

"Very impressive," he said, taking the seat next to her.

"I'm not sure how to apologize for that," she said through her hands.

"You don't have anything to be sorry for. It was a reasonable hypothesis. You want to know where you went wrong?"

She sighed quietly. "Sure."

"Lisa. She was brilliant and beautiful and made me feel good about myself as a person and not just as a human calculator. I spent most of my childhood with counselors and shrinks falling all over themselves to get into my head. Not because they gave a crap about me but because they had some theory they wanted to prove or some paper they wanted to write. And after I'd spent fifteen years as a lab rat, not a single one of them ever succeeded in understanding what made me tick. Lisa was the only person who ever did."

It was the genuine pain in his voice that finally made Quinn look up.

"My parents were intimidated by me, other kids thought I was a freak, the art world wanted to use me, and a lot of people in science wanted to see me fail. Lisa was the only thing in my life that was worth anything."

Quinn reached out and put a hand on his, but he didn't seem to notice. He looked right through her. "Kind of funny. It's only been about ten years, but now it's hard for me to picture her. It's like she's been pushed out by everything else. All I can re-member now is how much trouble her death has caused me . . ."

"You knew her for . . . what? Two years? And you've spent the last decade paying for it. You've had to live with the suspicion, you had to leave your home . . ."

He let out a sharp breath through his nose that could have been a bitter laugh, but she wasn't sure.

"I couldn't stand the stares, you know? If I was working late, women would make excuses not to be alone in a room with me. And then there was that son-of-a-bitch cop from Baltimore . . ."

"Renquist?"

Eric nodded. "He kept hounding me, asking the same questions over and over, thinking up excuses to call anybody I managed to put a relationship together with. He spent all his time trying to trip me up instead of looking for the person who actually killed Lisa. To this day, the only friends I have are people who knew me before all this happened and never believed I was guilty. And there aren't many of those."

He fell silent and looked down at the file lying on the floor between them. Quinn took her hand off his, thinking he was ready to reach for it, but he didn't. Instead he leaned back in his chair and examined her thoughtfully. "But enough whining. What about you?"

"What do you mean?"

"You know my whole life story, the deepest recesses of my mind, and I don't know the first thing about you."

She shrugged. "Nothing much to tell. My life hasn't been as interesting as yours."

He remained silent, prompting her to go on.

"I grew up on a small dairy farm in West Virginia. When I graduated from college I got out of there as fast as I could."

"Why?"

"You've obviously never **been** to a small dairy farm in West Virginia."

"So you wanted to see the world?"

"You could say that. When I got to D.C. I took a job as a computer programmer. About a year later I took a clerk job with the FBI because I wanted to be an agent."

"Really? I don't see you as the FBI type."

"I could do the job as well as anyone," she said defensively.

"I meant that as a compliment. Why on earth would you want to be an FBI agent?"

"I already told you, it seemed like it would be an exciting way to make a living."

"Is that why you didn't just send these files back? Excitement?"

She shook her head slowly. "Maybe that was part of it, I don't know . . . But the bottom line is that people are dying."

He seemed satisfied with her answer. "Married?"

She shook her head.

"Boyfriend?"

"Not anymore."

He started tapping his lower lip with the end of his pencil but didn't take his eyes off her. He sat that way for almost five minutes before Quinn couldn't stand it anymore and broke the silence.

"So what do you think? Do you believe me now? Or do you still think I'm crazy."

"I don't think you're crazy. But I've got to admit that I can't make any of this fit together. There's got to be a simple explanation you've missed . . ."

"Like what?"

He reached into his pocket and pulled out a rubber band, using it to tie back the long hair framing his face. "I don't know. You've spent more time with these files than I have. Is there anything that all the women have in common other than the fact that they're all about the same age and body type?"

"All of them? No. Not that I can find."

"So nothing would suggest that they were killed for any logical purpose. It was random. Some kind of psycho."

"On the surface, that would seem to be the answer." She nodded toward the file on the floor, feeling a little guilty for prodding him. "You know that case as well as anyone. Maybe you'll be able to make a connection. See something that I couldn't. That the police couldn't."

"I don't know. It's been a long time," he said, leaning over and scooping it up. He ran a hand slowly over the cardboard cover but didn't open it.

Quinn stood and started for the door. "Why don't I see if I can track us down some coffee?"

He'd loved Lisa Egan; it was obvious from the way he spoke about her. Quinn already felt almost physically ill at forcing him to look at the gruesome photographs of her body and relive the most painful time in his life. No need for her to be there to watch.

26

A lengthy mathematical equation filled most of his computer screen, but Dr. Edward Marin didn't see it or feel it. They used to be alive to him. They drew breath, sang, and whispered their secrets; they had beauty and emotion. But now they were dead. Lifeless symbols that had no real meaning anymore.

He turned and looked out at the main research facility, visible through the glass that made up the north wall of his office suite. It, too, had shrunk to insignificance—a sterile cavern filled with pointless mechanisms that represented ten years of his life. Ten wasted years. How had he let it happen? How had he allowed himself to be imprisoned for so long?

The quiet hum of a printer starting disturbed his

introspection and he spun around in his chair to face the noise.

She had her back to him. A lab coat hid her thin, athletic body, though that unfortunate fact was oddly balanced by the way the white fabric so violently contrasted with the dark hair flowing down her back. She was wearing jeans today and gray tennis shoes.

In the beginning, she'd rarely come in on Saturdays. But now he used whatever excuse he could find to bring her here—data that needed to be compiled, a computer problem, a last-minute memo that had to be typed and sent off. Anything to be able to watch her against the backdrop of the empty building. Just the two of them . . .

"This is about done, Dr. Marin," she said, looking seductively over her shoulder. "Do you want it on your desk?"

"No, I'll take it here, Cynthia."

He watched her glide toward him, the primitive grace of her movements apparent even when surrounded by all this technology.

Despite her bright mind, the truth was that she was a little young and inexperienced to be his primary assistant—and that did occasionally create frustration. But such inconveniences were meaningless compared with the benefits her youth offered. The small, perfect breasts, muscular legs, flat stomach. All hinted at but never completely revealed as her lab coat flowed over her body.

He took the printout from her hand, listening to the sound the paper made as it slid along her smooth skin.

"Is there anything else I can do for you, Doctor?"

She took a half step back as she spoke. And in that half step, he got another brief glimpse of the end.

When he'd hired her, she had been in awe of him. And as time passed, he'd watched that awe turn to attraction. It had reached its apex about six months ago: the avoidable physical contact, the barely perceptible self-consciousness when she knew he was watching, the awkward attempts to start a conversation when there was nothing to be said.

Now those signals were gone, replaced by a vague nervousness. He doubted she knew why she suddenly felt the way she did or even consciously recognized the change. It was probably nothing more than the intuition women were so famous for. And that worried him. But it also exhilarated him.

"Just a couple more little things, Cynthia," he said, unwilling to let her go just yet. "I—"

The mechanical buzz of the phone interrupted him, and his assistant picked it up. "Dr. Marin's office . . . Yes, he is . . . Fine, I'll tell him, sir."

"For me?" Marin said as she replaced the receiver.

"General Price would like to see you, Doctor."

He shook his head with mock gravity. "Great. That should be good for wasting the rest of the day."

She smiled at his attempt to be disarming, but the effort was weak. Nothing more than a polite gesture.

"Okay," Marin said, rising from his chair and reluctantly starting for the door. "Tell you what, we'll call it a day. Go do something fun and I'll see you first thing Monday morning."

Marin didn't think he could remember ever seeing Richard Price's outer office empty. Normally, it was wall to wall with bureaucratic drones waiting for an audience with their king. Even the shriveled old secretary, who so jealously guarded her master, was absent.

"I'm surprised to see you in here, Richard. Shouldn't you be spending the day with your beautiful family?" Price looked like he always did: gray suit, red tie, white shirt. Men like him couldn't live without some kind of uniform. It made them feel safe, a part of something. They drew their authority from it.

"Have a seat, Doctor."

There was an authoritarian air to the invitation, though Price still had the good sense to tread lightly. Marin nodded his consent and sat down, content for now to give Price the illusion of control. It was his full expectation that this meeting would prove to be interesting at worst, entertaining at best.

Price sat quietly for a few moments, never looking directly at Marin. Finally, he spoke. "You're not living up to our agreement."

Marin had never been able to decide whom he disdained more. Was it the politicians whose hypocrisy was so carefully planned, or the soldiers whose hypocrisy was so indignant? He allowed a hint of a smile to transform his face. They hadn't spoken of this in almost a decade. Price liked to pretend that it didn't exist, that he was a patriot. He undoubtedly spent his nights philosophizing about the "needs of the many" and "acceptable losses" and whatever other clichés men like him used to disguise their ambition.

"We can't afford any more unauthorized activity."

"Unauthorized activity," Marin repeated quietly. The words rolled from the tongue with such detachment; such lack of meaning.

General Richard Price finally looked directly at him, placing his palms flat on the desk, as though he was bracing himself against some imaginary onslaught. "This isn't a game, Doctor. We have an agreement and you are honor bound to live up to it."

Honor.

"Keeping things from us," Price continued, "has put us in a difficult position. One that could force our hand. One that could hurt us both."

It had been subtle, but in the combination of syntax and tone there was a threat. The beautiful, and apparently nimble, Quinn Barry was still evading Brad Lowell and his band of sycophants. Of course, Marin knew all about her. After so much time spent compromising Price's communications, he knew just about everything. He knew that she had the files of five of his young women, that she had discovered ATD's modifications to CODIS, that she had escaped Lowell's poorly conceived efforts to ensnare her, not once, but twice.

The timing couldn't possibly have been better. He sincerely hoped he would have an opportunity to meet this young woman before it was all over.

"Haven't we provided you with everything you've asked for?" Price said, still braced against his desk. "Is there anything you've needed that we haven't given you?"

Marin didn't respond. How could a man with such a hopelessly limited intellect and imagination even begin to understand? He had provided nothing. Nothing.

It had been more than ten years but the memory was still painfully vivid. The police had closed in so much more quickly than he had foreseen—coming to his home, calling him. The questions about Lisa Egan had been innocuous at first but quickly became more pointed.

Her death had been such a tragedy; she had been so beautiful, so perfect. And he'd waited so long for her. He could still hear the knock resonating through her neat, feminine-smelling apartment. At the time he had been relatively inexperienced and in his momentary surprise, he had lost control of her. He'd watched in horror as she took a deep breath, preparing to unleash a scream that would have been heard throughout the campus. The profound sense of loss that he had felt when the delicate skin and sinewy muscle of her neck split beneath his knife had been almost indescribable.

To this day, she was always with him, more than any of the others. He woke up at night thinking of her—of an opportunity forever missed. What might she have shown him that the others hadn't?

"Remember where you would be without my help, Doctor. The police were on to you. If it weren't for me . . ."

"I would be dead," Marin said. His tone was calculatedly neutral, offering no hint as to whether he was grateful or angered by Price's intervention. The general seemed unsure how to respond.

In the end, what Price had offered was a trap. Marin had known it from the start, but there had been no choice. He couldn't let it end like that. With a whimper.

When Price spoke again his voice had gained in confidence, as Marin knew it would.

"Without going into detail, Doctor, I have to tell you that we are in a very dangerous position. I have to know: can I count on your cooperation?"

Price made it almost too easy. He wanted—needed—to believe so desperately. Marin considered toying with the man, making him beg, but knew that it would prove to be a pointless and ultimately tedious exercise. He would have Price on his knees soon enough. "You can, General. I give you my word."

The phone started to ring before Marin was even out the office door. Price didn't immediately reach for it, instead watched the man walk smoothly into the outer office and back toward the lab.

It had gone better than he'd expected. Marin's arrogance had seemed uncharacteristically subdued. He would push, but in the end, he knew what he had and wouldn't be anxious to give it up. Price's instincts told him that there would be no more trouble from Dr. Edward Marin. At least not in the short term.

After confirming that the call was coming in on a secure line set aside for Brad Lowell, Price picked up. Perhaps his luck would hold and it would be good news.

"Have you found her yet?"

The reply wasn't as immediate as he would have hoped. "No, sir."

"Where do we stand, Brad?"

"Our surveillance has provided no contacts, sir."

"But it's fully implemented?"

"Yes, sir. Though we've been unable to locate Eric Twain. My men have been through his house and there is no indication that he'll be gone for any length of time. We have someone on-site."

Price pulled a cigar from the humidor on his desk and began chewing the end of it nervously. "Could she have contacted him?"

"Based on the information we know she has, I think it's unlikely, sir. If anything, she'd suspect him."

Price was silent for a moment as he tried to calculate his position. "We need to find him, Brad. We can't risk leaving anything to chance."

"I understand, sir. We're doing everything we can."

"Keep me informed of any—**any**—new information."

"Of course."

"And, Brad?"

"Sir?"

"You understand that nothing can happen to Twain. He's to be protected at all costs."

27

The Styrofoam cup steamed satisfyingly, though a quick sip revealed the coffee inside to taste like a botched chemistry experiment. Quinn ripped open another packet of sugar and dumped it in. Another sip suggested little improvement: it now tasted like an overly sweet botched chemistry experiment. What the hell—she didn't really drink the stuff anyway. She'd just needed an excuse to escape for a while.

She glanced up again at the large convex mirror that provided a slightly distorted view of the rows of junk food behind her. The man had moved back a few feet and was pretending to consider a rack of potato chips while positioning himself to get a clearer view of her.

Quinn shoved lids onto the two cups and carried

them toward the refrigerators in the back. Except for the cashier, a young girl with a hairdo that looked like it had been designed to catch wind, he was the only other person in the store. Quinn started to feel like she was involved in a bizarre dance as she stepped behind a display of brightly colored sweets and peeked through them.

His hair was cut short and he was wearing wire-rim glasses and a well-kept but unstylish gray suit. Quinn felt her heart jump a little when his head rose a few inches and his eyes started to search for her.

This was crazy. Men had been staring at her since she was fourteen. She was already up to her neck in paranoia and there was no way she was going to let herself drown in it.

She grabbed a package of doughnuts and purposely chose a path to the register that took her as close to the man as possible. He ignored her with a noticeable effort.

"Is that it?" the girl at the counter said.

"I think so."

He was looking again, no longer trying to hide it. She could see him in the mirror above the counter.

"Keep it," Quinn said, sliding a ten across the counter and scooping up her purchases. She was out the door before the man behind her could move.

She walked as quickly as she could without letting her gait become unnatural, but it was already too late to win the race against the coming night.

Almost all the cars on the sparsely traveled street had their lights on now, partially blinding her and filling the narrow alleyways she passed with impenetrable shadow.

When she reached the steps of the library, she realized she was almost jogging. Her breath was coming a little heavy as she ran up them and ducked inside. The glass doors behind her acted as mirrors, forcing her to step close to them to see back out into the street. He hadn't followed. The sidewalk and steps she'd come up were completely empty.

"Get a hold of yourself, for God's sake," she said loud enough to earn a stern look from the woman behind the circulation desk. Quinn shot her an apologetic smile and then made her way to the room she'd left Eric in.

"You okay?" she said, closing the door quietly behind her and pushing one of the cups toward him. When she sat down, she saw that the file was lying open in front of him but didn't see the pain she'd expected to be etched across his face. Instead his lips were clenched and his eyes had narrowed. The detachment that had been so evident in him since they'd first met had completely disappeared.

"Eric?"

He slammed the file closed and jumped to his feet, immediately starting to pace back and forth in the small room.

"That son of a bitch!"

"What?"

"He wasn't even **trying** to find who really did it!"

"Who are you talking about?"

"Roy Renquist," Eric spat out. "Meanest bastard I ever met and probably one of the dumbest . . ."

"Look, Eric, I don't mean to defend him but he had good reason to suspect you. Statistically speaking—"

"Don't tell me about the statistics, Quinn. I know all about them. If somebody's going to cut you apart with a chain saw, chances are it's going to be someone you love, right? I accept that. And I acknowledge that it was partly my own fault that I was such a good suspect." He jabbed a finger in the general direction of the file. "But this . . . It's a classic case of the kind of thinking that helped create the Dark Ages. First, come to a conclusion, and second, make the evidence fit it. I mean, it's unbelievable! Any line of investigation that doesn't have to do with me just kind of peters out. Based on half the shit he wrote about me, he wasn't even paying attention when I was talking. He was just sitting there figuring out a way to screw me."

Eric finally stopped pacing and fell into a chair, his anger at least partially spent. "No wonder they never caught anyone. The guy who killed Lisa could have taken out an ad in the paper confessing and Renquist wouldn't have paid any attention."

Quinn slid the file into her lap and flipped

through it, avoiding the photographs of Lisa Egan's dead body. "So you're saying there's nothing? Nothing in here that could help us?"

"There's nothing in there intelligent enough to even bother with."

She continued to turn the pages, focusing briefly on the statistics, scientific analysis, and conjectures it contained, but not really registering any of it. There had to be something she could do, something she could learn. Someone she could trust. "Where does that leave us?"

"I don't know," Eric replied. "But it leaves Lisa dead. Just like she was an hour ago."

"Eric . . ."

He didn't seem to hear.

"Eric. Would you please look at me?"

When he did, his expression had softened a bit.

"I understand that you don't really know anything about me and you don't know what to believe. But I'm asking for your help."

He looked like he was about ready to get up and walk away. Quinn tried to will him not to, and for once, it seemed to work. He took a deep breath and settled a little deeper into his chair.

"Okay. What do we know?" he said.

"Huh?"

"Always start with what you know."

She didn't bother to disguise her relief as she pulled a few blank sheets of paper and a pen from her knapsack. "All right. What do we know? We know that there's a man, or men, running around the country raping, torturing, and killing young women. And we have an intentionally compromised computer system at the FBI covering up that fact. Right?"

He seemed to have slipped away again.

"Eric. Are you with me?"

"Yeah. Okay. What can we safely assume?"

That was a more difficult question. "That there are at least two people involved."

"Why?"

"The people who attacked me."

"Oh, right."

She ignored his thinly veiled skepticism and continued. "At least one of them would have to be highly organized and intelligent. Not only did they manage to compromise CODIS, but they found out that I was going to see my father and rigged my car to die on the loneliest part of the road. That also suggests they have access to the parking lot at Quantico."

"So you think it's an FBI agent," Eric said.

She took the pen out of her mouth and wrote "UNSUB"—unknown subject—in bold letters across the top of the blank sheet of paper in front of her. "What do we know about this guy? The MO varies with each killing, which is common as a killer perfects his scenario, but we can probably assume that the signature remains the same."

"You lost me."

"MO is how the killer commits the crime—the

boring details. Like if he goes in a window or through the door, or if he wears gloves. Signature is what he does to . . . well, get off. That won't vary really 'cause he has to do what excites him or there's no point to committing the crime. In this case, he ties them, rapes them, and tortures them with a knife or blade of some sort."

"Where are you getting all this? I thought you said you were a computer programmer."

"I, uh, read up on it."

He frowned a bit but didn't say anything.

"I think we can assume that we don't have the entire picture. I doubt that the killing in '89 was the first."

"What makes you say that?"

"The individual state crime labs only recently got federal funding to start DNA-typing evidence from old case files. Most of them have only made it back to the late eighties at this point. I mean, it could be a coincidence that the first DNA evidence we have comes from that time period, but I doubt it. My guess is that as the states keep going back, this guy's going to keep turning up."

"Assuming that DNA evidence was collected."

"Right. He tried to cover up the '89 killing. If he did the same for prior crimes—if he made it look like an accident or just didn't leave a sample, then it wouldn't register on the database."

"So you're saying this guy could have killed a hundred women for all we know."

For some reason, hearing that number threw her. It took her a moment to regain her train of thought.

"If you look at the early deaths, we can see that the killer's got a victim profile he likes. Mid-twenties, well educated, physically attractive. That would be very important to him. He's staging a fantasy and the victim is like an actress. He's going to be very visual."

"You're getting all this from a book you read?"

She cleared her throat nervously. "Uh, skimmed, actually. But it was two books."

"Two books? Oh. Well. In that case, please go on."

"Hey, I don't need this," she said, letting a little anger creep into her voice. "If you think you can do better . . ."

He held up his hands. "Take it easy, Quinn. I don't. I don't think I can do any better."

"Okay, then. He's probably a white male. I doubt he'd have started killing before his mid-twenties, so now he's at least thirty-five, probably older. He's going to have a dominant personality, probably very self-centered, and have the ability to be quite charming when he wants to be. Definitely above-average intelligence, probably college-educated. Most likely he takes souvenirs away from the killings so he can relive them at home. Could be anything—pictures of the victim, maybe even video. Clothing, jewelry, body parts—though that's not indicated here. He'll probably also collect sado-masochistic pornography."

She glanced up from her pad and saw that Eric was starting to look a little pale. "You all right?"

"Sure. Fine."

"Okay. Over the time period we have data on, he's been getting cockier. In 1989 he goes through the trouble of making the girl's death look acciden-tal. But he doesn't cover up the 1991 murder—ei-ther because he can't or because he just doesn't bother. Then in 1992, he gets interrupted. Another indication that he's getting sloppy. Perhaps he's los-ing control. Or maybe he's found that he's con-trolled the situation too well and that he needs the risk to get his rush."

"But then it all changes," Eric cut in. "Remem-ber the 'catharsis' of me killing my girlfriend?"

She winced slightly when he brought up the pro-file she'd written on him. "I think maybe getting interrupted scared him. Maybe enough to signifi-cantly change his method . . ."

"But you aren't sure."

She shrugged. "The first three were all within a few hours' drive of one another and probably close to his home. Mostly these kinds of killers like to operate where they're comfortable. Maybe he thought the cops were getting too close, so he spread out geographically."

"Okay, I'll buy that. But what about the choice of a victim? You said killers like this want a specific type to act in their play. The last two women are uneducated and have a very different look than the first three—"

"But they **are** around the same age and build."

"Yeah. But could he change? Even that much?"

"I don't know," she said, shaking her head slowly. "It makes logical sense to change to a victim who is already at risk for violence and where there would be an obvious suspect . . ."

"But psychos, kind of by definition, aren't logical."

Quinn leaned back in her chair and tossed her pen onto the table. "I'm not trying to pass myself off as an expert here."

"But you've obviously put a lot of thought into it. I assume it's leading somewhere?"

"I don't know."

"Sure you do, you're just not saying."

She'd been spending too much time around David and his Neanderthal friends. She wasn't used to men reading her so easily.

"We're not back to me, are we?" Eric said.

"**No,** we're not back to you. Combine what I just told you with what we know about the cover-up."

"Oh, right. Your mysterious FBI agent."

"You have a better idea?"

"I wasn't being critical."

She sighed quietly. "Sorry. I'm really tired."

"So where are you going with this, Quinn? Somebody in the FBI with enough juice to get CODIS programmed around his DNA profile, right?"

"When you think about it, that also fits the other stuff we know," she said. "An FBI agent would have information on at-risk women from access to police reports—so he'd have known where to go to find those last two victims."

"And he'd have access to Quantico to sabotage your car."

She nodded.

"Don't leave me in suspense, Quinn. Who's our killer?"

She was finding it hard to say out loud. But there seemed to be no other explanation. "My old boss. Louis Crater."

Eric raised his eyebrows but didn't speak.

"He had the bottom-line authority to transfer me," Quinn started. "He was involved with CODIS from the beginning, he would have known to watch me in Quantico to see if I continued looking into this thing. He's a white male, about the right age and personality type. He was the one who got rid of the outside contractors that were administering CODIS and consolidated the system fully under him . . ."

Eric just stared at her, tapping his front teeth again, this time with his fingernail. There was still something about him that made her a little uncomfortable. Despite everything she knew about him from the file, it was like he was looking at her through a two-way mirror. Was he seriously considering what she was saying or was he just humoring her, playing around because he had nothing better to do than go back to an empty house?

"Okay," he said finally. "Let's say you're right. How would he enlist people to help him? Assuming your boss was in the car that tried to chase you, who was the guy who tried to grab you?"

It was a good question; one she hadn't been able to satisfactorily answer. "An accomplice? There's actually a precedent for sadistic rapists working in teams. Or maybe he just lied—enlisted an agent to help him."

That could also explain David's involvement, assuming that he was involved and she wasn't just crazy.

Eric shook his head. "Not an accomplice. They'd have had to program around his DNA signature too, and you only found one embedded subroutine, right? And not an agent. The killer wouldn't risk exposing himself unnecessarily. He'd just do away with you personally. Hell, you're pretty close to fitting his victim profile."

That fact had been hanging at the edge of her consciousness almost since the beginning of this thing. So far she'd been successful at fending off the image of herself wired naked to the floor with a knife-wielding psychotic hovering over her, but it was getting harder and harder.

"What about felons?" Eric said, thinking aloud. "Someone he let go and now they owe him? You say he pretty much controls CODIS, right? What if he just buries a little evidence now and then and uses it as blackmail?"

"It's possible, I suppose."

"Okay. So let's call the guys who created the system and ask if this Crater guy told them to put in that subroutine? Voilà. You have your answer."

Quinn took a sip of her coffee and forced herself to swallow. It wasn't any better cold, but the sugar and caffeine would still do the job. "No way. Even if I knew specifically who did the original programming, why would they talk about a confidential government contract with me? Particularly if Crater told them not to—and I'm guessing he has."

Eric frowned, obviously in agreement with her logic. "For some reason, I know I'm going to regret asking," he said. "But just what is it you think we should do about this?"

28

Does this seem inordinately stupid to you? 'Cause it sure does to me."

Eric Twain adjusted his position to take better advantage of what little cover was available. They were standing in Louis Crater's carport, which in turn was situated in the middle of a rather dense swath of suburbia about thirty minutes from D.C. Fortunately, the carport was sunk a little below the level of the street and had a vehicle parked in it. Of course, it was a damn Mazda Miata, so it didn't exactly provide a whole lot of cover.

"I told you," Quinn said, continuing to examine the wood-and-glass door leading into the kitchen. "Louis is in Atlanta at a conference."

"I don't really care if—" Eric suddenly realized how loud he was speaking and lowered his voice to a whisper. "I don't really care if he's orbiting the earth in the space shuttle. He's an FBI agent and you can believe me when I tell you these guys don't have a sense of humor about this kind of thing. If you think he's guilty, why don't we just get on the phone and call someone?"

It was impossible to read her expression when she looked back at him; her face was striped by the intermittent light working its way down to them from the street lamps.

"Who would we call, Eric? There were a lot of very powerful people involved in the development of CODIS. What if I'm wrong and Louis isn't the man we're looking for? What if we contact the wrong person? All I'm saying is that it makes sense to be sure."

She turned her attention to the paper bag at her feet and emptied its contents into her hand.

"**That's** what you bought at the hardware store? Quinn, really . . . we have to talk."

She ignored him, sticking a suction cup to one of the panes in the door and working around it with the glass cutter.

"Shit," Eric mumbled to himself as he looked up toward the street. The neighborhood had been completely deserted a few minutes before, but now he could see shadowy figures moving in the distance. Dog walkers, he guessed. People who used the visual distortion of late dusk to mask their movements as they let their pets loose on their neighbors' lawns. None was close enough yet to see them and none seemed to be moving in their direction. Probably smart enough to concentrate on yards owned by people who didn't carry guns to work.

By the time Eric had satisfied himself that they would be okay for another few minutes, Quinn was already reaching through a small hole in the glass and flipping the lock. A moment later she was standing in the dark kitchen staring out at him. "You coming?"

He just stood there examining the open door. He'd been stupid enough to come this far, he might as well go all the way. It was better than standing around in the carport waiting for some old lady with a poodle to spot him and call the cops. When he started moving again, Quinn turned and disappeared into the house.

The kitchen he entered was spotless, with nothing on the counter but a bucket full of cleaning products. The edge of the living room was visible through the gloom and looked similarly unlived in.

When the complete idiocy of his situation finally hit him full force, he stopped and leaned against the refrigerator, refusing to let himself go further. He'd spent pretty much every day of the last ten years trying to avoid cops. And now he'd let himself be talked into breaking into the home of an FBI agent by a woman who had probably just escaped from an insane asylum for the terminally gorgeous.

"Smart. Real smart," he said under his breath just as Quinn reappeared around the corner and motioned urgently to him. He sighed and started forward again, following her up a set of stairs to the second floor.

She stopped midway down the hall and pointed to a small bathroom. "Start in there. We're looking for hairs with good follicles, fingernail clippings—anything we can get a solid DNA sample from."

He nodded without enthusiasm and flipped the switch on the wall. The sudden burst of light made him feel even more nervous, though all the shades in the house seemed to be safely shut.

The sink was clean to the point of looking sterile. He wasn't going to find anything there. He dropped to his knees only to find the bathtub basin similarly buffed. He was craning his neck around the back of the toilet when Quinn crept up silently behind him.

"Eric!"

He jerked upright, banging his head into the edge of the commode and sending another jolt of adrenaline into his already jittery heart. "Jesus!" he said in a whisper that had almost the volume of a shout. "Are you nuts!"

He sat down on the edge of the tub and rubbed the back of his head, imagining that he could already feel a bump rising through his thick hair.

"Take a look," she said, completely ignoring his

distress and proudly holding up a copy of **Penthouse**. "What did I tell you—collects pornography."

"You said sadomasochistic pornography. That's a **Penthouse**."

She flipped open the centerfold, which depicted a woman wearing only a pair of black leather boots and sitting in a less than ladylike position. "Are you kidding? This is gross."

"Come on, Quinn. I'll grant you that it isn't art, but half the men in America subscribe to that magazine."

She turned it around and gave the picture one last disgusted look before slamming it shut. "You find anything?"

Eric shook his head. "I don't even think he uses this bathroom. How about you?"

"Not yet, but I will. It doesn't help that he's almost completely bald and anal-retentive as hell," she said, starting down the hall. "Why don't you check out his office."

"Yes, ma'am," Eric muttered when he was sure she was out of earshot.

"I heard that."

The office wasn't exactly elaborate—nothing more than a desk with a computer on it and a single bookshelf, half-full. Eric stood in the middle of the room for a moment, not sure what to do. It was one thing to crawl around a man's toilet, but going through his office somehow seemed really, really wrong.

On the other hand, he was pretty sure that the young woman in the other room wasn't going to let him leave until she was satisfied that they had turned every stone. He shrugged to himself and sat down in front of the computer. A quick search of the hard drive found no pornographic pictures and the browser didn't indicate any recent access to adult sites.

The closet turned out to be just as neat and well organized as the rest of the house, allowing him to go directly to the interesting stuff. None of the Visa bills he found listed anything like Mistress Inga's Love Palace and there were no videotapes or photographs at all. No women's underwear. No jewelry. An examination of a stack of old calendars netted him pretty much nothing. What had he been expecting? **Torture young woman to death, 4 P.M. sharp. Pick up laundry on the way home.** This was just nuts.

Eric was flipping through Louis Crater's passport when he thought he heard something downstairs. He was in the process of telling himself it was just a figment of his overstimulated imagination when it came again, this time much clearer. He swallowed hard and stood, padding silently down the stairs and peeking around the corner toward the kitchen.

The woman was Hispanic, probably in her early fifties. He remembered the feather duster in her hand as having been in the bucket of cleaning products on the kitchen counter. The good news was that she was completely oblivious to his presence, just dusting along happily, swaying to the music coming over her Walkman. The bad news was that she was effectively blocking all the house's exits.

Outstanding.

Quinn didn't look up from her position on the floor until Eric closed the door quietly behind him, trapping them both in the tiny master bathroom.

"What are you doing?" she said, gazing past him at what had been the only way out of the room. She suddenly looked a little uncertain. Maybe even a little afraid of him. Served her right.

"Find anything?"

"Uh, yeah. I found a few hairs," she said hesitantly. "Nothing great, though. Why are you standing in front of the door like that?"

He ignored the question and stayed right where he was. "I figured out why the place is so clean."

"Really?"

"He's got a maid."

"How do you know?"

"She's downstairs dusting."

Quinn jumped to her feet. "No way! What kind of maid works this late?"

"The kind that's downstairs."

Her eyes darted back and forth and she ran a hand through her short blond hair. "A window," she said finally. "We'll go out a window."

"Good idea. **That** won't attract any attention," Eric said sarcastically.

She took a deep breath, held it, and then slowly let it out. "What if she comes upstairs? We've got to get out of here. Where is she? Do you think we can slip out a door when she isn't looking?"

Eric shook his head. "Got that open floor plan down there, you know?"

Quinn gnawed on her thumbnail for a few seconds. "Feel free to help out anytime here, Eric. Aren't you supposed to be, like, the smartest guy in the world?"

He frowned and bounced his back off the door, brushing past her to grab a container of shampoo off the edge of the tub. "I can't believe I let you talk me into this."

She followed him back down the stairs, looking even more worried when he motioned for her to stay where she was. He slipped around the wall and walked quickly up behind the woman who was now working her feather duster gracefully over a shelf full of china.

In one swift motion, he flipped one of the earphones from her ear and clamped a hand over her mouth. With his other hand, he pressed the end of the shampoo bottle into her back. "Don't move."

She completely locked up. Stiff as a board. Clearly a woman who could follow instructions.

"Now, I'm not going to hurt you, do you understand? But you have to do exactly what I say and stay completely quiet." She didn't react, so he repeated himself in Spanish. That got a short nod.

He could feel the sweat breaking out around her mouth as he maneuvered her toward a closet. "Open the door," he said, sticking to the Spanish that she seemed to understand.

She did as he told her but with difficulty. The poor lady's hand was shaking so badly she could barely get a hold of the knob.

"Don't turn around," he said, pushing her gently into the closet. "I'm going to shut the door and you're going to count to five hundred. Don't come out until you get to five hundred. Okay?" He knew he should threaten to shoot her or something but couldn't bring himself to do it.

"Uno, dos . . ." he started. She joined in as he pushed the door closed and left her in the dark.

"So can I assume that this is the silent treatment?" Quinn said. She was behind the wheel of Eric's Honda, propelling it out of the quiet subdivision and onto a busier, strip-mall-lined street. He folded his arms across his chest and pretended not to hear.

"Come on, Eric, I said I was sorry—"

"You probably don't even work for the FBI," he

cut in. "You probably got that ID out of a box of Cocoa Puffs they gave you with your medication."

"The ID's real, Eric."

"Well, then maybe you're an agent. And you're trying to get me busted for something so you can sweat me."

"Come on. You know that's not true. Quit being such a baby."

He turned toward her, his mouth hanging open. "A baby? **A baby?** I just mugged an old lady."

Quinn sighed. "I know. And I'm **sorry**."

They sat in silence for a while.

"Thank you," she said finally.

"For what?"

"For getting us out of there."

His anger started to fade and he sank a little deeper in the seat but kept his arms crossed indignantly. "You're welcome."

"At least it wasn't for nothing," Quinn said, trying to sound cheerful. "I got a few hairs. They aren't great, but I think they'll work."

"Forget it."

"What?"

He pulled Crater's passport from his pocket and waved it in the air as Quinn looked on in horror. "You stole his passport?"

"After attacking his maid, I figured what the hell." He pointed out the front windshield. "Watch the road."

"Why?"

"So we don't crash."

"Why did you take his passport?"

Eric flipped toward the back, stopping on a page with two prominent stamps on it. "Entry into Frankfurt on July fifth, 1995. Returned to Chicago on July twentieth, 1995."

Quinn had to think for a moment to grasp what those dates meant. "The last girl . . ."

"Killed July seventeenth, 1995, in Oklahoma. I never forget a date."

Quinn stared at the headlights coming toward her in the other lane and tried to blink away the wide halos glowing around them. How could that be? Everything pointed to Louis . . .

"What if those stamps are fake," she said, reaching under her glasses and rubbing at her eyes. The adrenaline rush of breaking and entering was starting to fade and had left her with an empty tank. She was starting to forget the last time she'd slept.

"Come on, Quinn. Why would he? Face it, Louis Crater isn't your man. By the way, where are we going?"

"I don't know," she admitted, her voice barely a whisper. What now? She tried to get her mind to focus on the problem and didn't notice that she was drifting onto the shoulder until Eric reached over and took hold of the wheel.

"You all right, Quinn?"

She shook her head violently and sucked in a

deep breath, taking control of the car again. "Yeah. Fine."

Eric reached out and took her chin in his hand, gently pulling her head a little to the side so that he could see her eyes. "You don't look all that great."

"Just a little tired, you know?"

He nodded with what looked like genuine concern. "Why don't you pull over and let me drive."

Her initial instinct was to protest, but she knew it would be stupid. As a computer programmer, she was all too familiar with the effects of trying to blow off sleep for too long. Everything had that hazy look and her head felt like it was full of gauze. It wouldn't be long before she completely crashed.

She pulled the car to the edge of the road and scooted across the seat as Eric jogged around the front. She saw him briefly illuminated in the headlights before leaning her head against the passenger-side window and closing her eyes.

"Okay, Quinn, this is ours," Eric said, grabbing the hotel-room key off the dash and stepping from the car. He was partway across the parking lot before he realized she wasn't behind him. When he finally turned around he could see through the windshield that she was still unconscious in the passenger seat.

He made his way back to the car and opened the

back door, pulling her knapsack out and throwing it over his shoulder. He was about to open the passenger door when he realized that she'd probably fall out if he did. He had to reach through the back and steady her as he opened it.

"Quinn? Rise and shine." He shook her shoulder. "Quinn?" Her breathing didn't break from its deep rhythm.

Eric sighed quietly and reached into the car, lifting her out with surprising ease. Despite her being nearly as tall as he was, she was mercifully light. He kicked the door closed and started back toward the hotel, wondering what the hell it was he was doing.

The answer, of course, was pretty straightforward. He was walking through a hotel parking lot carrying a woman he didn't know and a bag full of undoubtedly stolen police files, fresh from breaking into an FBI agent's home and attacking his maid. How much more trouble could one person generate in such a short life?

Fortunately, the elevator was empty, as was the third-floor hallway. Getting the key into the door and her through it was a challenge, but it turned out to be a manageable one.

He deposited her on one of the beds and lifted off her glasses. Except for the dark circles painted beneath her eyes, she was nearly perfect. Strong, straight features, smooth, if slightly pale skin, athletic build . . .

Stop it.

He squeezed his eyes shut and turned away from her. He'd had one meaningful relationship in his life and that had ended violently when he was only seventeen. There had been women since, of course, but nothing more than brief encounters. He'd learned never to let himself expect more than that. In the end, they always found out. Best to just face that his life was never going to resemble a breath mint commercial.

He folded the bedspread over her, reminding himself that her physical appearance was nothing more than a random piece of genetic coding and media hype. It didn't mean anything. It didn't mean she wasn't paranoid, or setting him up, or completely nuts.

He knew that the smart move was to leave now, to go back home to the prison he'd spent so much time building for himself. Back to the paintings no one would ever see and the music no one would ever hear. Back to the elaborate gourmet meals that he'd taught himself to cook in single portions. But he couldn't. Not yet.

He picked up her knapsack and started pawing through it, ignoring the files and reams of computer paper it contained. He found her wallet near the bottom and pulled it out. With one last glance over his shoulder to confirm that she was completely dead to the world, he emptied it out on the floor. Who was Quinn Barry?

29

The red symbols hovered steadily in front of her but she didn't immediately comprehend them.

8:32

Quinn kicked the covers off and tried to untangle her legs from her skirt as she rolled onto her back. Why was she sleeping in her clothes? And why was it so dark? A few moments passed before she registered the thin blade of light working its way through the curtains and the dimly lit room around her. Another few seconds and she recognized it as a hotel room.

Eric Twain.

The events of the last few days came flooding back to her, culminating with her switching seats with Eric on the Beltway. She closed her eyes and concentrated but it didn't do any good. Everything after that was a blank.

She sat up, feeling strangely dizzy, and looked around. The bed next to hers was empty except for the now-familiar case files lying amid the covers. Two grocery bags were stacked precariously on top of the television and the streak of light coming through the window glinted off the ice and Coke cans overflowing from a trash can on the floor.

Quinn flipped her legs off the bed and stood, feeling a dull pounding begin in her head. Where was Eric? Had he bailed on her?

She started through the semidarkness and pulled aside a set of full-length curtains, revealing a sliding-glass door that led to a small deck overlooking Washington, D.C.

Eric was out there, sitting in a plastic chair, wearing only a pair of jeans. She didn't immediately open the door, instead watching him as he propped his bare feet on the railing and continued to flip through the file in his lap. She hadn't seen the second tattoo when she'd first met him. It covered his right shoulder blade, visible next to the long ponytail running down his back. A black grid pattern twisted into a shape that was visually confusing enough to make her blink. It seemed vaguely familiar to her. Something from a physics class maybe . . .

Eric twisted his head around when she opened the door and he followed her with his eyes as she took a seat in the chair next to him.

"Coffee?" he said, reaching down for a pot plugged into the wall next to his chair.

"Is there any herbal tea?"

"Uh-uh. I had orange juice but I drank it all. How about a nice doughnut?" He held a greasy bag out to her. "I got you some of those really nasty ones with the chocolate glaze and cream filling."

She grimaced and shook her head. "How did we get here?"

"The normal way. Cars, elevators, hallways."

She was about to ask for a few more details, but before she could, he tossed the file onto the deck and disappeared into the room. When he returned, he was holding a grocery bag.

"We've got Pop-Tarts, Cocoa Puffs, Cap'n Crunch, and Malto-meal."

"Malto-meal? What the hell is that?"

"I dunno. Looked kind of gross, though—I thought you'd like it. Most programmers I know have the same dietary requirements as those really big Asian cockroaches. Hang on . . ." He dug deep in the bag and pulled out a banana. "I was saving this for later."

She accepted it a little hesitantly. She wasn't accustomed to waking up in hotel rooms with men she didn't know. Particularly one who, until forty-eight hours ago, she'd thought was a psychotic murderer.

"You're one of those people who get up with the sun, huh?" she said, making a feeble attempt at small talk to cover up her discomfort.

"Not really . . . You realize it's Monday, right?"

"What?"

"Yeah, you kind of missed Sunday."

"Monday! Why didn't you wake me up?"

"I tried. You hit me with a pillow."

She put the banana down and started rubbing her temples, trying to relieve the throbbing in them and get her mind working at normal speed again.

"You okay?" Eric said.

"I'm fine. What have you been doing all this time?"

"Reading through the files again. Oh, and there was a Clint Eastwood marathon on TNT. Caught some of that."

"Have you found anything? What do you think?"

"I'm thinking that either **Pale Rider** or **High Plains Drifter** was a ghost. Maybe both."

She glared at him. "Anything else?"

"Not really."

They sat in silence for a while, Eric looking out over the city and Quinn trying to analyze the week's events, sorting through what she knew, what was an educated guess, and what was just fantasy.

"It didn't have to be Louis," she said finally. "There were a lot of people involved in the development of CODIS."

That didn't get any reaction at all, though she knew he'd heard her. They were only three feet apart.

"I still think we're on the right track," she continued. "Louis was the most obvious, but—"

"We're not breaking into any more FBI agents' houses, Quinn. I don't know if you noticed but we're not good at it."

She opened her mouth to defend herself, but then just closed it again without speaking. He was right. Besides, she didn't really know who the other people were; she'd still been in college when CODIS had been rolled out. On the brighter side, though, Eric had used the word **we**. Quinn examined his face, wishing again that her normally impressive ability to read men worked on him. But since it didn't, she'd have to rely on a more direct approach.

"Does this mean you believe me?"

He didn't respond.

"You have to answer."

His head rolled around on his neck as he tried to formulate a response. As far as body language went, it wasn't a great sign.

"I see what you've put in front of me and it looks real."

"That's not an answer."

"Do I think that there's a psycho FBI guy running around cutting up women with an army of blackmailed convicts watching his back? I don't know, Quinn. Seems pretty far-fetched."

She stared down at the concrete beneath her feet. "That's okay. I understand."

"Hey, don't get all depressed. I'm trying to keep an open mind, okay? Like I told you, I owe Lisa a lot. If I have any chance at all of finding the guy who killed her, I will."

For some reason, hearing that relaxed her a little bit. She still didn't really know anything about Eric Twain, but at least she wasn't completely alone. Misery loves company, she remembered, grabbing the banana off the table again and starting to peel it.

"So what's our next move?" Eric said.

The truth was, she had no idea. She'd been so sure that everything pointed to Louis, she'd never really considered a backup plan. "I don't know."

Eric picked up the file at his feet and dropped it in his lap again. She recognized it as the one that concerned him and Lisa Egan.

"What about Renquist?" he said.

"What about him?"

"There were definitely FBI guys running around while he was harassing me. Renquist played it down in his reports to make it look like he was doing all the work himself, but the FBI was definitely a presence."

"So?"

"So if you were the killer—and an FBI agent— wouldn't you try to keep up with the case?"

She thought about that for a moment. It made a certain amount of sense. "You . . . you think you might have met him?"

"The killer? I doubt it. I mean, he probably wouldn't show his face, but he'd be asking questions behind the scenes, don't you think?"

"Do you remember who any of the agents were?"

He shook his head. "I'm not so good with names and faces. Too bad they didn't give me badge numbers. But I figure Renquist would have it in his notes. Maybe one of the agents who helped him on the investigation remembers someone at the Bureau who had an unusual interest in the case." He shrugged. "It's not exactly the most brilliant plan in the world, but then, this isn't really my thing. If you've got a better idea—and by better I mean one that doesn't involve us in a felony—I'm open to suggestion."

30

The room was comfortably small—no more than ten feet square and the same stark white as the lab. There was nothing on the walls, no carpet, no file cabinets. Only a low-lying counter with five computers lined up on it, and a single chair.

It was originally designed to be a storage area for his office suite, and Edward Marin had commandeered it as a private retreat some time ago. No one but him had access and no one but him had entered since the workmen had completed the modifications he specified. Even Richard Price, whose monotone voice was playing over one of the computers' speakers, had never set foot inside. His override codes would be rejected by the tiny keypad on the door, though he was undoubtedly not aware of this.

Marin jabbed at the keyboard in front of him, silencing the speakers. Through ATD's mainframe he had the ability to record the conversations taking place over any phone in the complex. In fact, he had the ability to do just about anything. But, as always, the phone taps were so much less interesting than the e-mail. Price and his brethren placed complete faith in their encryption technology—faith that in most cases would have been well founded. It had taken even Marin years to compromise it.

His practiced eye could discern the importance of Brad Lowell's poorly composed reports from the first few lines. The one up on the screen had an urgency about it that Marin rarely saw.

Eric Twain still hadn't surfaced. A more thorough search of his home had been performed but still revealed nothing. Everything suggested that with no planning or preparation, he had simply disappeared.

Despite Lowell's stupid rationalizations and self-serving speculations, the truth was obvious. Eric had finally found himself a new woman to replace the one Marin had taken from him. The beautiful, and apparently extremely clever, Quinn Barry would undoubtedly prove to be very entertaining to both of them.

Marin closed his eyes and let his mind float. It had all been so perfect. And that perfection, he now realized, had been the fatal flaw. He'd spent years planning, preparing, organizing. In the end, though, his diligence had been ill-conceived. He'd hopelessly dulled the edge of unpredictability and fear that was so important. And now Eric Twain and his new friend were going to restore it.

Marin cleared the screen in front of him and turned to focus on the computer situated at the far end of the table. He'd tied it into one of the complex's security cameras and the terminal was now outputting real-time images from a hallway in the administrative wing. Still nothing.

He let time fall away from him, watching the movements of insignificant men and women as they came and went, living their dead little lives. And he fantasized. About the women he'd taken, about the one that was next. He smiled. She had grown into a formidable woman but without losing the vulnerability her eyes had always conveyed so earnestly. She was a young doctor, hoping for a surgical residency at George Washington. She was close to her parents but not as much to her sister, who had recently moved to Nebraska. She had been voted most popular in high school. In college, she'd been a member of a sorority and played field hockey . . .

The heavyset man flashed onto the computer screen wearing a pair of jogging shorts and a sweatshirt, then just as quickly disappeared from the camera's limited field of view. Marin jumped up, throwing open the only door to the room and darting into the main suite.

"Dr. Marin? Sir?" His assistant, Cynthia, chased after him for a few feet but quickly gave up. He was completely focused, and on this rare occasion, barely saw her.

"Charlie!" Marin said, stepping directly in front of the man and blocking his path to the exit. He was on his way to the jogging track that circled the ATD facility. He would walk one mile and tell everyone he'd walked two, just as he did every day. "How are you?"

Charles Bank's reaction was one of relaxed pride—a far cry from the near panic he'd displayed at their first meeting. It had taken almost three months for Marin, a man known for avoiding interactions with the people around him, to cultivate what was now an easy acquaintance with the man. Something he assumed the pathetic little man bragged about to his coworkers.

"I'm good, Doc. How 'bout you?"

Marin leaned over a water fountain and took a drink, partially for effect and partially because his mouth had suddenly gone dry.

"Not bad. Hey, Charlie . . . you know . . . Could I ask you a favor?"

"Sure, Doc. What do you need?"

"I got my girlfriend a birthday present . . ."

Bank reached out and whacked Marin in the

shoulder with the back of his hand. "I didn't know you had a girlfriend, you dog."

Marin had been prepared for the reaction and smiled a little self-consciously, careful not to betray the revulsion he felt at being touched by the man. "Yeah, I admit it, I do. And a nosy one at that—she finds every gift I buy for her no matter where I hide it."

Bank laughed and shook his head knowingly.

"Anyway, would you mind if I kept it in the trunk of your car for a couple of days?"

"No way she'll find it there, huh, Doc?" Bank said, swinging at Marin's shoulder again. This time Marin stepped out of range, creating a moment of confusion in the man.

"Uh, sure, Doc," Bank said, not even bothering to ask Marin why he didn't just keep it in his office. "Let me go grab the keys for you."

Marin scrubbed away a thick film of sweat building on his upper lip as Bank hurried off. His was the last one—the last key Marin needed. He'd copy it and place it on the chain around his neck along with the other two. Every time they rattled against his bare skin, it would remind him that it had started. After all this time it had finally started.

31

"Pull over here," Quinn said, crumpling up the torn phone book page in her hand. "That's it. Six forty-three Crowheart."

Eric turned his old Honda down a side street and eased to a stop next to the curb, leaving them with a distant view of the house. A call to the Baltimore police earlier that morning had told them that Detective Roy Renquist had retired two years ago and was now living a quiet life of golf and fishing.

"Nice neighborhood . . ." Eric mumbled, the bitterness clear in his voice.

He was right. The empty streets looked newly paved and the houses were all a little larger than she'd expected. The driveway held a Corvette no more than a couple of years old.

Quinn stepped from the car, walking around behind it and stopping where she couldn't be seen from Renquist's house.

"How're you going to play it?" Eric said, coming around and leaning on the rear door of the hatchback.

"Same way I played it with you. The FBI's re-opening the Lisa Egan case based on some new evidence that might connect it to other murders. I'm doing the initial footwork."

He nodded, examining the conservative navy blue jacket she was wearing and slightly less conservative matching skirt beneath it. "Okay, hit me with it."

She cleared her throat and dug her ID from her pocket. "Mr. Renquist. I'm Quinn Barry. I do research for the FBI and was wondering if you'd have a few minutes to answer some questions about a case you once worked on."

Eric nodded. A little gravely, she thought. His mood had darkened noticeably as they had driven from D.C. to Baltimore and Renquist's home. She couldn't blame him really. At an age when normal boys were running around playing baseball and worrying about their grades, Eric had been teaching college physics and spending his free time being persecuted by the Baltimore police.

She didn't resist when he reached up and pulled the glasses from her face. "Horn-rims," he said, looking down at the plastic. "I admire the fashion statement but it doesn't scream FBI to me. Can you see without them?"

She nodded. "They're just for distance."

"Okay. Turn around."

She did as he asked.

"Told you."

"What?"

"The skirt works. If you get an opportunity to walk away from him, it might help."

She frowned deeply, still regretting that she had allowed him to talk her into buying a size too small.

"I'm serious," he said, pulling an apple from the pocket of his jacket and taking a loud bite. "This guy's not too complicated. Nothing but a redneck, really. A little leg'll go a long way."

"I'll keep that in mind," she said coldly.

Quinn had to struggle to keep her breathing in an easy rhythm as she jogged across the street and up Renquist's driveway. It wasn't so much that she was nervous about interviewing the old cop; it was the possibility that he might not know anything that was really bothering her. If this turned out to be a dead end, she had no idea what her next move would be. Her credibility with Eric was shaky at best and he'd probably give her a sympathetic pat on the back and then ditch her at the first opportunity. And as much as she wanted to be mad at him for that, she really couldn't. This all seemed crazy to her, too.

She stopped in front of the door and smoothed her skirt nervously, trying to put the thought of being completely alone again out of her mind.

Nice and easy.

She grabbed the brass knocker and gave it a couple of authoritative raps while she rehearsed her greeting again. Renquist had undoubtedly worked with hundreds of FBI agents during his career. She had to make this convincing.

The man who answered was pretty much what Eric had described: short dark hair parted severely on the side, a thick layer of fat around his midsection that was in the process of spreading to his face, a nose that looked like it had been broken a couple of times.

His brow furrowed a bit as the door opened. He didn't speak, instead leaning out and squinting as he examined her.

"Mr. Renquist?" she said, reaching into her jacket for her ID. "I'm Quinn Barry. I do research for the—"

His mouth broke into a crooked smile—a sneer, really—as she spoke. Quinn fell silent, looking into his deep-set eyes and seeing recognition there. When she took a hesitant step backward, he shot a hand out and tried to grab her. Age and the extra weight he was carrying made him just a fraction of a second too slow; his fingers slid ineffectually from her arm as she jerked away.

By the time she heard the unmistakable sound of

splintering wood, she had already kicked her shoes off and started to run. She dared a quick look over her shoulder when she made it to the street and saw that the man chasing her now was neither old nor fat. The front door to Renquist's house was hanging open, partially torn off its hinges by the force of the man who had burst through it.

She was at full speed now, running as fast as her bare feet would allow, but he was gaining quickly. When she saw him start to reach into his jacket, she faced forward again, ignoring the pain and forcing herself to go faster.

"Eric!" she screamed, praying that he'd been watching. "Eric!"

The sudden flare of pain in her head came completely without warning. The world around her blurred and she felt herself falling forward onto the asphalt. She immediately began struggling to get back to her feet but lacked the strength. Despite a desperate effort, all she could manage was to roll on her back and prop herself into a half-sitting position. The lack of movement as she looked toward Renquist's house confused her until her head cleared enough to process the blurry images in front of her.

The man chasing her had stopped and was standing motionless some twenty-five yards away. She blinked hard, trying to clear her vision and regain enough of her equilibrium to stand. When she opened her eyes again, she was momentarily blinded by an intense red light.

A pair of arms suddenly wrapped around her torso from behind and she felt herself being dragged backward. Her vision continued to clear and now she could see that the man was crouched in a classic shooting pose, holding a gun with a red laser emanating from it. She looked down at the arms clamped across her chest and saw that one was illuminated with a single red dot.

The dot disappeared and the man was sprinting in her direction again, his gun still gripped tightly in his hand. He got close enough for her to read the resolve in his face before she felt herself being flipped around and thrown into the backseat of a car. The sound of squealing tires was accompanied by the thump of a body slamming into the side panel.

Bright red hit her eyes again, but not blinding this time. It took her a moment to realize that it was blood. When her face finally sank into the vinyl seat, she knew that she wouldn't have the strength to lift it again. She assumed that she was dying but wasn't coherent enough to figure out how she felt about it.

32

Quinn!

"Quinn! Can you hear me?"

She didn't open her eyes, instead closing them tighter, trying to force herself back into oblivion. She didn't know where she was or when, and she didn't care—all she wanted was to fall back into silence and escape the excruciating pain chipping away at her unconsciousness.

"Quinn!"

She suddenly jerked fully awake and lashed out instinctively, only to feel someone catch her wrist in a gentle grip.

"Relax. It's me. You're okay," the familiar voice said. She felt herself being pushed back onto the soft mattress.

The form hovering over her and the details of the

small room slowly started to come into focus. She blinked hard a couple of times and found herself staring into Eric Twain's worried face.

"Can you follow this?" he said, holding up a finger and moving it around in front of her. It was difficult at first, but as long as he didn't go too fast, she could. He closed his hand and retreated until his back was pressed against the wall. A loud rush of air escaped him as he slid down onto the floor amid what looked like a disassembled case file.

His head sank into his hand and his long hair fell across his face in matted clumps. It took a few seconds for her to put that together with the other stains on his skin and clothing. Blood.

"Eric . . . are you . . . are you all right?"

He pushed his hair out of the way and looked up at her. "It's not my blood."

She froze for a moment but finally gained the courage to steal a glance down at herself. She was still wearing the navy blue skirt she'd had on earlier, though the matching jacket had been replaced with a white T-shirt. Blood covered a good portion of both and was still wet in places. She reached around to the back of her throbbing head and ran a finger across a bandage. "Owwwww."

"Do you know how lucky you are, Quinn? The bullet just glanced off. You've probably got a mild concussion, but I don't think there's any permanent damage. But then, my doctorate is in physics."

She felt around the edges of the bandage. It was

a few inches long and maybe an inch wide. He was right. She should be dead. "What happened? How did we get away?"

"Fancy driving and both our lifetime allotments of luck." He shook his head miserably. "I'm sorry, Quinn, this is my fault. I almost got you killed."

"Your fault? What are you talking about?"

He picked up a handful of the papers strewn out around him. "It's all here. I thought Renquist was a moron—that he had some kind of vendetta against me; that he was too stupid to follow up on obvious leads . . ." His voice trailed off for a moment. "But it's not random, there's a pattern. The son of a bitch was in on it."

Eric dropped the documents in his hand and began searching through a stack to his left. Finally, he came up with a single sheet of white paper and leaned forward, dropping it next to her on the bed. Quinn picked it up, staring into what looked like a black-and-white photo of a man's face. It took her a moment to realize it was actually an incredibly realistic pencil drawing.

"That's the guy who shot you. Is it the same man? The same one who tried to grab you last week?"

She shook her head.

"You're sure?"

"He was much older. Maybe this is the guy who was in the other car . . ."

Eric pushed himself to his feet and started pacing, slowly at first, then with greater urgency as the nervous energy bottled up inside him started to escape. He jabbed a finger in the direction of the drawing in her hand. "What the hell's going on, Quinn? That guy tried to kill you in broad daylight! **He actually tried to kill you!**"

She watched him move back and forth across the tiny room for a few moments, but the motion was making her queasy, so she lay back and closed her eyes. "I told you, they already tried once. But you thought I was making it up, didn't you?"

When she heard him stop moving she opened her eyes again.

"I don't know what I thought," he said, running his fingers through his tangled hair. "I thought you were kind of cute. I thought maybe you were a little nuts. I thought you were the first person I'd met in almost ten years who didn't immediately label me a homicidal maniac. Jesus . . ." He started pacing again, so she tilted her head back and stared at the ceiling, trying to put some logic into what had happened.

She remembered the look on Renquist's face and him trying to grab her arm. She remembered running, and the other man, the one in Eric's drawing, bursting through the door and coming after her. Then the pain in her head, the disorientation. Eric's arms wrapped around her from behind. The red dot on his arm . . .

"Why didn't he?"

She heard Eric stop again. "Why didn't he what?"

"Why didn't he kill me?"

"Your thick skull. It sure as hell wasn't for lack of trying."

"No. When you grabbed me, he had a gun aimed right at us. But he didn't shoot. He just started running at us again."

"I don't know," Eric said. "Maybe he thought I was an innocent bystander."

The sound of the door opening startled her, breaking her concentration. She bolted upright as a pale face appeared around the jamb.

"Quinn! Take it easy," Eric said, holding his hands out in front of him. "This is Tony. He's a friend of mine."

Tony didn't actually look at her, instead focusing on the floor and then on Eric. "Is she going to be all right?"

"Looks like it," Eric said.

"Do you need anything?"

"I think we're okay for now. Thanks."

Tony bobbed his head and then pulled back out of the room, closing the door behind him.

"Where are we?" Quinn said when she was sure the man was gone.

"Baltimore. This is Tony's house."

She started to try to get out of bed but found that her muscles still weren't completely ready to obey her orders. "We've got to get out of here. They'll trace us—"

Eric crouched down and laid a hand gently on her knee. "Don't worry about it, okay? We've still got time. Tony didn't start at Jet Propulsion Labs till after I'd moved to D.C. We met at a physics conference a few years ago. We play video games over the Net and swap e-mails now and then. Other than a few people in the physics community, nobody even knows we're friends."

She stayed where she was, halfway off the bed, trying to decide what to do.

"Trust me," he said. "We're okay for a little while. And we need the time to figure out what we're going to do. Running out of here with no plan would be stupid and maybe could even get us killed. Right?"

Quinn sank back into the pillows propped up behind her, but didn't say anything. She just wasn't sure. She wasn't sure of anything anymore.

"Look, I'm going to go get cleaned up," Eric said. "Why don't you rest, and when I'm finished we'll talk about what we're going to do. Who we're going to call. Okay?"

"Okay."

Quinn slid her feet toward her and then back again as he disappeared through the door, flexing the muscles in her legs and trying to ignore the pounding in her head as her heart reacted to the movement. She kept at it and in less than a minute her mind and body were starting to work more or less in unison again.

There was no doubt that Renquist was involved. He'd known damn well that wasn't an FBI operation—agents weren't in the habit of shooting unarmed women in the back. How had he been coerced? Money? Not on an FBI agent's salary. Blackmail of some sort?

And what about the idea of there being only two men involved in this? Who was covering her home? Her dad's house? Her office? All more likely stops for a woman in trouble. The theory that the killer was a high-level FBI agent who had used his position somehow to coerce criminals to help him was getting more and more believable . . .

Her head hurt too much for this. She swung her newly cooperating legs over the edge of the bed and stood cautiously. Her balance was still a little off but wasn't too bad, considering. She picked up a towel from the nightstand and tried to wipe the dried blood off her neck and face, but without success.

The skirt and sweater she'd been wearing earlier were there, too, lying on the nightstand looking like they'd been washed and pressed. She reached out for them but then thought better of it. A shower first.

She opened the door and walked out into the hall, moving unsteadily down it until she came to the cluttered room at the other end. Tony Colier spun around in his chair at the noise behind him, but upon seeing it was her, returned his eyes to the floor.

"Hi, Tony."

He dared a quick look up at her. "Are you okay?"

"Eric tells me it's not as bad as it looks. I think I'm going to live."

She looked around her as she made her way to a worn sofa pushed up against the wall. Ninety percent of the equipment clogging the room was familiar—expensive, cutting-edge computer stuff. The other ten percent she wasn't sure of. "So are you another one of these geniuses?"

He shook his head. "No. Not a genius. Just high on the RFS scale."

"The what?"

He covered his mouth with his hand and giggled. "Real Fucking Smart."

"What's the difference?" she asked, dropping onto the couch and examining her host. He seemed to be about her age—certainly no older than twenty-six—with an amazingly bad haircut and wide eyes that made him look perpetually surprised.

"Geniuses see things differently than other people. Like Einstein, or da Vinci, or Newton . . . Or Eric."

"Eric?"

He nodded. "Yeah, he's one of them."

"How well do you know him?" she said, deciding to take the opportunity to get another perspective on the man she'd put so much blind faith in. Tony was the only person she'd met who actually knew

Eric Twain. Not a report written by a cop or a journalist who had met him only a handful of times, but a flesh-and-blood friend.

"Not that well," he admitted. "We play video games together. And he lets me bounce things off him when I get stuck. He's great about that. He's a really cool guy, but you know he doesn't have that many friends 'cause . . ." He went silent and stared down at the floor again.

"I appreciate you helping us, Tony," she said, making a conscious decision not to dredge up Eric's past. She doubted there was anything Tony could tell her about the death of Lisa Egan that she didn't already know.

"How . . . how'd you get hurt?"

Quinn heard a shower go on somewhere in the back of the house and turned in the direction of the sound for a moment. "It was nothing, Tony. An accident. Just a stupid accident."

33

Edward Marin pressed the phone to his ear and listened to it ring. He was about to hang up when he heard the unmistakable click of someone picking up and then the disappointing clatter of the handset being fumbled.

"Hello?"

He frowned. The voice was groggy. Half-asleep.

"Put Quinn Barry on the phone," he ordered.

"Quinn Ba—Who the hell—Jesus, it's two in the morning, man. You have the wrong number." Another audible click as the handset was slammed down.

Marin adjusted himself into a more comfortable position against the side of the bed and crossed the name and phone number off the pad in his lap.

He'd compiled the list partially from memory

and partially from the outbox on Eric Twain's personal e-mail program. Despite his lack of success thus far, Marin wasn't concerned. The gods were with him. He dialed again.

This time the reaction was a little more encouraging. It was picked up on the second ring.

"Hello?"

Marin had already abandoned his position at the University of Virginia in favor of an anonymous existence at ATD when Tony Colier entered the scientific community. They had never actually spoken, so there was no risk that Tony would recognize Marin's voice.

"Hello? Hello? Is anyone there?"

Trepidation colored with a bit of confusion. It was just what Marin had been looking for.

"Put Quinn Barry on the phone."

A long silence.

"I . . . I'm sorry. I don't know who you're talking about."

Marin tossed the phone list onto the floor next to his open portable computer, struggling not to laugh. The gods continued to smile.

"I can have people at your front door in three minutes, Anthony. Put her on the phone. **Now**."

The sound of a hand clamping over the phone and then more silence. Marin glanced over at his laptop and the lengthy e-mail report he'd intercepted glowing from its screen. He skimmed it again, reveling in the details of the third botched attempt on Quinn Barry's life. Apparently, Eric Twain had gotten in the way. It was really just too perfect.

Breathing replaced the silence over the phone, but this time it was a little faster, higher pitched. Feminine.

"Quinn?"

"Who is this?" He knew she had been injured but couldn't hear it in her voice. She was trying to be brave. How wonderful.

"I'm a friend. Are you all right? Are you seriously hurt?"

He was reluctant to fill the silence that ensued. Instead he leaned over the woman lying on the floor next to him. Beautiful young thing. A doctor. In fact, she had just started her residency two weeks ago.

He reached out and ran his fingers along the coat hangers securing her hands to the bed frame and heard her breath catch at his sudden attention. Quinn seemed to be playing a waiting game, trying to force him to speak again. Good for her. He let his fingers slide from the cold wire to the warm skin of the woman's hand. There was still no sound over the phone, so he rocked to his knees and continued moving his fingertips along her naked body, feeling the muscles tense beneath them. Down her leg, to the wire securing her ankle to the heavy bookcase along the wall. He hadn't put her gag in yet—it was so much more exciting this way. Knowing that she could cry out at any moment, ruin everything. But she wouldn't. His power over her was complete. He was her entire world.

"I'm not hurt," Quinn said finally. "Not badly anyway. Why should I believe you're a friend? I don't have many friends these days."

The woman beneath him tried to jerk her hips away when his hand made its way back to the top of her thigh, but her bonds kept her almost completely immobile. Tears began to flow down her cheeks as he ran his fingertips gently through her pubic hair.

"If I wasn't your friend, there would be men at your door right now, wouldn't there?"

"How did you know where I was?"

He closed his eyes, trying to put motion and life to the photograph he'd seen of Quinn Barry. He imagined what it would be like to feel her break down beneath him—to watch as all her courage and reason slipped away from her. To see her bright young eyes beg him.

"It's not important," Marin said. "Can you talk? Are you alone?"

Another long pause. Then, "Tony, could you excuse me for a moment?"

The sound of receding footsteps at the other end of the line was briefly drowned out by a violent intake of breath from the woman beneath him as his finger penetrated her.

"Is Eric there?"

Another moment of silence as Quinn tried to calculate how much to say. Did he know Eric Twain was with her or did he just suspect? What should she give away?

"He's in the shower."

"Good. Now listen to me very carefully. This is important. You're in great danger. Do you know what Eric does for a living?"

"He's a physicist. He works for a university."

"Is that what he told you?"

"Yes."

"While it's true that he's still on staff at Johns Hopkins, that isn't where he spends most of his time . . ." Marin let his voice trail off. He'd make her ask.

"Where does he spend his time?"

"Working for Advanced Thermal Dynamics, the company responsible for creating the FBI's DNA database."

He could tell that she was struggling not to believe him. It wouldn't take much to push her over the edge.

"Do you believe me, Quinn?"

"No."

He smiled and glanced at the laptop, again confirming the details of her most recent escape. "The man who chased you into the street in front of Renquist's house. He could have shot you both, couldn't he? But he didn't. Why do you think that is?"

She didn't respond.

"It's because they need to know what you know, Quinn. Who you've told. Eric Twain is there to find those things out. To make you trust him."

"That's not true!"

"Come now, Quinn. An emotional outburst? That's beneath you."

"Who are you?"

"That's not important."

"Then why should I believe you?"

He could tell from her voice that she already knew the answer to that question but needed a little more help in order to make the leap he was asking of her.

"Because I have nothing but credibility, Quinn. But if you need further proof, I'll give it to you. Do you know where Eric lives?"

"Yes."

"On the first floor he has a desk. Look in the lower right-hand drawer. Your proof is there. But go now—it's critical that you get away from him. If he were to suspect that you know . . ." Marin didn't articulate the possible penalty, leaving it to her imagination.

"No. No way. You'll have people there waiting for me."

"Don't be so obtuse, Quinn. It doesn't suit you. I know where you are right now, don't I? You have my word that the men you fear will not be waiting for you there."

Actually, that was the truth. Lowell had decided days ago that watching Eric Twain's house was a poor use of his limited manpower.

"Quinn, you have to trust me."

"Why should I? You won't even tell me who you are. Why do you want to help me?"

This time he didn't answer right away, giving the illusion that he was struggling with the decision of how much to tell her.

"Because this is so much bigger than you can imagine. I don't have the courage to bring it down. But I sense that you do."

When he replaced the receiver, he saw that the young woman next to him had regained some of the composure that she so wonderfully exhibited in her life. He gazed at her well-muscled legs, her flat stomach, her small but perfectly round breasts, and then finally let her have what she wanted—eye contact. He kept his own expression completely passive. It wasn't time to show himself to her. Not yet.

"Please," she said. "I won't tell anyone about this. I swear. My father . . . he's sick. I'm the only one left who can take care of him—"

Her voice got lost in her throat for a moment when he pulled his fingers out of her and opened the cooler next to him. He took out a thick canvas apron and slid it over his head, then removed an IV bag full of blood.

"What are you doing? Please . . . Please talk to me."

He remained silent as he hung the bag on one of the bedposts. She jumped a little when he slid the needle into her arm and secured it with tape.

"Please . . ." she sobbed as he laid an X-Acto knife down on her abdomen and then stood, stepping back far enough to take in her entire body at once.

Getting her blood type had been more difficult than he'd planned, but in the end it would be worth it. Blood loss was always what killed them. But worse, it took away their fear and pain, and let them float away.

He stepped over her and walked out of the bedroom. He hated bedrooms; the women looked so much more stark, so much more naked, against the backdrop of a living room or a kitchen. But there was nothing that could be done.

He could hear her trying to reason with him, the words drifting out to him on the still air. Telling him more about her father, her plans for her life. God, how he loved the sound of their voices. Each one so uniquely expressive, so effective at increasing the suspense and anticipation that finally consumed him.

He leaned against the iron railing and gazed down at the ground floor. It was really very impressive—the enormous paintings, the brightly colored pipes, the remnants of industrial machinery still growing from the walls. All the more depressing that he had to confine his activities to the relatively conventional surroundings of Eric Twain's bedroom.

He glanced down at his watch, mentally calculating how long it would take Quinn to arrive. Four hours, perhaps a bit less. He'd never kept one alive for that long. It would be a record.

Quinn stared at the phone, standing motionless until it started to beep loudly. She hung it up, but still couldn't think clearly. Her head, already throbbing, was now starting to swim.

She just couldn't make sense of any of this. It was too much. Too much for her. Women being tortured to death. Mysterious people trying to kill her. The FBI's computer system compromised. And now . . . And now the only person she'd found any reason to trust wasn't who he said he was.

She wanted to go to Eric, to talk to him. To get an explanation. But how could she? The man on the phone obviously knew where she was. If he'd been part of the group who wanted her dead, she would be. Right?

She put her hands against her temples and pushed, as though she was physically trying to hold her head together.

Right?

There was a soft clunk in the house's plumbing as the shower was turned off. She looked at the closed door in front of her and sucked her lower lip between her teeth.

Make a decision.

"Are you all right?"

"I'm fine, Tony," she said, jogging past him and back into the bedroom she'd woken up in. She slammed the door and stripped off her clothes, replacing them with the skirt and sweater lying on the nightstand and finding her tennis shoes next to the bed.

Through the thin walls, she could hear Eric rustling around in the bathroom. She tried to will him to stay put as she collected the loose papers and photos strewn across the floor and shoved them back into her knapsack along with the other files. Throwing the pack over her shoulder, she grabbed his keys off the dresser and pushed through the door.

Tony hadn't moved; he was still standing there in the middle of the cluttered hall, obviously unsure of what to do. She took him by the arm and dragged him along behind her until they were far enough from the bathroom door that Eric couldn't hear.

"Tony, I need to get out of here for a little while . . ."

He looked at the dried blood still painting her neck and hair. "I don't think—"

Quinn squeezed his arm, effectively cutting him off. "Look, I just need some air. A little drive to clear my head, okay? Where's Eric's car?"

His eyes shifted toward the bathroom and Quinn moved her hand to his cheek, forcing him to look at her. "It's okay, Tony. I swear. Where's the car?"

34

She decided to cover the last half mile on foot. The sun hadn't quite made an appearance yet but the east had turned a deep red, casting a malevolent glow over the crumbling industrial park. The good news was that she could see where she was going. The bad news was that so could anyone else. Quinn moved quickly through the piles of twisted metal and machinery, finally taking refuge behind the rusted remnants of a car. From there, she could see the old warehouse that Eric called home, but couldn't bring herself to complete the last two hundred yards that would take her into its courtyard. She looked around her again and strained to hear something that might indicate she wasn't alone—a vibration, the clink of metal on metal, the crunching of dirt beneath rubber. There was nothing.

The sun broke over the horizon and she was suddenly surrounded by the distended shadows of dawn. What was she waiting for?

She ducked through the stone archway guarding Eric's property and ran, half-crouched, through the sculptures in the courtyard, finally stopping short when she got to the door.

It was wide open.

She hovered there for longer than she should have, not knowing what was inside and not sure she wanted to. She'd already resigned herself to the fact that the best she could hope for was to find exactly what she'd been told she would. And then her only friend in the world would be an anonymous man on the other end of a phone line.

She forced herself forward, pausing again at the threshold and then slipping inside. The brick walls of the hallway seemed to close in on her as she penetrated deeper into the building. She wanted to turn and run. But to where? She had no choice but to keep going.

The enormous room that made up most of the building was a little better illuminated than the hallway, thanks to the morning sunlight streaming through its windows and skylights, but it was still hard to discern individual details in the visual chaos Eric had created. She hovered at the room's edge, scanning it and the walkway that circled the wall twenty feet up. Once again, there was nothing. Or at least the skillfully created illusion of nothing.

She moved silently, picking up a hammer lying on the floor and allowing herself to take a little comfort from its weight and the smoothness of the wood handle against her palm.

The desk was where she remembered it, pushed up against a wall covered in graffiti-like mathematical symbols. She took a deep breath and opened the lower right-hand drawer, finding it full of neatly labeled hanging folders. She started to flip through them, having some difficulty because of her reluctance to let go of the hammer. Nothing particularly interesting at first: taxes, insurance, product receipts, house receipts, credit card information. Toward the back she came across a folder labeled with nothing but a series of dollar signs. She pulled it out and emptied the letters and check stubs it contained onto the desk. Most of the stubs were for around five thousand dollars and were from companies like TRW, Raytheon, and Boeing. There were also regular checks from Hopkins.

Near the bottom, Quinn found what she'd hoped wouldn't be there. The bright blue logo at the top of the letterhead was easily legible in the strengthening light. Advanced Thermal Dynamics. Her hand hovered over the letter for a moment before she flipped it over and looked at the attached stub. Thirty-five thousand dollars. A quick search of the remaining documents revealed no less than twenty payments from ATD—the smallest of which was for fifteen thousand.

Quinn sank into the chair behind her, suddenly feeling too weak to stand. She pulled a handful of credit card receipts from the drawer and checked the signatures on them against a deposit slip Eric had signed, already knowing what she would find. They matched.

The sound seemed to come from behind her but was almost inaudible—just an undefined vibration in the air. She jumped from the chair and spun around, holding the hammer out in front of her and scanning the room. Had it really been a sound? Maybe it was just her imagination . . .

No. She knew what she'd heard.

She skirted the perimeter of the room, moving quickly toward the hallway that led to the open front door. She was halfway there when she slowed and then finally stopped. What if she made it? What if she ran through the door, got back to her car, started the engine, and floored it? She didn't even know what direction to go in.

It came upon her too fast for her to immediately recognize or control. Her anger and frustration suddenly flared, blotting out the fear and uncertainty that had plagued her for the last two weeks. She purposely banged her head into the wall behind her, the pain amplifying her sudden fury.

"Who's there!" she heard herself yell. Predictably, there was no answer, but she was glad she'd done it. She was tired of running, of not knowing. It was time to take a stand.

Still convinced that the ground floor was deserted, she walked purposefully through it toward the spiral staircase near the far wall. She didn't bother trying to mask the sound as she ran up them and jumped out onto the open walkway. Empty. She squeezed the hammer a little tighter and started toward an open door at the other end.

It was a bedroom.

There was a large bookshelf that took up most of the far wall and a nightstand, both partially hidden by the unmade bed in the center. She inched past a chest of drawers—the only other piece of furniture in the room—and jumped into the doorway just beyond it, swinging the hammer threateningly.

A bathroom. Also empty.

She turned and started with equal caution around the bed toward the open closet.

The scream erupted from her before she could squelch it. She clamped her free hand over her mouth and stumbled backward a few steps but managed to catch herself before she fell.

The woman was completely naked, her hands and feet securely bound with wire. Blood was everywhere—soaked into the carpet and the quilt hanging from the side of the bed, pooling around the base of the nightstand, splattered across the lower shelves of the bookcase.

Quinn remembered the way she'd felt when she'd first seen the photographs of the other victims. Now she knew they were nothing—plastic reproductions that couldn't possibly capture the reality of it.

She took a deep breath and forced herself toward the open closet, letting the hammer lead as she edged across the wet carpet. A few steps and she could see everything inside—clothes and boxes, nothing more. The relief she felt was brief.

"He's still here," she whispered to herself.

The realization hit her with an almost physical force. Her muscles tensed and she spun around to face the open door leading onto the walkway. He was in the house with her. The man who did this was still in the house.

She ran at the door, slamming it shut and clawing desperately at the lock. When it finally clicked, her stomach revolted. She fell to her knees, coughing loudly and feeling the muscles in her abdomen begin to spasm. But there was nothing in her to throw up.

She had no notion of how long it took, but she finally got control of herself and managed to get some air into her lungs. She looked over at the bed and crawled toward it again, not allowing herself to stop until she was within a few feet of the woman.

Quinn squeezed her eyes shut, momentarily blocking out the image of the woman's slashed skin and the blank expression on her untouched face. When she opened them again, she crawled forward a little more and felt the still-warm blood soaking through her skirt and oozing around her knees.

"Oh no . . . No . . ."

The stream of saliva running down the woman's cheek was moving. Every few seconds tiny bubbles would appear at the corner of her mouth and then shrink away. Quinn leaned closer, looking into the woman's open eyes. They didn't seem to see, but when she touched her neck, she could feel a hint of warmth and a weak pulse.

"Oh God . . ." She withdrew her hand and looked down at the needle in the woman's arm, following the tube growing from it to an empty IV bag under the bed. It was still tinged pink.

"Can you hear, me? Hold on. I'm going to try to get help."

There was a glimmer of consciousness in the woman's eyes, but it lasted for no more than a second. That brief moment of recognition seemed to take the last of her strength. Her breath caught audibly in her chest and then she went completely slack.

Quinn realized that she was crying, the tears mercifully blurring the image in front of her. She put a hand on the woman's naked chest to start CPR but then fell back onto the wet carpet. The woman didn't have any blood left to pump.

Quinn struggled to her feet, wiping the tears from her eyes with the sleeve of her sweater, and jumped up onto the bed to avoid having to step over the woman's body. She grabbed the phone off the nightstand, already sure that it would be dead. She was being played with and she knew it.

It took her a moment to process the fact that there was actually a tone. She dialed 911 and, miraculously, a human came on almost immediately.

"A . . . a woman's been killed. I don't—"

"Ma'am, can you give me your name?"

"Quinn Barry . . ."

"Where are you?"

"I'm in an old industrial park at the end of Talisman Street in Northwest. I don't know the address. It's the only building that isn't falling down . . ."

"We're dispatching someone immediately. Can you tell me what happened?"

"She's dead . . ." Quinn's mouth had gone completely dry and she was finding it increasingly difficult to speak. "Someone killed her . . ."

"Killed who?"

"I don't know . . ."

She looked down at the young woman's body and felt the tears well up again. The cuts grew progressively sloppier as they moved from her breasts to her hips and down each leg, as the man who had done this to her had become too excited to work precisely. There was so much blood. Even though she was dead, her wounds were still oozing; red streams being dragged to the carpet by gravity. The transfusion . . . he'd given her a transfusion to keep her alive while he . . .

It had been him; it had to have been. **He** was the

one who had called. Had he been killing her—raping her—while they talked?

"Ma'am? Ma'am! Are you still there?"

The woman's shout pulled her back into the present. "Yes . . ."

"I have confirmation that we have a unit on the way. Now I need you to tell me what happened."

"I . . . I came upstairs. And found her. She was still—"

The crash downstairs was audible even through the locked door.

"Oh, my God," Quinn said, dropping the handset onto the bed.

"Ma'am. Ma'am!"

Quinn hung up the phone, afraid the killer would hear the tinny shouting of the woman at the other end, and ran to the door. With her ear pressed against it, she could clearly hear footsteps. They were still downstairs. And they were running.

She jumped back onto the bed and grabbed the edge of the window that made up much of the back wall. She pulled with everything she had, but it didn't budge. Breaking it would be impossible—the glass sandwiched thick wired screen.

The footsteps took on a metallic ring as they started up the spiral staircase. He was coming. The police would never get there in time.

She jumped to the floor and picked her way around the dead woman, being careful not to leave bloody footprints as she stepped into the closet. The quiet rattle of the hangers seemed loud enough to burst her eardrums as she pulled the door closed until there was only space enough for her to see out.

The first impact came almost immediately. The second shook the bedroom door visibly. She could almost feel the third.

Quinn tightened her hand around the handle of the hammer as the doorjamb started to separate from the brick wall. No fear, she told herself. Her only hope was to kill him. With a little luck, she could surprise him and sink the hammer into his skull before he even knew what was happening. She'd never even thought about killing someone before, but she knew she could do it. Not only to save herself, but for what he'd done to the others.

The door finally gave way, and Eric Twain came bursting into the room.

"Quinn!" His voice was a harsh whisper, easily audible.

She watched him run into the bathroom and pulled back slightly when he turned and looked directly at the closet door. Her hand tightened a little more on the hammer as he started to approach, though the resolve she'd felt a few seconds before was fading quickly. He worked for ATD and she couldn't trust him; she knew that. But she also didn't think she could hurt him.

He had barely cleared the edge of the bed when he fell backward onto the floor.

"Shit!"

He kicked his feet out in front of him, trying to back away from the woman's body, but got tangled in the quilt. He yanked it off his legs and withdrew a few more feet before he stopped, hyperventilating.

"Christ," he said, catching his breath and pushing himself to his feet. He stood still for a moment, staring down at the body, growing paler and paler. Then he just turned and disappeared through the door. About a minute later he reappeared, backing slowly across the threshold.

"Spread out!"

It was a man's voice, floating up from the ground floor. Anything else he might have said was cut off when Eric quietly closed the broken door behind him. He jumped up onto the bed, just as she had, and started pulling desperately on the fused window.

Quinn tried to think as she watched him try to escape. He couldn't have faked his reaction to the dead woman—she was sure of that. What did it really mean that he worked for ATD? Maybe something. Maybe nothing. Was part of the killer's game turning her against her only ally?

Quinn stepped silently from the closet and walked up behind the bed. In one quick motion, she jumped onto it and clamped a hand over Eric's mouth, leaning forward enough for him to see her face before he could use his superior strength to break free.

"Jesus Christ, Quinn," he whispered when she pulled her hand away. "What the hell is going on?"

She didn't answer, instead grabbing hold of the window. He took the hint and put his hands on top of hers. "On three. One . . . two . . ."

"Sir, you'd better come up here and take a look at this."

Colonel Brad Lowell looked up at the man hanging over the balcony, making sure that he revealed none of the emotions that were raging inside him. This was Eric Twain's house. **Fucking Eric Twain's house!** He was going to cut that psycho's heart out for this.

When he reached the top of the stairs, he found his man standing in front of the shattered door to the bedroom. That wasn't right. Marin never broke anything. And he never used bedrooms. Living rooms. Sometimes kitchens. But never bedrooms.

"He didn't use a dropcloth, sir." Susan Prescott's voice. He stepped over the threshold and found her busy unwiring the dead woman from the furniture. None of this was right. The apron was there, but where were the used condoms?

"Did you see that?" Prescott nodded toward a bloody IV bag as she yanked one of the woman's lifeless arms free.

"John," Lowell said, speaking to the man standing behind him. "Get on a cell phone and run the plates of the car out front."

"Yes, sir."

Lowell put a hand to his earpiece as it came crackling to life.

"Sir, this is Geller. We have a police cruiser pulling in up front . . . Okay. Both cops are out. We've got one coming through the courtyard. It looks like the other's going around back."

Lowell touched the microphone attached to his neck. "Everyone that's in the house. Second floor. Now."

He waited for all his men to clear the stairs before he descended. He was halfway down the hall, moving toward the front of the building, when he heard a metallic pounding just ahead. He took a deep, cleansing breath and then slid the front door up on its rails.

The cop was about six feet tall, a heavyset black man. His gun was in his hand but aimed at the ground.

"Could you step out of the building, sir?"

Lowell manufactured a surprised expression and did as he was told. "What's going on, Officer?"

The cop seemed to relax a bit. Not a surprising reaction, when faced with a forty-three-year-old white male in a thousand-dollar suit and an eight-hundred-dollar topcoat.

"Sir, we had a report of a murder at an unspecified address in this area. Are you the owner?"

"A murder? Here? Are you sure?"

"Sir, are you the owner?"

Lowell shook his head. "No. Eric Twain is. I work with him; he's meeting me here."

"Do you mind if I have a look inside?"

"Of course not. Come in," Lowell said, leading the cop down the hall. "I'm an art dealer," he said when they reached the main room. "I represent Eric. We're supposed to go over some of his new pieces . . ."

The cop nodded and took a quick turn around the ground floor. "Do you know what's upstairs?" Lowell listened to the footsteps approaching from behind him but didn't turn around. "Actually, I've never been up there."

The second cop was significantly smaller—a balding Caucasian. He holstered his gun as he approached, though his partner kept his in his hand.

"What's going on, George?"

"He says he's an art dealer. He's supposed to meet the owner."

The white cop nodded thoughtfully. "Sir, how long have you been here?"

"Maybe fifteen minutes."

"Do you have any identification?"

"Sure." Lowell reached into his coat and wrapped his hand around the handle of his nine-millimeter pistol.

The first cop made a valiant effort to raise his gun, but he was much too late. The second didn't do anything. He just stood there looking confused until the bullet pierced his heart and he sank to the ground.

Lowell pulled down his collar and tie, pressing his finger against his throat mike again. "Burn it."

Despite the advanced age of the half-collapsed roof, the smell of tar still hovered in the air above it. Edward Marin breathed it in and made sure his linen slacks touched nothing but the blanket beneath him. When he was satisfied that they were not at risk of being stained, he poured some wine into a crystal glass and returned his attention to the scene below.

He really hadn't thought it possible to time Quinn Barry's arrival to coincide with the arrival of Lowell and his cleanup crew. But now things had degenerated beyond even his wildest imaginings. The surprise arrival of Eric Twain and the police. The gunshots.

He raised his glass to the gods that seemed so enamored of him and took a tentative sip. He'd been saving the Latour for a long time. He wasn't disappointed.

The smoke was subtle at first—disguising itself as dust blowing in the gentle breeze—but it didn't take long for it to gather color, density, and direction. Marin sat mesmerized, watching it rise steadily into the clear morning sky.

35

No! Through here," Eric whispered, pulling her toward the large brick building next to the one he lived in. The side entrance was covered with a sheet of old plywood, but enough of it had rotted away to allow them to slip through noiselessly. Perhaps as a result of her concussion, Quinn was having trouble adjusting to the sudden gloom and she had to rely on Eric to lead her through the debris that littered the floor.

"Where's my car?"

The interior of the building was starting to come into focus: light bleeding through the broken windows and holes in the walls, the fallen beams partially blocking their path, the abandoned machinery.

Confident that she could make her way unassisted now, Quinn pulled away and stopped next to an old crane. She put a hand out to steady herself and leaned forward. Her light-headedness was getting worse.

Eric turned around, but didn't stop, walking backward through the rubble. "Come on, Quinn. Where'd you park my car?"

She didn't answer.

He finally halted, staring at her through the semidarkness. "I don't know if you've been keeping up on current events, Quinn, but it's time for us to be gone from here." He swung an arm toward the far side of the building in an exaggerated motion. "Do you mind?"

"I guess I'm just not in as much of a hurry as you are. How did you find me?"

"Tony was listening in on the phone. He's kind of funny that way. All right? Can we discuss this somewhere else?" He turned and started walking again, not allowing himself to look back and confirm that she was following.

Quinn still wasn't sure if she could trust Eric Twain. What she **was** sure of, though, was that the men back at his house weren't particularly sympathetic to her predicament.

"Why didn't that guy shoot you?" Quinn said when she caught up.

"Quinn, could we prioritize a little here? **First,** let's get out of here without getting our heads blown off, **then** we'll discuss the nuances of our situation. See how the order works there?" He stopped at a hole in the back wall and peeked out. "Okay, it's clear. Ladies first."

She shot him a suspicious glance and then got down on all fours. Before she could start crawling through the hole, though, he grabbed the back of her skirt. "Once we get outside, there's not much cover. We're going to have to move fast. Is there some reason I shouldn't know where you parked my car?"

The shadows were playing across his eyes, making him even harder to read than normal. In the end, though, she really had no choice. "It's near a body shop about—"

"Okay. Good. That's not far. We'll cut through the junkyard. Go left out of here. Stay close to the wall."

She crawled out into the sunlight and started along the side of the building with Eric not far behind. When they cleared the wall, they both looked back and saw the smoke starting to rise from the roof of his home.

"There's your answer," he said, taking her arm and pulling her behind the same burned-out car she'd used for cover on the way in.

"Answer to what?"

"To why that guy didn't shoot me. They needed a scapegoat."

Quinn looked him directly in the eye and shook her head. "I'm not buying it, Eric. That's just too easy . . ."

"Now's not the time to get into this. Are you feeling okay? Can you go on?"

She answered by edging around the car and sprinting for the body shop.

Thankfully, it hadn't opened yet; they were still completely alone as they ran into the gravel parking lot. Eric stopped at a pay phone and picked up the handset. "I left Tony's car out in front of my house," he explained. "They'll run the plate—if they haven't already. I've got to call and warn him."

She nodded and turned to go get the Honda but he grabbed her. "You're not going to take off and leave me again, are you?"

"I'm not sure."

He held her for a few seconds but then let her go to jog across the parking lot and jump into his car.

In the rearview mirror, she could see that he was following her with his eyes as he spoke into the phone, watching her back out into the middle of the lot and start toward the road. He actually looked a little surprised when she stopped and threw the passenger door open. He slammed down the handset and jumped in, kneeling backward on the seat as Quinn accelerated down the road.

"Shit."

Quinn glanced in her mirror again and saw the flames beginning to billow through the windows of his house. Surprisingly, she felt a twinge of sympathy for him as he turned and fell into the passenger seat. She tried to force it back, to stay detached. "Did you reach him?"

"Yeah."

Neither of them spoke again until they made it to the Beltway and were reasonably sure that no one had followed.

"Who do you work for, Eric?"

He lifted his head from the passenger-side window and looked over at her. "Tony told me the guy on the phone talked about Advanced Thermal Dynamics."

"You told me you work for Hopkins."

"I do," he said earnestly. "I'm on staff there; call them if you want to. But I also do freelance consulting."

"You forgot to mention that?"

"Give me a break, Quinn. I do stuff for NASA, Raytheon, TRW, Lockheed Martin, and a whole lot more. Why would I bother to tell you that? Why would you care?"

She eased the car around a semi and depressed the accelerator almost to the floor. Another ten minutes and they'd be clear of D.C. Still no one behind them that she could see.

"What do you do for them?"

"For ATD? Theoretical stuff mostly. Nuclear fusion containment systems. They pay really well. So what?"

"Remember when I told you I got transferred and they brought in the original contractor to fix the CODIS search engine?"

"Yeah."

"The original contractor was Advanced Thermal Dynamics."

Out of the corner of her eye, she saw his brow crinkle as his mind started to work that through. He seemed surprised, but there was no way for her to know if it was genuine.

"I hadn't thought much about ATD," she continued. "I'd assumed they were just following the programming parameters that the FBI had set out. But now . . ."

Eric turned fully in his seat and studied the side of her face. "So where do we stand?"

"I don't know. Maybe ATD—"

"No. Where do **we** stand? You can't possibly think I have anything to do with this. Why would I go through all this trouble if I was involved?"

"Maybe you're trying to figure out what I know, if I've said anything to anyone," she said, parroting what she'd been told—most likely by a psychopath.

"Oh, come on, Quinn. I just lost everything I own and the cops are going to find a dead woman in my apartment. That's not going to do much for my reputation now, is it? If I was involved with those guys, why wouldn't I just turn you over to the killer? You'd tell him anything he wanted to know. Anybody would."

Quinn gripped the wheel a little tighter and concentrated on the road. She wanted to trust him. But was that logic or desperation?

"I haven't told anybody anything," she said finally. "There. Now you know."

He folded his arms across his chest and went back to staring out the windshield. "Fine."

"Fine."

The angry silence lasted all the way to Fairfax, Virginia. The longer it went on, though, the more the image of that dead girl in Eric's bedroom tried to force its way back into Quinn's mind.

"Did you see any of the men downstairs?" she said finally. "Was one of them the guy who shot me?"

He shook his head. "I don't know. Maybe. I didn't get a good look at them. There were three or four men and one woman . . ." His voice trailed off.

"And?"

"It was weird, Quinn. They were really clean-cut—wearing suits and all. They didn't look like a bunch of blackmailed criminals to me—what they looked like was a bunch of FBI agents."

She thought about that for a few moments but didn't get anywhere. The more they learned, the less any of it seemed to fit together. "Did they say anything?"

"Something to the effect of 'spread out and find the body. Let's get this cleaned up and get out of here.'"

"They didn't know we were there," she said.

"That'd be my guess. But they knew that poor girl was. It's like they're some kind of maid service for psychos. I just can't figure any of this out. Does it make any sense to you?"

She shook her head. "He's playing with us, though. That I can tell you."

"Who?"

"Whoever killed that girl. It was him on the phone, I'm sure of that. He wanted me to come to your house and find her. Then he called those men—his cleanup crew—down on top of me."

Quinn was suddenly aware of the slight tightness in the skin on her knees where the girl's blood had dried, and she reached down, trying unsuccessfully to scrub it off with the fabric of the skirt. What kind of . . . thing . . . could do that to another human being? She felt her forced calm slipping a little as she started to think about the phone call: his voice, how easily he'd manipulated her. The fact that he'd known where to find her.

"Quinn, are you all right?"

"He thinks he can pick us off anytime he wants."

The worry on Eric's face seemed genuine. He seemed to be thinking the same thing she was—

that she fit the killer's profile almost perfectly. He undoubtedly had plans for her.

"If he's messing with us, then he's doing it to them, too," Eric said, making a valiant effort at sounding upbeat. "All we have to do is figure out why . . . And who 'them' is."

36

Edward Marin turned down the heat on the grill built into his granite countertop and listened to the hiss of the cooking steak fade. A few more minutes.

He padded into the dining room and retrieved a meticulously pressed linen place mat, smoothing it out on the dining-room table. The complex rhythms of Mozart's **Jupiter** Symphony swirled around him as he began to polish his silverware with a soft rag.

It was the same ritual every night: the cooking, the careful setting of the table so that each crystal and silver implement glowed with unblemished purity and rested in its precise place. It was a mindless task that, for some reason, he truly enjoyed. In fact, it was one of the very few things in his life that he could derive pleasure from anymore.

And today it was that much better. He was still enveloped by the memories of the girl—the way she had looked spread out on Eric Twain's bedroom floor, the way she smelled. The sound of her soft skin splitting, magically audible beneath the screams working their way around her gag. The all-encompassing defeat in her eyes near the end when he finally pressed himself against her pain-racked body and entered her.

The transfusion, combined with her fierce will to live, had come together magnificently. She had still been alive after almost four hours of his constant attention. A truly sublime achievement.

Marin walked back into the kitchen and busied himself with the pans on the stove, stirring, seasoning, carefully adjusting temperature. The large windows to his right continued to darken with the setting sun, obscuring the dense foliage covering the twenty acres around his house and leaving a black mirror that reflected his image with increasing clarity.

After neatly arranging his food on a plate, he returned to the dining room and used a touch-screen remote to shut off the music. Always silence when he ate—nothing to mask the quiet clink of silver on china, the sinking of tooth into flesh.

So far there had been nothing but silence from Advanced Thermal Dynamics. Quinn Barry and

Eric Twain had once again escaped; he knew from an intercepted e-mail that Lowell had been completely unaware the two were ever at the house. Marin also knew that the burned-out shell of Eric's home now contained not only the blackened remains of the girl, but the bullet-ridden bodies of two policemen. The good colonel would be scrambling to solidify Eric as the prime suspect and Price would be resisting, frantically trying to regain control of a situation that he was too stupid and arrogant to accept was beyond his control. Marin reached for his glass, smiling to himself. Richard Price certainly was not going to be happy with the day's events.

The loud crack of splintering wood was followed quickly by the sound of people running. Marin took a sip of his wine and let the tannins tease his palate. No, not happy at all.

"Doctor."

Marin didn't look up from the steak he was cutting, using his other senses to follow the men fanning out around him.

"Colonel Lowell. I was just having dinner." He slid a bite of the meat into his mouth and laid down his silverware.

"You're to come with us, Doctor."

Marin continued to chew and swallowed before he spoke. "As I said. I was just having dinner."

Lowell gave a short nod and a moment later Marin felt someone grab his shoulder from behind.

He spun around and, in a single violent motion, wrapped a hand around the man's throat and held the point of his steak knife to the man's eye.

"Stop!"

It was Lowell's voice. Not aimed at Marin, but at the four remaining men, all of whom now had their guns drawn.

"Let him go, Doctor!"

Marin tilted his head a bit to the right, watching the reflection of the man's eye in the knife and listening to him try to take air into his constricted throat. Marin's gaze swept downward and he saw the man's feet suspended half an inch above the carpet. It had all been completely instinctive—no effort or thought at all. It was coming back. The years of captivity hadn't dulled him.

"Dr. Marin!"

He considered pushing the knife into the young man's brain but quickly decided against it. Stupidity and unpredictability were too closely linked. While Price's, and perhaps even Lowell's, reaction would be easy to foretell, the men around him might be more rash. It wasn't the time.

"I'm sorry, Brad. I'm afraid I don't like to be touched."

He relaxed his arm and released the man, who staggered back, his hand pressed to his throat.

Marin turned and smiled politely at Lowell, who was making a pathetic attempt to maintain the illusion that he was in command.

"You're to come with us," he repeated.

Marin sat down at the table again and wiped away whatever the young man's eye might have left on his knife. "I look forward to it, Colonel, but first I'd like to finish my dinner. If you and your men will wait outside, I'll be out momentarily."

Lowell didn't move, except to clench his jaw so tightly that Marin imagined he could hear the teeth grinding. Lowell undoubtedly wanted to kill him. He had wanted to do so for years. But that was impossible—contradictory to his orders. It hadn't gone far enough yet for Price to remove his leash. Not yet.

Lowell finally jerked his head in the direction of the door and his men followed him back out as Marin sipped his wine.

37

Quinn let out a frustrated grunt and jabbed her index finger at the enter key on Eric's portable computer. She was sitting cross-legged in the middle of a king-size bed, staring at the small screen as she navigated the Internet. The task she was performing should have been simple—a ten-minute no-brainer. But like everything else over the past two weeks, it was turning into an impossible mess.

She looked over at Eric, who had parked himself on a stool at the far end of the spacious hotel suite he'd sprung for. His normally dark skin had taken on a slightly pale hue and he looked a little shaky, but the room's well-stocked bar seemed to be helping.

"I can't find **anything**," Quinn said.

He tossed back a shot glass full of something or other. "Told you."

"I mean, I've used every search engine I know of. As far as the Net is concerned, there is no such organization as Advanced Thermal Dynamics."

He shrugged.

"Come on, Eric. You work for them, for God's sake. You must know something."

"I got hired over the phone, Quinn. It's not that unusual; most people want what I can provide but aren't anxious to get too close to a guy who supposedly slit his girlfriend's throat. They give me specific problems—usually pretty focused and specialized—and I send them the answers through e-mail."

She perked up a little. "E-mail? What's their address?"

"Don't bother. I've already looked. It's a dedicated mail server. If you try to pull it up with a browser, it just comes up blank."

She shut down the laptop and tipped herself back into the soft pillows propped against the headboard. Closing her eyes, she tried to let some of the tension fall from her shoulders and back but knew it was probably hopeless. She couldn't shake the feeling that a clock—her clock—was ticking; that the freak who had killed those women was watching her; that he knew where she was; that he was waiting. Planning.

She squeezed her eyes shut a little tighter. "You said you do work for them on fusion . . ."

"Inertial containment systems for fusion reactors, to be precise," he said.

"Tell me about that."

"Not too much to tell. Fusion is a nuclear reaction that combines particles instead of splitting them apart like our nuclear reactors do now. The sun is an example of a fusion reactor. The combining of atoms releases a lot of power, and it's a much cleaner, safer process than fission."

"Then there's a lot at stake in its development. I mean, it could be really big . . ." She didn't know where she was going with this, but she needed to go somewhere. There had to be a way to put this together that made sense.

"Sure, I guess," he said. "Someday it may be a great thing. But right now we're years away from finding a practical way to harness the energy a reaction produces."

She opened her eyes. "What about the military? Is there a military application?"

"If I've learned anything being involved in science for this long, it's that there's always a military application. The army could figure out a way to kill people with a comfy chair, you know? Actually, the detonation of a hydrogen bomb involves fusion, but the stuff I'm doing couldn't really be used in that way. Besides, I don't really think anyone—even the military—sees much of a need for bigger bombs, do you?"

"But what if they've—"

"Quinn. Trust me here. This is a subject I know something about."

He turned and poured himself another drink. "I've been thinking, what if we've been going in completely the wrong direction on this thing? Your profile of the killer seemed pretty reasonable and it did fit an FBI agent, but there are other ways to interpret it. It seems to me that Renquist was somehow paid off. Do you agree?"

She nodded.

"What if somebody at the FBI is being paid off, too? That would go just as far to explaining how your car got sabotaged in the Quantico parking lot and how CODIS was compromised. And as far as FBI agents having access to information on women who were already at risk for abuse, well, a lot of people would have that information. Hell, you could probably read it in the paper."

"So you're saying we should be looking at ATD?" Quinn said.

"Think about it. Who were those guys at my house?"

Quinn rolled on her side and propped her head in her hand. "Originally, we said ex-cons that had been blackmailed into helping the killer. But you don't think so anymore."

He shook his head. "I wish you could have seen

them. I can almost guarantee you that those guys weren't a bunch of criminals."

"Who, then?"

"I don't know. Remember what you asked me when we were in the car? Why the guy at Renquist's house backed off when I got in the way? I mean, he didn't seem to have any moral issues with shooting you . . ."

"ATD," she said.

He shrugged. "It's just something I've been mulling over. If that guy was working for Advanced Thermal, there's a good chance he'd have been told not to hurt me. I don't want to sound arrogant, but I do things for them that no one else can . . ."

Quinn played with the bedspread for a few moments, thinking about what he'd said. "It would have to be someone high up in the organization. They'd have to have enough power to go after the CODIS programming contract and a lot of money to spread around."

"High-tech millionaires are a dime a dozen. There are a lot of people out there who could have set up a company like ATD."

Quinn slid off the bed and grabbed her sweater off the floor. "I don't know, Eric. There are still a lot of pieces that don't fit. I mean, what is ATD and why is there no information on it anywhere? If they'd been set up specifically to compromise CODIS, I'd be more inclined to think you were on the right track. But you're telling me they also do expensive research into fusion reactors and God knows what else. And then, of course, you have to consider the source of all this."

"The source?"

"Who gave us the ATD angle? The guy who left that woman in your bedroom. What if the ATD thing is just a coincidence and the killer is using it to throw us off, to make me suspect you? Are we just playing into this guy's hands? Doing what he wants us to?"

She pulled the sweater over her head.

"Are we going somewhere?" he asked.

"I'm hungry."

"Let's just order room service. We—"

"No. I've got to get out of here. Get some fresh air. Go somewhere I can think."

38

Everything white.

Four walls, ceiling, floor, a tiny cot, a toilet. Scrubbed, polished, and pressed with the mindless military efficiency Marin had become so accustomed to. In this case, though, the effect was startling. An accidental masterpiece.

He sat on the floor, feeling more and more part of the stark emptiness around him. How long had he been there, imprisoned in the tiny brig built into an unused corner of the Advanced Thermal Dynamics facility? Not long. He could still feel the weight of food in his stomach. Somehow the sensation was uncomfortable, alien.

After sending Lowell and his men out, he'd finished his meal, but it had been a hollow experience. The taste, the sounds, the smell had faded into an overwhelming blandness. The comforts of his home, his work, his genius had become empty, meaningless. There was nothing left for him in the present. There was only the future and the past.

He'd always had a gift for remembering the women. But now he found he had the ability to fall back into them, to recall each one with all the intensity and detail that had existed at that precise, perfect moment in time.

The first had been in 1983, when he was only twenty-six. It had been clumsy by his current standard, completely unplanned. He had knocked her unconscious with a bottle and for a time thought he wouldn't be able to wake her. Finally, though, her long lashes had begun to quiver and she had shown him the depth of her green eyes.

What he'd done to her, his technique, had been hopelessly crude—using only what implements he'd found in a toolbox in her basement. She'd slipped one of the ropes securing her while he was using a pair of pliers on her and he'd barely managed to regain control before she could pull her gag out. Marin smiled as he felt his heart jump, just as it had at the moment it had happened.

That first time had been all uncontrolled passion. All heat and flash. In many ways, he'd never again matched the raw intensity of it.

But that didn't matter; he'd compensated with the refinement of his technique. The fear and nov-

elty slipped a little further away with every year—
there was no stopping that. But each time he
learned a little more. How to inflict the pain more
efficiently, how to keep them alive and conscious of
what was happening to them for longer and longer
periods of time. How to control them to such an ex-
tent that they thought only what he told them to
and felt only the agony he provided.

Ten years ago that delicately maintained balance
began to falter. He found that every time he needed
more and they gave him less. He'd finally let everything fall away: society's conventions, his humanity, his work, his future. For a short time he'd been
truly free.

And that's how it should have ended—with him
above human weakness, with limitless power, lust,
and rage. He'd become something else; he knew
that now. Something indescribable.

Enter the Baltimore police and then his would-be
savior, General Richard Price. His offer had appealed to the tiny intellectual spark that Marin had
allowed to remain, the final shreds of human reason
that he had been afraid to completely release. Price
offered him everything, and that spark had turned
to flame again. Everything he had become crum-
bled and he'd once again seen through human eyes.

And that's how he'd lived the last decade of his
life. With nothing but the memory of what had
been. The women were rare now and the experi-

ences had been scrubbed to a sterile, antiseptic nothing with the same robotic precision that had created the room around him.

It was a mistake he wouldn't make again. There would be no spark left to destroy him this time. He would be completely pure.

39

Can I refill that Coke for you?"

The waitress was more or less beaming at Eric. She was all of about nineteen, with longish hair dyed an intentionally unnatural black and a gold nose ring. For some reason, Quinn found herself wanting to resist making the observation that she was a striking, strangely beautiful girl.

"That'd be great. Thanks," Eric said, sliding his still half-full glass across the table. Quinn considered pointing out that her water glass had been empty for the last fifteen minutes but was pretty sure the young woman didn't care.

The waitress remained focused on Eric as she backed away, finally coming to a stop after she'd made it only a few feet. "I'm sorry. Don't I know you from somewhere?"

Quinn rolled her eyes.

"Wait. Don't you play in that band Faith Void?"

"No."

"Man, this is driving me crazy. I've seen you somewhere."

"Do you ever watch **America's Most Wanted**?"

He spoke with such calm sincerity that she didn't know how to react. A smile started across her face then abruptly stopped. When she finally turned to walk away, she was even more under his spell than before.

"If you want to keep her, Eric, you're going to have to promise to feed her and walk her every day."

"No, I won't. They never stay that long."

Quinn winced, regretting opening her mouth. With everything that had happened—and was happening—it was easy to forget where she'd found Eric. Alone in an old warehouse in that forgotten corner of D.C. She wondered how long his most serious relationship had lasted. How long before the woman became acquainted with Detective Roy Renquist and the memory of Lisa Egan.

"I'm sorry, Eric. It was just a stupid joke," she said, not sure it was entirely true. It wasn't like her to say something like that without thinking.

His smile seemed sincere. "I know."

The waitress reappeared and set the full glass on the table. "Have you made a decision yet?" she said, focusing entirely on him again.

"I'll have the grilled chicken sandwich and she'll

have the pasta special," he said, handing her their menus. "Thanks."

Quinn watched the girl weave expertly through the crowded brew pub for a moment and then turned back to Eric. "I can't seem to shake the feeling that we're diving into a pool without looking to see if there's any water in it."

"I know what you mean. But it's the only lead we've got."

"I think calling it a lead is a little optimistic, don't you? Basically, we're playing right into this freak's hands, and we're not even doing a good job of it. We haven't been able to find out anything about ATD—"

"That's not really true."

"It isn't?"

"Of course not. We know they're a high-tech company involved in nuclear energy and computer programming—probably other things, too. I think we can also be fairly certain that they focus on classified work for the government."

"Why do you say that?"

"Well, they aren't exactly jumping up and down trying to attract clients. And they must be pretty well funded. Fusion is an expensive area to research and they never even bothered to negotiate with me on my fee—I alone jack them for something like a hundred and fifty grand a year. I think it's safe to say they're some kind of a joint venture between big contractors—or maybe one of those weird quasi-governmental organizations that are floating around doing stuff that nobody really wants to be directly involved in."

Quinn shrugged. "Great. Very clever. But where does that get us?"

"Not very far," he admitted. "But we both have contacts in their industry. Maybe we know someone who can tell us more."

"I don't mean to sound negative here, but what if they do? What if we find out it's a joint venture between Boeing and TRW to build a bomb that can blow up the earth? Or that ATD is just a cover for the navy or the CIA? What then? Even if we assume this guy works for one of those organizations, we've only narrowed it down to about twenty thousand people."

Quinn was finding it harder and harder to keep her frustration in check. The depressing truth was that after no fewer than three near-death experiences, she didn't really know any more than she had two days after she'd found the files.

"I think it's at least worth looking into."

"I'm not sure I do," she said. "Whoever this son of a bitch is, he's smart. Really smart. If we go in that direction, I think we're either going to find nothing or we're going to find exactly what he wants us to find."

"So what do you suggest?"

"We need to do something unexpected."

"Like what? The cops?"

She shook her head. "We can't trust them—we've learned that. Besides, they might . . . get the wrong idea about you."

"You don't have to walk on eggshells around me, Quinn. Just say it: when they finish sorting through what's left of my house and find that girl, they're going to crucify me."

"I'm sorry, Eric. I'm sorry I got you into this."

"It's okay. My life wasn't all that great to start with." He spoke with a depressing fatalism. "So what's the plan, Quinn? Plastic surgery? A move to Antarctica? Maybe a tall glass of hemlock?"

"I don't know." She leaned back against the cold vinyl of the booth, trying to shake off the sense of dread that was tightening its grip on her. No time for that now. "I think we should forget ATD and focus on the killer."

"Sounds good to me. How?"

"It goes back to what I was telling you before . . . something I've been thinking about. These types of guys are always control freaks, right?"

"You're the expert."

She frowned but couldn't actually detect any sarcasm in his voice. "They're also hunters. That's a big part of this for them—finding just the right victim to act out their fantasies with. Let's say we were right and this guy forced himself to settle for less perfect victims after he was almost caught . . . uh . . ."

"Killing Lisa," Eric said, finishing the sentence she hadn't wanted to.

"Yeah. Sorry. So we can assume that his early victims were his ideal—young, beautiful, well educated. Those kinds of women don't grow on trees—"

"Tell me about it."

"So how's he finding them? They were all in different fields, came from different parts of the country, worked for different companies. It seems like a guy efficient enough to reprogram CODIS wouldn't leave something this important to chance."

"So you're telling me that he has a system," Eric said. "Like he has a job that puts him in contact with these women."

"Exactly. Maybe he works, say, in personnel for a company they all applied to but didn't go to work for?"

Eric began spinning his spoon on the table. It looked like he was trying to hypnotize himself. "Maybe. It could also be something more trivial. What if they all won spelling bees as kids? Or they all had phenomenal SAT scores."

They fell silent as the waitress approached and slid their food onto the table. "Can I get you anything else? Refill on that Coke?"

40

"Come on, Quinn. This is crazy," Eric said. "Even worms are smart enough to learn from their mistakes."

She had to admit that the sense of déjà vu was a little uncomfortable. The neatly kept houses and mature trees that lined the street didn't really look any different from the ones that made up Roy Renquist's neighborhood. And it wasn't so easy to forget that the asphalt there was probably still stained with her blood.

Once again, they found themselves standing next to Eric's car on a narrow side street, studying a white two-story house. There were two cars in the driveway and the shades were open, though it was impossible to see past the bright sunlight glinting off the windows.

Eric pushed his index finger into the center of her forehead. "This time they're going to make sure they put the crosshairs right here."

"Is that helpful? I don't think that's helpful." She looked down at the new gray suit she was wearing, smoothing the skirt and brushing some imaginary lint from the jacket. She was just stalling now, and she knew it.

"How do I look?"

"At least let me go with you."

She reached over his shoulder and gave his ponytail a gentle tug. "You think I don't have credibility . . ."

"Five minutes with a pair of scissors and I'm the poster child for the Young Republicans," he said.

She shook her head. "You know it's safer like this. It worked the last time."

"Barely."

"Come on, Eric," she said, moving her hand to his shoulder. "Don't worry so much. I'll be back in a few minutes."

She started off at a casual pace but had unconsciously sped up to a slow jog by the time she crossed the street. Her head moved from side to side, scanning the quiet neighborhood in the flat morning light. It was completely quiet. Empty. Just like last time.

"Hello," she said quietly as she stopped on the front stoop and stared at the closed door. Her voice shook a little. "Hello," she said, a little louder. That was better.

She took a few steps back after ringing the doorbell to give herself a head start should she need to run. A quick glance over her shoulder calmed her a little. She could see the outline of Eric's head through the windshield of his car and a hint of exhaust coming from the tailpipe.

"Hello, young lady."

He was older than she had expected. Gray hair and skin, a little hunched over. She could see the mild suspicion on his wrinkled face but there was no threat or recognition in it. She allowed herself to relax a bit—he probably thought she was a Jehovah's Witness or something.

"Mr. Tanner?"

He nodded.

"I'm Quinn Barry, with the FBI." She dug her ID out of her jacket pocket and held it up. "I was wondering if I could have a few minutes of your time."

Now he really looked perplexed. "What's this about?"

"It's about your daughter, sir. Catherine."

The muscles in his face seemed to lose their strength at the mention of her name. Quinn wasn't sure he was going to agree to talk to her until he shuffled aside and opened a path wide enough for her to enter.

"Pete? Who is it?" A woman's voice from somewhere in the back of the house.

Tanner remained motionless in the entryway, staring at Quinn as she moved past, but not speaking.

"Pete?"

The woman who appeared on the stairs seemed much younger than her husband, though Quinn guessed that they were probably about the same age.

"Hello," she said.

Quinn offered her hand. "Mrs. Tanner? I'm Quinn Barry with the FBI. I wanted to talk to you and your husband about Catherine."

"Catherine," she repeated. Her voice was soft but her handshake revealed none of her husband's apparent despair. "Please," she said, motioning toward the living room. Quinn followed her in and took a seat on the sofa. Mrs. Tanner sat down across from her, but her husband just stood at the edge of the room.

"What about Catherine?"

"Well, ma'am, we've reopened the inquiry into her death . . ."

"The FBI? Why would the FBI be involved in a car accident?"

Catherine Tanner was the earliest victim Quinn had information on—the one whom the killer had burned in her car.

"We've uncovered some evidence that suggests . . . well, that it may not have been an accident."

"Evidence. What kind of evidence?"

Quinn saw no reason to lie. "There was blood found at the scene that wasn't your daughter's.

Based on some new technology, we've been able to link that blood sample to a number of crime scenes involving other young women."

"Oh, my God. Are you—"

"No!"

The surprising volume of Pete Tanner's shout drowned his wife out and caused both her and Quinn to turn toward him.

"It was an accident! It was ten years ago. She died in an accident. That's what you people told us."

"I'm sorry, sir—"

"Don't tell me you're sorry! None of you were sorry! You didn't do anything! And now you come in here—"

"Peter!"

He fell silent but his eyes lost none of their furious light.

"You're being rude to our guest. This young lady was still in grade school when Catherine passed away."

His head fell forward and he stared down at the carpet.

"I left our breakfast on the stove," his wife began. "Why don't you go check on it for me?"

Quinn watched him walk from the room, his shoulders seeming to bow even further, as though the memory of his daughter had physical weight.

"I'm sorry about that," Mrs. Tanner said, after he had disappeared around the corner.

"There's no need to apologize, ma'am."

"He's never gotten over Cathy's death. Neither of us has. You probably know from your files that we never thought it was an accident, that we tried to get the police to keep the case open. It's taken years to accept what happened. And now here you are . . ."

"Why didn't you think it was an accident?"

"The normal reasons, I suppose. That she was a careful driver, that there was no reason for her to be on that road . . ." Her voice faded for a moment. "I suppose that we just didn't want to believe that she died because of . . . because of nothing. That we lost her to turning up the radio, or being a little drowsy, or . . . I know it's been said many times before, but losing a child is probably the most agonizing thing that can happen to a person. You'll do anything to try to mask what you're feeling, to put off really facing it. And for a while, looking for someone to blame helps."

Quinn's discomfort at dredging up this woman's pain was starting to overshadow her nervousness at being there. She had to stay focused, though. The sooner she was gone the better it would be for everyone involved.

"I'm sorry to have to put you through this, Mrs. Tanner, but you understand that it's very important."

"Of course I'll do whatever I can to help."

Quinn smiled gratefully. "I'm particularly interested in any papers or records Catherine might have kept. Letters, things from school, résumés, records of job interviews . . . Would you have kept anything like that?"

Mrs. Tanner nodded slowly. When she spoke again, she sounded a little distant. "We kept everything."

41

Marin didn't move when the door to his temporary prison swung open and three young men entered and surrounded him. They stared down at him in silence, hiding behind what they assumed was their absolute anonymity. Of course, that anonymity was an illusion. He knew their names, who their parents were, where they lived, their levels of education, their psychological test results. He knew everything.

Marin rose from the floor slowly and moved through the open door, aware of the men falling in behind him as he started down the hall. He didn't acknowledge the respectful nods and murmurs of the people he passed—none of them existed to him anymore. They had served their purpose and were now something to be discarded.

The three men didn't follow him into General Price's office, instead taking positions outside the door and pulling it closed. Marin padded across the thick carpet, not bothering to acknowledge Brad Lowell, who was standing in the far corner with his hand concealed suggestively in his jacket. A bit theatrical but at least it showed a glimmer of imagination.

"You think you're indispensable."

Marin sat, looking past Price at the eight-by-ten photograph sitting on a low table behind him. He'd only seen it a few times before, and only when he arrived unannounced. Normally Price removed it before their meetings.

It depicted Price with his wife, a woman almost thirty years his junior, and their young daughter, who was born to him when he was fifty-two. A pathetic attempt at immortality by an old man whose usefulness and power were waning.

"I **am** indispensable," Marin answered, still focused on the photograph. Rachel. His daughter's name was Rachel. She was a beautiful girl: long, blond hair, impossibly smooth skin, small breasts only hinting at what they would become. She was a sophomore at Falls Church High, where she was doing very well.

"You overestimate yourself, Doctor," Price said in a tone that Marin had never heard before. Authoritative, emotionless, slightly condescending.

His command voice. "Your system is not the only option the military has open to it."

"But it's the only one that will work." Marin leaned back and crossed his legs. "I am the military, General. The time of the uniformed thug is over. Now they're only useful for posturing in front of cameras or as pawns to be sacrificed while people like me fight the real war."

"People like you?" Brad Lowell blurted. "You're nothing but a sadistic psychopath who gets off on killing helpless women! How could you ever possibly understand what it is to be a soldier—"

"Brad," Price cautioned.

"Ah, the honor and dignity of war," Marin said. "The courage it takes to fire missiles at helpless villagers. The inestimable bravery it takes to bomb technologically backward countries from the stratosphere." He adjusted his position in his chair so that he could face Lowell. "How many children have you set on fire, Colonel? And how did it make you feel? To kill thousands with the touch of a button; the stroke of a pen? Did it make you feel like God?"

"Shut up, you fucking piece of shit!" Lowell's hand fell from his jacket, sadly empty, and he lunged forward.

"Brad!" Price yelled, jumping up from his chair. "Enough! That is enough!"

Lowell came to a stop with less than five feet between him and Marin, who hadn't bothered to react to the potential attack. There had never been any real danger. Price could still be trusted to see to that.

"This all stops now, Dr. Marin," Price said, continuing his ridiculous effort to gain the upper hand.

"I'm sorry. I'm not sure what you mean."

"You will submit to constant surveillance by the colonel's team. You will be escorted from your home to work and back again. You will not leave your house except to come here. You will do nothing but work to complete this project."

Marin nodded, pretending to consider the man's words.

"And if I can't work under those conditions, General? What then? You and I both know that there's only one other person with the capacity to complete a project like this. And Eric Twain won't knowingly work on weapons systems."

There was a slight flash in Price's eyes at the mention of Twain's name, as Marin knew there would be.

"Don't overestimate my patriotism, Doctor. I'll shut this project down so fast it will make your head spin." The implied threat was obvious, as it was meant to be. The end of the project would also be the end of Dr. Edward Marin. But it was hollow. Price's patriotism was irrelevant. His ambition wasn't. And Marin didn't believe it was possible to overestimate that. He reconfigured his face into something that hinted at uncertainty. His plan, though still not a completely finished work, assumed that things at ATD remained constant for a little longer.

Price saw the change in him and assumed that he was finally gaining control, as he was meant to. "You mention Eric Twain, Doctor. We believe that he's involved with a woman who is investigating this . . . situation. We believe she contacted him because he was implicated in the incident at Johns Hopkins."

Situation. Incident. Marin hid his amusement at Price's reliance on such bloodless euphemisms.

"It's critical that we find him." Price paused dramatically. "For both our sakes."

Marin nodded slowly, as though he was struggling with a decision.

"I think I can help," he said finally.

Price's smile was nearly imperceptible as Marin leaned forward and took a pad off the large desk in front of him. He wrote on it for a few moments and then slid it back toward Price.

"What's this?" Price said, reading through the list of twelve names. "Tyrell Darien? Doesn't he do work for us?"

"Three of those people do," Marin answered. "I think there's a chance that Twain will contact one or more of them."

"Why?"

Because he himself had told Quinn about the

ATD connection. He assumed that Eric would call
people involved in various scientific fields to try to
dig up information on the company. In fact, it
wasn't out of the question that he and the beautiful, beautiful Quinn Barry already knew his identity. Of course, it wouldn't be practical to tell Price
any of this.

"Call it a hunch, General."

42

I really wish you hadn't done that," Quinn said, though she knew that she was more or less talking to herself. She'd come to recognize the slightly lowered head and glazed eyes that accompanied Eric's bouts of intense concentration. He had been completely motionless for over a minute, staring at the foot-high letters scrawled across the hotel room wall in black Magic Marker.

HIGH SCHOOL
SATs
JOB SEARCHES
UNDERGRAD
GRAD
SECURITY CLEARANCES
OTHER STUFF

Quinn crawled across the floor and retrieved another one of the boxes containing the history of Shannon Dorsey's short life and dragged it to the section of carpet she had claimed as her workspace.

As it turned out, Shannon's parents had been no more inclined to discard their dead daughter's belongings than Catherine Tanner's had. They had been a little more cautious in their agreement to let the FBI—Quinn—borrow them, but in the end had acquiesced.

"I think . . . yup. I got Shannon's SAT score," Quinn said, centering a stack of papers on her lap. "Thirteen-ninety. Not bad."

That seemed to break Eric from his trance. He crossed the room and tore open the flaps of another one of Catherine's boxes. The oppressive odor of mildew surrounding them was suddenly stronger.

"What did you get?"

Eric pressed his back against the wall and sank to the floor, holding an old trophy and a stack of colorful notebooks. "Huh?"

"On the SATs. What did you get?"

"Oh, uh. Fifteen-eighty."

"Really?"

"You sound surprised."

"I guess I figured you for a perfect sixteen hundred."

"Missed something on the verbal, I guess." He shrugged. "I was only nine."

. . .

"That's it," Quinn said, pushing her glasses up onto her head and rubbing her eyes. The clock read four P.M. That meant they'd been at it for almost five hours. She shoved a stack of Shannon's love letters into a box full of tiny stuffed animals and crawled across the carpet to where Eric was still propped against the wall.

"Coffee," she said, sagging against him.

He flipped another page in a pile of old performance reviews from Catherine Tanner's job at her college's dining hall. "Thought you didn't like coffee."

She scowled and leaned across him, covering what he was reading with her body and lifting the pot off the box next to him.

"Anything I can do to help?" she said, pouring herself a full cup.

He poked her gently in the side, trying to get her off the papers in his lap. "Well, this is a little distracting."

"Right. Sorry." She pulled back and licked the spoon she'd been stirring with, grimacing at the bitter taste. "Seriously. What can I do?"

"Nothing. There's not much more."

She lay down on the floor and propped her head against his leg. It was a little difficult to drink from that position, but she could feel the cramped muscles in her neck start to loosen.

Most of the boxes had been refilled and were now stacked on the bed they had pushed into the corner. At the base of one of the walls, beneath the headings Eric had written on it, were neat stacks of the dead women's documents.

Despite the warmth of the room and her drink, Quinn couldn't help feeling a little chill. It was just kind of spooky to be surrounded by all this stuff—paper-and-ink reminders of flesh and blood, of young women who'd breathed and worked and learned and felt, and then died horribly for no reason.

They'd been lucky to get their hands on it, though. As near as she could tell they had everything that remained of the killer's first two documented victims. Unfortunately, getting Lisa Egan's things wasn't going to be possible; her parents had moved to California after she died. In a way, though, Quinn was grateful for that. Every now and then they would pull out an old photograph, or something that still held a hint of perfume, or an old note recounting some joy or triumph, and for a brief moment the women came to life. It was hard enough to stay objective as it was.

She suddenly realized that the sound of shuffling paper behind her head had been replaced by the impatient drumming of Eric's fingers. He tried to scoot his leg out from under her, only to find himself trapped by the boxes stacked around him. "This isn't doing much for my concentration."

"Shhh. I'm thinking," she mumbled, closing her eyes and laying her coffee cup on the carpet next to her.

"Done."

Quinn opened her eyes, confused for a moment. Had she been asleep?

"What?"

"That was it. The last box."

"Did you find anything else?"

"Nope."

"So what do we have?" she said, propping herself up on an elbow.

"Let's find out." Eric crawled across the floor and settled in front of the papers lined up against the wall. Under each heading he'd scrawled was a stack of documents with the exception of one. He tapped at the empty carpet beneath the words SECURITY CLEARANCES.

"Doesn't look like the FBI ever had a reason to do a background check on either one of them. And there was no copy of a job application to the FBI in Catherine's stuff."

Quinn frowned. "No mention of the FBI in Shannon's things either," she said. "What about Lisa?"

He shrugged and shook his head. "As far as I know, she was a professional student. Nothing but odd jobs outside of that."

"So our FBI connection continues to slip away."

"Fast."

Quinn sighed quietly and took a sip of her now lukewarm coffee. "Okay, then. What else have we got?"

Eric scooted to the pile beneath the words HIGH SCHOOL.

"They went to different schools hundreds of miles apart," he said, shuffling through the pages. "Based on the report cards we've got, both did well. Lisa and I never really talked about it, but I assume she did, too, since she went to Princeton for her undergrad."

"What about other activities?"

He held up a stack of ribbons bound together with a rubber band. "Catherine was a swimmer. Neither Lisa nor Shannon was athletic. They all seem to have received academic awards, but in different areas and from different organizations. Catherine was in **Who's Who**, but Shannon wasn't. Don't know about Lisa . . . I don't think there's anything here."

"What about the SATs?"

He shrugged. "They did well but not spectacularly. Besides, how would someone working at the SATs know what these girls look like?"

"What about the person who administers the tests?"

"How would he know what they scored?"

Quinn frowned. "You're right. Too complicated.

I see this guy as having a system that's a little more . . . I don't know . . ."

"Elegant?"

"Exactly."

"Moving on, then. Jobs. Any big government contractors?"

He shuffled through the stack and shook his head. "Shannon's got stuff in here from three pharmaceutical companies—all big ones I've heard of. And I found some letters from South America, where she did an internship studying salamanders or something. Catherine signed with Intel before she graduated."

"And you said Lisa was just a student."

He nodded. "This is starting to look like a waste of time."

"No. There has to be something connecting these girls. There has to be. What about college?"

" 'Undergrad,' " he read off the wall as he scooped up a tall stack of documents and crawled back over next to her. He gave her anything relating to Shannon and kept everything else himself.

"Okay," Quinn said, starting to leaf through them. "Catherine went to MIT. There's a copy of an application to Hopkins"—she looked up at him, but he just shook his head—"but I can't tell if she ever sent it. Acceptance letters from Princeton and the University of Virginia. She got turned down by Yale."

Eric suddenly seemed a little distant.

"You all right?"

Shannon went to Caltech," he said, quietly. "I've also got acceptance letters from Stanford and Harvard. And the University of Virginia."

Quinn jerked upright and grabbed his leg. "UVA? Did Lisa apply there?"

"I . . . I have no idea. I guess it's possible."

"Oh, my God. This could be it!" She jumped to her feet, but wasn't sure what to do.

"Calm down, Quinn. They're both from this area and UVA's a major school. It could be nothing but a coincidence."

"What about Lisa's parents?" she said. "They'd know, right? How can we get in touch with them?"

He looked a little confused, like he couldn't quite process what was going on. "Eric! How can we get their number? Information? Do you know where they live? What about the Net?"

She was pacing back and forth now and didn't notice him scribbling on a scrap of paper until he grabbed her by the leg. "Try this number. It's ten years old, but they might still live there."

She froze for a moment and then snatched the paper from his hand. "Why the hell didn't you tell me you knew it!"

"I just did."

"Should I call or you?"

"I think you. I'm not exactly on speaking terms with Lisa's parents, you know?"

"Oh. Right."

The phone on the other end was on its third ring when Quinn started her chant. "Please be there, please be there."

"Hello?" A woman's voice.

"Hello . . . Mrs. Egan?"

"Speaking."

"Mrs. Egan. This is Quinn Barry with the FBI."

Silence.

"Are you there?"

"I'm sorry, did you say the FBI?"

"Yes, ma'am. I apologize for springing this on you over the phone, but we've reopened the case relating to your daughter's death."

Another silence.

"Are you all right, ma'am?"

"Did you find some new evidence? Have you . . . have you arrested Eric Twain?"

"Uh, no. Actually, Mr. Twain is no longer a suspect."

Eric's smile was a little sad, but he managed to give her a weak thumbs-up.

"No longer a suspect?"

"No, ma'am. We have proof that he wasn't involved. We think that Lisa's death might be connected with the deaths of a number of other young women . . ."

"Oh, my God. But the police told us—"

"I need to ask you a question," she said, cutting the woman off. "It's very important. Do you recall if your daughter ever applied to the University of Virginia?"

She didn't answer immediately, and with every second of silence, Quinn's heart rate notched a little higher.

"I believe she did, yes."

"She did?"

Eric stood and walked over to her, putting his ear near the phone.

"Yes, she did. She didn't go there, though. She just applied as . . . what did she call it? A backup."

Eric moved in front of her and mouthed the word **interview**. Quinn nodded her understanding.

"Did she ever physically visit the campus or go for an interview?"

"Um . . . no. She never did."

Eric suddenly looked a little deflated.

"Thank you, Mrs. Egan, you've been very helpful. We'll keep you informed."

"Wait! Could—"

Quinn replaced the receiver and watched Eric start pacing around the room again.

"How would he know?" he said.

"What?"

"What she looked like? She was never there."

Quinn chewed her thumbnail and then picked up the phone again and dialed information.

"What city?"

"Charlottesville. The University of Virginia Admissions Office. Could you just connect me, please?"

There were a few clicks over the line.

"Admissions, this is Carla. Can I help you?"

"Hi, yeah. I had a question about your application procedure. Do you ask for a picture of the person applying?"

"A picture? No."

"You don't?" Quinn suddenly felt a little weak and sat down on the box behind her. She'd been so sure this was it. That they'd found the connection.

"No, ma'am. We took that off the application in 1998. You understand that it was always optional and that the university didn't—"

"Score," Quinn said, replacing the handset.

"No way—they ask for a picture on their application?"

"Until 1998."

"Jesus." He started pacing again.

"This has to be it," Quinn said. "He must have worked at UVA in some capacity that gave him access to undergrad applications. He'd pick the ones he was interested in—smart, pretty girls. Then he'd wait . . ." Her voice trailed off as she felt the hairs on the back of her neck start to stand up. The thought of some freak poring over the pictures of little girls, looking at their grades, reading through their essays, deciding whether or not they would make entertaining victims . . .

"And he'd watch," Eric said, completing her thought. "He'd see what they did with their lives. How they turned out. And if they still interested him when they got old enough . . ."

Quinn leaned forward and propped her elbows on her knees, only half listening to what he was saying. This was it. They finally knew something about the killer. For the first time since all this had started, they had an edge. But she knew it wouldn't last.

"What do you want to do, Quinn? We've got enough now, don't you think? All someone has to do is go through the employment records at UVA and find the white males who had access to that information over the right time period. Then find the one who works for Advanced Thermal Dynamics."

"Who's 'someone'?" Quinn said.

"What?"

Quinn looked up at him. "Who do we call? You left part of the description out. Someone who worked for UVA and is now a powerful member of some organization with serious resources. Remember CODIS? Remember Renquist?"

"There must be someone at the FBI we can call, Quinn. Someone who isn't connected with CODIS. Someone we can trust."

She shook her head. "I don't know . . . Maybe. There's a guy named Mark Beamon . . ."

Eric stopped pacing. "Where have I heard that name before . . . ? Isn't he the guy who got in all that trouble over those phone taps? It was in the papers."

"Yeah. He's the head of the FBI's Phoenix office now. Word is, he's kind of a nut. But he's not for sale."

Eric waved a hand toward the phone, but she didn't move.

"What about the men who burned down your house, Eric? You said they looked like the government."

"I think anyone who wears a suit looks like the government. Doesn't necessarily mean anything."

"But what if you're right? What if there isn't anybody being paid off at the FBI? What if the FBI's involved?"

He considered that for a moment but then shook his head. "I think that's kind of a long leap."

She leaned back against the wall, but didn't say anything.

"Quinn?" he said a little hesitantly. "It **is** a long leap. Right?"

She still didn't answer.

"You're not telling me something. What is it?"

Finally, she sat up straight again and met his gaze. "Promise you won't be mad?"

43

eady?"

Susan Prescott held her automatic pistol up next to her face and gave a short nod as Brad Lowell slid the key card into the lock. He looked around him at the empty hall one more time and then threw the door open, jumping into the hotel room with his gun held out in front of him. Prescott cut efficiently behind him, dragging the closet door open as she ran into the small bathroom.

"Clear," she said.

"Shit!" Lowell moved to the center of the room and turned in a slow circle, examining every corner. Quinn Barry had been there as little as two hours ago, when she had called Lisa Egan's parents to ask questions about the University of Virginia.

"All right, Susan. Let's see what we can find."

All the furniture that wasn't bolted down had been shoved against the wall. Lowell looked under the bed and went through the tangled blankets as Prescott opened the drawers in the bureau.

"Anything?"

She pulled out a pencil and shaded a pad of cheap hotel stationery to see if anything had been written on it. "Nothing."

"God **damn** it."

"They didn't check out at the desk, sir. They may be back."

He shook his head and pulled a cell phone from his pocket. "No. They're gone."

She continued halfheartedly to search the room, dragging the bed away from the wall as he dialed.

"Sir? You'd better take a look at this."

He stepped forward and read the words scrawled on the wall in black marker.

HIGH SCHOOL
SATs
JOB SEARCHES
UNDERGRAD
GRAD
SECURITY CLEARANCES
OTHER STUFF

"Get a picture," he said as the phone at the other end rang twice and was picked up.

"Hello?"

"There's no one here. What've you got?"

"They contacted two of the other families as well, sir . . . In person."

"Christ."

The families of Marin's victims had been too low priority to waste valuable manpower on. He'd been forced to rely strictly on phone taps. "Which ones?"

"Dorsey and Tanner."

"And?"

"Barry identified herself as an FBI employee and told the parents that the Bureau's investigating a possible connection between their daughter's death and the deaths of other young women around the country. They asked to see the victim's personal effects. They were particularly interested in written records and documents."

Prescott had moved most of the furniture away from the wall to get a clearer angle for a photograph and Lowell looked again at the writing. "Let me guess. Stuff relating to high school, college, and jobs they had."

There was a brief silence over the phone. "Yes, sir. How did you—"

"Did they get them?"

"Yes, sir. They left both houses with a number of boxes."

Lowell nodded into the phone. That would explain why the furniture had been moved; they used the floor to organize what they'd been given. "And we've got nothing from the families of the other women?"

"No, sir. Should we reassign some men to their houses?"

He thought about that for a moment. Quinn Barry was proving to be an extremely persistent and unexpectedly clever adversary. What would she do?

"No," he said finally. "But take Sanderson off Barry's father's farm and send him to UVA."

"With any particular orders, sir?"

"Just tell him to keep his eyes open—Quinn Barry may make an appearance. Any activity on the other phone taps?"

"None, sir."

Lowell cut off the connection just as the flash on Susan Prescott's camera went off.

"Got it?"

"Yes, sir."

"And there's nothing else here?"

"Not that I can find."

"Then let's get the hell out."

44

Eric leaned a little farther under the hood but had no idea what he was looking at. He adjusted the baseball cap and sunglasses he was wearing and shot a sideways glance across the engine of the rented Suburban.

They'd been stopped on the side of the Washington Beltway, about ten miles from Langley, for a half hour now. The space between cars flowing by seemed to be increasing by about an inch a minute as rush hour slowly waned, but it was still only up to about six feet. Why on earth had he agreed to this? It seemed that all Quinn needed to do was bat her eyelashes a few times and he'd agree to set his hair on fire. Resistance was futile . . .

At least there were no police. Not yet, anyway. But the longer they stayed there, the better the chance that their luck would run out. Quinn had told him what to say to a cop about the engine and had promised to come and bail him out if the questions got too tough. At this point, though, that didn't make him feel a whole lot better. In the situation they currently found themselves in, it was probably best not to act any more suspicious than absolutely necessary.

"Eric!"

He worked his way around to the left until he could see her hanging out the passenger-side window.

"That's him! Come on! Let's go!"

He slammed the hood and jumped behind the wheel, immediately starting to accelerate down the shoulder. No one seemed particularly inclined to let him in, so he found a meticulously maintained Jaguar and forced his way in front of it.

"Where?" he said over the frustrated horn blasts coming from behind them.

She was scanning the thick traffic ahead, concentration etched deeply into her normally unlined face. "I . . . I lost him. I don't see him!"

"Take it easy, Quinn. He didn't get far in this mess." Eric forced the truck over into the center lane. It seemed to be moving a little faster.

"There!" Quinn said, finally. "The Lexus SUV five cars up. Do you see it?"

"I got it. How much farther to the exit?"

Quinn leaned over and looked through the steering wheel at the trip odometer. "Four point three miles."

"Okay. No problem."

He tried to make his multiple lane changes as smooth as possible, concerned that he might start to look suspicious to anyone paying attention. In the end, though, he wasn't driving any more erratically than anyone else. Just a typical government worker anxious to get home to his big-screen TV and fridge full of Miller Lite.

After three miles, they were still two cars behind.

"Come on, Eric! There's just over a mile to go. You're gonna lo—"

"Quinn!" he said. "You're making me nervous, okay?"

She fell silent, but continued to grip the dash with white-knuckled ferocity.

He managed to squeeze into an opening and gun the truck forward. With less than a half mile to go, he closed to within a few feet of the Lexus in the lane to its right.

"Okay, just stay here," Quinn said. "He's going to have to get over. All you have to do is let him in."

Eric glanced in his rearview mirror and saw a generic-looking blue sedan ease in behind him. There were two men inside, both wearing suits. It didn't mean anything, he told himself.

Everybody within fifty miles of D.C. looked like that.

"This is the exit," Quinn said excitedly.

As if its driver had heard her, the Lexus's signal went on. Eric tapped the brake and let the car in, then followed it to the exit. Another quick look in the rearview mirror confirmed that the blue sedan was still there.

"See those guys behind us?"

Quinn twisted around in her seat for a moment. "You recognize them?"

He shook his head. "Can't see their faces. They just seem like the type."

"Do you want to call it off?"

Damn right he did.

"No."

Eric could just barely make out a traffic light at the end of the off-ramp. It turned red and they rolled to a stop. About a minute later it went green and allowed them to move forward a bit before they were forced to stop again.

"Okay," Quinn said. "Six cars are getting through. That means four more lights."

Eric could feel the sweat building on his lip and he tried to wipe it away without her noticing.

"Are you scared?" she said.

"I guess. A little. You?"

"Yeah."

They moved forward again and stopped.

"This is going to work, Eric. Don't worry."

"I didn't say I was worried. Just scared."

They sat in silence until the light ran two more cycles.

"Okay," Quinn said. "This is it. Give us some room."

Eric slowed and let the Lexus open up a fifty-foot gap before it was forced to stop again. He ignored the sound of horns as he inched forward.

"Thirty seconds," Quinn said, staring at her watch.

He gripped the wheel a little tighter.

"Fifteen . . . GO!"

He slammed the accelerator to the floor and turned the wheel hard, listening to the squeal of rubber as the truck drifted sideways and stopped ten feet behind the Lexus. Quinn threw her door open and had already cleared the truck when he slammed it into reverse and centered it, broadside, between the concrete barriers on either side of the ramp.

He was out and halfway over the hood when he heard the sound of a gunning engine behind him. When he looked back, though, it wasn't the blue sedan he'd expected. It was an old VW two cars back. The little car was running up the small shoulder, throwing sparks as its door scraped against the concrete barrier.

He slid off the hood of the Suburban and started running full speed toward Quinn and the Lexus.

She was well ahead of him, and he watched her yank the passenger door open at precisely the same time he heard an explosive impact behind him.

He dared a look over his shoulder but continued to run.

The Suburban **had** been long enough—but only barely. The VW had hit it full force, trying to throw the back end around and squeeze through. Thanks to Galileo Galilei and his elegant laws of inertia, though, the VW was now stuck—wedged between the Suburban and a few tons of concrete.

The back window of the Lexus was open, so Eric didn't bother with the door. He just dove in.

"GO! GO!" he heard Quinn yelling as he rolled on his back and struggled to get his legs fully inside. When he finally succeeded, he knelt on the seat, facing the back window. Someone had emerged from the VW, and whoever he was, he was fast. He'd already cleared the Suburban.

"What the fuck!" Eric heard the man behind the wheel say. It was then that it registered with him that the car wasn't moving. He pulled a knife from his back pocket and spun around, putting it to the man's throat. "Step on the gas or I'm going to kill you. Do you understand?"

In reality, it was just a dull piece of silverware he'd stolen from room service. Even more pathetic was the fact that it was still stained with mashed potatoes. He hypothesized, though, that all knives felt sharper and shinier than they really were if pressed against your jugular.

His theory proved correct and the car started to accelerate, running the red and turning onto a busy street lined with strip malls.

"Left here," Quinn said.

The driver did as he was told and they eventually found themselves cruising through an expensive-looking residential area.

Quinn twisted around and looked out the rear window. Before falling back into her seat, she glanced at Eric and rolled her eyes, exhaling loudly.

"You want to call off your dog, Quinn?"

She nodded at Eric and he pulled the knife away.

"David Bergin. I'd like you to meet Eric Twain."

Their eyes locked in the rearview mirror.

"Watch where you're driving, David."

His angry stare lingered for a few more seconds and then returned to the road. "What the hell is going on, Quinn? Where have you been? Why didn't you show up that night in the park?"

"I was there," she said. "I was watching you while we talked on the phone. Who'd you call after I hung up?"

"What? I don't know . . . I don't remember."

It was an obvious lie, and from what Eric could see of Quinn's face, she knew it.

"Who did you tell that I was going to see my dad for the weekend?"

"What the hell are you talking about? Quinn—"

"Answer my question!"

"Who would I tell? Who would care? Have you gone nuts? You had this asshole hold a knife to my throat and cause a car accident—"

"Someone siphoned my tank and jammed my fuel gauge that night, David. And then, when I ran out of gas, they stopped and pulled a gun on me."

"Quinn—"

"Then, a few days later, someone shot me." She pulled off her baseball cap, wincing a little as she did, and showed him the bandaged wound on the back of her head.

Bergin didn't seem to have an indignant response for that.

"If it weren't for Eric, I'd be dead."

Bergin glanced in the mirror again as Eric settled into the soft leather of the seat. "If that's true, then I guess I owe you."

The possessiveness in his voice was meant to be obvious. Eric raised his hand and extended his middle finger. The fact that this arrogant, buttoned-down prick had dated Quinn Barry was definite proof that all was not right with the world.

"Who did you call, David?"

"Quinn, I have no idea what you're ta—"

"Don't give me that, David! We were in that park at three in the morning. You're going to sit there and tell me you can't remember who you called? Try thinking real hard."

He turned right and came out on a narrow road densely lined with trees. Quinn spun sideways in her seat and was glaring at him so intently Eric could almost feel it. He figured no one could hold up to that for much more than a minute. Bergin lasted only about thirty seconds.

"Military Intelligence."

"What? Oh my God."

"Is that who was following you?" Eric said. "In the VW?"

Bergin shook his head. "I don't know . . . I didn't know anybody was following me . . ."

"What's going on, David?" Quinn said. "Just tell me what's going on."

He was silent for a moment, trying to decide what to do. "You're suspected of stealing FCI information from the FBI's computers . . ."

"You have **got** to be kidding," Eric said, leaning up between the front seats. "What does the government give you for betraying a friend, David? Do you get a better parking space or something?"

"Hey, fuck you! I—"

"Stop it!" Quinn yelled. "Both of you. Just shut up!"

"Asshole," Eric mumbled, falling back into the seat again and folding his arms across his chest.

"FCI, David. What's that?"

"Foreign counterintelligence. Look, Quinn . . . When they came to me and told me this, I knew you had nothing to do with it. I thought if I did what they asked, I could help prove that. I could make sure nothing happened to you."

She gazed out the window, considering his words. "You bastard. That day I came home and found you in my apartment . . . You weren't there to apologize. You were searching it and didn't expect me home that early."

"Quinn—"

"And then you fed me that bullshit story about your brakes going so you could take my car and search it."

He just hung his head as she twisted around and looked at Eric. "What do you think?"

"I think we have serious problems." He jerked his head toward Bergin. "He's CIA. As for that guy in the VW, take your pick. Military Intelligence, CIA, FBI. You know this dweeb better than I do. It's your call."

Bergin shot him another angry look, but all Eric could do was shake his head. Despite everything that was going on, there was no guilt or concern in his expression. Just jealousy.

"If I tell you what's really happening, David, will you help us?"

He didn't react immediately but finally gave a short nod.

"David. Look at me."

He sighed quietly, but did as she asked.

"Will you help us?"

"Yes, okay? Yes."

"I think we should tell him, Eric. He wasn't directly involved with them trying to grab me on my way to my dad's. He would have known I'd figure out what was wrong with the car."

"Like I said. Your call."

She took a deep breath and started. "Okay, David, here it is. When the CODIS system was originally programmed, it was designed not to recognize a certain DNA signature. That signature belongs to a man who has killed at least five women."

"What are you talking about?"

"It was deliberate, David. Somebody doesn't want anyone to find out this . . . this psychopath exists."

"Who? Why would anyone want to cover up something like that?"

"I don't know why. But obviously the military is involved. And they've involved the CIA and the FBI. But it all seems to revolve around a company called Advanced Thermal Dynamics. Have you ever heard of it?"

He shook his head.

"I realize you probably don't believe any of this right now; all I'm asking is that you look into it. And when you find out I'm telling the truth, you help us figure out what to do, who we can trust. Will you do that?"

He drummed his hands on the wheel as they continued to glide along the quiet road. "I can make a few calls."

"Hey, don't put yourself out," Eric said, but Quinn held her hand up and silenced him.

Bergin jotted something down on a small pad stuck to his windshield and tore the page off. "This is the number for my secure line. Call me tomorrow evening around seven. I'll know something by then."

She nodded. "Okay. Stop here."

"What?"

"Stop here."

He did as she asked, pulling into a shallow clearing in the trees.

"Get out."

"Quinn, come on—"

She leaned over him and threw his door open. "You heard me. Out!"

Eric climbed up through the seats and dropped behind the wheel as Bergin jumped down onto the gravel shoulder and slammed the door shut.

"Could I borrow your cell phone for a second, David?" Eric said as he rolled down the window.

Bergin reached into his jacket and pulled out his phone, placing it in Eric's outstretched hand. He promptly threw it over the top of the truck into the woods.

"Goddammit!"

Eric ignored the outburst and dangled a set of keys out the window. "These are to that Suburban. Don't dent it, okay, Chief? It's rented."

45

Brad Lowell wasn't sure if the problem was that the lock was particularly stubborn or if it was that the slight shaking in his hands was throwing him off. He knelt, bringing his face even with the knob of Edward Marin's front door and tried to let his mind go blank. For a moment he was able to squelch his anger and nervous excitement. It turned out to be long enough. The door clicked open and he entered, watching his team spread out around him.

Everything in its place.

Lowell moved slowly, studying Marin's living room with feigned detachment. The sparse furniture was meticulously polished and arranged in a perfectly aligned pattern. No dust, no marks on walls or carpet. It was as if Marin kept the house, and himself, hermetically sealed. But all that was about to change.

"Geller, you're in the basement; Susan, upstairs," he said. "I'll take the main floor."

Lowell walked up to an elegant grandfather clock filled with gleaming crystal, and in one swift motion, pulled it over. The sound of splintering wood and shattering glass was like music to him. Two solid kicks broke open the back and he used gloved hands to rip out the gears and wheels inside.

"Search everything."

At that, his men disappeared, and in less than a minute a symphony of destruction floated to him on the still air. Lowell almost managed a smile as he unsheathed a long military knife and started in on one of the two leather sofas that dominated the room. Price had tied his hands as far as Marin's physical well-being was concerned but had been wonderfully nonspecific in his orders relating to this operation.

Ten more minutes of wanton vandalism revealed that nothing of interest was hidden in the living room. But then, he'd already suspected that.

The kitchen was next. He used his arm to sweep the expensive china and cooking utensils from the counter, letting them crash to the tile floor as he began emptying the cabinets.

Nothing.

He walked into the dining room, hearing the broken glass crunch beneath his boots, and began forcing the drawers out of an antique sideboard.

Marin was laughing at them. Price chose to ignore it, but he was laughing at them. He was steadily, purposefully pushing—testing his boundaries. And every time they did nothing, he knew he could push just a little further. But this would be the end of him. Price wouldn't be able to turn away from this. He'd finally have to act.

The glass display cabinet that covered much of the wall took almost no time. Lowell opened it and threw every ornately decorated bowl and vase it contained against the hard mahogany of the dining table, making sure each was completely destroyed.

"Sir?"

He could barely hear the voice in his earpiece over the sound of shattering porcelain.

"Sir?"

Lowell pressed two fingers against his throat mike. "Go ahead."

"I might have something in the basement."

Lowell sighed quietly and dropped the delicately painted soup bowl in his hand. He'd hoped it would take more time.

· · ·

"It was under the stairs, sir."

Lowell took the last two steps to the basement floor somewhat reluctantly, seeing that it, too, was obsessively arranged and antiseptically clean—with one exception. A heavy metal box sitting alone on a low bench. Covered with dents and scratches and beginning to rust in the slightly humid air, it seemed completely out of place. Only the stainless-steel lock hanging from the front looked new.

"Sir, should we take it to . . ."

Geller fell silent when Lowell reached into his jacket and pulled out his nine-millimeter.

"Sir?"

He dove to the floor when Lowell fired, covering his head with his hands and not daring to move again until the echo of the shot had completely subsided.

Lowell ignored Geller's shocked stare as he stepped forward and pulled the broken lock off the front of the box.

"Sir? Are you all right?"

Lowell didn't answer, instead digging a handful of soft silk and nylon from the box.

"Should I call off the search upstairs, sir?"

Lowell stared down at the bloodstained panties in his hand for a moment. "No. Let her keep working. No reason not to be thorough."

What he was looking for was near the bottom—a thick manila envelope, nearly worn through at its edges. He held it up to the naked bulb hanging from the ceiling, feeling its weight and looking at the dark shadow of its contents.

"Good-bye, Dr. Marin."

46

Every minute, the clock seemed to be moving a little slower.

Quinn adjusted herself into a more comfortable position on the sofa and stared at the ceiling, trying to listen simultaneously to the television and to Eric's muffled voice coming from the hotel suite's bedroom. Neither was completely intelligible, but the noise was somehow comforting.

Most of the last five hours had been a waste of time. She'd talked to no fewer than five people at the University of Virginia, none of whom was even remotely interested in giving out personnel records over the phone or by any other electronic means. Eric had protested violently when she'd suggested pointing the car toward Charlottesville, where her overused FBI clerk's ID might get them further.

And, in the end, she'd decided he was right. First, she wasn't convinced that it would do any good. How could she, or anyone else, be sure exactly who'd had access to undergraduate applications that long ago? And even if she did get some reliable information on this particular subject, how many names would there be? A hundred? Five hundred?

And then there was the question of safety. Whoever was after them seemed to turn up in the most inconvenient places. Was someone waiting for her at UVA? Based on what she'd learned over the last few days, it seemed possible. Maybe even likely. Before they did anything that might get them killed, they needed more information.

Eric had an intense distrust of David—and rightfully so—but still, it made sense to sit tight until they heard what he had to say. If she could be sure of anything anymore, it was that David had always been a terrible liar. She generally believed what he had told her in the car, though Eric was wholly unconvinced.

After striking out at UVA, she'd spent two hours calling old friends in the computer business, hoping that someone would be familiar with Advanced Thermal Dynamics. Another swing and a miss. Forget about specific names, places, or projects—no one had even heard of the company. Eric was still working through his contacts in the scientific community. Hopefully, his luck would be a little better. It couldn't be much worse.

The only thing she'd done the entire day that might be even remotely helpful was to refine her profile of the man they were after—and who, it seemed, was after them. She glanced down at the yellow legal pad in her lap again, examining the mark-outs, arrows, and boxes that almost completely obliterated her original notes. Despite the visual chaos, it seemed to be finally coming together. Or at least the individual pieces were starting to loosely relate to one another. With a few scraps of information on ATD—to be provided, she hoped, by David later that evening—she might be able to wrap everything up into a coherent theory. Though she was becoming less and less sure she wanted to.

Something familiar suddenly caught her attention and she turned toward the television, sitting upright quickly enough to dump the legal pad onto the floor.

". . . until three days ago, this was the home of Eric Twain, a renowned physicist employed by Johns Hopkins University."

The newscaster was walking slowly to her right as she spoke, allowing the camera to pan the length of the blackened pile of brick and wood that Eric had put so much of himself into.

". . . according to anonymous law enforcement sources, there was a 911 call the morning of the fire, placed from Twain's home and reporting a murder. Two officers were dispatched and called in their arrival, but then there were no further communications. When their backup arrived, they found the building already ablaze. The last report we have is that three bodies have been pulled from the rubble. Two appear to be the police officers and one is as yet unidentified—possibly Twain."

Quinn watched, transfixed, as the woman continued walking, framing out the firefighters picking through the rubble for a more subdued background.

"This will only serve to intensify the controversy surrounding Eric Twain, who, when he was only seventeen, was investigated for the brutal murder of a woman he was involved with. Due to lack of evidence, he was not indicted, but that murder remains unsolved . . ."

Quinn heard movement to her left and turned to see Eric standing in the doorway. His hands were gripping the top of the jamb and he was partially using his arms to support himself as he stared at the television.

"Eric, I . . . I'm so sorry . . ."

"Why? It's not your fault."

"I called the police, I . . ."

Her voice trailed off as his hands dropped from the door frame and he walked silently back into the bedroom. What was there to say? When the police discovered that the unidentified body belonged to a young woman, their decade-long suspicion of Eric would be confirmed.

She fell back into the sofa again, closing her eyes tight and covering her face with her hands. By what seemed to be silent mutual consent, they still hadn't talked about what David had told them. They had driven to the hotel in uninterrupted silence, their minds trying to grasp the involvement of military intelligence and the CIA, but not yet prepared to speak of it. It was almost as if saying any of it out loud would make it real.

But now they knew that two policemen were dead. The men that had burst into Eric's home had efficiently killed and burned them with no apparent fear of reprisal or discovery . . .

Quinn squeezed her eyes shut tighter, until she could see bright pinpoints of light flashing on and off behind her eyelids. The throbbing in her head, unrelenting for two days now, intensified, filling her entire body.

What had either of them ever done to deserve this?

When Quinn opened her eyes again, the throbbing in her head had faded almost to nothing. The shades were drawn and the television had been turned off. She pushed herself into a sitting position, noticing the blanket covering her only when it dropped to her waist.

She looked down at her watch, barely able to read it in the dim light. Five o'clock.

Quinn padded across the room in her stockinged feet and slipped quietly through the bedroom door, finding Eric with his feet propped on the bed and a phone pressed against his ear. She crawled across the bedspread and flopped down on it.

"Are you all right?" he mouthed, running his fingers through her short hair.

Quinn answered by taking his hand in hers and pressing it against her cheek.

"Hello?" he said. His hand slipped away and he used it to press the phone harder to his ear. "Hello? Yes. Stephen Hawking, please."

Quinn felt her eyebrows rise at the name but wasn't sure why she was surprised. She lifted a pad of hotel stationery from his lap and looked at it while he was waiting to be connected. The first two pages were full but completely illegible. Sentences were written with no regard to straightness, often looping around on top of other sentences and running off the page. Even individual letters seemed to be from a different alphabet than the one she knew.

"Jane? Eric Twain. Is Stephen in? Thanks."

He looked up at her for a moment and crossed his fingers. "Stephen? Eric." Long pause. "I'm good. Question for you. Is anyone in your department doing math for a company called Advanced Thermal Dynamics?" Another long pause. "You're sure." He sighed quietly as he listened. "Yeah. I'm hoping to be there . . . Uh-huh . . . Okay. I'll see you then. Thanks."

"**The** Stephen Hawking?" Quinn said as he replaced the handset.

Eric nodded. "But he didn't know anything."

"What's all this?" Quinn said, handing the pad back to him. "I can't read a word."

"Two hits," he said.

"Really? You found something?"

"Celestial mechanics and a computer programming problem. I don't have any details on the first yet, but the second has something to do with artificial intelligence. There are a lot of university people I couldn't reach—they were in class. I left messages and they're going to get back to me."

"Do you think that's safe?"

"I didn't leave a number, just my e-mail address. No way to trace us to a physical location with just that."

"What did the two people you talked to say?"

He shrugged. "Not much. They work the same way I do—they don't really know anything about the company."

"What about the stuff they're working on?"

"I don't know yet. I woke both of them up—one was in Japan and the other India. We should get the details later tonight."

They both fell silent for a moment.

"Eric, about what happened . . ."

"It wasn't your fault, Quinn."

"I called the police. I—"

He stood abruptly and reached out to her. She

took his hand and let herself be pulled off the bed. "I would have called the police myself if I'd been in your position. I'm sorry for what happened to them . . . But I'd be a lot sorrier if it was you back there."

The pay phone was thirty miles from their hotel, next to an all but abandoned Dairy Queen. Eric wanted to go even farther but she had finally convinced him to stop. Even if she was wrong about David and he was going to betray her again, they'd be long gone before anybody made it out to this backwater. She finished dialing and leaned in close to Eric, partially so he could hear and partially to keep warm in the cutting wind.

"Perry," came the voice on the other end of the phone. She was confused for a moment; David had given her this number and told her to call at seven P.M. She looked at her watch. Seven on the dot.

Eric stepped away and started jabbing a finger in the direction of the phone, trying to get her to hang up. She shook her head.

"Hello?" the voice said. "Is there anyone there?"

"Kenny?"

The frustrated breath escaping between Eric's teeth was audible even over the wind. She shot him an apologetic look as he moved in again and put his ear close to the handset.

"Quinn? Is that you?"

"Yeah, Kenny. It's me."

She'd known Ken Perry for almost a year. A short, pudgy man who looked ten years older than the thirty-two she knew him to be, he had been one of the few people she'd met through David who'd always been nice to her.

"What are you doing on a secure line?"

"David gave me this number. Is he there?"

Eric clamped a hand over the mouthpiece. "He's stalling us!"

She pulled away.

"Kenny?"

"You haven't heard . . ."

"Heard what?"

No answer.

"Heard what, Kenny?"

"David . . . he was car-jacked yesterday."

Quinn looked at Eric and rolled her eyes. "Car-jacked. Really? Is he okay?" she said, affecting surprise.

"Quinn . . . I'm so sorry to have to tell you this. He didn't make it."

Her mind went blank for a moment and it took her a few seconds to get it back on-line. "What . . . what are you talking about?"

"We don't have a lot of details yet, Quinn. The eyewitness accounts say a man and woman blocked traffic with a Suburban, jumped in his car, then took off. They, uh, they found him by the side of the road about ten miles away. He'd been shot . . . Quinn? Are you there?"

She leaned her forehead against the metal edge of the booth and let the phone fall from her hand. She could hear Kenny's tinny voice calling her name as Eric picked up the handset and hung it up.

"Oh God," she mumbled. "Oh God."

Eric pulled her against him and held her as she started to sob. She tried to regain control of herself, but it had gone beyond that now. David, the woman in Eric's apartment, the seemingly omnipotent men trying to get to her—it all flooded out of her in uncontrollable waves. "We're never going to get out of this," she sobbed. "Never."

He pulled her closer and she could feel the warmth of his chest melt into hers.

"Don't give up now, Quinn. You're about all I've got."

He held her for a few more seconds then pulled away, looking directly into her eyes. "I'm sorry, but we've got to get out of here. There's just no time for this right now."

47

They stayed so much closer now.

Marin glanced in the rearview mirror and saw the black Ford cross a double yellow line to pass the car in front of it and once again settle in twenty feet from his bumper.

He'd always known they were there, of course. But it had been so much more subtle—an occasional glimpse, an intercepted surveillance report detailing his activities, an out-of-time click on his telephone. All that had changed now. As he knew it had to. His ever-present watchers would never again retreat to a respectful and discreet distance.

He smiled to himself as he turned off the quiet rural highway into his driveway. He increased his speed slightly, watching them drop back as he negotiated the winding eighth of a mile to his house.

The Ford never reappeared from the last bend; undoubtedly it was stopped in the narrowest point of the tree-lined corridor, making it impossible for him to leave without the driver knowing. The sudden intensification of his relationship with Price's brood was exhilarating.

Marin parked the car in front of his garage and started for his house through the fading sunlight. He'd left ATD early that day and spent the past three hours just driving. The work would continue to pile up—reports, queries, theoretical data from far-flung consultants—but he couldn't focus long enough even to pretend anymore. It was all too close now.

Marin reached out to slide his key into the front doorlock, but when he touched it, the door drifted back a few inches. He didn't move for a moment, finally coming back to life when he heard the crunching of leaves behind him. He turned and watched the two men approach.

"After you, Dr. Marin," one of them said. He actually wasn't sure which—his mind was too busy recalculating his position. He had anticipated the more obvious presence of Lowell's men, but hadn't expected them to go this far.

"Sir," the man behind him prompted again.

Marin straightened, rising to his full height, and reconfigured his expression into one of complete calm as he stepped across the threshold.

Richard Price was sitting in the middle of the

living room on the only piece of furniture that was still intact: a straight-backed chair that had been brought in from the dining room. Brad Lowell stood behind him, an arrogant smile playing at his lips.

Marin swiveled his head from side to side as he continued toward Price, taking in the utter destruction of what had once been his perfectly ordered home and trying to hold back the unfamiliar sense of uncertainty that was suddenly gnawing at him. Was this meant to be some sort of punishment? No, Price would never do anything so vulgar and pointless. Then why?

"General Price," he said in a tone thick with a confidence that he no longer felt. Had he pushed too far? "Welcome to my home."

Price didn't answer and didn't move from his chair, instead watching silently as his men took up positions at the edges of the room.

"It appears that we didn't understand one another last time we spoke, Doctor."

They stood staring at one another for a long time. Marin wasn't sure what the correct reply was, so he said nothing. The situation was still too murky to commit to a strategy.

Price reached into his pocket and held out a five-by-seven photograph. "Take it."

Marin didn't normally react to orders, but it was perhaps time to defuse the situation. Besides, he was curious.

"Does it mean anything to you?"

Marin examined the photograph carefully. It depicted a wall in what looked like a hotel room. Someone had written on it in tall block letters. He had to bring the picture close to his face to make out the individual words.

"Eric Twain," he said, stepping forward and handing the photograph back to Price.

"What?"

"Eric Twain," Marin repeated. "When he first started at Hopkins he actually used crayons. After a year I don't think there was an inch of his office that didn't have an equation scrawled across it in some color or another. I would have hoped he'd outgrow—"

"Do you know what the words mean?"

They meant that Eric and his stunning companion were getting close. Very close. Wonderful. Their timing couldn't have been better. "I'm sorry to say that I don't."

Price nodded gravely and slid the photo back into his pocket. "Maybe I can be of help. Quinn Barry went to visit the families of Catherine Tanner and Shannon Dorsey, whom, I'm sure, you recall. She left with many of their personal belongings. Later she called Lisa Egan's mother and asked her if her daughter ever applied to the University of Virginia. Why do you think she did that?"

Marin considered his next words carefully. Price

was, of course, fully aware that he had worked at UVA for many years. Was denial still plausible?

"I have no idea."

"No idea," Price repeated. "I see. Well, I have one more thing that might help jog your memory."

Marin felt his breath catch in his chest when Brad Lowell bent over and pulled an old metal box from behind Price's chair.

"Is something wrong?" Lowell mocked as he opened it.

Marin took a half step forward but managed to stop himself. He tried to restore the passive mask he'd worn a moment before, to pull his eyes away from the box, but it was impossible. His stomach rolled sickeningly and he felt bile burning his throat as Lowell put his hand inside the box and began emptying it. He paused cruelly with each handful, running the colorful material slowly through his fingers, stealing from Marin what was his only—the soft, delicate sensation of silk, nylon, and cotton and the memories it provoked. The color of their eyes, the smell of them, their sweat-dampened skin. Their fear.

Marin stood frozen, the taste of blood now overpowering the burn of bile as his clenched teeth cut through his cheek. He took another half step forward, a jerky, graceless movement that he knew was beneath him. He was forced to stop again when the men surrounding him pulled their guns from their jackets and aimed at him in unison. Theatrics? He wasn't sure anymore.

And then, finally, it was over. Lowell let a pair of white cotton panties printed with roses fall from his fingers and produced a manila envelope from the bottom of the box. He extracted copies of the college applications it contained and handed them to Price.

"Do these ring any bells, Doctor?"

Marin's entire being was focused on Lowell, who stared back with near-equal intensity. It could end here. Marin knew he could cover the five feet between them in less than a second. He could almost feel it—Lowell's head in his hands, the snap of his neck, the dull ache of bullets piercing his body. What Lowell had taken from him would be returned in an instant. It would be his alone again.

No.

He could still control the situation. It wasn't time to let himself go. Not yet. He redirected his wet eyes to Price and gave him a respectful nod.

"Are there any more secrets between us, Doctor?"

"No more secrets."

Price clearly didn't believe him but seemed confident in the strength of his position. He had no way of knowing how fleeting it would be as he leafed through the applications in his lap, looking at the carefully reproduced photographs stapled to each.

"Such beautiful girls," he said. Marin's teeth clenched again as Price pulled a lighter from his jacket and set the stack of papers on fire. They burned quickly, finally falling from Price's hand and filling the room with the acrid odor of ash and burned carpet. It didn't matter, he told himself. Not anymore. It was just another example of entropy—all things descended into chaos eventually.

Brad Lowell pressed the device beneath his collar as he followed Price down the steps and out into Edward Marin's driveway. "Bring the general's car."

"We'll walk."

"Sir, we can have—"

Price waved a hand dismissively and continued on, trying to squelch his emotions and concentrate. There were too many unknowns now. How much longer could he allow this to go on? Control was slipping away, as he had always known it would. The hallmark of a leader was to know when it was about to slip so far it would become irretrievable. To know where that line was drawn.

He walked faster, trying unsuccessfully to draw calm from the still air and twilight surrounding him. If any of this ever became public, he would be abandoned and then crucified by the very men he served. And the American people would be all too happy to play along. Every night they expected to go home and crawl into their nice safe beds, but didn't really want to know what it took to keep them that way. They would wrap themselves in

their carefully crafted naïveté, and they would con-
demn him.

"Barry and Twain?" Price said as Lowell jogged
up alongside him.

"They're smart, sir. More resourceful than we
ever imagined. They aren't giving us much of a trail
to follow and they aren't taking the obvious route.
But I'm getting closer. I'll find them."

"When?"

"I can't answer that, sir."

"There's no telling how much damage they can
do. How much they've done already. We have to
find them, Brad. Alive if possible. If not . . ." He let
his voice trail off.

"Twain?"

"Do what you can to keep him alive. But it's no
longer a priority."

"Yes, sir."

"What about Marin?" Price said.

"We're making our presence known now—keeping him in visual contact, per your orders. It will be
much harder for him to slip us now."

"Make it impossible. You have to stay with him,
Brad. Mistakes are too expensive now."

"Am I to understand that there are no longer any
restrictions on my methods, sir?"

"None whatsoever," Price said, stopping and
grabbing hold of Lowell's arm. "I understand and
sympathize with your personal feelings on this,
Brad. Perhaps more than you know. But I need you

to put them aside. You understand how important he is, don't you? You understand that?"

"I do, sir."

"Then I can trust you with what I'm about to say. I can trust that you won't take advantage . . ."

"I've always carried out your orders to the letter, sir."

Price released the man's arm and put a hand on his shoulder. "I know you have, Brad. I know you have . . ."

"What is it, sir?"

Price sighed quietly. There was no choice anymore. "If Marin slips you again, track him down and get rid of him."

Lowell's face betrayed no reaction at all. "I understand."

48

Had he known the man who killed him?

What had David felt when he saw the gun? When he knew that the careful plans he had made for his life meant nothing? That the thirty-one years he'd already lived was all he was going to get?

Quinn covered her tear-filled eyes with her forearm, listening to Eric's unintelligible voice as he spoke on the phone in the other room. Unlike her, he was still working—trying to come up with something solid on ATD. Trying to get them out of this mess.

She finally forced herself to sit up, wiping her eyes with the sleeve of her sweater. Enough of this. The bastards who had caused all this were still out there and they weren't going to stop because she was crying. They'd keep coming. And unless she and Eric figured out who these men were and how to stop them, they would both end up like David.

She scooped up her legal pad from the floor and ripped off the mess of a profile she had been working on, leaving herself with a clean page. She'd hoped that David could fill some of the holes, but that obviously wasn't going to happen. She was just going to have to fill them herself.

Quinn was too engrossed in what she was doing to hear Eric approach. She didn't register his presence until he knelt behind the sofa and rested his chin on her shoulder.

"You okay?"

"I guess," she said, scanning the pages in her lap again. For the first time she had a profile that more or less fit together into one insane theory. But there was no way to know if it was even close to being accurate. In a way she hoped it wasn't.

Eric circled the sofa, falling into a chair next to it. "I'm not getting anywhere."

"What?"

"People are out of the office in the States and it's too late in Europe and too early in Asia."

"Did you find out anything new?"

He shook his head. "I haven't checked my e-mail yet, though—I left a lot of messages. What about you?"

She looked down at the pad in her lap. "I think I finished it."

"Finished what?"

"The profile I've been working on."

"Anything that can help us?"

She shook her head slowly. "I don't know. Maybe."

"Well, then why don't you hit me with it."

She took a deep breath and tried to focus on what she'd written. It was still about half voodoo. But it was the best she could do.

"White male between the ages of thirty-five and fifty. I'll amend my theory of him having above-average intelligence to suggesting that he is brilliant. He'd have been on staff at UVA in some kind of hard science that interests the government—or more precisely the military. For years he'd been killing young women who applied to UVA but didn't attend, and cleverly covering up their deaths. But sometime in the early nineties he starts getting cocky, or maybe starts losing control. He leaves evidence in one killing and a body in another. That all culminates in his attack on Lisa Egan, where it looks like he was interrupted."

"And he gets scared and changes his victim profile," Eric said. "We've been through this before."

Quinn hesitated for a moment. "I don't think he got scared. I . . . I think he got caught."

"Excuse me?"

"Think about it for a minute. During the police investigation, the real killer starts to come under suspicion. And at some point the military find out. They give your friend Renquist money, or in some other way coerce him to not pursue the real killer and to subtly change the evidence and direction of the investigation to focus on you. But not enough to get you into a court, where things might get examined too closely."

Eric leaned forward, resting his elbows on his knees. She seemed to have his full attention.

"So in 1992, shortly after Lisa's death, he'd have quit UVA and gone to work for Advanced Thermal Dynamics, which, as you said, is probably some kind of quasi-governmental organization . . ."

Eric suddenly looked a little distracted. His eyes were trained somewhere in front of him, but didn't seem to see anything.

"Are you listening?"

" 'So in 1992, shortly after Lisa's death, he'd have quit UVA and gone to work for Advanced Thermal Dynamics, which, as you said, is probably some kind of quasi-governmental organization . . .' " he repeated. It was like a recording, every inflection exactly in place, but she still wasn't sure he'd really heard.

"Okay. Things are quiet for a while after he starts with ATD. They saved him from prison and in return he works on whatever it is they're doing. But after a while he'd start obsessing, losing his ability to concentrate—guys like this rarely just stop. Maybe he attacks another woman—kills her perhaps—and they cover it up. Then they find out that he's all fat and happy and back to work."

"So they start feeding him victims," Eric said, finally breaking out of his self-induced trance. "Ones that won't cause a lot of suspicion. They'd use their contacts with law enforcement to find women already at risk. Basically fitting the physical type he likes, but poor and uneducated. After he kills them, they send those sons of bitches that were at my house to clean up and the body disappears . . ." He fell silent and Quinn picked up where he left off.

"And the police would naturally assume that the woman just took off, or that her husband or boyfriend or whoever killed her and dumped the body. But, with the advent of DNA evidence in the late eighties, it becomes impossible to totally clean a crime scene. So when CODIS goes into the planning stage, ATD makes the low bid and designs the system so that it won't recognize their man's DNA signature."

Eric jumped to his feet and started circling the room. For some reason, he almost looked like he was in pain.

"Eric. Is something wrong? Should I go on?"

He jerked his head forward in something that resembled a nod.

"Now for a little voodoo," she started slowly. "I'd guess this guy is arrogant and manipulative. It's fun for him to toy with these women, and us, and even his own cleanup crew—who he hates. He'd hate anyone connected with the military."

"That doesn't sound right," Eric protested. "He'd love the military. They feed him victims. Isn't that what you said?" He seemed to desperately want her to agree with him. But he wasn't thinking.

"We've talked about this. These kinds of crimes are about control. He's lost that. He no longer gets to hunt—he's just fed. And not even the right women. Victim profile and the hunt are very important to this guy. He needs to control all aspects of the experience. He likes highly intelligent, classy-looking young women and now he's forced to settle for women he would consider poor white trash . . ." She let her voice fade as the speed with which Eric was circling the room increased. "Eric, really. Are you okay?"

"Marin," he said in a voice almost too soft for her to hear.

"What did you say?"

He stopped suddenly and spun around to face her. "Nothing. I didn't say anything. I mean, you're not a profiler. Shit, you're just guessing."

"You **did** say something. What was it? Marin?"

He seemed to be unable to move, except for his eyes, which darted randomly around the room. It was a bizarre enough image to make Quinn walk over to him and slide a hand through his long hair.

She squeezed the back of his neck comfortingly. "Eric, what's wrong with you?"

He chewed his lip for a moment before he spoke. "Edward Marin."

"Who?"

He cocked his head and looked at her like he wasn't sure what she meant. **"Edward Marin."**

"You're not making any sense, Eric. Come on, let's sit down." She led him to the sofa. "Who is Edward Marin?"

"Dr. Edward Marin is a white male, about forty-five years old. He used to be the head of UVA's physics department and is one of the most brilliant men in history. People used to call him the Alien— partly because they joked that he was stealing alien technology and partly because of his personality, which I think you'd describe as arrogant and reclusive."

Quinn scooted back into the sofa, thinking through what he had said. "Do you . . . do you know him?"

"I met him a few times when I was a kid. But I wouldn't say I knew him. He quit UVA and just kind of disappeared years ago. Everyone figured he finally cracked up and went to live in the New York City subway tunnels or something."

"When? When did he disappear?"

" 'Ninety-two," he said. "I remember . . . because it was just a few months after Lisa died."

Quinn looked down at the coffee table and the profile she'd written. "Oh my God."

"No," Eric said, jumping to his feet and starting to pace again. "This is stupid. We're talking about fucking Edward Marin here. I mean the guy won the Nobel Prize for physics with a paper that **didn't have any footnotes.** Do you understand what that means?"

She shook her head.

"It means he wasn't building on anything—it was totally new. It was like when Einstein said that the speed of light was constant but the flow of time wasn't . . . There's just no way."

Quinn felt a pang of sympathy as she watched him march back and forth across the room. This Marin was obviously a personal hero to Eric— someone he'd grown up admiring and wanting to be like. But it all fit together.

"Why would a man like that work for UVA?" she prompted. "It's not exactly a big physics school . . ."

He slowed and finally stopped. "Everybody used to wonder about that. Make jokes . . ."

"I'm sorry I have to say this, Eric, but could it be because schools like MIT didn't ask for photographs on their undergrad applications?"

He jabbed a finger in her direction but seemed to lose his focus somewhere between action and speech.

"Why, Eric? What could he be working on that would be worth . . . this?"

He shrugged weakly and then fell into the chair next to the sofa again.

Quinn waited for him to say more, but when it became obvious that he wasn't going to, she walked over to his portable computer and connected to his e-mail account.

"You got some back," she said, looking over her shoulder. "Eric? Did you hear me? You got some mail back."

There were six messages in all. The first two were one-liners saying that the writers had never heard of ATD. When she pulled up the third, though, it was over a page long.

"Eric. This one's from someone named Falco. Is he the guy you told me about? It says he's doing celestial mechanics work for ATD." She scanned the body of the text, but it might as well have been in Swahili.

She minimized it and continued going through the others.

"Got another one! It's from a guy who calls himself Wolverine. Looks like he's e-mailing from Sony in Japan. It says he's working on something called mechanical harmonics . . ." She looked over her shoulder again. "Are you listening?"

He nodded weakly. "She."

"What?"

"Wolverine's a girl."

Satisfied that he was paying attention, Quinn opened the last e-mail. It was the least complicated but the most confusing. "This one's from a guy named Tyrell Darien at Stanford. It just says, 'Kiss my ass.'" She turned around to face him. "Why would he say that?"

The hint of anger in his nearly blank expression grew until he finally pushed himself out of the chair and came up beside her. He turned the computer toward him and jabbed angrily at the keyboard, scanning the two e-mails she'd told him about.

Quinn jumped when he suddenly grabbed a vase off the desk and threw it across the room. It shattered on the far wall. "Son of a bitch!"

"Would you talk to me, for Christ's sake!" Quinn shouted at him. "What!"

"Think about it! Mechanical harmonics?"

"I don't know what that is."

"But you do know a lot about cars. When you start one up, why does it vibrate?"

She shrugged. "'Cause of all the moving parts?"

"Right. What if you made all the moving parts go in perfectly balanced opposite directions."

"Uh, I guess it wouldn't vibrate."

"And the celestial mechanics problem relates to gravitational effects on orbiting bodies."

She shrugged. "I have no idea what you're talking about."

"Maybe this will help. The work I did for ATD was in the field of inertial containment systems for fusion reactors. Another word for that would be **lasers**."

That was it. The final piece.

"Star Wars?" She ran a hand though her hair, trying to think back. "I studied that in school. I mean, it died when we were kids, right? During the Reagan era. It was a total waste of money—"

"Hardly," Eric said. "It succeeded in bankrupting the Soviet Union, didn't it?"

She considered that for a moment. "I never thought about it that way. But technologically wasn't it a complete bust? Besides, don't we have those Patriot missiles they used in the Gulf War?"

"They don't work," he said simply.

"But they hit almost everything they were aimed at."

"You shouldn't believe everything you read," he said. "Actually they couldn't hit the broadside of a barn. Missed every time. But the military certainly wasn't going to tell the press that, and frankly, the press didn't want to know. After Vietnam, Americans just don't like to hear about the failures of their military. I mean, think about it. The whole concept is absurd. It's like two people shooting at each other and hoping they'll be saved by the bullets colliding in midair."

"But space-based lasers **will** work?"

He grabbed a laser pointer from his computer carrying case and ran to the opposite side of the room, then turned it on her and shook his hand slightly. The faded red dot jumping around on her body brought back some not-so-happy memories.

"Star Wars circa 1984," Eric said. "But if you correct the mechanical jittering . . ." He steadied his hand and the dot centered on her chest. "Then you correct the power and atmospheric distortion problems . . ." He moved forward until he was only a couple of feet from her. The dot darkened and its edges became sharply defined. "And I don't have to tell you about the advances in computer power over the last fifteen years."

"But why keep it so secret?"

"Treaties," he said. "The Russians don't have the money to compete anymore. A few years back we told them we wanted to start looking into this again—on a very limited scale. The idea was to design something that could pick off a couple of missiles launched by Afghanistan or some other 'rogue nation.' The Russians weren't crazy about the idea, but as long as we promised to keep the scale real small, they didn't look like they were going to kick up too much dust."

"So you sort of prove my point," Quinn said. "Why keep this so secret?"

"Based on the e-mails we got back, they're not **starting** research, they're **finishing** it." He aimed the pointer at her feet. "And one more thing. The Russians aren't much going to like the laser I helped develop . . ."

Quinn stared down at the little red dot centered on her foot. "It'll hit the ground?"

"It'll leave a crater about thirty feet deep. And with the computers we have now, I'm guessing they've designed a targeting system that will let them hit just about anything they want."

"Oh, my God. Didn't you know? Didn't you know what you were working on?"

He shook his head angrily. "It was all theoretical stuff—a bunch of equations. There wasn't anybody who could twist them into a long-range weapon . . ."

"No one except Edward Marin."

"No one except Edward Marin," he said, reaching around her for the phone.

"Who are you calling?"

"Tyrell. He's one of the most talented mathematicians in the world and he must know something or he wouldn't have sent that e-mail."

She leaned in and listened to the phone ring on the other end.

"Yo! You've got Tyrell Darien live, you lucky bastard." The voice was deep and masculine, with a pleasant urban drawl.

"Tyrell, it's Eric."

"Well, well. Eric Twain. Calling to rub it in, are you?"

"What are you talking about?"

"Don't play dumb with me, you grandstanding motherfucker. I'll come out there and kick your scrawny white ass."

"I'm serious, Tyrell. What are you talking about?"

Darien started to sound a little uncertain, but he still seemed to think he was being set up for some kind of joke. "I sent in some math on heat dissipation to ATD a few weeks ago. Took me two months to work it out. The next day I got it back, with corrections. That screams Eric Twain to me, you officious little prick."

"Wasn't me."

"Bullshit. **Nobody** corrects my math . . . Nobody but you."

"I'm telling you, it wasn't me."

There was a brief silence over the phone. "You're serious."

"Yeah."

"Holy shit . . . could this be it? A bona fide Marin sighting? Oh, man! I got to go, I got to get this out on the gossip line—"

"Tyrell. Tyrell! Don't hang up! You can't tell anybody about this. I'm serious, man. Nobody."

"What's gotten into you, boy?"

"Listen. What do you know about ATD?"

"Nothin'. A bunch of rich white boys in unimaginative suits would be my guess. They e-mail me problems. I do 'em and e-mail 'em back. And for that they send me an embarrassingly large amounts of cash."

"Do you know anybody else doing work for them? Where they're located? Anything."

"Huh-uh. You all right, man? You sound kind of stressed out."

"Yeah. Yeah, I'm fine. Okay. Thanks."

"No problem, bro. Now what—"

Eric replaced the receiver, cutting his friend off, and walked to the windows on the far side of the room.

"How do we find him?" Quinn said.

"There **is** no way."

"What are you talking about?"

"People have been trying for years to track Marin down. Hell, I tried a while back when I had a problem I couldn't figure out. Jesus. I still can't believe this. Maybe we're wrong. Maybe there's something we missed. I mean, we're talking about **Edward Marin** here."

"It makes sense, Eric. You know it does. Are you sure there's no way to find him?"

He shrugged.

"Then we're back to ATD," Quinn said.

"What do you mean, 'back to ATD'? We don't know anything more about them now than we did yesterday. Nothing that could lead us to them anyway."

"Maybe, maybe not. I might have an idea."

He turned away from the window and faced her. "Is it going to get me shot at?"

"Probably not."

"Put in jail?"

"I doubt it."

"Okay. Let's hear it then."

"I've been thinking . . . Maybe we've gotten too reliant on technology and the Net—too used to having everything at our fingertips. Maybe it's time we get low-tech."

49

Do you sell tea here, ma'am?"

The woman looked over her glasses at him as only a librarian can and pointed lazily to her right. "It's over there. Leave a quarter now, young man. That's how we pay for it."

"Yes, ma'am."

He found the pot of hot water without any trouble, but after pouring it into a cup, all he could do was stare blankly at the various colorful boxes lined up next to it. He never drank the stuff himself, and that, combined with having been pretty much banished from polite society when he was only seventeen, left him at a loss.

He finally decided that the one called Awake was probably the most appropriate under the circumstances and tossed a bag of it into the water. A little cream, then a little powdered stuff and a couple of spoonfuls of sugar turned it a generally unattractive color.

Quinn was sitting toward the back of the library, beneath a conveniently burned-out light that kept her mostly in shadow. As he approached, he could see the outline of her typing furiously on one of the library's terminals. She didn't acknowledge him when he walked up behind her and slid the Styrofoam cup onto the table.

"Anything?"

She shook her head and smacked the enter button. The blue of the screen lit up her face and deepened the lines of concentration as she began to read the text that appeared.

Eric reached around her and picked up a couple of loose sheets of paper from the table. He read through them for what must have been the fifth time, though he knew he wouldn't find anything more. Thank God for Quinn Barry. Despite a truckload of childhood tests that put him firmly in the super-genius category, he'd never have thought of this in a million years.

She'd checked out the obvious states first—Nevada and California for their reputation in the field of scientific research, then all the states in which women had been killed. Then Texas—Marin's home state. But in the end, she'd found what they were looking for right in their own backyard. Advanced Thermal Dynamics, Inc. had been chartered in Virginia. And its articles of incorporation as a Virginia business were a matter of public record.

Not that they provided much information. Nothing about what the company did, or why. No physical address—just a PO box in Richmond. But there was one useful item. It was signed by the president and CEO. One Richard W. Price.

Quinn reached past him without looking up, feeling around until she found the cup of tea. She took a sip but then grimaced and shook her head violently. "What is that?"

"Not how you like it?"

She screwed up her face and pushed the cup away, continuing to maneuver through the screens.

"Wait a minute . . ."

Eric looked up from the document in his hand. "Did you say something?"

"Okay, okay . . ." she mumbled. "Oh yeah. Got ya."

"What? What have you got?"

"**General** Richard W. Price," she read.

"Where are you getting that?"

"It's an article from an old issue of **Science** . . . It seems that General Price used to be the director of the BMDO."

"BMDO?"

"Ballistic Missile Defense Organization."

Eric put his hand on her shoulder and leaned in toward the screen. "You're kidding."

"Nope. And according to this, he retired from the military in 1989 to, and I quote, pursue other interests."

"Other interests," Eric repeated quietly as she continued to scroll down. "Anything else?"

She shook her head. "This is mostly a bunch of technical stuff about using missiles to intercept other missiles. Price was just quoted as a source." She tapped the down arrow a few more times and reached the end of the article. "That's it. That's all there is."

"It's got to be him."

She nodded. "Who better to quietly run an SDI project for the government?"

It was just starting to rain when Eric lifted the handset of the pay phone outside the library and cradled it between his cheek and shoulder. The fine droplets were dampening the top sheet of the pad in his hands but weren't heavy enough to smear the list written there: seventy-eight phone numbers from Virginia, Maryland, D.C., North Carolina, and West Virginia, all belonging to men named Richard Price.

"I don't get it," Quinn said, looking cold and more than a little worried. "What are you going to say? 'Hi, do you run Advanced Thermal Dynamics, a top-secret company working on SDI? Oh, and while we're on the subject, are you protecting a murderous, sadistic freak?' "

Eric smiled as he dropped in a couple of coins and dialed the first number on the list. "My plan is so much more elegant than that," he said as it rang.

"Hello?" A man's voice.

"Hello? General Price?"

"Huh? This is Dick Price. But I sure as hell ain't no general."

"Oh. Sorry. I must have the wrong number."

Quinn slapped a palm into her forehead as he hung up. "I'm an idiot."

"Maybe. But you have so many other charms." His smile widened slightly. "It's gonna take a whole lot of quarters but we may get out of this yet."

50

"Don't look so depressed," Quinn said, stepping into the empty hotel elevator. "There was no way it was going to be that easy."

Eric shuffled in behind her and pressed himself into a corner without speaking.

They'd called every number they had and the closest they'd gotten was a former marine sergeant. And with that, the dim light at the end of their tunnel had flickered out.

"It's not exactly a shocking concept that a guy involved in ultrasecret research and the murders of God knows how many young women wouldn't be listed in the phone book," Quinn said, jabbing the button for their floor.

"I guess."

"We'll get him when everything opens in the

morning. We know who he is, what he used to do for a living, what he does now, and roughly where he lives. There must be a directory of retired generals or something. We'll get him."

Her little speech didn't seem to have the intended effect; Eric was looking increasingly deflated. "So what if we do?"

"What do you mean 'so what if we do'? An hour ago you were on fire to find this guy."

"An hour is a long time. Let's say we do manage to get an address. What are we going to do with it? Drive up to his door and confront him? What's he going to say? 'Oops, you got me'?" Eric's tone turned a little sarcastic. "No, wait. I've got a better idea. Why don't we just find the research facility. You and I could overcome the hundred guards protecting it, climb the fence, and make a citizen's arrest. Sure. Why the hell not?"

"We still have the files," Quinn said, lowering her voice as the doors slid open and they stepped out. "All we have to do is find this Marin guy and get a DNA sample. Then we have proof."

"I ask you again. What are we going to do with it?"

The truth was, she hadn't completely worked that one out yet.

"What about that guy you were talking about at the FBI?" he said.

"Mark Beamon?"

"Yeah. You still think he's an option? I mean, based on what we know now?"

She stopped in front of the door to their room and pulled the key card from her pocket. "I don't know anymore . . . I mean I've never even met him. Based on what people say about him, I'd say yes. But . . ."

"Maybe it's time to call him. We don't have to tell him who we are. Just feel him out. Open a line of communication. What can it hurt?"

She slid the key card into the door and pushed it open. "Maybe you're right. We'll call him. But not from here. From a pay phone."

Quinn turned to close the door behind them but saw that it was already swinging shut, seemingly by itself. A moment later the man behind it was revealed, as was the barrel of his pistol, which was leveled at her face.

"Eric?" Her voice came out barely a whisper.

"Oh, shit."

"Now let's all just relax."

Quinn turned slowly away from the door and toward the strangely familiar voice. "That's him, Eric. The one who tried to grab me on the way to my father's place."

The man made a show of twisting his arm back and forth. "Still hurts."

She barely heard him, instead concentrating on the pistol in his hand. It, like the one held by the man behind her, had an unnaturally long barrel—a modification she recognized from movies she'd seen. Silencers.

"Why don't you have a seat, Mr. Twain," the man said. He was older than the other two in the room and clearly in charge.

Eric didn't seem sure what to do. He looked around him but otherwise didn't move.

"Eric. Do what he says," Quinn managed to get out. "There's nothing we can do."

"She's right," the man said. "There's nothing you can do."

Finally, Eric acquiesced. Quinn watched him move cautiously forward as a hand came to rest on her shoulder. She didn't bother to resist as she was pushed toward the sofa and forced down next to him.

The man in charge took a seat in the chair across from them and reached out to pluck a mint from a dish on the coffee table. "Who are you going to call, Ms. Barry?"

He'd obviously heard part of their conversation about Mark Beamon, but hadn't caught the name.

"Nobody," she said, fighting to stay calm.

He nodded thoughtfully as he popped the mint into his mouth. "Somehow I thought you'd say that."

51

Why don't you try to get some sleep?" Eric said. "I'll stay awake."

Quinn pressed herself a little harder against him and he responded by wrapping his arms around her. The cot they were on was barely large enough to fit them both; he was leaning against the wall and she had her back against his chest. The warmth of her, the smell of her hair, was strangely comforting. They'd been separated on the long drive into the Virginia mountains and he had been certain that he would never see her again. Now, though, with the two of them reunited in this tiny cell, some of his fears had faded a little. It was an illusion, of course. It had been a hell of a run, but now it was over. They were dead.

Quinn turned her face up toward him and made

a weak effort to smile. "Looks like I've done it to you again, haven't I? I don't suppose you have any brilliant ideas?"

"I'm thinking we should start seeing other people."

She tilted her head back against his shoulder. "Maybe."

The truth was, their options were pretty much nonexistent. The walls of the tiny room were concrete. The only door looked to be made of solid steel, interrupted only by a small Plexiglas window that looked like it belonged in the side of a ship. And, as near as he could tell from their drive in, a well-guarded razor-wire fence surrounded the entire complex.

Quinn's breathing started to deepen and he moved his head so that he could see the side of her face. Her eyes had finally closed. Good. At least she could escape the sense of doom hanging over them for a little while. He, on the other hand, was wide awake.

An odd thought suddenly occurred to him. He might never sleep again. At twenty-six, he'd never really considered the possibility of his own death. Time had always been something that stretched so far out in front of him he hadn't yet caught a glimpse of its end.

His watch had been taken from him, so he had no idea how long they sat like that—long enough for him to slip into a thoughtless trance staring at the blank wall. At first, the electronic buzz confused him, but when the door started to swing outward, he pushed Quinn off him and jumped to his feet.

"What," he heard her say, obviously still groggy. "Eric—"

The man who stepped into the cell was probably in his sixties, but his broad shoulders and trim waist made it impossible to be certain. Eric heard the quiet creaking as Quinn rose from the cot. She came alongside him and slipped her hand into his, squeezing almost hard enough to cause him pain.

"It's okay," he said. "It's not him."

Her grip loosened. "General Price?"

"Retired," the man replied as the door shut behind him. "You continue to impress me, Ms. Barry. You've been a surprising adversary." He nodded toward Eric. "But now I'd like to have a word with your friend here. You won't mind if we excuse ourselves for a moment?"

She didn't respond.

"I'll just stay where I am, if you don't mind," Eric said.

"It might be easier if you heard what I have to say in private."

"No, thanks."

Price shrugged. "As I'm sure you know by now, you've been an important part of our team, Eric. We don't want to lose you."

"SDI."

"I'm afraid so, son. For obvious reasons, it's a

project that's been kept very quiet. But in the end, I think you'll agree that it will be recognized as the most important military advance since—"

"The atomic bomb?"

Price smiled. "I was going to say the bow and arrow."

"I don't do weapons."

"It seems time that you reexamined that prejudice. You know as well as I do that it won't be long before the American mainland will be within the range of rogue-nation missile launches. The system we're working on will neutralize that threat."

"Spare me, General. I'm the one who developed the theory your new toy is based on. I should know what it can do."

"Clever boy. Of course you're right." He leaned back against the wall, looking thoughtful for a moment. "You've dealt with the military enough, I think, to understand that most of its officers lack, well, a certain creative spark . . ."

"They're a bunch of sadistic dinosaurs," Eric said.

"Possibly a little harsh, but not entirely inaccurate. My peers seem to be stuck in the past. All they want is heavier metal and larger calibers—things that you and I both know are obsolete before they even come off the assembly line. The future is about speed and precision. And our—your—system is the embodiment of those principles. Frankly, we're already ahead of schedule, but if you were to come on board full-time, I think we could push things forward even more."

Under normal circumstances, Eric would have told him to go fuck himself, just like he had every other uniformed hack that had shown up on his doorstep. Clearly, though, these weren't normal circumstances.

"I'll work for you on one condition. Quinn walks away from this."

Price's face took on a vaguely artificial expression of pain. "I'm afraid the offer extends only to you, and that there's no room for negotiation. You see . . . while it would be convenient to have you, we don't really need you."

"Marin."

That ironic smile again. "What can I say? Once again, I'm impressed."

"There's no deal without Quinn."

Price opened his mouth to speak, but Quinn cut him off.

"Eric, wait. Think about this. If you can—"

"No," he said. "There's nothing to think about."

She grabbed his shoulder and pulled him around to face her. "Eric, he's offering you a way out."

"No, he's not. He's offering me temporary slavery and then a painless execution." He turned back toward Price. "Isn't that right, General?"

Price's nod was almost imperceptible.

"That doesn't seem like a good deal to me," Eric said. "I'll pass."

"I'm sorry to hear that. But I respect your courage and sense of loyalty."

That finally pushed Quinn over the edge.

"What the hell would you know about courage and loyalty?" Eric made a grab for her arm, but she slipped him and walked right up to Price, staring directly into his eyes with an intensity that clearly surprised the man. "You help him. Don't you? **Don't you?** You feed him women so he can torture them to death and build your stupid machines."

"Quinn," Eric cautioned. She ignored him.

"Have you ever seen one of them, General?"

Eric started forward when she actually poked Price in the chest, but stopped when the man didn't react.

"You haven't, have you? You just read about it in a report and bark orders. You don't have the **courage** to face what you do."

"You think I enjoy this?" Price said, following her with his eyes as she started to circle him like a cat. "That I condone it? Let me assure you, I don't. But I don't have the luxury of moral outrage. I have two hundred and fifty million people in my care."

"Is this where you tell us you were only following orders?"

He shook his head. "I'm afraid I don't even have that excuse. I've done what I've done because I felt that I had no other choice."

Eric was ready for what happened next. He lunged forward and intercepted her before she could get her hands around Price's throat. She fought with surprising power but he managed to push her to the back wall and pin her there. "Quinn. Calm down! This isn't going to get us anywhere."

"I'm afraid I have a meeting in Washington in a few hours," Price said as the latch buzzed again and the door swung open.

Quinn stopped struggling and Eric released her, turning back toward the door just in time to see three formidable-looking men come through it.

"You understand that I have to know everything," Price said as he exited into the hall. "And I'm afraid the best way to do that is separately."

At that, the three men charged, hitting Eric hard and sending him to the concrete floor. He swung a fist and connected with enough force to stagger one of them, but the other two were quickly getting a grip on him that would be impossible to break.

"Let go of him!" Quinn yelled, getting an arm halfway around one of the men's necks before being thrown to the ground. Eric saw the man he'd hit grab her arm and start dragging her toward the open door.

"Eric!"

He caught one last glimpse of her before his face was shoved into the floor. It seemed that all his thrashing had accomplished was to allow the men on top of him to tighten their grip.

"I'm sorry, son," he heard Price say. "I really don't have any choice."

"Everyone has a choice," Eric managed to get out.

"I wish the world was still that simple. I really do."

The weight on top of him was suddenly gone, but by the time he struggled to his feet, Price and Quinn had disappeared and the two men who had pinned him to the floor were backing out into the hall. He lunged forward, already knowing it was too late. The steel door slammed shut just before he hit it, resonating with the impact of his body and then going silent. He pressed his face up to the glass but couldn't see anything.

"QUINN!"

Two hours.

That was his best guess as to how long he'd been sitting motionless on the cot listening to the silence. They were trying to get to him—to allow time for his imagination to run amok. He'd tried to fight it, to keep his mind occupied with math tricks and impossible physics problems, but it didn't take long for his fears for Quinn to break him down.

Marin was here. Somewhere close. Surely they wouldn't . . . they wouldn't give her to Marin.

No, he told himself. Price wouldn't; he couldn't.

He'd fed Marin women in the past, but that had been different. He'd never met them. Like Quinn had said, they were just words on a report to him, statistics. Price had spoken to Quinn, touched her, looked into her eyes. He couldn't turn her over to Marin. He couldn't.

Eric's head sank slowly into his hands. "Oh God."

52

Quinn ran her hand along the edge of the door, but wasn't really sure why. The cold steel was no less than an inch thick and secured to the concrete walls with hinges that looked like they could stop a tank. She tried again to get her fingers behind the keypad set into the wall, succeeding only in ripping part of her nail off and starting the blood flowing down her hand.

She knew that Eric wasn't far away—no more than a hundred yards in her estimation—but it might as well have been a thousand miles. They'd never see each other again. She was sure of that now. Like her, he would be questioned, and when Price and his men were satisfied, he would be killed. And it was her fault. If she hadn't been so stubborn, so starved for excitement, he'd be sitting in his house right now, carving on that stupid table of his. A short, bitter laugh escaped her and she shook her head. Excitement. The naive and bored little girl she had been two weeks before seemed so distant now.

An audible but ultimately indecipherable sound coming from the hallway intruded on the stillness of her cell and she pressed her face up against the tiny window in the door. Nothing—the hallway looked empty.

The buzz of the lock startled her and she jumped back as the door began to swing open. The man who came through was completely unfamiliar. She studied his face for a moment before he turned and tapped a few numbers into the tiny keypad on the wall. The air pressure in the room increased enough for her to feel it in her ears when the door slammed shut.

When he faced her again, she was able to get a longer look at him. He was extremely good-looking. Probably in his mid-forties, with longish gray hair and straight white teeth. His meticulously pressed linen slacks and cotton shirt were stylishly formless, hanging perfectly on his thin frame.

The expression on his tanned face was strangely enigmatic. His mouth curled into what should have been a smile, but expressed no joy or humor. She tried for a moment to see something hidden there, but her eyes were drawn to the long military knife hanging from his left hand. She stared down at it, watching the blood spattered across the blade collect at the tip until a single drop finally fell to the floor.

"Marin," she whispered. Careful not to make any sudden moves, she started to back away from him. After about five feet, though, she bumped into the wall.

"Quinn. I can't tell you what a pleasure it is to finally meet you." She felt a surge of adrenaline as he took a tentative step forward. "You know, the pictures of you . . . lied. Do you know what it takes to be photogenic?"

She shook her head. Was it the same voice? Was this the man who had called her from Eric's apartment? She tried to remember but found it impossible to concentrate.

"It takes a person that is dead inside," he said. "That way a camera can capture everything they are. No camera could ever hope to record you."

Quinn slid along the wall, keeping the distance between them constant as he kept inching forward. She was squeezed into a corner when he finally got close enough to touch her. It seemed that every muscle in her body seized when he ran his index finger gently down her cheek. The strange expression he'd worn when he entered was gone—replaced by an aura of serenity and kindness. Her mind reminded her of the knife in his hand, but it seemed to lose its meaning as she looked into his eyes. "Who are you?" she heard herself say.

He turned away from her and crossed the room, sitting down on the cot.

"Who are you?" she repeated.

She heard the knife hit the wall almost before she saw it. In one blinding motion, he had embedded it in the cinderblock behind him. But it wasn't the act that made her legs suddenly go weak. It was what she had seen in his eyes at the moment of impact. Hate, cruelty, fear, rage. Evil. She tried to shove herself deeper into the corner but her feet temporarily lost their traction and she barely managed to keep from falling.

When she focused on him again, he was smiling warmly at her.

"You . . . you killed them," she said.

"Yes. I'm afraid I did."

Quinn looked over at the steel door and then at the cement walls surrounding her. There was nowhere to run. No one to help her. The image of the dying girl in Eric's bedroom suddenly came rushing back at her. She couldn't breathe.

"Why?" she stammered.

The question seemed to interest him. "Why? Because I like it." His expression turned thoughtful, but still betrayed none of the malice she'd seen moments before. "I wouldn't expect a woman to understand . . . but your friend Eric would. What do you think he feels when he looks at you?"

She didn't answer.

"Love, perhaps? Tenderness?" He shook his head.

"Those are emotions peculiar to the female of the species; illusions rooted in humanity's early struggle for survival. Women love. Men lust. When he looks at you, he imagines what it would feel like to have you naked beneath him, ramming himself inside you. The sound of your screams. Your body wet with perspiration, sliding against his as you fight to get away . . ."

"You're wrong," she said. "You—"

He silenced her with a wave of his hand. "Oh, of course he suppresses those feelings, twists them, convinces himself that they don't exist. Thousands of years of civilization won't allow him to submit to his deeper instinct—to have complete control over you. To have you helpless, submitting to whatever he wants to subject you to. I, on the other hand, don't deny myself those sensations."

He followed her gaze to the knife stuck in the wall behind him and his smile widened. "Do you want this?"

She had to use her tongue to suck enough saliva into her mouth to speak. "How many?"

"How many what?"

"How many women?"

"Thirty-two—every one unique and perfect in her own way. I remember them all; every detail. It's really quite remarkable. Almost as if all five of my senses record the experience precisely—no nuance missed. Do you know what that's like? Can you even imagine an experience with that kind of intensity?" He fell silent, making it clear that his question required an answer.

"No. And I don't think I'd ever want to."

"Come, now, Quinn. Try to be a little less dense; I know you have it in you. I don't mean the killing per se. I'm speaking of emotional intensity. I can guarantee you that nothing compares—not love or hate or faith. Maybe death. I don't know, I've only been at the very edges of it."

Quinn managed to regain a more natural rhythm to her breathing, and that, for some reason, helped to mask the fear that had nearly paralyzed her. "You're wrong. You're dead already; you have been for years. The fact that you'd put hate in the same category as love and faith proves you've never experienced either."

She knew from the books she'd borrowed from the FBI that arguing with him was probably the wrong thing to do, but it didn't matter. This man—this **thing**—had already decided her fate. There was nothing she could do to change it.

"Have you considered the possibility that the emotional intensity you get from torturing and killing is no more powerful than what normal people feel every day? Every time they look at their children, or hear beautiful music, or go to church?"

He pulled one of his legs toward his chest and propped his foot casually on the edge of the cot. "Wonderful. You're so much more than I ever could have hoped for, Quinn."

When he finally rose to his feet, Quinn's instinct was to press herself farther into the corner. She refused to give in, though. She wouldn't give him the satisfaction. He took two steps toward her, but then turned and walked to the door. He punched another code into the pad on the wall and followed the door as it swung out into the hall.

Quinn wasn't sure what had just happened. She moved forward a few feet when the door failed to close, but saw nothing. She was about to take another step when Marin's head reappeared around the jamb. "Are you coming?"

She froze.

"You're safe from me today, Quinn. I give you my word I won't harm a hair on your beautiful head."

It didn't take long to run through her choices: stay and submit to "questioning" and execution, or go and face the unknown.

He must have seen the decision in her eyes because he pointed to the knife still stuck in the wall. "Don't forget that."

She kept her eyes locked on him as she grabbed hold of the hilt. It took all her strength but she finally managed to work it free.

"Where's Eric?" she said, holding the knife threateningly out in front of her. He laughed and shook his head. "I truly admire your spirit, Quinn. You really are magnificent. Do you know that?"

53

Richard Price slowed his car and leaned close enough to the window to be seen clearly by the uniformed marine standing at the side of the road. After snapping to attention and saluting, he disappeared into a small guardhouse and the razor-wire-topped gate began to swing open. Another salute sent Price through and onto a narrow dirt road cut from the Virginia forest.

It was eight miles to the first paved road and another ten to the highway. The ATD campus, nestled in the mountains far from any population center, was for all intents and purposes impregnable. The mountainous terrain surrounding it was bristling with cameras, listening devices, and motion detectors. No fewer than twenty-five well-trained men took turns manning a sophisticated monitoring station and physically patrolling the area. In the ten years the company had occupied this corner of nowhere, there had been only three perimeter alerts. All had turned out to be lost hunters whose stories and backgrounds had withstood intense scrutiny.

The oppressive level of secrecy and security could be difficult at times but unfortunately was necessary. It was impossible to predict how word of ATD's research would be received by the world at large. If the Russians were aware of the progress that had been made, they would be fighting it tooth and nail. No longer able to afford the billions it would take to build effective countermeasures, they would use the only weapon still available to them—their frightening desperation. And in the face of that, America's cowardly politicians would buckle.

But if the system was rolled out complete and ready for operation, the Russians and the rest of the world would be completely unprepared. There would be some saber rattling, of course, but it would be too little too late. In the end, the men in charge of what was once the mighty Soviet Union would throw up their hands and crawl back into their pathetic little holes.

Price rolled down the window a few inches and felt the cool wind dry the thin film of perspiration from his face for the first time in days. The past few weeks had been the most dangerous since the inception of the project. It seemed that everything that could go wrong had. But that spate of bad luck seemed to be over now—control had been regained. Quinn Barry's five police files had been burned and steps were being taken to see that the originals were destroyed and all references to them eradicated from state and federal computers.

There were significant risks in taking that action, of course. Numerous law enforcement officials still remembered the murders, and certainly the victims' families hadn't forgotten. But over the short term, the benefits outweighed those risks.

The questioning of Barry and Twain would undoubtedly be successful—though Price didn't expect to learn anything new. He was confident that he was aware of their recent activities and that any damage done could be contained. It was possible that their deaths could cause unforeseen complications, but these wouldn't be insurmountable.

Price slowed his car again and reached into his glove compartment, depressing a button built into the side. An old fence constructed of what appeared to be rotting logs began to swing open on hidden hinges. He glanced at his watch and realized that he was already behind schedule. Unless traffic around D.C. was unusually light, he was going to be late for his meeting with Senator Wilkenson. He'd considered taking the helicopter but knew that he needed the two-and-a-half-hour drive to re-calculate the project's time line. The loss of Eric Twain was undoubtedly going to translate into a delay. His unknowing contributions to the project had been second in importance only to Marin's.

Marin.

Price felt his lip curl involuntarily at the thought of the man—if he could indeed be called that. The psychological profiles that Price had commissioned at the beginning of this project labeled Marin in-sane, suicidal, deluded. He had never put a great deal of faith in them, though. To him, Marin seemed too calculating to be truly insane. He was always watching, studying, testing.

But with the girl he'd killed in Twain's house, he had finally crossed the line—and he knew it. Price remembered the fear in Marin's eyes when he had been confronted with the souvenirs of his killings. And with that, Price's utter contempt was complete. Marin was nothing—a coward, a sadistic pervert who liked to inflict pain on the helpless. But he was afraid now, and that could be used to focus him, to help counteract the loss of Eric Twain.

Price was confident that the major theoretical problems plaguing the project could still be solved within a year and a half. Then the individual parts could be broken up and farmed out to Lockheed Martin, TRW, Boeing, and the like. At that moment, ATD would cease to exist. And so would Edward Marin.

Price couldn't help smiling at the thought. He visualized Marin's lifeless body being thrown into an unmarked grave somewhere in the Virginia wilderness, never to be seen again. It was a ceremony he would attend personally.

54

There's a guard," Quinn whispered.

Marin leaned out around the corner for a moment and then pulled back. "So there is."

"What are we going to do?"

"Perhaps you should run. I can get you out of here without anyone interfering. But we don't have much time . . ."

"And where does that leave Eric?"

"Oh, I suppose dead, don't you?"

"I'm not leaving him."

Marin nodded thoughtfully. "I'll tell you what. I'll go talk to the guard, divert his attention. How would that be?"

Quinn looked into his dead smile for a moment, suddenly a little confused. "But . . . I thought . . ."

Marin raised his eyebrows. "You thought what?"

She was just as terrified of him now as she had been when they first met—making their current alliance a rather uneasy one. What was his motivation? He wasn't helping her out of the goodness of what was left of his heart.

Marin walked calmly around her and started down the hall. She leaned around the corner again, clutching the heavy knife in both hands, and watched as he approached the guard.

"Is Eric Twain in there?" His voice echoed through the corridor as he skillfully maneuvered the guard around until his back was to Quinn.

"I'm afraid I'm not at liberty to say, sir."

"Oh, for God's sake," Marin said. "I need to speak to him for three minutes about a problem we're having."

"I'm sorry, sir. I have my orders."

"Why don't you call General Price and get permission, then. I don't have time for this."

He was serious; all he was going to do was talk. She had at least thought she could count on him to deal with any necessary violence. It was the one benefit to having a psychopath temporarily on your side.

When he glanced in her direction, his growing amusement was immediately obvious. He was trying to force her hand, making it clear that if Eric was going to be saved, she was going to have to do it.

"Give him a call," Marin said again, pointing in

her direction. "There's a phone right around the corner."

The guard didn't immediately respond, considering his position. There was no more time. If he decided to make the call, he would walk right up on her. It was now or never.

She stepped out into the open and padded silently down the hall, cocking the knife back in her hand. When she was only inches from the guard, she froze. Marin was obviously becoming impatient and made a show of redirecting his gaze over the man's shoulder and staring intensely at her. She struck, swinging with everything she had, just as the guard started to turn.

The impact reverberated all the way up her arm as the heavy metal hilt connected with the back of his skull. He crumpled to the floor with a muffled grunt, leaving her face-to-face with Marin.

"Very good, Quinn. Now finish it."

"What?"

"When he wakes up, he'll sound the alarm. Then they'll track you down like an animal."

"Kill him? You want me to kill him? . . . No."

"Well, if you don't care about yourself, at least think of Eric. It's your fault that he's in this situation, isn't it?"

"I'm not killing him."

Marin looked more than a little disappointed as he slid a key card into a slot in the wall. "Your decision."

"Eric!"

He jumped up off the cot and threw his arms around her. "Quinn! Oh, my God. Are you all right?"

"I'm okay. You?"

He pulled away and looked into her eyes for a moment but then spotted the bloody knife in her hand. "Quinn, what the hell is—"

He suddenly grabbed her arm and pulled her behind him. When she looked up, she saw Marin moving smoothly through the door.

"Eric Twain," he said, sinking casually onto the cot. "Look at you. All grown up."

"Marin." Eric backed up a few feet, making sure to stay in front of Quinn.

"How long has it been, Eric? I hardly recognize you. Last time I saw you, you couldn't have been any older than fifteen."

"You killed her, Edward. You killed Lisa."

Marin rolled his eyes and pointed lazily at Quinn. "You should thank me. Look how much better you've done for yourself."

Quinn pressed herself against Eric's back and wrapped her arms around his stomach, partly to comfort him and partly to keep him from doing anything stupid.

"You son of a bitch! How could you do it? What gives you the right—"

"Must we resort to name-calling, Eric?" Marin waved his hand around him. "And as far as what gives me the right, you already know that, don't you? The United States government gives me the right. They give me that, and much more. And in return, I make them feel safe in the world they've created. It seemed like a perfect arrangement—particularly when the alternative was prison and perhaps even execution . . ."

"But the reality turned out to be less attractive than the fantasy," Eric said.

"That always seems to be the case, doesn't it?" Marin stood and started for the open door. "I think it's about time we go. Follow me."

When Marin had disappeared into the hallway, Eric spun around. "What the hell's going on, Quinn?"

"He's helping us."

"No, he's not. He's helping himself. You know what he is."

She shook her head. "What choice do we have, Eric? I don't want to go with him, but I also don't want to stay here."

"Quinn—"

She grabbed his hand and pulled him through the door, knowing what he was going to say and not wanting to hear it. Marin was waiting on the other side, holding two plastic badges similar to the one clipped to his shirt.

"Put these on."

They did as he told them and waited to see what came next. Marin just stood there for a moment and then pointed to the guard lying on the floor with a touch of exasperation.

Eric took the hint and dragged the unconscious man into the small cell. Marin was already starting down the hall when he reappeared and closed the door behind him.

"What about the surveillance cameras?" Quinn said, when they caught up.

"I've locked them out of the mainframe—none work."

"Won't somebody fix them?"

"I'm sure they'll try."

The hallway eventually wound its way to a security checkpoint. The desk was empty and the monitors next to it were displaying nothing but static.

"You're going to go down this hallway," Marin said, stopping and pointing down a narrow corridor to their right. "It's quite a long way and travels beneath the complex for a while. Take your second left and follow that hall to its end. There will be a security station like this one, but with a door to the outside . . ."

Quinn was vaguely aware of Marin's voice trailing off as both he and Eric followed her gaze to the door behind the security desk.

"Oh, my," Marin said. "That does look a bit suspicious, doesn't it, Quinn? . . . Quinn?"

She broke from her trance and looked up at him.

"Are you wearing anything under your sweater?"

"What?"

"Back off, Marin," Eric said. "I swear I'll—"

Marin shushed him.

"I want you to give me your sweater. But only if you have something on under it, of course."

Quinn pulled her sweater over her head and handed it to him, leaving her in just a T-shirt. She wasn't sure what else to do.

He nodded politely and walked behind the desk, dropping the sweater on the floor and pushing it around with his foot trying to sop up the deep puddle of blood flowing from under the door. When he'd gotten as much up as he could, he opened the door and shoved the sweater inside.

The guard, who had undoubtedly been sitting behind the desk earlier that day, was now sitting on a stack of complex circuitry and computers packed efficiently into the small space. His head was thrown back, revealing a wide gash in his throat.

Marin closed the door and turned back toward them. "Where was I? Oh, yes. After you leave the building you'll be faced . . . Are you listening?"

Quinn tried to focus on him.

"You'll be faced with a large parking lot. Turn left and follow along the building. When you go around the corner you'll see a blue Isuzu parked against the wall." He held a set of keys out in front of him. Quinn couldn't seem to bring herself to move close enough to take them. Fortunately, Eric could and Marin dropped them in his hand. "It belongs to my assistant. She won't be needing it."

Marin took off his watch and reached out to Quinn. She jerked back, but he caught her hand and began slowly fastening it around her wrist. Eric didn't interfere but watched intently, waiting to see where all of this was going.

"At exactly four o'clock," Marin continued, "there is going to be a lab accident that destroys this entire building. That gives you ten minutes. I suggest you don't waste them."

"You're going to destroy it?" Eric said.

"They imprisoned me here. Everything you see was stolen from me—from my mind. I'm not going to leave any of it."

"Why are you helping us?"

Marin's only response was to turn and walk back the way they had come.

The corridor was quiet, but not completely empty. The badges Marin had given them were effective at deflecting suspicion, though, and the most attention they'd received was a nod and a smile.

"Five minutes," Quinn said, looking at the watch on her wrist.

They had stopped in front of a bright red fire extinguisher and an alarm recessed into the wall.

"Do you have any idea how many people might be working here?" Quinn said.

"No. Could be hundreds."

"They'll all be killed."

"Yeah."

She reached up and grabbed hold of the alarm lever but didn't pull it, looking to him to see if he agreed. He chewed on his lower lip for a moment and then put his hand on top of hers. "I can't believe we're doing this."

55

The sound was muffled by the thick walls of his windowless retreat, but Marin could still hear the shrill, wavering tone as it flooded the complex. He stood in the middle of the room, scanning the computer monitors that littered the tiny space. These five screens were the only ones remaining that could output the data from the complex's countless surveillance cameras. He watched them, mesmerized, as they switched smoothly through the different sectors of the campus.

ATD's employees were performing just as they had been trained to. Techs were manning every PC and terminal, deftly working through the screens necessary to send the day's work to a fireproof storage facility as their colleagues moved like cattle toward their designated exit.

Marin reached out and turned off the lights, bringing sharper contrast to the monitors as he watched the young techs complete their tasks, shut down the systems, and follow their friends toward the safety of the outside world. Marin finally turned, focusing on the single screen behind him. Unlike the others, the view remained static, glowing with the image of his assistant shuffling nervously through the papers on her desk, occasionally glancing up at the clock. She had removed her lab coat and he could see that she was wearing a green silk blouse tucked neatly into a short skirt. She wasn't wearing any panty hose, having been forced to abandon them years ago as he had notched the temperature in the outer office higher and higher. She'd been a little self-conscious that first day without them, he remembered. But when he hadn't protested her lack of formality, she'd never thought about it again.

He saw her stand abruptly and begin pacing back and forth, the muscles in her young legs flexing visibly even on the small black-and-white screen. He looked past her at the large glass pane that made up the far wall of the office suite. The main lab was deserted; only the silent machines remained.

His assistant's movements gained urgency at the same pace as his own excitement. She didn't want to evacuate the building without him but also didn't want to approach the innocuous little door that guarded his retreat. He had made it clear that he was never to be disturbed there and that no one—no one—was ever to enter.

Another thirty seconds and her pacing stopped. He saw her glare at the door and then march toward it. The camera lost sight of her just before he heard the knock.

Marin felt his throat go dry and he swallowed hard as he reached for the knob. Four years. Four years he'd watched her, spoken with her, smelled her. He'd even touched her, though he'd only allowed himself brief brushes against soft fabric—never skin. The anticipation of her had been nearly unbearable as it was.

When he opened the door, he found her standing directly in front of it, shifting her weight self-consciously from foot to foot.

"Dr. Marin. I'm sorry to disturb you. Can you not hear the alarm in here?"

"I can, Cynthia." He waved behind him at the darkened room. "But for some reason I lost the lights in here and I have papers everywhere. They're all originals."

Her mouth tightened in frustration and she glanced over her shoulder at the empty building. "We have to hurry, Dr. Marin. Will you let me help you?"

He hesitated for a moment, as she would have expected. Other than him, no one had been in the room since it had been converted from its original purpose.

"We don't have much time, Doctor," she prompted.

He stepped aside and she rushed by, starting to collect the notes and papers strewn out across the counter that ran the length of the wall. He closed the door and moved up behind her, slipping his hands into the pockets of his slacks. Each contained a single syringe. When she leaned over to pull a notebook from behind one of the computers, he jabbed one of them through the wool of her skirt.

She screamed and he barely managed to pull the needle out of her before she spun around. She just stared at him for a moment, unsure of what had just happened. It didn't take long, though, for her to see the empty syringe in his hand. To her credit, she didn't hesitate at all, striking out at his face with a vicious blow. Wonderful.

He evaded it easily, of course, and let her run past him to the door. He watched as she grabbed hold of the knob and began pulling futilely on it. When she finally came to the realization that the door wasn't going to open, she turned and pressed her back against it. She was starting to look a little wobbly.

Marin reached out for her, purposely moving slowly enough for her to dodge him. The motion turned out to be too violent for her impaired balance and she tripped over her own feet, falling gracelessly to the floor. He watched, transfixed, as she rolled onto her stomach and tried to crawl away.

She let out another, weaker scream when he grabbed her ankle and pulled her foot against his stomach. Her thrashing did little except to cause her skirt to slide up her thighs and reveal the narrow strip of white nylon and lace between her legs. It seemed to glow in the gray light emanating from the computer terminals as they flickered out the images of the empty complex.

"Stop," she breathed out as he dragged her back a few inches. "Please . . ."

He'd chosen the drug and dosage carefully. It was enough to rob her of her strength and coordination, but not so much as to hopelessly cloud her mind. She understood what was happening to her and, more importantly, that she was helpless to prevent it.

She rolled onto her back and kicked at him with her free foot, the blow glancing off his thigh and hiking her skirt farther up her hips. He could see the dark pubic hair through the sheer material now. Just a hint of it. A promising shadow.

Marin reached into a drawer behind him and pulled out three pairs of handcuffs. He attached one to her left ankle and then dropped her leg and sat across her abdomen, pinning her to the floor. When she raised her hands in a pathetic effort to fight him, he attached the second pair of handcuffs to her wrists and secured them to the counter behind her head.

"Dr. Marin . . ." she managed to get out as he turned and crawled down to her feet. "Stop . . . Please . . ." He grabbed the handcuff hanging from her ankle and pulled her leg toward the far wall.

He remembered the workmen's confusion when he'd insisted on this particular modification to the room. In the end, though, they had done as he asked and installed two heavy steel loops in the wall near the floor, exactly three feet apart. Marin clamped the free end of the handcuffs to one of the loops and quickly secured her right ankle to the other.

Prying her mouth open was an unusually simple matter. The muscle relaxers kept her jaw from clamping shut, allowing him to stuff a rag in and secure it with a piece of tape. He could see the lazy motion of her eyes as they struggled to follow his hand to the X-Acto knife lying on the floor behind her head.

He started with her blouse, cutting off the buttons and then slicing the full length of each sleeve, until it fell off her without his ever actually touching the material. It was too soon for that. He brought the knife up between her legs next, feeling the resistance of the wool as the razor-sharp blade cut through it, leaving her in only her bra and panties.

Her nipples, visible beneath sheer white material, were a little darker and larger than he'd imagined but no less beautiful. Her hips bucked weakly as he slid the knife beneath the edge of her shimmering panties. She was right. Not yet. He withdrew his hand from the blade, leaving it trapped between the fabric and her skin, and pulled the other syringe from his lab coat. He watched her face carefully as he slid the needle into the muscle of her thigh and depressed the plunger.

The stimulant went to work quickly—her eyes cleared and she sucked in a loud breath through her nose.

Now she was ready.

#

When they finally broke out of the hall into the security area Marin had described, it was crammed with people shuffling toward the glass double doors at the other end.

"How long?" Eric said.

Quinn glanced at the watch on her wrist and tried unsuccessfully to push the people in front of her forward. "Less than a minute."

They were through the doors with fifteen seconds to spare, darting to the left to get clear of the path of the glass, in case it shattered outward. The flow of traffic from the building was lessening and the parking lot was overrun with people congregating into well-organized groups.

"Three, two, one!" Quinn said. They both

crouched and covered their ears in anticipation of the blast.

Nothing.

"That was it," she said, letting her hands fall to her sides.

"Are you sure?"

"I can tell time, Eric. Maybe somebody found the bomb? Maybe Marin screwed up? Who cares? Let's get the hell out of here."

She started forward again, but stopped after only a few feet when it became clear that Eric wasn't following.

"What are you doing? Come on!"

He just stood there scanning the parking lot and the people milling around in it.

"Eric!" She grabbed his arm and started dragging him along behind her. "What's wrong with you? This is the first shred of luck we've had since we met. Let's use it!"

"Why did he tell us he was going to blow this place up?" Eric said, planting his feet and bringing them to an abrupt halt. He slipped her grip and took a few tentative steps toward the crowded parking lot.

"What? I don't know—because he wanted us to escape?"

"We were leaving anyway."

Quinn pointed back at the door they had come through. "Look. They're all out—they'll be okay! We've got to move!"

For a moment Eric seemed to fall into the trance-like state she had come to recognize as concentration and then he suddenly started jumping up and down and waving his arms wildly. "Get out of there! Get out of the parking lot!"

Quinn threw her body into his, slamming him against the wall and trying to clamp a hand over his mouth. "Are you crazy?" He shoved her away and continued to shout at the top of his lungs. "Get the hell out of there!"

Quinn looked out at the mass of people in the lot and saw that most had stopped talking and were now staring directly at them. A moment later two men burst from the crowd, sprinting in their direction. She recognized both of them.

Instead of turning and running, Eric started toward them, continuing to shout nonsensically. She grabbed him around the waist, but knew that it was too late. The men were only twenty feet away now and closing fast.

The blast caught her completely unawares. She felt the force and heat of it for a split second before Eric dragged her to the ground. Two more blasts followed almost immediately, but the sound was muffled by the ringing in her ears, and by the fact that Eric was completely covering her with his body.

The rumble of the last explosion faded into the sound of crackling fire and car alarms, but Eric didn't move. She tried to push him off but couldn't get enough leverage.

"Eric! Eric! Can you hear me? Are you all right?"

She felt him shift his weight slightly. "I . . . yeah. I think I am."

He rolled off her onto the asphalt and lay there on his back looking into the smoke-filled sky. Quinn pushed herself to her knees and ran her hands along his body, looking for wounds or burns. The only obvious thing she found was a deep laceration along his side. She tore a piece of cloth from the bottom of her skirt and pressed it against the wound.

"Jesus!" Eric coughed.

"Are you all right?" Quinn said, helping him rise to a sitting position.

"Yeah. Yeah. I'm fine."

His face was briefly obscured by a wave of smoke. It smelled strange. Like gasoline, but with an underlying sweetness to it. When the haze thinned again, she turned and looked around the parking lot.

There were fires everywhere—some towering as high as fifty feet as the cars were consumed. Some bodies were still recognizable as human but many had been completely torn apart and were now just unidentifiable hunks of flesh blackening in the flames. The two men who had been running at her and Eric were now lying facedown on the pavement only a few feet away. Their backs hadn't been close enough to the blasts to burn and instead were bristling with carpentry nails.

Quinn swallowed hard and stood. "Eric, can you walk?"

"I think so," he said, letting her help him to his feet. She was repositioning herself so she could help support his weight when she saw that one of the two men she had taken for dead had regained consciousness. He was still lying on his stomach but his head was raised and he had a gun aimed directly at them.

"Eric?"

"I see him."

In stark contrast to the condition of his back, the man's face was completely untouched. He was still clearly recognizable as the one who had been in command when they were captured in their hotel.

His hand jerked but he didn't fire. Instead he used the last of his strength to beat the grip of the gun on the asphalt in a fit of rage. Finally, the gun dropped from his hand and he laid his head down on the asphalt to die. But before he did, he said something. She couldn't be sure, but it sounded like "Good luck."

Quinn spotted the fatigue-clad man running up the dirt road just as she sent the tiny Isuzu into a four-wheel drift. She jerked the wheel right, missing him by only a few feet and nearly sending the car into the trees that bordered the sharp curve. When she looked in the rearview mirror, she saw that the soldier had stopped and was staring at them through the dust. She tensed, expecting him to pull a gun and fire at them. Instead he turned and started running again toward the black smoke rising from the forest behind them.

"Damn! Do you think we can get through that?" Quinn said as they closed on a tall chain-link gate topped with razor wire.

"I don't know," Eric said.

She slammed the accelerator to the floor and closed her eyes involuntarily just before impact. When she opened them again, the car was through the gate and jumping wildly as the condition of the road suddenly worsened.

"Quinn! Slow down."

She couldn't. For the first time since all this had started, she felt a true, undiluted panic take hold of her . . . she thought of the people torn apart by the bombs, bombs that she and Eric had sent them walking into . . . the brief moment when Marin had let her see what he really was . . . what he'd said to her: "You're safe from me today." She understood then that he was still in complete control—that he was manipulating their every move. And when he wanted to, he would find her, and then . . .

She saw the hard right turn ahead of them, but what it meant didn't really register with her.

"Quinn!"

The motor suddenly revved uncontrollably and

she jerked forward as the car slowed. Eric had pulled the stick shift into neutral and grabbed hold of the emergency brake. She tried desperately to pry his hand loose but couldn't make him release it.

"Are you crazy! Let go!" she yelled as the car drifted to a stop. "We've got to—"

"Quinn!" he shouted, setting the brake and grabbing her by the shoulders. "Look at me."

She did, managing to draw a little bit of calm from his dark eyes.

"There's no one left to chase us."

"Marin," she said. "He—"

"Marin's not interested in us right now." Eric reached out and gently gripped the back of her neck. "We're okay. Do you understand? We're okay."

"I . . . I'm sorry. You're right."

He gave her a reassuring squeeze and stepped from the car, walking back down the road in the direction they had come. He stopped about twenty feet away and stood staring up at the smoke rising from the trees. Quinn leaned her forehead on the wheel and took a few deep breaths, feeling her ability to think rationally slowly coming back to her. When she was ready, she pushed the door open and started walking toward him.

"Eric? What are you doing?"

He pulled his shirt over his head, wadded it up, and used it to stanch the trickle of blood still oozing from the wound in his side.

"Eric? Come on. We've got to get you to a hospital."

"It's nothing. I'm okay."

"We can't stay here," she said, stopping next to him. "Even if Marin isn't coming, someone is. The guards, the survivors . . ."

He shook his head solemnly. "No one will live through the next explosion."

She moved in front of him, blocking his view of whatever it was he was staring at. "What are you talking about?"

"Remember what he said? He said that it was all stolen from him—that he wasn't going to leave any of it."

"Eric. He was lying to us; he knew we'd pull the alarm. He just wanted to—"

"No. He had this planned the whole time, we just made it more fun for him. He'll wait for the guards to get there and for some of the people who weren't killed to go inside, then he'll blow the building."

Quinn held her breath for a moment and squeezed her eyes shut, trying to push back the fear, hate, and guilt that were building inside her. "We've got to go back," she heard herself say. "Enough people have died, Eric. We've got to warn them."

He shook his head. "It's too late."

The second blast came only moments later, just as he had prophesied. Quinn spun around as the dull rumble shook the ground beneath them. Chunks of flaming concrete and steel arced gracefully through the sky as the explosions came one after another. She didn't know how long it went on—but it was certainly long enough for her to know that Marin had succeeded and that nothing of Advanced Thermal Dynamics, and the people who worked for it, remained.

"Do you think . . . do you think he's dead?"

Eric just turned and started back toward the car.

57

Only about half the streetlights worked, illuminating partially constructed sidewalks and the
large mounds of dirt piled alongside them. There
were a few completed homes in the fledgling subdivision—large Colonials designed to tastefully re-
flect the wealth and stature of their occupants. He
was moving toward the largest, situated on the
highest point in the area and surrounded by an
open field of vacant lots.

Marin killed his headlights and coaxed the car up
Richard Price's steep driveway, navigating by the
light emanating from the house's large windows.
He examined himself in the rearview mirror for a
moment. The expression of calm benevolence and
self-consciousness that had served him so well over
the years wouldn't fully come. It was there on the

surface, but beneath there was a strange emptiness. Soon, he knew, he would have trouble holding on even to that. But for now, it would be enough.

He straightened his collar and looked down at himself. His lab coat had, for the most part, protected him. Other than an innocuous bloodstain on his cuff that had already faded to brown, and the faint smell of smoke clinging to him, nothing was amiss. He reached out and touched the tiny stain, letting himself relive for a moment the experience that had caused it, but carefully controlling the intensity. Years of fantasizing, planning, restraining himself; he had assumed that she would never be able to live up to his time-bloated expectations. Nothing could have been further from the truth. Cynthia had been magical. As magical as his first . . .

Marin stepped from the car and started up the driveway, careful to avoid the mud flowing into it from a recent rain. The door was lit by a single carriage lamp and he stood in its glow for a moment, trying to decide whether to knock or ring the bell. For some reason it seemed important. Every detail was important now.

The muffled chime was quickly followed by the rhythm of footsteps inside. A moment later the door cracked open a few inches, stopping when the chain across it pulled tight. He could see only a sliver of a face in the narrow crack—a blue eye, half a small, straight nose. A hint of blond hair.

"Hi," Marin said, a friendly smile spreading

across his face. "You must be Rachel. Is your father home?"

"He's not. Hang on." She closed the door and he heard the chain rattle. When it opened again, he was provided a full view of her.

"You don't look much like your picture," he said.

"Picture?"

"The one on your dad's desk. You're standing next to a tree with—"

She grimaced energetically. "Oh God. He still has that? It's **awful**."

The photo, Marin knew, had been taken two years before, when she was barely fourteen. Since then, her hair had grown to shoulder length and her body had begun to curve seductively.

"Well, I don't know. I thought it was cute." He offered his hand. "I'm Dr. Marin. Your father and I work together."

Her hand was just a little damp. Judging from the dish towel slung across her shoulder, probably with water and soap, not sweat.

"Do you know when your father's going to be back? It's kind of important that I talk to him."

"Maybe, like, an hour?"

It wasn't much time, but there had been no alternative to cutting it this close. While he was confident that he had completely destroyed ATD's communications capabilities, there would undoubtedly be survivors. In fact, he assumed that the majority of the guards stationed at the campus's perimeter were still alive and lucid. They would have no real access to Price, though; only upper management would know how to contact him at home or in his car, and they would be in no condition to do so. Of course, there was no way to be certain of any of this. But then, that was all part of the excitement.

Marin let a hint of worry darken his expression. It had the intended effect.

"Would you like to come in, Dr. Marin? If you don't mind sitting around for a while, you could wait . . ."

He made it look like he was considering the offer for a moment. "You know, maybe I should."

"So are you, like, a doctor doctor?" she said as she led him through the vestibule and into a spacious living room. Her jeans were worn enough to have turned white where her buttocks met her thighs. The outline of her bra was clearly visible through the thin white T-shirt, but Marin couldn't help wondering if it was really necessary to contain her small breasts.

"If I understand your question correctly, the answer is no. I'm a physicist."

She turned to face him with the grace of a gymnast, which, in fact, he knew her to be. "**Really?** How awful."

The smile that spread across his face actually held a hint of sincerity. Her unguarded countenance and barely harnessed energy were mesmerizing. He suddenly realized that he'd never really spent any time around girls her age. Even during his years as a college professor, they didn't make it to his classes until they were in their twenties.

"Awful? Why do you say that?"

"I have a physics test tomorrow. And I am completely clueless. Gravity. Black holes. I'm sorry, but who cares about that stuff?"

Marin pointed to her feet. "You should. Gravity's what keeps you from hitting your head on the ceiling."

She grimaced again. Apparently the subject was even more painful than that of the photograph on her father's desk.

"May I?" Marin said, pulling the dish towel off her shoulder. "Gravity's easy. Come here, I'll show you."

He put one edge of the towel on a table against the wall and secured it with a heavy bowl of fruit. "Okay, hold on to this for me." She did as he asked, taking the other side of the towel and holding it taut.

"Let's say that this towel is space. Are you picturing it?"

"I guess," she said.

"Good." He took an apple from the bowl and set it in the middle of the towel. "The apple's a planet, okay?"

"Okay."

"Let's see what happens." He placed a grape on

the edge of the towel and they watched it roll toward the indentation made by the apple. "Voilà. Gravity. Put it in three dimensions and that's all there is to it."

Rachel looked down at it for a moment and then smiled. "Really? That's it? What about a black hole?"

"Just as simple. What if that apple was a tenth the size and weighed a thousand pounds? What would happen?"

"Uh, I guess it would tear a hole in the towel."

"The what?"

"I mean, space."

"And what would happen to the grape?"

"It'd fall through."

"Exactly right."

She considered that for a moment. "But where does it go? It's got to come out somewhere."

"A very intelligent question," Marin said, genuinely impressed. "I don't know. Maybe another universe. Wouldn't that be neat?"

"Yeah. I guess it would kinda . . ."

"Rachel! Who are you talking to down there?"

Marin heard the woman's voice float down the stairs behind them, temporarily breaking the spell the young girl had cast on him.

"Is that your mother?"

Rachel nodded.

"Why don't we go up and see her?"

58

The glare from the oncoming headlights seemed to be timed perfectly to the dull throbbing in Richard Price's head. He looked away, focusing on the right edge of the road and maneuvering the car using only his peripheral vision.

Six hours. Six hours of posturing, cajoling, and endless explanations had achieved exactly nothing. Every time he sat through one of those meetings, he left telling himself that they couldn't get any worse. And every time he was proven wrong.

In the beginning, it had just been the typical political bullshit; arrogant elected officials—who hadn't read the materials he'd provided and whose daddies had gotten them out of military service—telling him where the next threat to America would come from and the best way to defend against it. Of course, their strategy had nothing to do with patriotic fervor and everything to do with whether or not a particular weapons system was manufactured in their state.

But now the meetings had slipped to a level of absurdity that was almost surreal. At first, the changes had been fairly subtle, but now, as the deployment of ATD's system became imminent, the shift in focus had become painfully obvious.

It was clear that these men were completely unprepared for the political ramifications of a fully operational space-based defense system. They had assumed ATD was just another bottomless pit to throw taxpayers' money into. And now they were beginning to panic—throwing up budgetary roadblocks and changing their demands and expectations almost daily in an effort to stop, or at least delay, the inevitable.

Price was grateful for the quiet darkness that descended over the car as he pulled off the highway and onto the street that led to his neighborhood. He navigated mostly by memory, replaying the meeting in his head one last time. They had cut off a substantial portion of his funding—effective immediately—in a last-ditch effort to slow him down. It wouldn't work. With the unpredictability that Marin introduced into the project, it had always been clear that an interruption in the flow of money could be devastating. Every minute that Marin was able to contribute to the project was precious and had to be exploited to its fullest. The contingency fund Price had secretly created would be sufficient to complete the project. Admittedly, it would be tight, but with the major theoretical hurdles cleared and Marin momentarily docile, it would be enough.

Price eased into his driveway, frowning when he was forced to squeeze past a car he didn't recognize in order to get into the garage. If that belonged to a friend of Rachel's, they damn well better be studying. One more C in science and she'd find herself grounded until she was twenty.

Price stepped out into the garage and moved around to the back door to retrieve his briefcase, but then decided against it. No more work tonight. He just wanted to take a shower and slip into bed.

"Connie! Are you home?" he shouted, stepping over a pile of laundry in the mudroom and continuing toward the door leading to the kitchen.

"Connie! Are you—"

Price threw an arm out and managed to brace himself against the refrigerator before his legs collapsed beneath him.

"I'm sorry, General. Did you say something?" Edward Marin's torso moved back and forth, like a tree swaying in the wind. Or a snake. He was standing directly behind Rachel, his body framing what Price could see of her face over the large island that dominated the kitchen.

"No." The sound that came from his mouth wasn't really a voice—more of a structured breath.

Price moved slowly to his left, careful not to make any sudden moves and keeping his eyes locked on Marin. He was almost unrecognizable. His normally perfect hair was tangled and matted with sweat, his mouth was curled into a cruel smile that showed his teeth in a way that didn't seem human. Price had seen hints of this before, brief flashes. But he'd never considered what it would be like to see what was inside Marin come fully to the surface.

When Price finally came out from behind the tall counter and saw what had been done to his little girl, he felt the muscles around his stomach clench uncontrollably. He doubled over, almost bringing up the dinner he'd been served two hours before.

"Is something wrong, General?"

She was naked, secured to a kitchen chair with coat hangers. Her pale skin was crisscrossed with narrow slits beginning just below her neck and stopping at her knees. The blood had begun to clot in some of the shallower gashes, but others still flowed red down her body. Price blinked hard, trying to block the images of his daughter's birth and life that were beginning to clog his mind.

"I'm sorry, General. I'm being rude. You're probably worrying about your wife. She's upstairs. But I'm afraid she . . . died."

"You son of a bitch." Price found his voice as the

adrenaline started to flow through him. "I'm going to kill you."

He took a step forward but then stopped when he saw the flash of the X-Acto knife. Marin wrapped his hands around Rachel from behind and began smearing blood in slow circles around her right breast. Her head moved slightly when he began rolling her nipple between his index finger and thumb. She was alive.

Price reached into his jacket and pulled out his nine-millimeter. "Get away from her! Do it now!"

Marin leaned in a little closer to Rachel, brushing her hair back with his lips and whispering something in her ear. He took her chin in his hand and pulled her head up. Price saw her eyelids flutter, but he refocused on Marin again before she could fix her eyes on him. "I said move away!"

Marin continued to play thoughtfully with her nipple, keeping his knife close enough to her throat to make it impossible for Price to risk firing.

"Do you have anything you'd like to tell her, Richard? She's still conscious. You've given me a lot of practice at keeping them conscious."

"I said get the fuck away from her!" He'd managed a shout this time, but it didn't carry any real force. Tears began to blur his vision and he was forced to wipe them away.

"I don't understand, Richard. You seem upset. The laser's still important, isn't it? It was important enough to sacrifice those other fathers' daughters."

Marin took a deep breath, seeming to drink in the scent of Rachel's hair. "I don't want you to worry, though, Richard. I told her your story. And I know she's proud of you for the sacrifices you've made for your country."

"Get away from her!" Price screamed. "Please!"

Marin finally did as he was told, taking a single step to his left. As he did, though, he drew the knife across her throat.

"No!"

Price watched helplessly as the blood rolled down his daughter's breasts and stomach, finally flowing down between her naked thighs and cascading to the floor. She didn't seem to completely comprehend what had happened. She just stared at him, confused, until the light that had shone so brightly in her eyes finally went out. But just before it did, there was a brief flash of understanding. Of accusation.

Price's stomach finally rebelled and he doubled over, vomiting uncontrollably and struggling to keep his pistol trained on Marin. When he was finally able to straighten up, he saw that Marin hadn't moved. He was just standing there with a mockery of sympathy on his face.

"You can't kill me," he said as Price leveled the pistol at his chest. "Think of your duty. Think of America."

Price ran at him, firing as fast as he could make his finger squeeze the trigger. Marin jerked backward, struggling to maintain his balance, and then crumpled to the floor. Price dropped to his knees, his mind registering the holes in Marin's shirt directly over his heart, but it wasn't enough. He dropped his gun and began swinging his fist over and over into Marin's face, feeling his knuckles contact with bone, flesh, and teeth, seeing the blood spatter from his split lips. But that wasn't enough either. He picked up the gun again and swung it down, butt first.

It never connected.

Marin's hand shot out, catching his wrist in a grip that seemed impossibly powerful. Price could feel his bones grinding together and slammed a fist into Marin's chest, trying to free himself before they began to crack. When his hand impacted, he felt the dense padding of a bulletproof vest.

"Did you really think I'd make it that easy?" Marin said, the blood rolling from his mouth as he spoke. "You disappoint me, Richard."

59

Are you sure this is it?"

"No."

Quinn could barely see the outline of Eric's face in the dim light. The streetlights that had been erected in this part of the subdivision were widely scattered and in various stages of completion, as were the houses. Everything looked dead, abandoned. Everything, that is, except the large home towering above them on an unlandscaped hill. There was a dull glow coming from the windows— not quite enough to see if you looked directly at it, but undoubtedly there.

Eric had been the one who'd finally turned up the address. Between them, they'd talked to every military and pseudomilitary organization in the phone book, finding them all equally tight-lipped. Calls to golf and video clubs, and even to an old college friend of Quinn's who worked at the IRS, had also proven to be a waste of time. The turning point had come when Eric had phoned a long-retired professor of mathematics who had consulted for the U.S. Space Command. It seemed that he still exchanged Christmas cards with the elusive Richard Price and had his home address.

Quinn pressed up against Eric and let the warmth of him overcome some of the chill she felt. It had started to rain again—not hard, but enough for the cold mist to begin working its way through her T-shirt. "What do you think?"

"I think the same thing I thought an hour ago— that we should go to Phoenix and find that FBI agent of yours."

"What would we go to him with? We don't have the files anymore and I think we can be pretty sure that the originals are a pile of ashes by now. ATD and most everyone who ever worked for it are gone too. And you're wanted in connection with the deaths of at least four people . . ."

He sighed quietly. "Okay, maybe we lack a certain credibility, but—"

"I think that's kind of an understatement, don't you?"

"Fine. Let's say we do this. And let's say Price is home. What then?"

She'd given that a fair amount of thought but still hadn't come up with any hard answers. Finding Price seemed to be the only path left to take. Marin, if he was still alive, would undoubtedly make himself disappear. He had no family, no home anymore, and soon would have an army of trained professionals trying to find him and blow his head off. Price, though, couldn't so easily disconnect himself from the world.

"We talk," she said.

"We talk," he repeated. "And what are we going to say?"

"I don't know."

She saw his head move toward her, but her eyes still hadn't adjusted to the darkness enough for her to read his expression. "A few hours ago this guy was getting ready to spend his day burning us with cigarettes . . ."

"And yet now he seems to be our best friend in the world."

"I'm serious, Quinn."

She shrugged. "So am I. Look, all his people—everything he was out to protect—are gone now. And that leaves us with something in common."

"Marin."

"As long as he's alive, you, me, and Price are going to be waiting for him to pop out of the woodwork. I don't know about you, but I can't live like that."

Eric was silent for what seemed a long time. The cold continued to seep into her, but she didn't rush him. The truth was, she didn't want to go up that hill any more than he did.

"And what if he doesn't see it that way? What if he hasn't changed his mind about us?"

She didn't answer.

"That's what I thought."

"Eric, we **have** to get through to him, it's as simple as that."

"I'm sorry to say that I don't share your faith in humanity." He pushed her away and slid something from beneath his shirt. As its outline became visible, she recognized it as the handle from the jack in his car.

"What's that for?"

"Guess."

"Eric . . ."

"What choice do we have? If he isn't with us he's against us, Quinn. With him gone, there's a good chance that there won't be anyone from ATD still alive who knows about us. Then all we have to worry about is Marin. And as far as I'm concerned, that's enough."

Quinn looked away from him and concentrated on the house hovering above.

"Can you do it?" she said finally. "Could you just kill him?"

"I don't know," he admitted. "Could you?"

"I don't know."

She followed him along the street and then up the steep driveway to Price's front door. The light was strong enough there to see a shaky resolve form in Eric's eyes as he held his makeshift club in one hand and turned the knob with the other.

The door swung open silently and they both examined the wide entryway, listening for movement. There was nothing, though. Nothing but wood floors and tasteful furniture.

Eric stepped through first, moving along the hall toward what seemed to be the only source of light in the house. Quinn followed, walking backward so that she could see anyone coming up behind them. She could feel her heart pounding in her chest and tried to slow it by telling herself that the men who had been trying so hard to kill her were dead. It didn't work.

When Eric stopped at the end of the hallway, she almost ran into him. He turned and looked into her eyes for a moment. The communication was silent, but completely clear. The point of no return.

She saw his knuckles whiten around the tire iron as he stepped across the threshold into the next room. He froze after less than two feet. "Oh, Jesus . . ."

Quinn moved out into the room and instantly felt the tears well up in her eyes. The source of the glow bleeding through the windows of the house was a single track light. It had been turned to spotlight a naked, blood-soaked girl wired to a chair.

"Leave her," Eric said, grabbing Quinn's shoulder as she tried to get past him. "She's dead. And we've got to get out of here."

Quinn tried to pull away. Maybe she wasn't dead. Maybe she was hanging on, like the girl she'd found before. They could call an ambulance, paramedics . . .

"Quinn!" His voice was a harsh whisper. "Quinn! Look at her! There's nothing you can do."

She felt herself being pulled toward the front of the house, but couldn't seem to take her eyes off the girl. Her untouched face was completely smooth and stark white, in contrast with the drying blood that covered the rest of her. Even in the horrible state she'd been left in, it was obvious that she was only in her middle teens. How many more? How many more would there be before . . .

Eric came to a sudden stop just as they reentered the vestibule. "General Price?"

Quinn turned her head slowly, looking past him. The outline of the man standing in front of the door was dim but unmistakable, as was the outline of the gun in his hand.

"General Price?" Eric said again. In response, the shadow moved forward and let the light catch his long, gray hair.

"You never disappoint, do you?" Marin's voice seemed to come from everywhere at once, an uncomfortable quivering in the air. They backed away as he advanced.

"I knew you'd find me."

"What do you want?" Eric said as they entered

the kitchen again, keeping the distance between them and Marin constant.

"What do I want . . . I don't really know anymore. Isn't that wonderful?" He stepped into the light and Quinn could see that his face and clothes were streaked with blood. His hair was matted to his forehead, darkening his eyes and partially obscuring the bruising and swelling that was beginning to mar his handsome face. She tensed when he swung the gun in their direction but he only used it to point to the floor behind her. "Don't fall, dear."

"**Jesus!**" Quinn shouted, jumping to her right to avoid stepping on Richard Price. He was lying motionless on his back in a pool of blood that was slowly making its way across the wood floor.

"I have to thank you both for your help earlier," Marin said. "I believe you succeeded in killing nearly everyone."

"Why?" Quinn said. "Why do all this? Why hurt those people?"

Marin thought about that for a moment, scratching his chin with the barrel of the gun. "They turned me into a pet, Quinn. Enslaved me, used me. Held my freedom over me."

"At least that's what they thought," Quinn said, trying to keep him talking; trying to keep him from carrying out whatever scheme it was that had kept him there, waiting. "But you've been planning this for years . . ."

"Unconsciously, probably from the first day. And now I've succeeded. I've completely erased ten years of research and development in the span of a few hours. The Afghans and North Koreans can let their missiles fly without having to worry about them being destroyed in their silos. The world's more exciting that way, don't you think?"

Quinn yelped when Marin suddenly threw his gun to Eric, who was forced to drop the tire iron to catch it. He stared down at it for a moment and then took unsteady aim at Marin.

"The answer to the question you want to ask is yes. It is loaded," Marin said, edging closer to them as he spoke. "You know, Eric, the one thing that weighed on me through all this was the thought of being killed by some cretin. By Renquist, or Price, or that pig Lowell. You don't know how relieved I am to know that there's no longer any chance of that."

"Don't come any closer," Eric warned. "Just stop right there. Move back."

Marin did as he was told, stepping backward until the wall stopped him. "Is this better?"

"Just . . . just stay right there, Edward. Don't . . . don't move."

"Pull the lever back," Marin suggested.

"What?"

Marin made a motion like he was cocking the gun and Eric followed his instructions, chambering a round.

"Are you ready, Eric?" Marin bounced his back off the wall and looked over at Quinn. "What about you?"

"Eric. Shoot him," she said.

Marin started moving toward them again, weaving gracefully back and forth with his eyes locked on the gun in Eric's hand.

"Shoot him!"

"Edward, don't come any closer."

"ERIC! SHOOT HIM!"

Quinn was about to grab for the gun when it bucked in Eric's hand. Marin jerked out of the way with almost supernatural speed and the bullet embedded itself harmlessly in the wall.

Eric pulled the trigger again but the gun just clicked.

"No second chances," Marin said, starting forward again. Quinn backed away and he adjusted his trajectory a little, seeming to forget that Eric even existed.

"Quinn! Run!" Eric scooped up the tire iron and swung it with everything he had, but Marin dodged the blow and clamped a hand around Eric's throat. Quinn stayed where she was for a moment, watching Eric claw uselessly at the finger digging into his neck. He tried to swing the tire iron again, but Marin caught it and yanked it from his hand.

This was her chance. She could run—make it to the car and disappear. The price for her escape, though, was Eric's life.

Quinn ran at the two men, grabbing Marin by the hair and trying to drag him off Eric, who was starting to weaken. She went for his eyes with clawed fingers but was knocked to the floor when an elbow connected with her temple. The blow wasn't especially powerful, but combined with the mild concussion she had already suffered, it made getting back to her feet surprisingly difficult. She watched helplessly as Marin hooked an arm between Eric's legs and lifted him off the floor, carrying him toward the sofa in the center of the room, raising him up a few more feet, and then smashing him down on the coffee table. His body crashed through the glass top and he lay unconscious, tangled in the table's iron frame.

"Quinn? Are you all right? You're not injured, are you?" Marin said, as he turned back toward her.

She made it partway to her feet and stumbled toward the hallway. When she looked back, she saw that he had dropped to the floor and was crawling toward her at a speed that made him look almost like a videotape in fast forward. She made it a few more feet before his hand clamped around her ankle and she was dragged to the ground. He moved over her like a giant spider, crawling up her back and immobilizing her with practiced efficiency. When he spoke, she could feel his lips brush her ear. "Don't cry, Quinn. Not now. Not yet."

60

Are you hungry?"

Quinn couldn't bring herself to look at him but didn't dare turn completely away either. She stared directly through the windshield, trying futilely to extract some comfort from the normalcy speeding by—the shops, the restaurants, the people. None of it seemed to be part of her world anymore. Her entire universe had shrunk down to the interior of this car and the man hovering at the edge of her vision.

"Are you hungry?" Marin repeated.

She twisted around in the passenger seat a few inches, intensifying the pain in her tightly handcuffed wrists. His face had continued to swell and darken, but it was hard to tell how much of the distortion was the result of his injuries and how much was the result of what was left of his humanity slipping away.

She wanted to speak, to say something that could stop this. Her books said that this type of killer could be appealed to, that she should try to make herself seem real and not just an unwilling prop in his fantasy. But she knew that there was nothing left in him to appeal to. He would just enjoy it.

"We have to keep your strength up," he said, turning the car off the road and pulling into a McDonald's drive-through.

He never took his eyes completely off her as he leaned out the window and spoke into the microphone. "Two cheeseburgers, two large fries, and . . . I think root beers. Two medium root beers."

He picked up the X-Acto knife lying on the console between them as he pulled the car forward. Quinn held her breath when he reached down and touched her bare shin just below the hem of her skirt. His hand—and the knife—ran slowly up her leg, lifting the fabric as it went. By the time the car had rolled to a stop next to the pickup window, he had the blade pressed up between her legs hard enough to cut through the fabric of her panties. She could feel the cold sharpness of it.

Quinn tried to control her obvious trembling as he turned toward her and smiled. The act pulled his split lips apart and sent blood drooling down his chin. Despite this, she could see that his eyes had undergone a miraculous transformation back to something that approached normalcy—though it wasn't as complete as the metamorphosis she had seen at ATD. His ability to create the illusion of benevolence and gentleness seemed to be slipping away along with everything else.

"That's eight dollars and twenty-three cents, please . . . Jeez, mister. Are you all right?"

"I'm fine. Thank you for asking."

Quinn couldn't see the girl's face, only her hand as Marin exchanged a ten-dollar bill for the bag of food.

"Keep the change."

She wanted to scream but found herself mute. There was no car in front of them; if she made any sound at all, she knew, he would use the knife between her legs. But not enough to kill her. He would cut her and then simply step on the gas. They would be gone before the girl in the window knew what had happened. And his rage would be further fueled.

Marin's eyes melted back into a malevolent blankness as they pulled away, but with one additional component—a deep satisfaction that verged on sexual release.

He removed the blade with agonizing slowness, seeming to have already forgotten the bag of food and the two cups on the dash. This is what it was about for him. Control. He had given Quinn an opportunity to defy him and she had been too afraid to take it.

"What do you want from me?" she heard herself say after a few minutes of silence. As much as she didn't want to know, as much as she wanted to lie to herself until the last possible moment, she couldn't bear the anticipation any longer. Images of the dead little girl they'd just left, of the woman she'd found in Eric's house, of the pictures in the police files played relentlessly across her mind.

"I have a treat for you—for us, really," he said.

Quinn closed her eyes tight and felt the warm tears run down her face. There was no one left to help her. No one knew Marin existed—and even if they did, they wouldn't be able to find him unless he wanted them to. She saw Eric's body draped across Price's smashed coffee table, and the pain and death that surrounded him. There was a part of her that hoped he was dead. In the end, it would be easier for him that way.

61

Eric Twain wasn't sure how long it took for the darkness to fade to white or for his mind to finally grasp that he was staring at the ceiling. The process of untangling himself from the frame of the table took a lot longer than it should have, but at last he was able to rise unsteadily to his feet. He touched the back of his head and then his injured ribs, unsure of the source of the worst pain.

Looking around him, he saw that nothing had changed—except that Marin and Quinn were gone. Price was still lying on the floor and the young girl was still wired to the chair, dead. He let out a low groan as he walked through the broken glass to the center of the room.

He glanced up at the clock, estimating that he had been unconscious for no more than twenty minutes, and then looked down at himself. Miraculously, he didn't seem to have been cut. The deep gash in his side had started to ooze again and there was an impressive bump swelling from the back of his skull, but that was it. He had escaped being thrown like a rag doll through a coffee table with nothing much more than a splitting headache.

"Quinn!" he shouted, more to push back the silence than in any real hope of a response. He took a dish towel from the stove and used it to slow the bleeding in his side as he moved methodically through the ground floor of the house.

"Quinn!"

Nothing.

He went for the stairs but stopped at the first step.

For a brief moment he thought the woman sitting on the second-floor landing was staring at him. The illusion passed when it became obvious that she was beyond seeing.

Much older than the girl in the kitchen, she was still wearing a green blouse, though she was naked from the waist down. Across the inside of her right thigh was a deep gash that had severed her femoral artery and sent her life cascading down the stairs. Other than that, her only injury seemed to be the cuts that had opened on her wrist beneath the handcuff securing her to the railing.

Eric didn't want to think about what had happened to her as he moved through the blood on the steps, but he couldn't help himself. She must have been Price's wife—and that little girl's mother. Had Marin cut her first and let her die trying to free herself? Or had he just secured her to the railing and then gone to work on her little girl?

When he got to the top step, he discovered the truth. The pinkish-white of bone was visible beneath the handcuffs—she had been forced to listen to her daughter being tortured and raped, and she had nearly severed her own hand trying to stop it.

Eric looked away as he stepped around the woman's body, doing his best to shut off his emotions. Once past her, he searched every room and confirmed what he already knew: Quinn was gone.

He went through a medicine cabinet and came up with a roll of athletic tape. As he descended the stairs, he secured the dish towel tightly to the gash in his side, slowing the bleeding to the point where it could clot.

"What now?" he said aloud. "Think."

He had to find her before Marin had time . . . Eric shook his head violently, not letting himself consider the consequences of failure. He needed an unclouded mind to reason this through. All that mattered now was finding Quinn.

But how? Marin could do whatever he wanted, go wherever he wanted. No one knew he existed. Even insane and focused solely on his own twisted fantasies, how long could he survive before he was discovered and tracked down? A month? Two? Six? How many women would die?

Eric bent forward at the waist when he felt the blood starting to rush from his head. There had to be an answer. He had to think. Even in apparent chaos, there was always a pattern. Where would Marin have gone . . . ?

The siren was almost inaudible at first. Eric turned his head slowly, bringing his ear in line with the sound and realizing that it was growing louder.

"Shit!" he mumbled, and started moving around the room as quickly and efficiently as he could. There was no way to know if that cop was coming here or just driving by, but what was certain was that he couldn't afford to be found. Not yet. Quinn's clock was ticking and she didn't have time for him to explain all this.

Thirty seconds of searching didn't turn up the gun. Marin must have taken it. Eric dropped to his knees and moved his hands along Richard Price's body, looking for a weapon. He found a holster, but it was empty.

"No!"

Eric fell backward, barely avoiding being hit in the face by a wild swing from Price's right arm. He kept scooting away, his heart racing uncontrollably, until his back hit the island in the center of the kitchen.

A slow wail escaped the man. It had no real volume but carried a depth of despair that seemed almost infinite. A moment later Price's eyes opened and he lifted his head a few inches off the floor.

"You aren't dead. Why aren't you dead?" Eric said,

and then realized how obvious it was. Why would he be? Marin would want Price alive so that he could suffer, so that he would remember that he had caused the death of his own family and would spend the last years of his life wondering exactly what Marin had done to his daughter before he had killed her.

Eric crawled back over to the man and grabbed him by the front of his jacket, lifting his back off the floor. The sirens were getting louder.

"Wake up, you son of a bitch!"

Price's body remained limp but his eyes started to track. Eric saw a hint of recognition begin to spark in them.

"Get the fuck up!" Eric shouted, dragging the man to his feet. Price swayed slightly but looked like he could stand under his own power.

Other than his back, which was soaked through with blood, and a darkening bruise on his forehead, he looked uninjured. In fact, Eric wasn't dead sure that the blood Price had been lying in was his own.

"We're getting out of here," Eric said. "Now!" He grabbed hold of Price again and tried to drag him toward the back of the house, but the man resisted with surprising strength. "My . . . my wife."

"She's dead."

"No, she can't be. I—"

Eric curled his hands through the lapels of the man's jacket again and moved in until their noses were nearly touching. "You can trust me on this, General. Thanks to you, I'm an expert on dead."

Price pulled away and stumbled backward, inadvertently turning toward what was left of his daughter.

Eric caught him before he could crumple to the ground. The man's sobs went silent when Eric wrapped an arm around his neck and partially cut off his air. Price reached out toward his daughter, but didn't have the strength to resist as Eric dragged him back. The walls of the house were starting to swirl in an eerie red and blue as a police cruiser came up the driveway.

The answer to the question Eric had asked himself earlier came to him as they crashed through the back door into the cold rain. If Price couldn't, or wouldn't, help find Quinn, Eric knew what he would do. He'd strangle the life out of the bastard. And he'd enjoy every minute of it.

Dragging Price's nearly dead weight through the deep mud became increasingly difficult as they moved farther into the darkness. It got even worse when Price suddenly snapped from his stupor and started to struggle, writhing wildly and clawing at the arm around his neck. Eric tightened his grip and kept moving, sinking at least six inches into the topsoil with every step.

The ground beneath them turned solid again as they entered a thick stand of trees about two hundred meters from the house, allowing Eric to move a little faster and Price to thrash even harder. Another thirty seconds and they'd reached a wooden fence surrounding the backyard of a well-lit house at the edge of the trees. Eric twisted violently, slamming Price face first to the ground and landing hard on top of him.

"Stop it!" Eric whispered through clenched teeth. Price kept trying to free himself, so Eric shoved the man's face into the wet earth and held it there. He wasn't proud of the satisfaction he felt when Price's air was finally completely cut off, but he didn't really care anymore. When he felt the man's writhing start to lose its urgency, Eric released his head and listened to him gasp for air.

"Do we understand each other now, General?"

He thought Price was going to try to fight again but his body just went limp and his head sank slowly to the ground.

"The only reason I don't kill you now is because I need you to help me find Quinn."

When Price finally spoke, his voice was barely audible. "You think I care?"

The authority, confidence, and power that he had exuded at their first meeting was completely gone now. He sounded small. Weak.

"Yeah. I think you care," Eric said. "Because if we find Quinn, we find Marin. I assume that you have something you'd like to say to him after what he did to your family? Or do you not care about them either?"

That got a reaction. Price tried to twist around but didn't have the leverage or strength. Eric shoved his face back into the ground, then released it almost immediately. This time Price spit out the mud and grass with a little more enthusiasm.

"Where is he?" Eric said.

"How the fuck would I know?"

"Think! Does he have another house somewhere? A relative? A night job? Did you schedule a victim for him? Think!"

Price stiffened but didn't try to break free again. His breath was coming shorter and harder as his mind processed what had happened.

Anger. Good. He could use that.

"Don't move," Eric ordered as he climbed off the man. He shoved Price's jacket up and tore his shirt, exposing a surprisingly muscular back. The blood was definitely his—the narrow gashes in his skin were visible in the light coming from the house next to them. Eric used the edges of the torn shirt to wipe away the excess blood so that he could get a better idea if any of the cuts were life threatening.

None looked particularly deep. He pressed on the ones that were still seeping for a few seconds and then pulled back to see if the bleeding was under control. When he did, he finally saw the pattern. The cuts weren't random—Marin had carved something in the man's back.

An address.

62

Quinn tried to cram herself farther into the gap between the seat and the car door as Marin's hand passed her and flipped open the glove box. A moment later the garage door of the small suburban home in front of them began to open. She closed her eyes as they pulled inside, hearing the sound of the car's engine replaced by the loud hum of the motor closing the door. And then silence as she was completely cut off from the outside world.

She opened her eyes again as Marin stepped out of the car. The garage was neatly arranged, with everything stored on a high shelf that circled the walls. It was all too normal: bicycles, a pair of skis, worn cardboard boxes with XMAS scrawled across them. This wasn't his house. She was sure of that.

"Come." He leaned in through the open door and held a hand out toward her. She didn't move.

"Don't do this, Dr. Marin. You're . . . you're one of the most brilliant men in history. You know it's wrong. You don't want to be remembered for this."

She knew she was just babbling. What could she possibly say that would stop him? Over the last twenty-four hours he had been responsible for hundreds of deaths. And in the decades before, he had raped, tortured, and killed another thirty-two.

She twisted around and kicked at him over the console when he tried to grab her. "NO! Don't touch me! Stay away!" She missed his face by less than half an inch, allowing him to catch her ankle in a grip that she knew would be impossible for her to break.

"Stop! Let go!" she screamed as he dragged her across the seats. She thrashed violently, ignoring the handcuffs tearing at her wrists, and trying futilely to get a hand around the steering wheel.

She took a deep breath as his fingers dug into her thigh and she was forced out onto the concrete floor. The scream that she prayed the people sleeping in the surrounding houses might hear was stifled when he clamped a hand over her mouth.

He waited for her to exhale and then pinched her nose shut. She panicked, struggling against him even harder, but quickly began to weaken from the lack of oxygen. Just as bright points of light started flashing before her eyes, the hand over her mouth withdrew. She gasped for breath, but when she did, he forced a rag into her open mouth. A moment later it had been efficiently secured with tape and she was desperately taking in air through her nose as he dragged her into the house.

She felt her strength coming back to her as she was pulled across the kitchen floor, but didn't bother to fight. There was nothing that could stop this now. She had known it the moment Eric had crashed through that table. How long would it take before she finally died? An hour? Two?

Please, not more than two.

Marin released her and sat in the small of her back as he handcuffed her ankles together. It wasn't until her feet were pulled up behind her and secured to the chain between her hands that it occurred to her that this wasn't right. This wasn't how Marin tied his victims.

She was pulled roughly to her knees and saw Marin's face hovering in front of her. "Quinn!"

She was having a hard time focusing.

"Quinn!"

She saw the pink of his teeth as his swollen lips curled into a smile. "Are you back with me?"

She couldn't speak around the gag but her expression seemed to satisfy him. It was when he began walking back toward the garage that Quinn saw her.

She was only about three feet away. Probably a couple of years older than Quinn, with long dark hair and a thin but curvaceous body that was completely exposed. Her hands were wired to a kitchen table that had been nailed to the floor and her feet were similarly secured to two thick eyebolts screwed into the wall.

Quinn squeezed her eyes shut for a moment, trying to block everything out. When she opened them again, the woman was looking directly at her. She could see the terror in her eyes, and the dull streaks where tears had flowed down her temples and dried.

"I see you two have met," Marin said when he returned. He passed by Quinn and stepped over the woman, placing a cooler on the floor next to her. "I told you I had a treat for you," he said, pulling an IV bag full of blood out and hanging it on the table. "For us, actually."

Quinn turned her head away while he located a vein in the woman's arm. She saw the woman's feet had turned completely white beneath the wire securing them. How long had she been there? How long had he been planning this?

Quinn heard a muffled grunt come from the woman. At first she thought it was a response to the needle, but when she looked back, it was already taped into place and Marin was putting on a thick apron.

Quinn knew what the woman wanted, but resisted. She couldn't handle any more. She couldn't.

Finally, Quinn raised her head and met the

woman's gaze, looking directly into her eyes. The contact seemed to calm the woman a little.

"Beautiful, aren't they?" Marin said.

Quinn maintained eye contact, trying to convey strength and courage that she didn't think she had anymore.

"It's amazing," he continued. "The brightness in their eyes when they're like this. How alive they look. She's working on her Ph.D. in geology—by all accounts a brilliant woman. She understands what's happening to her. Not like those **things** Price tried to satisfy me with. They never looked like this. They were half-dead already. Stupid. Weak. Boring."

The girl screamed pathetically through her gag when Marin's hand came up between her legs and explored her there, but she didn't break eye contact. Quinn wanted to cry, but she didn't have any tears left.

"Look at me, Quinn. Quinn?"

The woman didn't want to let her go and whimpered quietly when Quinn did as Marin asked.

"I want to tell you the rules." He took an X-Acto knife and a pair of pliers from the pocket of his apron and laid them on the woman's quivering stomach. "Every time you look away, I'm going to remove one of your fingers. Not with the knife, though. With the pliers. Do you understand?"

She just stared.

"It's important that you understand. Do you?"

She finally managed a short nod.

"Good."

Quinn looked into his victim's face again, trying to comfort her and not let her eyes betray what she knew was about to happen.

"No, no," Marin said, running a hand through the woman's hair and gently turning her head toward him. "Don't look at her. Look at me."

63

General! No!" Eric slammed on the brakes, trying to hit Price with the door as he jumped from the still-moving car. Price dodged it with ease that belied his age and injuries and began running up the driveway toward the nondescript suburban house.

Eric stepped from the car a little more cautiously—not so much out of fear for his safety but out of fear for what he might find. The address that had been carved into Price's back had initially led them to a gas station on the other side of town. After a ten-minute search, they had turned up an envelope with the address of another gas station. And the envelope they found there had led them to this house—almost four hours after Marin had abducted Quinn.

"General?" Eric said, stepping across the threshold of the open front door.

No response at first, then an unintelligible shout from Price and the sound of shattering glass. Eric ran forward, ripping a heavy wooden lamp from the wall and trying to forget Marin's superhuman strength. If Price could hold Marin's attention for just a few seconds, that would be all he would need. He would use the lamp to crush Marin's skull, finally putting an end to one of the most brilliant and horribly twisted minds in history.

When Eric burst into the kitchen, though, he found Price sweeping the contents of the kitchen counter onto the floor.

"General, where is he? Where's Marin?"

Price was out of control, overturning a shelf full of dishes, ripping cabinet doors off their hinges. The cuts in his back had started to seep again and his shirt was matted against his skin.

Eric moved forward cautiously, and as he did, the legs started to emerge from behind a wall dividing the kitchen from a small dining area—naked and crisscrossed with narrow wounds. He dropped the lamp and forced himself to keep moving, staring down at the woman's body as it was revealed.

"Not her," he heard himself say. "Please, not her."

When the long dark hair came into view, he let out the breath that he hadn't been aware he was holding. He'd never seen this woman before in his life.

He felt a touch of guilt at the relief he felt as he

stood over her. The narrow slashes seemed to cover every inch of her skin, except her face and neck, which remained completely untouched. The empty IV bag hanging from the kitchen table was still attached to her arm.

The sound of splintering furniture coming from behind him faltered and went silent as Eric crouched down and closed what he could see had once been beautiful green eyes.

"She's fucking dead!" Price said, taking up a position directly behind him "And he's long gone. We're wasting time."

The corpse was in the same condition as the others—the woman who had been killed in Eric's bedroom, the ones he had seen in the police photos. But with one glaring exception. This one had been released. The hangers were still wound around her wrists and ankles, but they had been detached from the table legs and from the two eyebolts in the wall.

"I know she's dead," Eric said with undisguised hatred. "But she's also untied. He left us another message."

When Price reached for the dead woman's shoulder to flip her over, Eric lashed out, backhanding Price full in the face and almost knocking him over backward.

"Don't touch her!"

Price regained his balance and looked like he was going to rush forward again, but then seemed to think better of it.

Eric took a deep breath and gently slid his hands beneath her, but immediately withdrew them.

"What the fuck's the problem—"

"Shut up!" Eric shouted. "Just shut the hell up!"

Eric turned back to the woman and slid his hands beneath her naked body again. He hadn't been prepared for how sickeningly cold she'd feel. This time, though, he was able to roll her over.

It was there, as he knew it would be. He used his sleeve to wipe away the excess blood and reveal the letters and numbers carved much more deeply into her than they had been into Price.

"What is it? What does it say?"

"It's an address. In Annandale."

Annandale was one of the countless Virginia suburbs that surrounded Washington, D.C. Eric glanced at his watch. It was two in the morning, so there would be no traffic. His best guess was that they could be there in an hour.

He fell back onto the floor and watched Price disappear down the hallway that led to the front door. He wanted to follow, to slam the accelerator to the floor and race across town. To find Quinn alive.

But that wasn't what was going to happen. It would be another gas station. And that would lead to another gas station. Finally, they would end up at another suburban house with another dead woman in it. Maybe Quinn, maybe someone else. And eventually, Marin would get tired of this little game and finish it.

As expected, Price reappeared after about a minute.

"Losing your nerve, Twain?" he hissed. "I thought you wanted my help? I thought you wanted to find him."

Eric didn't bother to look up, instead concentrating on the empty wall across from him. They would never track Marin down like this. They had to stop playing his game. Anticipate him.

"Give me the keys," Price said. "If you don't have what it takes to follow this through, I goddamn well do."

"And how exactly are you going to 'follow this through,' General? By doing everything Marin tells you to? By running around like an idiot until he gets tired of pulling your strings? This isn't just about your revenge. Quinn—"

Price's bitter laughter drowned out the rest of Eric's words.

"Quinn," he said. "Your little girlfriend's dead. **Dead.** You know that as well as I do. Marin tied her down and cut her apart."

Eric jumped to his feet, grabbing the lamp he'd brought in with him and lifting it above his head threateningly.

"Gonna kill me, boy? Do it." Price leaned forward, giving Eric a better angle on his head. "Go on. What's stopping you?"

Eric let the lamp drop to the floor. He still had a chance to save her. That's all that mattered now.

"How many, General? How many like this?"

"It doesn't matter," Price said. "I did what had to be done. The missile defense system . . ." His voice trailed off as the rationalization he had invoked so many times became lost in the image of his daughter's body.

"There is no more missile defense system. Marin lured everyone outside into the parking lot and blew them apart. They're all dead. Do you understand? They're all dead."

He could see that Price was struggling to process what he was being told. There was no point to any of this, Eric knew, but he couldn't stop himself. He wanted to hurt the man.

"The data, the machinery—"

"A pile of broken concrete and ashes, General. There's nothing left of ATD. All these women, your family . . . You killed them for nothing. **Nothing**."

Price stared at the floor for a moment and then started shaking his head.

"No. Our psychologists said that someday he might try to destroy what he'd created. There are backups."

"Wake up, General! Marin had control of everything in that complex, everything in the mainframe. It's all gone!"

Price continued to shake his head. "The prototypes and the on-site backups, maybe. But there's an off-site facility, too, and there's no computer access from outside—no lines in at all. We physically transfer tapes every two days. Except for the three people involved, no one knows about it. Not even Marin."

Eric stared at him, trying to understand what made someone like General Richard Price tick. His arrogance, his ability to rationalize what was so obviously unjustifiable, his blindness to anything outside the twisted reality he'd created for himself.

"What would make you say that, General? Is it because you've been so effective at outsmarting him so far?"

64

Quinn was lying on her stomach in the backseat of Edward Marin's car, hands and feet still
handcuffed and the rope connecting the chains behind her still in place. The numbness in her fingers
and toes had spread to her mind, and the slight vibration of the leather pressed against her cheek was
all she could feel. She was a child again, curled up
in the passenger seat of her father's truck, dozing in
the sun coming through the window, listening to
him sing along with the radio. Safe. Warm . . .

The police photograph of Shannon Dorsey's mu-
tilated body was the first image to jolt her, though
the garish colors brought out by the camera's flash
seemed to have faded now. It had been so shocking
when she'd first seen it, before she had transformed
it into a lifeless image with no past or future or con-

sciousness. A piece of information to be methodically analyzed but never considered too deeply. Her
brain had efficiently stored only the necessary
facts—dates, victim profile, methodology—and
had pushed the rest into a dark corner where she
had been afraid to go.

Quinn began to struggle, wrenching her hands
back and forth and thrashing uselessly as the pho-
tographic image was swallowed up by the emptiness that seemed to be all that was left inside her.
She needed to feel something—pain in her shackled
wrists and ankles, her heart reacting to the motion,
the cool trickle of sweat. Anything that could stop
her from falling back . . .

But it was too late. The woman was already with
her—green eyes glowing dimly in the darkness;
searching for human contact, comfort, release.
Pulling at her.

Quinn buried her face in the leather seat and bit
down on the inside of her cheek until she could
taste blood. But it wouldn't stop. The woman's
dead eyes glowed brighter still, suddenly sparking
with pain and terror. And then finally with hate—
aimed not at Marin but at Quinn, for not stopping him.

She had stayed alive and lucid longer than
seemed possible, feeling every cut, every abuse that
Marin had so carefully inflicted on her. Quinn had
prayed for her—for them both—to die, as it had
become harder and harder for her to separate herself

from the woman. She'd begun to feel the agony, fear, and humiliation with increasing intensity, her own identity becoming blurred. When the woman had finally, mercifully, slipped away, she had taken part of Quinn with her.

Quinn heard the quiet scrunching of leather as Marin turned to look at her over the seats and she opened her eyes. He seemed almost formless now, like smoke. In killing that woman, he had lost what little was left of his humanity. Any remaining shreds of compassion, intelligence, and humor had disintegrated as he'd hovered over her, fading so quickly and completely that it was impossible to imagine that they had ever really been there.

He had wet himself when his knife had finally worked its way down to the woman's hips, but hadn't seemed to notice. Finally, when his victim looked like she was in danger of becoming incoherent, and perhaps slipping into unconsciousness, he had stripped off his clothes and attacked what was left of her like an animal. And that's how she had finally died. With him on top of her.

The car eased to a stop and Marin rolled down his window. The cool air that blew in smelled vaguely of exhaust, momentarily clearing the humid mingling of blood, urine, and sex that was smothering her.

They started forward again but didn't go far. The

next time the car stopped, the engine died and Marin stepped out. There was another blast of air and then the cold of the asphalt as she was dragged out onto it.

Marin knelt, bringing his face to within inches of hers. He seemed to be reconfiguring his expression randomly, trying in vain to disguise the cruelty and hate visible in it, but succeeding only in adding to the visual distortion plaguing her. He began smoothing his hair and wiping the blood from his lips with strangely desperate motions, obviously troubled by his inability to reconstruct his mask. None of it meant anything to her anymore, though. She fixed her stare on the asphalt beneath her.

"We've arrived, Quinn. Look." He gripped the back of her hair and forced her head back. Powerful lights reflected with painful intensity off a small warehouse and then diffused, glinting dully off a chain-link fence before being swallowed up by the dark.

She saw the flash of the X-Acto knife and then felt her feet drop to the ground as the rope strung behind her came apart under the blade. A moment later her ankles were free and Marin was pulling her to her feet.

"Didn't you hear me, Quinn? We're here." His voice was thick, as though his throat was no longer fully equipped for speech.

She squinted at him, but wasn't sure what he'd said. Not sure anymore even who he was.

"One last thing to do," he said, sliding the knife into the waistband of her skirt and leaving it trapped there as he pulled her toward the entrance to the warehouse. "Then we can go meet the General. Maybe your friend Eric will be there, too. You'd like that, wouldn't you? You'd like to see Eric one last time."

As they neared the glass doors, Quinn could see a single security guard sitting behind a large curved desk. She instinctively tried to run toward him, but Marin anticipated her and wrenched the chain between the handcuffs, dropping her to her knees.

"No need to hurry," he said, dragging her into the shadows and out of the guard's line of sight. "There will be time for us to spend a few uninterrupted hours together soon enough."

65

Four-three-five-zero," Price said.

Eric leaned out the window and punched the numbers into a small keypad, then inched the car forward, keeping pace with the formidable-looking gate as it swung open.

"How many people are here at night, General?"

"Just one."

Eric felt a weak surge of adrenaline—probably all he had left in him—at the man's answer. There were two cars in the otherwise desolate lot.

He glanced over at Price, who was staring blindly at the dashboard, lost in himself. The emotional roller coaster the man had been riding for the past four hours seemed to have crashed, leaving a strangely dead-looking expression of resolve on his face, but nothing else.

Eric turned off the headlights when he cleared the gate and continued toward the single-story metal building in front of them.

This time, when Price suddenly came to life and jumped from the car, Eric was ready for it. He slammed the stick shift into neutral and threw his door open, sprinting up behind the man and dragging him to the ground.

"We do this my way," Eric growled into his ear, punctuating his words by grinding his knee into Price's injured back. "Do you understand?"

Price fought back this time, reaching around and getting hold of Eric's hair. It was a good effort, but he was too drained to overcome his opponent's leverage and youth. Eric rolled him onto his back, ignoring the pain as Price maintained his grip on his hair, and wrapped both hands around the man's neck.

He had never felt hate like this. Not for Renquist when the detective was so gleefully destroying his life, not even for Marin, who was clearly insane. Eric tightened his grip on Price's throat, imagining the suffering those women had endured before they died and knowing it was within his power at least to partially avenge them. After a few seconds Price released his hair and tried to pry his hands off, but the lack of air had robbed him of what little strength and coordination he had left.

No.

The dead women would have to wait a little

longer for their revenge. Eric loosened his grip slightly and leaned into Price's ear again, hearing the quiet wheeze of air being sucked into his still partially constricted throat. "Do I make myself clear, General?"

Price didn't have the strength to respond, or to resist when Eric pulled him to his feet and marched him toward the glass doors. Through them, a guard station was visible, as was a low bench running across the far wall. Both were empty.

Price steadied himself and punched a code into yet another keypad. The lock buzzed loudly and Eric pushed through, moving slowly and holding an arm behind him to keep Price back. There was no sound at all. No movement. He edged closer to the curved wall that made up the front of the guard station, finally getting near enough to lean over it.

He was dead, like the one at ATD. His throat had been cut and his life had leaked out all over the floor. Eric leaned in a little farther and saw the man's revolver. It had obviously been used to smash out the surveillance screens set into the desk and now lay on the floor, open and empty.

"He's here," Price said in a voice that was barely a whisper.

Eric spun around and grabbed him by the arm. "Don't **move**. Do you understand me? Not an inch."

"We've got the element of surprise," Price said. "It won't last. It never does."

"We don't have shit," Eric said, circling around the desk and sitting in the dead man's chair. "The computer opened the door when you punched your code in. He knows we're here. And he's ready— that's why he emptied the guard's gun and broke out these screens."

"He's running, then," Price said, starting to sound a little desperate. "There's a fire escape—"

"No, General. He won't leave. Not until he's finished. Do the surveillance cameras output any-where else?"

Price didn't seem to be listening. He was looking over his shoulder at the metal door leading back into the warehouse.

"General!"

"No . . . no," he said finally. "Just here."

Eric hit the enter key on the PC in front of him, bringing the undamaged screen to life. "What's the password?"

"Uh . . . it's **backlash138**."

Eric keyed it in and held his breath.

It worked. He went for security functions first.

"Shit."

"What?" Price said. He was starting to look a lit-tle more lucid. Perhaps it was finally getting through to him that this was probably their last chance—and that they were unarmed and appar-ently expected. Once again, Marin seemed to have dealt himself the winning hand.

"He's locked out security. Are there any overrides?"

Price shook his head.

Eric tried to pull up a diagram of the building next. Thankfully, that function was still available.

Price pointed to the screen. "We're here. The reception area."

"Where are the backup tapes stored?"

He moved his finger to a large room that made up the majority of the building and then back to a smaller room right in front of it. "And this is a control room—they use it for cataloging and clerical work. It's separated from the main storage facility by a Plexiglas wall."

"Goddammit," Eric said under his breath. "There's nothing to this building. A main entrance, a hall, a control room, and a bathroom. No clever way for us to get in, nowhere to rig an ambush . . . Is there anything I'm missing, General?"

Price just shook his head.

Eric came around the desk and walked to the metal door at the back, grabbing the handle and looking back at Price. "He's not going to give us a second chance. Are you going to be able to do this?"

"Bet on it."

Eric yanked open the door and Price jumped through into the narrow hallway.

It was empty.

"It's not far," Price said quietly as he started down the corridor. "Just up here."

When Eric caught up, Price already had his back pressed against the wall next to an identical steel door leading to the small control room in front of the storage facility. He used his fingers to count silently as Eric took up a position next to him. On three they both burst through.

Nothing.

The room was no more than ten feet by twenty, with a wall that was completely transparent except for the part of it occupied by a counter that ran its full length and the computer and office supplies it held. The lights in the room were off, making it easy to see into the main storage area in front of them.

It was much larger, with no fewer than twenty glass-fronted shelves filling the right half of the room. The left half was mostly empty, with the exception of another low counter running along the back and a computer similar to the one in the control room. In the center of the floor was a three-foot-high pile of computer tapes that looked like the makings of a bonfire.

Price pointed to the door they had come through. "Close it."

Eric didn't move.

"We don't know where he is and we don't want him coming up behind us," Price explained as he started forward, moving cautiously through the

only other door in the room and into the storage facility. He was right, but Eric still wasn't anxious to
do anything that might slow their retreat, should
that become necessary.

Finally, he reluctantly pushed it shut. The latch
was electronic, so there was no way to lock it. Instead, he slid a chair in front of it. While it certainly wouldn't stop Marin from coming through,
they'd at least hear him.

Price had stopped next to the pile of tapes and
seemed to be listening to the silence as Eric came
up beside him. He was about to speak when the unmistakable rhythm of footsteps started somewhere
among the tall shelves to their right. They both
turned toward the sound, tensing as it drew nearer.

"Very clever, Eric," Marin said as he emerged.
"I assume it was you who found me and not
this . . ."—he pointed to Price —". . . this thing."

Eric put a hand on Price's shoulder. "Steady,
General."

Marin was almost completely unrecognizable
now; his face was discolored with yellowing bruises
and hopelessly distorted by swelling and cuts.
Judging from the smell, the wide stain spread
across the front of his expensive slacks was urine.

"Quinn?" Eric said. "Are you all right?"

Marin had one hand firmly around the handcuffs
securing her wrists and the other around an automatic pistol.

"Quinn?"

She didn't respond and her stare never wavered from the floor. Physically, she looked unharmed, but her eyes reflected nothing but the room around her.

"What did you do to her?"

"Nothing," Marin said, moving slowly to his left and pulling Quinn along with him. "I've hardly touched her."

When he reached the room's only computer, he tapped a quick command into it. Eric jerked his head around toward the sound of buzzing locks. The door to the control room was still open, but the one leading to the hallway was now locked. Wonderful.

"Quinn?" Eric said, turning back toward her. He had no idea what was going to happen, but he knew that she would need to be coherent for it. "Come on, Quinn. Can you hear me?"

Her head didn't rise, but he picked up a slight flicker in her eyes.

"I told you, Eric. She's fine. Quit being such a worrywart," Marin said. He moved behind her, pressing his chest into her back and caressing her leg with the barrel of the gun. Eric let his hand fall from Price's shoulder and moved forward a step but checked himself when Marin aimed the pistol at him.

"I'm sorry, Eric. Is she yours? Tell me she's yours and you can have her back. Tell me you've been inside this beautiful little thing."

Eric remained silent, trying to figure out a way to close the ten feet between them without getting shot. But there was no way. As always, Marin was in control.

"No. Of course you haven't, have you? Bad luck with women, right?"

Price was inching forward and actually made it to within a few feet of Marin before the gun swung in his direction. "And you, General? Why are you here? Do you want revenge for your family? Or do you just want to save your precious career?"

The sharp light in Marin's eyes suddenly dimmed and his face went slack. "You know, I'd never really considered it, Richard—a girl that young. As you're aware, I've always waited—waited for them to gain a little experience, a little sophistication. I thought they'd be better equipped to understand what I was doing to them." He shook his head sadly. "I can't tell you how wrong I was. She understood everything. And she fought. She fought like none of the others. She wanted to live so badly. You'll be proud to know that she didn't give up until the very end. Not until I told her about you. About our . . . arrangement."

Eric didn't try to stop Price this time, knowing that it would be useless. Instead he followed, waiting for the sound of the shot and hoping that there would be enough time. A split second of vulnerability would at least give him a chance. He could grab the gun, wrestle it away . . .

He didn't get it.

Marin slammed the butt of his pistol into Price's face and sent the man spinning to the floor. Eric hadn't even closed to within five feet when the gun was once again centered on his chest.

Marin took a few steps back, pulling Quinn with him, as Price struggled to his feet. Eric felt his jaw clench when the gun swung to Price again, but instead of firing, Marin reached up and pulled the slide back repeatedly, ejecting the bullets onto the floor around him and finally tossing the gun aside.

"I think that makes things a little more interesting, don't you?"

Price got to him first but was stopped dead when Marin caught his face in his hand. Eric slammed a shoulder into Quinn, sending her stumbling backward, and then swung a fist as hard as he could at Marin's head.

It was close, but not quite close enough—his knuckles skimmed harmlessly off the top of Marin's skull. Concentrating too hard on lining up again, he didn't see the vicious backhand until it was too late. He heard a faint crunching sound in his head as Marin's fist crushed his cheekbone and he fell backward over the counter behind him, smashing through the computer terminal sitting on it. Sparks showered him and he was vaguely aware of them burning through his shirt as he tried to stop the room from spinning. A small flame lapped against his arm and he jerked away, the pain helping to clear his head.

Marin's hands were gripping Price's shoulders now as he drove him back toward the Plexiglas wall, ignoring the man's blows to his swollen face as though they were nothing. By the time Eric was able to stand without relying on the counter for balance, Marin was slamming the back of Price's head repeatedly against the wall.

Eric staggered forward, but hadn't even made it halfway across the room when he noticed the sound begin to change. The deep clang of Price's skull hitting the glass was starting to sound muffled, wet. He focused on the two men and saw that Price's eyes and mouth were wide open but that his body flopped around like a broken doll each time his head impacted. And each time it seemed to sink a little farther into the widening blood smear as his skull continued to give way.

The door.

The electrical fire Eric had started continued to grow, creating a mechanical-smelling cloud around him as he stumbled forward. Quinn was still on the floor where she had fallen and he wrapped his arm around her, pulling her toward the control room. She didn't resist but also didn't help, still locked in whatever world Marin had created for her. He wanted to speak to her, to try to get through, but was afraid Marin would hear.

The oddly comforting sound of Price's crushing skull stopped when they were only a few feet from the doorway. Eric fell through and twisted around, desperately trying to pull Quinn across the threshold as what was left of General Richard Price slid down the wall.

Marin ran at them, diving to the floor and sliding across it, managing to get hold of Quinn's ankle before Eric could get her fully inside. He watched in horror as Marin dragged himself hand over hand along her legs, his arms disappearing beneath her skirt as he worked his way upward.

"No!" she screamed, finally coming to life when he reached her thighs.

Her hands were still secured behind her but she began to twist back and forth, kicking with enough force to actually startle Marin for a moment. She arched her back wildly, causing her T-shirt to slip up and reveal the white of her belly and a shiny silver object the size of a pen tucked into her waistband. Eric released her arm and fell on top of her, grabbing the X-Acto knife and cocking his hand back to swing it. Marin tried to move out of range, but found himself tangled in Quinn's skirt. The knife penetrated only inches from his neck, embedding itself deep in the flesh near his collarbone.

The shriek that erupted from the man didn't sound even remotely human. He escaped from the folds of fabric and rose to his knees, grabbing the knife and trying desperately to pull it out.

That was all Eric needed; he gripped the door-jamb with one hand and rammed the other into Marin's chest, sending him toppling backward. A moment later he had Quinn fully inside the control room and was slamming the door shut. There was a satisfying click as the lock engaged.

"Quinn!" Eric said, climbing off her and starting to choke on the smoke filling the air around them. "Are you all ri—"

The sudden force of her knee connecting with his chest sent him rolling across the floor. By the time he recovered, she had crammed herself into a small space between the wall and a file cabinet.

"Quinn. It's okay," he said, crawling toward her. The dull clang of straining Plexiglas stopped him. He turned toward the sound and saw Marin standing with his palms pressed against the glass and his face close enough for his breath to fog it. The X-Acto knife was still stuck in him and looked like some kind of bizarre antenna growing from his shoulder.

The sudden blast of the alarm and the white fog spewing from the ceiling startled Eric enough to make him scoot back a few feet. The fire had continued to spread from the smashed computer console and was moving with surprising speed across the countertop. The combination of the swirling smoke in the air, the chaos of the fire suppressant billowing from the ceiling, and Marin's face against the glass looked something like Eric's notion of hell.

Marin suddenly turned and ran toward the now-diminishing fire, stopping in the middle of the room and dropping to his knees. Eric stood to get a better view of him crawling on the floor but didn't realize what he was doing until it was almost too late.

He dove to the ground in front of Quinn and covered her with his body just as the three bullets Marin had managed to find slammed into the glass. Quinn struggled beneath him, but he just held her tighter. When the barrage ended, he turned and saw the distinctive spiderweb patterns, each about six inches in diameter. He let the breath he was holding escape between his teeth. They hadn't penetrated.

Marin grabbed a still-smoldering chair from behind the counter and ran full speed at the glass. Quinn screamed when its metal bottom impacted.

"Quinn. We're all right. Okay? We're all right." He wanted to comfort her but there was no time. He watched Marin back up until he was nearly standing in what was left of the fire and ran forward again. The image was almost surreal—Marin's mouth was wide open and it was obvious that he, too, was screaming, but there was no sound except the wavering alarm.

Quinn seemed to have awakened from her stupor, though she still hadn't spoken. When Eric ran past her, he saw that she was on her back with her feet in the air trying to get her hands in front of her.

He grabbed the handle of the door that led to the hall and pulled on it with everything he had. It didn't budge. "Quinn! Help! We've got to get out of here!" His words were punctuated by another impact. When he looked behind him, he saw Marin drawing back again through the white fog still flowing from the ceiling.

"Quinn! Come on! Help me!"

Her hands were in front of her now and she was on her feet, but she didn't seem to be aware that he was in the room. Instead of coming to his aid, she ran to the room's computer. She didn't even look up when the chair hit right in front of her. The cracks extended from floor to ceiling now and the glass flexed noticeably.

"QUINN!" Eric shouted as she started tapping on the keyboard. "Goddammit! Help!"

She wasn't listening. "I can't get in!"

The sudden sound of her voice shocked him for some reason.

"He locked out security functions." Eric slammed his shoulder painfully into the heavy steel door. "You can't open the door from there."

She looked back at him. "You'll never—"

The sound of crunching glass silenced her for a moment, but she kept her eyes on Eric, resisting the urge to turn and look at Marin as he continued his attack on the wall. "You'll never get through that door. This is our only chance."

Eric stopped, breathing hard, and looked directly into her eyes. They were clear. She was thinking again.

"**Backlash138**," he said. "Try that."

He came up next to her just as the chair hit again. One of the legs penetrated fully this time, leaving a hole about two inches wide. Marin put his mouth over it, sucking the relatively clear air from the room with an ominous hissing sound.

"I'm in! I'm in!"

"Quinn, I'm telling you. He's locked us out of anything we can use," Eric said as she scrolled through the command functions, finally stopping when she got to **fire control**. Marin pulled away from the hole and was preparing to take another run at the glass when the fire suppressant falling from the ceiling suddenly stopped. He paused, looking behind him at the back wall. Most of the fire had been smothered but there were still no fewer than three places where the flames were burning almost a foot high.

When he turned back toward them, a smile had spread across his face. It was impossible to hear what he said, but Eric could read his lips.

Too late.

Marin ran at them again and slammed the chair into the glass. Another leg penetrated, but this time he didn't pull back, instead he wrenched it back and forth, widening the hole. Eric grabbed hold of it and tried desperately to find the leverage to shove it back through. A moment later the alarm went off, leaving only the sound of grinding glass and Quinn furiously tapping on the keyboard.

"I don't know what you're doing," he said. "But whatever it is, do it fast." The hole had widened to about three inches, and despite Eric's best efforts, Marin continued to work the leg in deeper.

The sudden crack of Quinn's hand on the enter key was followed by a hum that caused the entire building to vibrate. The lingering smoke and chemical fog in the storage room quickly dissipated as powerful ventilation fans in the ceiling came on at full power.

"Quinn! Jesus, what are you doing, man? He's gonna be able to breathe now! The smoke . . ." Then he saw it. As efficient as the fans were at clearing the air, they were even more effective at feeding the fire. Flames that had been petering out a few moments before suddenly leaped up and spread across the counter again.

Marin's face was only a few feet from Eric's, and for the first time he saw it clouded with uncertainty. Marin released his end of the chair and moved directly in front of Quinn, slamming his hands into the glass. For a brief moment Eric thought he saw her smile.

Marin finally pulled away and disappeared into the shelves that lined the right half of the room.

"He's going for the extinguisher!" Quinn said, tapping a few more commands into the keyboard. The ventilation units shut down and the smoke began to accumulate again. In less than a minute, Eric could barely see the shelves that Marin had run into. "Where is he? Do you see him!"

"The extinguisher's way in the back . . . He'll find it, but it won't be easy."

Another minute passed before Eric saw movement. He pressed his face to the glass as Marin ran through the smoke, coughing violently. "There! He's got it!"

Quinn was ready. She struck the enter key again and the ventilation system roared back to life. The flames had grown to five feet in places and had now spread all the way across the back wall.

Marin pulled the pin from the extinguisher and started to try to put out the fire, but it took him only a few seconds to realize that his effort was pointless. He turned and ran at them again, holding the extinguisher high over his head. It wasn't sharp enough to penetrate fully, but a section of the glass bubbled out and turned milky white beneath it. If he hit it in that same place again . . .

"He can't put the fire out, Quinn. Turn off the fans. If he can't breathe, he can't break through."

She didn't move; she just sat there calmly as Marin reared back and slammed the extinguisher into the glass again. The bubble gained depth, the glass barely holding.

"Quinn! For God's sake!" Eric leaned over her and went for the keyboard, but she grabbed his hand. "NO!"

"Are you nuts?" He pulled the chair she was sitting in away from the terminal, but when he did, she yanked the keyboard out of the CPU and threw it across the room.

"Oh, that's great, Quinn. That's just fucking great."

She moved to where Marin was attacking the wall, putting her hands on either side of the hole he was opening in the glass and watching him intently.

"Jesus Christ," Eric mumbled, finally understanding. She didn't want him to suffocate in the smoke. She wanted him to burn.

The flames were everywhere now. Richard Price's corpse was on fire, as were the tapes on the floor and the shelves that had contained them. Marin couldn't rear back more than a couple of feet for fear of stepping into the fire. Eric could see that his face had lost much of its cruelty and arrogance now. Desperation was all that was left.

Marin's fantastic strength was starting to wane. There was still very little smoke, but Eric could feel the heat radiating from the glass. Despite that, the metal edge of the extinguisher finally pierced the wall. Instead of trying to widen the hole, though, Marin pressed his face into it. His breath was ragged as he pulled the cool air into his singed lungs.

"Bitch!" Eric heard him gasp as Quinn leaned closer to him and stared into his eyes. Bloody spit hit her in the face, but she didn't react. Not to that, or to the hate in his voice, or to his shirt's finally catching fire, or to his muffled screams as he tried to smother the flames with his hands. And not to the silence when he was finally engulfed.

Eric approached her cautiously, taking her arm and pulling her away from the glass. When he looked into her face, he saw that it was a complete blank. He wrapped his arms around her and held her to him. After a few seconds she let out a quiet, choking sob and went limp.

EPILOGUE

For the first time in she didn't know how long, Quinn could feel the sun on her skin and take some pleasure from it. It was noon and around them the quiet courtyard was slowly coming alive as people streamed from the surrounding buildings in search of lunch. She leaned back a little farther on the bench, feeling the Arizona heat seep into her chest but keeping an eye focused on the entrance to the building in front of her.

"There! Is that him?" Eric said, nodding subtly toward a tall, well-dressed man with broad shoulders and a head of neatly trimmed curly hair.

"No."

She resisted the urge to let her mind go blank; she was getting too good at that little trick. She'd spent the major portion of the last three days behind the wheel of Eric's car, seeing only enough of the road to keep from drifting off it. She'd wanted to block it all out—the horrors that the case files had contained, the girl in Eric's apartment, the dead feeling that she'd almost drowned in after watching Marin at work. But most of all, the insane rage that had taken hold of her when she had seen Marin trapped in that storage room and the twisted joy she'd felt when he had finally burned. She wondered if she'd gotten a faint glimpse of what he must have felt when he killed those girls.

But in order to keep those memories at bay, she was forced to shut everything else off, too. And she couldn't live like that. She wouldn't let Marin take her life from her.

She looked over at Eric, examining his profile. He seemed to be a completely different person from when they'd first met. Overall, he looked the same, of course—the dark, smooth skin, the long black hair, the thin athletic body. It was something in his eyes . . .

No, they hadn't changed—they were the same shiny gray they'd always been. It was just that she could see deeper into them now.

He finally turned to face her, looking a little exasperated. "Stop it. You're making me nervous."

"What?"

"You're staring at me."

"Sorry. I was just wondering what you were thinking."

"I'm not thinking anything."

"Really?"

"My mind's a complete blank."

She smiled but didn't turn away. Eric was the real reason that she couldn't shut herself off from everything that had happened to her. If she did, she'd have to discard him, too.

"Quinn, seriously, you're freaking me ou—"

She leaned over and pressed her lips against his. When she pulled back again, he had another of those perfectly enigmatic expressions on his face.

"Not good enough?" she said.

"I, uh, well—"

She kissed him again, this time pressing her body up against his. It took a few seconds but he finally overcame enough of his initial shock to participate. He relaxed and slid his arms around her. She wasn't sure how long she'd wanted to do this, but it seemed like a long time. Maybe since the first time they'd met.

They were still locked in an embrace when she opened her eyes and caught sight of a man coming through the doors in the building in front of them. She moved her hands to Eric's chest and pushed him away. "That's him!"

"Great. Wouldn't you know," Eric said, following her gaze. "Where? I don't see anybody."

"Right there! He's the one lighting a cigarette by the fountain."

When Eric finally picked him out, his face

scrunched up into something that looked like a wince. Quinn grabbed his hand and dragged him to his feet, choosing to overlook his understandable disappointment. Mark Beamon's appearance didn't exactly inspire confidence. His face was thick, with a brow that jutted a little too far from his thinning hair and chubby cheeks that seemed ready to give up their battle with gravity. His suit was just a little out of style and looked like he'd purchased it when he was thirty pounds heavier.

Beamon started walking again, blowing thick smoke from his lungs and returning the respectful nods of passersby with a slightly self-conscious smile. His pace seemed a little too fast to be completely natural—almost as if he were trying to escape.

"Come on," she said, pulling Eric along behind her.

"Quinn, are you sure?"

"Yes, I'm sure. That's him."

Once Beamon had cleared the courtyard in front of the FBI's new Phoenix offices, he slowed to a stroll, dragging calmly on his cigarette and stopping occasionally to gaze into the windows of the shops and restaurants lining the street.

Quinn closed the distance between them quickly, slowing to match his speed when they were about three feet behind him.

"Mr. Beamon?" she said, trying to keep the nervousness out of her voice.

He turned and peered into her face. "Hello. Have we met?"

"Not really. No, sir."

"Well, what can I do for you?"

"I was . . . I was wondering if I could talk to you for a minute."

It seemed like a simple question, but he considered it as though it was a matter of life and death. "Are you a reporter?"

"No, sir. I used to work for the FBI. Technically speaking, I guess I probably still do."

Beamon looked over at Eric, his eyes lingering on the swelling and discoloration of his broken cheekbone. "What about you? What's your story?"

"I'm a physicist, actually."

Beamon shrugged. "I guess it's okay, then. I'm trying to decide where I want to have lunch. Why don't you walk with me?"